From Blossom herself:

I tell you, the world is so full of ghosts, a person wonders if there's a soul to be found on the Other Side, or anybody snug in a quiet grave. I've seen several haunts, and I've been one myself.

You've probably heard about me already. For a time I was the most famous girl in two countries. I've been called Ghost Girl and Fantastic Faker by turns. Numerous people have commented on my adventures in this world and others, but none could explain my Powers entirely, and many are liars outright.

My first glimpses into Worlds Unseen come as quite a surprise to me, among others. . . .

PUFFIN BOOKS BY RICHARD PECK

GHOSTS
I Have Been

RICHARD PECK

PUFFIN BOOKS

PUFFIN BOOKS
Published by the Penguin Group
Penguin Putnam Books for Young Readers,
345 Hudson Street, New York, New York 10014, U.S.A.
Penguin Books Ltd, 27 Wrights Lane, London W8 5TZ, England
Penguin Books Australia Ltd, Ringwood, Victoria, Australia
Penguin Books Canada Ltd, 10 Alcorn Avenue, Toronto, Ontario, Canada M4V 3B2
Penguin Books (N.Z.) Ltd, 182-190 Wairau Road, Auckland 10, New Zealand

Penguin Books Ltd, Registered Offices: Harmondsworth, Middlesex, England

First published in the United States of America by Viking Penguin Inc., 1977
Published by Puffin Books,
a division of Penguin Putnam Books for Young Readers, 2001

3 5 7 9 10 8 6 4

THE LIBRARY OF CONGRESS HAS CATALOGED THE VIKING EDITION AS FOLLOWS:
Peck, Richard. Ghosts I have been.
Summary: Blossom Culp's gift of second sight, which she discovers gradually,
leads her into some unusual adventures.
[1. Supernatural—Fiction.] I. Title.
PZ7.P338G [Fic] 77-9469
ISBN 0-670-33813-3

Puffin Books ISBN 0-14-131096-0

Printed in the United States of America

GHOSTS
I Have Been

° Prologue °

I TELL YOU, the world is so full of ghosts, a person wonders if there's a soul to be found on the Other Side. Or anybody snug in a quiet grave. I've seen several haunts, and been one myself.

You've probably heard about me already. For a time I was the most famous girl in two countries. I've been called Ghost Girl and Fantastic Faker by turns. Numerous people have commented on my adventures in this world and others, but none could explain my Powers entirely, and many are liars outright.

I lived a full fourteen years without thought to having any extra talents of my own. Psychic Gifts were to me the advantages certain other people had, like good looks or regular meals. So my first glimpses into Worlds Unseen come as quite a surprise to me, among others.

Whether you be born with the Gift or attain it is often debated. As you'll see, my Gift tended to creep up on me and would often pop out under pressure. Practice makes perfect, as the poet says. I seemed to refine my Powers as I went, much like learning to write a clear hand or driving one of the new automobiles.

All this was leading in a direction. At the start I was no more than a plain American girl with nothing going for me but spunk. Little did I know where my new-found talents would lead me—across tossing seas and into lives of high and low degree. I little knew the wickedness of this world until I saw beyond it.

Two fates were entwined: mine and the tormented ghost of a boy—a perfect stranger to me—who died a death I wouldn't wish on my worst enemy.

As I pen these words to leave a lasting record, I wonder myself where it all began. We start up in the mists of mystery, and there we all end. And Souls drift like ground fog across a hundred worlds and far frontiers.

Many's the ignorant person who claims that spirits and haunts have forsaken the modern age in this new twentieth century. But what they do not know would fill a book. And this is the book.

· 1 ·

THERE ARE GIRLS in this town who pass their time up on their porches doing fancywork on embroidery hoops. You can also see them going about in surreys or on the back seats of autos with their mothers, paying calls in white gloves. They're all as alike as gingerbread figures in skirts. I was never one of them. My name is Blossom Culp, and I've always lived by my wits.

My mama and me live hard by the streetcar right of way, on the down side. Ours is a two-room dwelling which we have rent free, it being abandoned. We had always lived off a hard clay garden and put by what we could against the winter. For extras, I've been on my own since I was knee-high.

My mama picked up a certain amount of loose change in palm reading, herb cures, and other occupations I will mention. But until I became famous, she never made her skills known. And in this modern age, if you don't advertise, the world doesn't beat a path to your door. Remember this. It bears on the story later on.

Since various people—newspaper reporters and suchlike —have asked me about my paw or if I have one, I'll just mention that Paw's a traveling man. We don't hear tell of him for long stretches. He doesn't figure in this present account, since to my recollection he didn't turn up at our place any time during 1913 or 1914. Still, I wouldn't be surprised to come in at any time now and find Paw stretched out insensible before the stove. As the poet says,

> *Not drunk is he who from the floor*
> *Can rise alone and still drink more;*
> *But drunk is he, who prostrate lies,*
> *Without the power to drink or rise.*

At intervals we get picture postcards from Paw, who lives his life answering the call of the open road. The name and address on the cards, merely "The Culps, Bluff City," are written in by a series of unknown hands. The spaces for messages are blank. Neither my paw nor my mama can read or write, though they have their talents like anybody else.

Here I have shown progress, for I am a quick study as to reading and other matters. My penmanship, as you can see from this page, is first-rate. My grammar is not perfect, but then whose is? As to spelling, I could cover my middy blouse with medals won at various bees.

None of these accomplishments will take you far, of course, if you lack what the world calls advantages. I consider that I was always well off without such advantages, as they tend to kill your initiative. As the poet says, necessity is what makes the mule plow. And I for one would not care to pass my life up on a porch, gazing into an embroidery hoop.

Naming no names, there are some people here in Bluff City who still say I do not know my place. How wrong they are. I know it well and always did. But I have always meant to better myself, and when you are on your own in this life, it is uphill work.

As the poet says, vanity has done more in this world than modesty. Now I am not vain when it comes to looks. If I was, a trip to the mirror would cure me. My eyes are very nearly black, particularly if I am roused to anger or action. My hair needs more attention than I have time to give it. And my legs, being thin, do not show to good advantage, as being fourteen, I am still in short skirts.

But I am vain about my resourcefulness. There is more to be learned about a town from the wrong side of the tracks than from the right. I made a study of this town long before I had the power to see beyond it. Bluff City is mainly divided into two camps: those who have already arrived and those who never will. So I am something of a misfit. But the advantage of a small town is that the rich and the poor live cheek by jowl. Just over the streetcar tracks lives a well-to-do family, name of Armsworth. They have a son, Alexander, who's in my same grade at school. He is getting to the lanky stage. However, being a boy, he's not as mature for his age as I am. Boys never are, which is a scientific fact.

Between his house and mine on the Armsworth property is a large outbuilding known locally as the Ghost Barn. You may have read about it in all the papers here and elsewhere last spring. Though the barn was haunted, it no longer is, thanks to me and Alexander Armsworth.

He had the Gift of seeing the ghost as plain as day. I had the talent for involving myself in other people's business. Between us, we got the ghost out of the barn and into a quiet grave. The whole business embarrassed Alexander considerably, though it did not faze me.

My name didn't figure in the local write-up. The reporter on the story was spooning at the time with Alexander's big sister, Lucille, so he featured the Armsworths strongly, leaving me out. His name is Lowell Seaforth, and I don't hold it against him. He's since married Lucille Armsworth, so I have no doubt he's paying for all his past sins.

The ghost which got such a big play last spring came to light entirely due to my mama. She was the first to perceive its presence. Gypsy blood runs in her veins, giving her the Second Sight and the Gift of seeing the Unseen, like Alexander but better. She's such a great hand at dealing in the supernatural that we were run out of Sikeston, Missouri, where we originated. They won't burn you for a witch in Sikeston, but they can make it hot for you.

The blood is running thin, though, and I doubted that I'd inherited any mystical gifts. At least they had not shown up yet. So here again, the only advantage I might have had seemed to pass me by. Anybody with a drop of gypsy blood in her veins would gladly lay some claim to mystical powers. But what's not inherited can sometimes be manufactured.

Halloween in Bluff City as elsewhere is a marvelous time of year for boys to play the fool. Nothing inflames them like an excuse to disturb the peace and a harvest moon to light their way. Mama and me were never troubled by pranksters. They paid us no mind generally, but on Halloween they went out of their way to shun us. Even now, no one is sure of the extent of my mama's Gift and how she might use it against you.

But I made it my business that Halloween of the year 1913 to be out and about myself. Boys will repeat the same tricks, never tiring of them. If there's anything more predictable than a boy, I haven't met it. I decided to give a certain gang of them something to think about. Indeed, I meant to scare them out of a year's growth.

My motive was not spotless. It involved Alexander Armsworth. Me and him had been drawn together over that ghost business. Directly after we'd settled it, though, he kept his distance. I was not sweet on Alexander. Still, a person does not like to be picked up and then dropped. I decided to let him know I was still a girl to be reckoned with.

Besides, he'd fallen in with a gang of rough types. Bub Timmons was one of them, and so was Champ Ferguson. The chief troublemaker was Les Dawson, a bully of more brawn than brain. Nobody cared to lock horns with him. I was shortly to do just that.

They were all older than Alexander, though Les Dawson was in our grade, being left back several semesters. It was entirely like Alexander to mix with an older crowd and be drawn into their doings.

Out in the Horace Mann schoolyard it was hard work not to overhear the gang's plans for Halloween mischief. They whispered about it every recess, boxing each other about the head and ears as boys do. Their Halloween plan was nothing more than to turn over people's outhouses. Progress in Bluff City is spotty. Only the chosen few have indoor plumbing. Much of the town on my side of the tracks is still dotted with privies. I had little trouble plotting the gang's course.

Since ghosts were still on the minds of many people, I planned a costume to feature myself as one. By dark on Halloween night, I had ready a garment made out of old bed linens. One ragged sheet provided me with a full skirt and trailing train. I devised two batwing sleeves from a pair of pillowslips. I shook a full cup of cake flour over my face and hair and worked it in. To complete my disguise as the shade of a dead girl, I draped a mosquito bar over my head as a veil. And I carried a candle in my hand and a box of safety matches in my shoe top to light up my frightful face when the moment was right.

As I stepped out into the evening, the town was alive with young children trick-or-treating from house to house. Half scared of themselves and each other, they kept to the roads and front walks. I flitted through backyards, not wanting to give the little ones a turn. Though it was a clear night, there were wisps of fog. I moved with small quick steps, and my white skirts billowed behind me for all the world like float-ing. Listen, I wouldn't have liked to meet *me* in a dark alley.

Glowing a ghastly white, I glided down garden rows and past woven-wire fences, lingering behind woodpiles to ob-serve how my drapings settled. There was a nip in the air, but I was warmed by my plans.

They were to figure out which of the outhouses Alexan-der's gang would push over first. I reflected on what a lot of trouble this gave innocent people and considered I was doing the property owners a favor. I might cure the gang of vandalism permanently.

The first privy I come to was on the back of Old Man Leverette's place. He's a retired farmer moved to town, but he keeps to his country ways and is not the type to invest in an indoor toilet. His outhouse stood like a sentry box against the rising moon. Here was a temptation the boys could not resist. I waited like a terrible statue for a time, seeming to hear the gang's stealthy footsteps in the distance. For the practice I sighed and moaned a little.

My intention was to step just inside the privy and pull the door shut. Then when the gang approached to tip it over, I planned to step out, with the lighted candle, and moan eerily. If this wouldn't strike them half dead with horror, what would? I grinned under my mosquito bar at my plans. Alas, I grinned too soon.

As there was no breeze that night, I fished the matches out of my shoe top and lit my candle as I stepped up to Old Man Leverette's privy door.

At this point, things went seriously wrong. I had one foot inside when I come face to face with Old Man Leverette himself. He was in his privy, using it. His nightshirt was hitched up about his hips. My candle threw dreadful shadows in the tiny room, and light fell on Old Man Leverette's startled face and on the torn pages of the Montgomery Ward catalogue in his aged hands.

Near enough to the grave himself, he let out a kind of Indian war whoop. He rose up, thought better of it, and flopped back down on the seat. I was as startled as he was, and the wind from his gasping breath set the candle flame bobbing.

"Whoooo, whoooo, whooo in the Sam Hill are *you*?" Old Man Leverette howled.

"I beg your pardon, I'm sure," I said, not wanting to identify myself. I took a step backwards, but his hand snaked out and grabbed my wrist. Pages from the catalogue fluttered away like moths. My presence of mind failed me and I said, "I just happened to be passing."

"So was I!" Old Man Leverette roared.

He could tell by grasping my wrist that I was human. Giving it a painful wrenching, he pushed me out the door, which closed between us. As I lifted my sheets to take flight, I heard his voice from inside still roaring, "Don't light out, missy! I got business with you!"

As near fear as I'd ever been, I waited until Old Man Leverette stepped out into the yard. Lit by the moon, we seemed a pair of ghosts, what with his white nightshirt and a shock of flowing white hair above his lion's face.

"If you're trick-or-treatin'," he said, still gasping, "you can go around to the front door of the house and take your chances like anybody else!"

My candle had gone out by then, and I'd thrown my veil back from my face. He fixed me with a watery eye, but couldn't place me. "And just who do you happen to be?" he said, and waited for an answer.

"Letty Shambaugh," I replied, naming a stuck-up girl in my grade whose name occurred to me.

"Explain yourself before I cut a switch and stripe your legs!"

It wasn't easy to explain to Old Man Leverette that I had his best interests at heart and only meant to save his out-house from a tipping over. And how would he like to be tipped over *in* it? I nearly added this, but didn't.

He is one of these people who don't like being convinced. But when I mentioned a gang of boys planning to knock over every outhouse between here and the city limits, he began to nod. I didn't name these boys, but I made it clear that I meant to teach them a lesson. If not in the Leverette privy, then in another.

My words began to work. Old Man Leverette worried the stubble on his chin with a gnarled hand. Presently he said, "There's sense to your plan, Letty. But I don't know but what I can improve on it. You can scare hell out of them in the privy, and I'll send 'em on their way with a plan of my own. Don't move. I'll be back directly." Then he stalked off to the house. His nightshirt strained around his big white legs.

He returned, marching down his punkin patch with a shotgun on his shoulder. "Now then," he said, taking over, "you can get yourself into the privy, and I'll hunker down over there behind my compost heap. I got a notion we won't have long to wait. Do your best, and I'll do the rest.

"And you just as well leave your veil up. You're spooky enough lookin' without it."

There was hardly enough air in the privy to get my candle going again. The atmosphere was close and unpleasant. I was reminded of mummies buried upright in their coffins before I heard the sure sounds of a gang of boys trying to be quiet. I drew my veil down.

The boys crashed through the undergrowth behind the privy. I hoped they didn't mean to tip from the back and flatten the door to the ground before I could float out of it. But they only lingered back there, egging one another on. A good example of cowardice is boys in a bunch. I had an idea this was their first privy of the evening. And with any luck at all, their last.

Giving the sides a shove or two, they circled around and went to work on the front. They began to rock my hiding place, but its posts were well sunk. It started to give, though, just as I pushed back the door and stepped out, nearly into the straining arms of Alexander Armsworth.

The candle flickered and guttered between my white veil and his suddenly white face. His arms fell from the door jamb, and he let out the high whinny of a fire-crazed horse. Bub and Champ were at work on the far side of the door and missed my entrance. But they couldn't miss Alexander. He keeled backwards and fell flat on the ground. "A HAUNT! I AM CURSED!" he screamed and lay on his back like a turned turtle, with his fists jammed into his eyes.

Bub and Champ were transfixed by this behavior. So was Les Dawson, who was standing farther off, supervising the job. I moved beyond the shadow of the door, pulled my veil tight at my throat, and held the candle directly beneath my chin. "Ohhhh! Woe to all here," I moaned in a far-off, cultivated voice, rather like that of our teacher, Miss Mae Spaulding. Bub and Champ gave me one look and ran directly into each other's arms. Then they stumbled forward, sprawling over Alexander, who was still on his back in the weeds. The three rolled together like puppies. Being farther off, Les held his ground. I raised a ghostly finger and pointed directly at him.

This moved him. Just as he wheeled in the direction of a high wood fence along the side of the property, Old Man Leverette reared up from behind him and let out another of his war whoops. It would have curdled milk and blood alike.

Already traveling, Les took a kind of skip in the air. The three on the ground were scuttling crab fashion toward the fence themselves, but they flattened when they heard the war cry.

Old Man Leverette's whoop had not died away before he aimed his shotgun in the air and fired off one barrel of rock salt. People later reported hearing the explosion as far away as the town square. There was a flash of flame from the muzzle, and for some seconds rock salt spattered like hail over the backyard and privy roof.

Les Dawson had hit the fence at his top speed by then, but crumpled down into a summer-squash vine, evidently thinking he was killed. In the next second Bub, Champ, and Alexander were on the fence, clinging to it a moment, and then over the top. Les, being gangly, made two tries at the fence top before he could heave himself over; he was sobbing aloud. For a long moment his backside was high in the air as he tried to calculate the drop on the far side of the fence. Temptation overcame Old Man Leverette.

He grabbed up his shotgun, jammed the butt into his shoulder, and squeezed off the other barrel of rock salt. His large target was Les Dawson's behind.

Of all the screams and whoops that rent the air that night, Les's was the loudest. He seemed to take flight from the top of the fence, like an aeroplane fueled by rock salt, and he fell in an arc on the far side, howling all the way to the ground.

Old Man Leverette whooped again, very nearly helpless with laughter. His shotgun clattered to earth. He gasped and called out, "Well, Letty, I reckon we showed 'em. You, Letty! You hear me?"

But I'd put out my candle by then and was making tracks toward home. I faded away behind a stand of dry hollyhocks, grinning as I went at the notion of Letty Shambaugh putting in such a night's work.

• 2 •

THE EVENTS of that busy Halloween night cast a lengthier shadow than I bargained for. In the long run many lives were changed, mine among them. But I little knew this the next morning. There's nothing like a night's work well done to set you up for the next day. I headed off for school with a cup of black coffee in me by way of breakfast and an apple in my skirt pocket for lunch.

As a rule I followed the streetcar tracks halfway to school, which is the long way around. Since I had to wear the same outfit in all weather, I would not parade myself down the best streets, like Fairview Avenue, lined with the large homes of such well-off old-timers as Miss Gertrude Dabney and, farther along, the Shambaughs. I have my pride just like anybody else. That morning, though, I trespassed across the Armsworths' property.

My success as a ghost had backfired on me in one way. I'd scared Alexander into believing he could see ghosts again, at least for a brief period. This would remind him of a time him and me had shared. But my disguise kept him from knowing who had set him gibbering with fear and showed up the thugs he was running with as a bunch of crybabies. Especially Les Dawson. I like to see credit given where credit is due. And if the credit's due me, so much the better.

Also, confession is good for the soul, as the poet says; though I'd have to catch Alexander before I could confess to him. It might take some while, but I was willing to wait. Still, with Armsworths on my mind, I made a shortcut across their territory.

Beyond the Ghost Barn their place rose up in all its glory. Autumn-red clinging vines twined over their many porches and towers. The morning sun caught the stained glass of their windows. The Armsworth place is the third largest house in Bluff City, with a lawn befitting it.

Drawn up to the side stood a new Ford automobile. This meant that Alexander's big sister, Lucille, was paying an early morning call. She's quite stout, so I guess she'd come around for a second breakfast. Lucille's the new bride of the newspaperman, Lowell Seaforth, who was soon to figure big in my fortunes. The Ford automobile was her paw's wedding present to the happy couple. Lucille Armsworth Seaforth was a well-known hazard around town all summer while learning to drive the Ford. She is headstrong but easily distracted, making her a poor candidate for a license.

While she was teaching herself to drive, the Ford got away from her and mowed down a line of shrubs on the Carnegie Library lawn. Veering the wrong way, she gunned the Ford up the front walk, and it tried to mount the library steps, destroying two stone urns. During this, Lucille rose in the seat and screamed "Whoa!" to the Ford.

Her paw paid all damages and said publicly that as to wedding presents, a set of silverware would have been a better bet.

Just beyond the Ford was a big dining-room window. From it came the sounds of the family at their breakfast. The smell of frying bacon drifted out, making me dizzy. The voices of Lucille and Mrs. Armsworth were raised in conversation. I took the sound of knives and forks to be Alexander and his paw silently putting their breakfast away. A hired girl was at their beck and call. Some people live high up on the hog and no mistake.

News travels fast in a schoolyard. There was considerable buzzing about the strange events and gunfire of the night before. As usual everybody had their own version of the story nowhere near the truth. But various parts of their tales were right enough; it would only need one intelligent person to put the puzzle pieces together.

Our grade at Horace Mann School was taught by the principal, Miss Mae Spaulding. She left nothing to chance, taking it on herself to whip us into shape before we moved across the road to the high school. And *whip* is a word you don't want to use lightly with Miss Spaulding. Though slender as a wand and ladylike, she has an arm on her like a bartender.

Les Dawson did not come to school till noon. I have an idea that his kin spent many hours picking rock salt out of him. A morning recess without Les was as good as Christmas for the smaller kids, for Les never missed a day of stealing their pennies and putting their lunch buckets in trees. When he did come to school, he was in a meaner frame of mind than usual. Alexander was subdued throughout the day. As to Bub Timmons and Champ Ferguson, I did not know, because they are across the road in the high school.

During Geography I noticed a worrisome thing. Miss Spaulding was saying, "And who can name me two principal exports of Egypt?"

Letty Shambaugh's hand flew up as usual. "Please, Miss Spaulding, sisal and jute!"

"Very good, Letty," Miss Spaulding said, and expanded on the answer.

I noticed that Les shot Letty a look. There was murder in his eye. It came to me that I'd passed myself off as Letty the night before. Old Man Leverette had called out her name just as the boys were encouraged over the fence. There is only one girl in town by the name of Letty. One is plenty.

This muddled my thoughts. Like the rest of the girls, Letty is no friend of mine. She's stuck-up and with very little cause, though her paw owns the Select Dry Goods Company. Letty is a walking advertisement for it. She has more shirtwaists, skirts, and shoes, all well fitting, than any five or six girls in school. She's also the president of a club of girls she founded herself. I knew nothing of it except for its name, The Sunny Thoughts and Busy Fingers Sisterhood. Only later did I learn how poorly it was named. For none of them had enough to do to keep their thoughts sunny or their fingers busy.

It looked like Les thought it was Letty who'd scattered his gang and caused him to be fired on. Anybody with common sense would know that Letty's not that enterprising. Besides, her people never let her out at night, let alone

Halloween. But if Les had common sense, he'd be graduated from the high school by now.

Whatever he planned for Letty might bring her down a peg or two. On the other hand, Letty was innocent of this. And I wondered if it was fair that she should suffer. A small amount of suffering would surely do her no harm, I reasoned. I put this problem aside in favor of Miss Spaulding's Egypt lecture.

At afternoon recess Les pounced. Letty was in a swing being pushed by one of her club members. Boys have gangs and girls have clubs, but they are much the same. Letty held her small feet close together. The lace of her many petticoats riffled in the breeze. Up and down she swooped, with a girl behind her straining to keep up the momentum. Letty's gold ringlets stood out from her round pink face, and her little rosebud mouth was pursed in pleasure. I was nearby, as I often am.

Les suddenly loomed up, snarling like a dog. She was swinging right into his ugly face before she saw him. He grabbed hold of her feet, and Letty's swing fell back without her.

She hit the dirt under a tent of collapsing petticoats, the wind knocked out of her. Les dropped her feet and set upon her, growling, "I'll larn ya," and several other words. Letty's half-smothered squeaks brought a ring of onlookers but no aid. Les flipped her over and rubbed her pink face in the dirt. Then he yanked off her enormous satin hair ribbon and ripped it to shreds. All the Sunny Thoughts and Busy Fingers girls squealed and wrung their hands.

To add to the confusion, up pounded Bub Timmons and

Champ Ferguson, even though nobody from the high school is allowed into our schoolyard, especially boys. They stood by, half satisfied and half uncertain. From the corner of my eye, I saw Alexander playing kick-the-can at the far end of the yard. He was well out of this.

Right then my better nature took command of the rest of me. Les was rubbing Letty's face into the playground, and her head seemed to be sinking lower into the earth. This might have ended in untimely death if I hadn't pushed through the crowd and come up behind Les. The big bruiser could have felled me with one blow. But who knew better than me how tender his rear must be, pocked with rock salt as it was? I kicked him hard where it would be most instructive.

He turned nearly inside out and yelled. But he let go of Letty. Then he was up in a crouch and wheeling my way. When he saw me with my thin legs braced and both small fists clenched, he broke into an evil smirk, though his eyes were wet with pain. Letty scrambled in the other direction. People said later that she took a few tottering steps and fell into a faint in the arms of her club. I'd saved Letty, but who would save me? I threw a few punches, but Les Dawson's hands closed around my throat and the world went dark.

Though I was only truly out for a moment, I remained where I sprawled. Somewhere nearby was the whistle and thwack of the paddle Miss Spaulding keeps for hard cases. Les was getting it again, and this time a systematic thrashing from Miss Spaulding's own arm. My mind drifted off then, for I was nearer strangled than I knew.

I come to in Miss Spaulding's private office, stretched out on a cot. Letty Shambaugh was on another cot just opposite. I let my eyes flutter shut again. If you must be in a principal's office at all, it's better to be unconscious.

But I had a glimpse of Letty still looking dead to the world. What a sight she was. Now you could have buried me up to my neck in hogmash and not done much violence to my bib and tucker. But Letty looked like the Wreck of the *Hesperus*. She was bright yellow with playground dirt, and her petticoat lace was hanging in tatters. Half her collar was missing, and her rosebud lips were gray. I sensed activity in the room and stayed quiet.

Time had passed, for school was out and Letty's mother had been sent for. Nobody thought to send for my mama, but that was just as well.

Evidently Miss Spaulding was trying to prepare Mrs. Shambaugh for her first sight of Letty. "Everything is under control now," Miss Spaulding was saying, "and I have thrashed the culprit soundly and expelled him from school."

"It seems to me," came Mrs. Shambaugh's voice, "that you'd have done better to expel him some while back. What Mr. Shambaugh will say when he— Saints in Heaven! Letty, honey, speak to me!"

Mrs. Shambaugh must have got past Miss Spaulding for her first view of Letty. In my opinion Letty was fully conscious, but playing the role for all it was worth. I glimpsed her head turning from side to side. When her mother blocked my view, Letty burst into piteous tears.

"Letty, precious, say something to Mommy!" Mrs. Shambaugh swooped down so that the furs hanging down her back swept across my nose. Letty had hysterics in earnest then, hiccuping and snuffling and carrying on. "Listen to me, Letty!" Mrs. Shambaugh yelled. "Can you move your arms and legs, and did that maniac of a boy get in under your skirts?"

"Oh no, no, nothing like that," Miss Spaulding moaned. "I checked her over myself."

"Oh yes," Mrs. Shambaugh said bitterly, "you have been a tower of strength, Miss Spaulding, I have no doubt!" Mrs. Shambaugh continued on about the dangers lurking in a school run by such as Miss Spaulding.

Never hearing a principal talked to like this, I forgot and left my eyes open. Clutching to Mrs. Shambaugh's skirts was a small boy, Letty's brother, who was dressed like Little Lord Fauntleroy, though getting too big for it. He wore a sailor's cap with ribbons and looked like he'd been carved out of lard.

Mrs. Shambaugh scooped Letty up in both hands. She's quite a large woman. She turned then and looked down at me over the head of Letty's brother, who is named Newton. The office seemed littered with bodies. I returned her gaze with glazed eyes. "And who might *this* be? Do not tell me the savage struck twice!"

Miss Spaulding cleared her throat. "Well, yes, in a manner of speaking. This is Blossom Culp, and the way I have it, she came to your daughter's rescue. There is surely more to the story, and I mean to get to the bottom of it."

I believed Miss Spaulding and thought of Alexander. If she found out everything, his name would come up.

"Well, I never!" Mrs. Shambaugh thundered. "Things have come to a pretty pass when two young girls can't go out on recess without being beaten half to death and are left to defend themselves the best way they can! And look here at this poor child's clothes. They are ruined too!"

Here Mrs. Shambaugh was somewhat misguided. My clothes had been in a pretty ruinous state before Les worked me over. "I will have my husband send out a new outfit from the store for this girl. She cannot go home looking like that! I would not like another mother seeing what *I* have seen!" Mrs. Shambaugh swept out then, cradling Letty, with Newton at her skirt-tails. "Though what Mr. Shambaugh will say, I do not know! Come along, Newton, and don't dawdle."

When the door closed behind them, Miss Spaulding let out a sigh. Then she said, "All right, Blossom, start at the beginning, and do not omit a detail."

I omitted only a few details. Miss Spaulding drew her office chair up to my cot and stared holes in me. She wears pince-nez glasses that perch on the nose and connect on a chain to a button on the bosom. Miss Spaulding has no bosom, so the button was planted at random on her chest.

The spectacles add years and dignity to her face, and she can look through you with them. She cares nothing for fiction. So I admitted most everything about dressing up as a ghost, and hiding in the privy, all to discourage Les Dawson's mob from causing destruction.

"This is all very interesting," she interrupted, "but I fail to see how your nocturnal activities incited Les Dawson to set on Letty."

"Oh, that," I replied. "Well, he seemed to confuse the two of us."

Miss Spaulding gave me a steady look. "Somehow I can't picture that, Blossom." So I had to own up to telling Old Man Leverette that I was Letty and how he called out her name in place of mine. I expected the worst from this. But Miss Spaulding's mouth worked, and she looked away out the window. She seemed to be swallowing a smile.

In any case, a delivery boy from the Select Dry Goods Company broke in on us about then, bearing a large box. My fingers faltered in getting through all the tissue paper. I'd never had a stitch of new clothes in my life. If it hadn't been for the rummage sale at the Foursquare Tabernacle, I'd have been wrapped in newspaper. My entire wardrobe was not enough to wad a shotgun with.

Miss Spaulding hung over me, interested, as I pulled out article after article. A starchy shirtwaist with tucks. A jacket with bone buttons. A tam-o'-shanter with a grosgrain band. A pleated skirt. Everything to match. With it two pair of stockings, white and tan, and a pair of shoes with pearl buttons. Stuck in one shoe top was a complimentary button-hook with SELECT DRY GOODS COMPANY FOR THE DISCERNING stamped on it. I'll say one thing for the Shambaughs. They are overbearing but not cheap. My eyes misted over.

Miss Spaulding touched my shoulder. "This is not charity, Blossom. You earned it. Now skin off your clothes, and let us see if these are a fit."

There are teachers who treat poverty like a crime, but not Miss Spaulding. While I was wiggling into my hard-won finery, she took up my old clothes. It was in her mind to pitch them out. But then she said, "You will want your other things for second best." This is a true lady speaking, who knows how to spare your feelings. Then she went out in the yard to give my old duds a good shaking to get the worst of the dirt out.

While she was absent, I happened to glance at the United States geography tests we'd lately taken. They were piled on her desk, hot from her grading pen. I only glanced at the top one and then the one beneath. They were the works of two girls in Letty's club: Nola Nirider and Ione Williams. Miss Spaulding's red-ink comments on them were in strong language. This was snooping, and I only mention it because it bears on future events.

When she returned, I was tricked out in my new togs. There was room to grow in the boots, but the rest fitted like a glove. Even the tam-o'-shanter fitted down well on my forehead. "Why, Blossom, what a transformation!" said Miss Spaulding, well pleased. And I was pleased too, in part that I hadn't revealed Alexander as a gang member. "You bob along home now," she said. "All's well that ends well."

But of course that was not an end. It was only a bare beginning. Nor was it the last time I was to see the inside of the principal's office.

· 3 ·

In earlier times I would have hastened to trap Alexander Armsworth in some out-of-the-way spot and there told him I'd saved him from a sure thrashing at Miss Spaulding's hand. She'd got the names of Champ Ferguson and Bub Timmons out of me with no trouble. She'd already dealt with Les Dawson. And she'd called him "Leslie" as she walloped him, adding insult to injury.

But my new refined appearance made me refine my methods as well. Alexander would put two and two together. Even he would figure that I was the Ghost in the Privy and that I'd had a private word with Miss Spaulding. Let him learn in his own time, and let him stew in his own juice. It would dawn on him that he owed me a favor, and I could wait. He knows I collect my debts.

At school next day I caused some comment but nothing direct. Though I was dressed better than most and entirely unlike myself, nobody came near. They were in the habit of paying me no mind. Still, many looked. I expect Letty

Shambaugh explained to all and sundry that my outfit was her mother's gift. But it didn't seem to dawn on her just how her fate and mine had entwined themselves.

Somewhere in my travels I'd come by a length of plaid taffeta ribbon. I tied my unruly hair back with it as best I could. And this was the crowning touch to my new appearance. I've already said I am not vain, but I was not far from it that day. Alexander seemed not to know me at all.

At lunch I laid out a nickel for a cup of milk and was having that with an apple when Letty Shambaugh came up, dragging her feet. There were purple marks on both our necks, souvenirs of the departed Les Dawson.

"Say, listen, Blossom," she said in a loud voice right in my face, "Mama says I should . . . well, anyway, you want to come over to my house after school today?" She eyed my new Select Dry Goods, and I could hear the ring of the cash register in her head. Her mama was clearly leaning on her to show me some friendship, and I enjoyed the pain Letty was having.

"I don't mind," I replied.

"You mean you won't come?" she said, brightening.

"I mean I will." And I did.

None of the Sunny Thoughts and Busy Fingers would walk me to Letty's house after school, not even Letty. I figured out my own way along Fairview Avenue, turning up late. As I climbed the porch steps, I knew I'd sooner face Les Dawson in a rage than a clique of stuck-up snips. But it's not my way to turn back.

Though the Shambaugh place is nowhere near as large

as the Armsworth mansion, it surpassed all my experience. There were rugs upon rugs, a profusion of overstuffed furniture, and of course electric lights. I walked in, supposing no one would answer if I knocked.

There in the front parlor all flopped on the floor with their skirts daintily tucked under their ankles were the club members: Letty, along with Nola Nirider and Ione Williams and Maisie Markham and Harriet Hochhuth and the Beasley twins, Tess and Bess, who are identical.

Now several of these were the very same girls who'd done me an injury back in fourth grade when I was new in town. And none of them had spoken a civil word to me since. Still, they were trying to act grown up. Harriet Hochhuth let out a strangled gasp and clutched her forehead when she saw me enter. Evidently nobody remembered to tell her I was included. But Tess and Bess leaned her way and whispered her into the picture.

Luckily for me Mrs. Shambaugh was passing among the group with refreshments. She had what Miss Spaulding would call "a civilizing influence" on them. "Why here is Blossom!" she cried. "Make room for her in your little circle, girls!" Letty's tongue shot out of her rosebud lips at her mother's blind side.

"How grateful we *all* are that Blossom was the *one* girl who stood up for Letty when she needed a *friend* the *most!*" boomed Mrs. Shambaugh. "I do *wonder* where the *rest* of her friends were in her *hour* of *need!*"

All the rest of her friends stared down into their little glass cups of apple juice.

There was a plate of finger sandwiches on the floor. And

as conversation languished when Mrs. Shambaugh was near, everybody chewed on them quietly. Though I was starved, I only had two. Maisie Markham wolfed down six, but she was soon to be sorry.

Finally Mrs. Shambaugh left us, and I wondered how a club worked. Nobody said much at first, though everybody shot everybody else looks full of meaning. At last Letty opened the meeting by putting down her cup and saying, "Oooo, I just hate apple juice, don't you?" And everybody agreed.

After more silence Letty sucked in her cheeks, saying, "Well, Blossom, you can't be here at the meeting without being a club member. And you can only belong for this one meeting." And everybody agreed.

This suited me well enough, since I didn't see much to it beyond the eats. "But you can't belong even for today without an initiation." And everybody agreed to this too. You never saw a group of girls more agreeable.

Letty could tell I didn't know what an initiation was. She twitched her shoulders importantly and explained. "You must entertain the group by showing off some talent such as singing or playing a piece on the piano. Or you can tell a story that is either very scary or about boys. Since you don't have any talents, you can start telling the story now. But keep your voice down, and if Mother comes back in the room suddenly, shut up."

I thought it was not wise to tell anything I knew about boys to a bunch who might know more. They were only waiting to laugh at me anyhow. So I tried to dredge up something scary to tell them. With such a simpering group,

I thought this might not be too hard, At once I recollected an experience my mama had, one of several similar and stranger than fiction.

I cleared my throat and began. "My mamá has the Gift of Second Sight."

"Oh, Heaven help us," Ione Williams said, "she's going to tell whoppers about her awful mother."

"Do you want to hear this story or not?" I inquired.

"Shut up, girls, and let's just see what she has to say," Letty remarked in her position as president.

Well, I told the story, which was an entirely true event. Mere white truth in simple nakedness, as the poet says. But I added little touches and extras to it. The bare bones of the story are these. When we lived down at Sikeston, my mama commanded respect for her powers and could sometimes help out the law when she felt like it. Sikeston is in many ways backward and largely lawless.

Now and again dead bodies turn up and lie unclaimed in the morgue, a tramp of either sex found in a ditch or bodies washed up on the riverbank. As I say, it is not an up-and-coming town, so there was no system of fingerprinting or the like for identification.

If a body hung around unspoken for in the morgue till it like to get ripe, the sheriff cut off its head and put it in a jar of alcohol for future reference. Anybody missing a relative could apply for a look through the jar collection. Certain people looked just for thrills. The rest of the body below the neck was buried at County expense.

One such a body turned up in a plowed field and excited comment, though the sheriff kept the details quiet. This was no ordinary corpse. It was a young woman of gentle birth and some beauty, now fading, wearing dressmaker clothes. And nobody claimed her, though a general notice went out.

Her severed head was in a jar on the sheriff's shelf before my mama got drawn in. The face on the head kept its beauty, even in death and alcohol. It bobbed in its jar before the sheriff's gaze. At last the mystery of it preyed on his thoughts until he called on my mama to identify the head with her powers.

She was brought into the room where the head reposed. By then the sheriff had pulled a croaker sack over the jar for his own peace of mind. Of course I was not along when my mama was sent for, but I can picture her in that chamber of death, dressed for the occasion. When she was about her business, she always threw a long shawl over her head. With her black eyes and dark lips and the gold crosses in her ears, she made an impression on all who saw her. Many would cross the street.

She stood before the shrouded jar and began to sway. Several witnesses were brought in and looked on. Mama told the sheriff not to show her the head until her Inner Sight had its chance. So they waited while she went into one of her trances.

After some moments a voice within Mama began to chant, "I see a young woman of breeding with hands unused to rough work. I see her too sheltered from the wickedness of this world to be proof against its dangers. I see her face before me, not in death, but as it was in life and is no more. She is past her first youth now, easy prey to any scoundrel who might cross her path and whisper lies into her ears.

"Her ears!" my mama moaned. "Oh, her pore ears, for

some beast of a man has jerked the emerald eardrops from her lobes, and left them ragged! And her eyes! Her eyes stare into mine, and they are her only natural imperfection. For one eye is robin's egg blue and t'other is hazel."

My mama fell silent then. And several in the room were unsure if she was playacting or not. But the sheriff reached over and pulled the sack off the jar. Pandemonium broke out then, and one man fainted. There were no ladies present, of course, except for Mama and the head.

Days before, when the sheriff had covered the jar with the sack, the eyes on the lady's head were closed. But when he whipped the sack off, the eyes on the severed head were wide open, staring into Mama's. And one of the dead eyes was robin's egg blue, and the other was hazel.

Some witnesses made for the door. But others stayed behind to see that the lobes on the staring head's pierced ears were torn indeed, just like Mama said.

She continued, still half in her trance, but addressed the dead head directly: "Yore people will find you now, for there is another feature which they will know you by. You have had a gold tooth in yore head since you was a girl. It's on the left side of yore mouth and chipped somewhat. What with that and them eyes, you will be reunited with yore loved ones, but naturally you won't know it, you pore cut-up thing."

At that, Mama seemed to come to herself and look around. She always knows exactly what she's said in any of her fits and swoons. Somebody urged the sheriff to lift out the head from the alcohol and check around in the clenched mouth to see if there was a chipped gold tooth anywhere in there.

"And while you are about it," my mama mentioned, "you will find a knot the size of two walnuts at the base of the skull beneath her back hair where she was knocked in the head with a bottle and killed by a tall man with a squint and a limp wearing a ring in the shape of a serpent."

The sheriff got the lid off the jar and reached down into the alcohol. He drew the ghastly head up; it hung by the hair in the air, dripping from the neck. All but the stoutest hearted turned aside while the sheriff explored in the head's mouth, drawing up one side. The mouth fell open, as if obedient. Sure enough, there was the gold tooth, slightly chipped in a mouth that seemed half to grin beneath them piercing eyes. The lump was on the back of the skull too.

A detailed description of the head went out to all the towns on the river. Shortly thereafter some well-to-do people of Stuttgart, Arkansas, answered the call. They were the dead woman's folks and come north for a view of her head. Not knowing she was dead, they'd never reported her missing.

She'd eloped with an implement salesman who'd killed her on her wedding night for the emeralds in her ears and the money in her purse. He'd spirited the body as far as Sikeston, where he'd dumped it. Then the crafty devil sent telegrams to the dead woman's kin from various places, signed with her name. Come to find out, he'd done this with many women and made a living at it.

He was a monster, and he was caught. For Mama seen him with her Second Sight: snake ring, limp, squint, and all. A man answering that description was rounded up in Texarkana. He was hanged there on the tree in Spring

Lake Park they keep for that purpose. Mama got very little credit and no reward. Still, a public demonstration of her skills brought people to her for advice and vision, though few could pay and fewer did. She was later hounded out of town by a more progressive element.

That's the sum and substance of the story I entertained the Sunny Thoughts and Busy Fingers girls with. They were an interested audience in spite of themselves. Though when I come to where the sheriff holds up the severed head and pokes into her green mouth for the gold tooth, it was too much for Maisie Markham.

I paused there because Maisie jumped up and made a run for the porch. We all watched from the window as she hung over the railing and threw up into the forsythia. Directly that interruption was over, Tess and Bess urged me to go on. They were so encouraging that Letty made a nasty gesture at them with one of her fingers. Maisie came back and stretched out on the couch to hear how the story ended.

When I finished up, they fidgeted but were speechless, except for Harriet Hochhuth, who said, "How do you suppose the head happened to open its eyes?"

But Letty said, "Oooo, that was *repulsive*. I wish I hadn't heard it."

"Well, you *said* it was to be scary," said Tess or Bess, "and it *was*." This was brave of her, but she soon fell back. Letty was sending her a silent message. It may have been that if everybody liked the story, I'd have to be made a life member of the club.

"It wasn't a story," Letty explained. "It was just a lot of Blossom's lies. She couldn't tell the truth if she tried." She waited then till everybody had to agree. This might not have got my dander up, but the next thing Letty said did. "There is no such a thing as Second Sight as everybody knows. And if there was, *Blossom's* family wouldn't have any. Heaven knows, they don't have anything else."

"That's a lie right there," I said. And then before I thought: "I have the Second Sight my own self."

"Aha! I saw this coming!" crowed Letty, jumping up. "If you have the Second Sight, Blossom Culp, let's see it. Haul off and do something spooky. Talk is *cheap,* Blossom, particularly yours. Prove it!"

"That's right. You'd better prove it, Blossom," all agreed. I liked to have fainted with the strain of the moment, because they looked ready to set on me and ruin my new outfit if I didn't deliver. Even Maisie was recovering fast and raising up from the couch. Her little pig eyes looked mean.

I didn't truly think they'd cut me up for bait. Not with Mrs. Shambaugh somewhere in the house. But I had to satisfy them or slink off in disgrace. Pride is a terrible thing sometimes. I racked my brains and played for time.

"We have to be in a dim room," I remarked. "It's too bright in here. After dark would be better."

"*Now,* Blossom," Letty said, and her little dimpled hands were on her hips, and her little dimpled elbows were fanning the air. "We can go into the room where Daddy smokes and pull the blind."

Everybody made a rush for this room, under the back stairs. Letty yanked heavy curtains across the window. "*Now* what do you need, Blossom, a crystal ball?" She poked the girls nearest her in the gloom to remind them to laugh.

I did just notice, though, that being in a darker place with me had quieted them down some. One more point in my favor and they might desert Letty completely, if only long enough to cover my retreat. Then I got a sudden inspiration, more secondhand than Second Sight. It was in regard to something I'd spied in the principal's office.

I pulled out a straight chair and sat down with my back to the door. As there weren't enough chairs to go around, the rest had to settle at my feet. So far so good, I thought. "It takes me a while to warm up," I mentioned.

"Don't be too long," Letty warned, "or we'll give you a broom, and you can fly home on it, ha ha."

I began to sway in my chair then, starting up slow. I always have been able to roll my eyes up into my head so only the whites show. As a kid I practiced that by the hour. "Oh, look what's happening to her eyes, isn't that sickening!" somebody said.

I moaned low in my throat, wishing I'd thought to ask for a candle. Candlelight always adds a touch. But I proceeded without it. In a far-off voice I began to moan a poem, working up from a whisper:

> *The . . . ghost . . . am . . . I*
> *Of . . . winds . . . that . . . die*
> *Alike . . . on . . . land . . . and . . . sea*
> *O Second Sight! O Second Sight!*
> *Send one small glimpse to me!*

Commencing with a real poem I have by heart, I added an ending to suit the occasion. By then my eyes were rolled so far back in my head I was looking at my brains. But you could hear a pin drop in the room.

"What is this vision I see before my inner eyes?" I asked, and waited as if for an answer. "A crime. A crime has been committed. A crime that will be punished with fearful retribution!"

"Oh dear," came Harriet Hochhuth's voice, "I don't really care too much for this sort of thing."

"And the criminal is not far off!" I continued. "No, wait! Two outlaws . . . and in this very room!"

"Make her stop," someone said in a small voice.

"I see the initials of one of the crooks. The letters are floating in the air before me."

There was stirring on the floor as, I suppose, everybody shifted around, on the lookout for floating initials.

"N. N. are two of the initials," I continued. "And the others are . . . I. and let me see . . . W.! Oh, what have these two been up to that will only lead them to a thrashing from a heavy hand?"

Whispers came from the floor around me as several came to their own conclusions about the owners of the initials. "They are cheats, these two," I moaned on, completely warmed up. "They've passed the answers on the United States geography test back and forth. But their crime has come to light."

There was a general intake of breath from the floor as I got more specific. Miss Spaulding had wound up our United States geography on Monday with a stiff test. I'd seen the papers on her desk, and I knew she'd caught Nola Nirider and Ione Williams red-handed. All their wrong answers were the same, and there were plenty of them. Miss Spaulding is not to be trifled with.

"Sacramento is the capital of California, not San Diego

as these two culprits both put down. And Robert E. Lee hails from Virginia, not Kentucky. There is more evidence before my eyes, but my powers grow dimmmmmm. I only see two more letters—a couple of Fs. But those are grades.

"But I can hear the sounds of bottoms being smacked and shrieks of pure pain!"

The curtain rings clattered as Letty swept the drapes back. Light flooded the room. I let my eyeballs roll forward to see Ione and Nola shrinking on the carpet in the midst of the rest.

"Did you two cheat on the test?" Letty barked, taking charge again with her usual bossiness.

"Certainly not," said Nola.

"What if we did?" said Ione, who is more brazen.

"Well, if that doesn't just about make me sick!" spat out Letty. "While all the rest of us beat our brains out studying, you two went off by yourselves and cheated! Then you had no more sense than to get caught."

"Just how do you know that?" said Ione, very sassy. "We don't even have the tests back yet, so how do you know?"

"Because Blossom said so," Letty snapped. Then she caught her breath. She'd given me credit and could not take it back. She shot me a look guiltier than Nola and Ione combined. For I had told—or foretold—something no living soul could know, except for Miss Spaulding. And I'd been believed. I had Letty in a cleft stick then, with no time to think. Both Ione and Nola looked plain scared, both of me and Miss Spaulding. Nola commenced to sob, anticipating pain.

But then something happened that even I could not explain. My eyes did not roll back, yet I seemed to go blind for a second. There was a peal of thunder that nobody else seemed to hear. Then a strange flash, like lightning at night —jagged and blue. The room and the girls flickered and faded from me, and I spoke without conscious thought:

"Oh dear," I said, "Newton just fell off the back of the trolley and was run over by Miss Dabney's electric auto."

Then I blinked and saw the room clear and all the girls' eyes staring at me. But only for a moment. The next second was split by a powerful shriek from Mrs. Shambaugh. Evidently she'd been eavesdropping behind the door the entire time. When I remarked that her little boy had just been run over—several blocks away—the shock of it nearly carried her off.

It was a confused hour later before it dawned on me. The blood had not run too thin. I had the Gift of Second Sight and the Power to See the Unseen. And maybe more.

· 4 ·

Sure enough, Newton Shambaugh, the apple of his mother's eye, had been run over by Miss Gertrude Dabney's Pope-Detroit Electric brougham. And while a cause for alarm, it was not a tragedy. I wondered at my Second Sight starting up over such a trivial matter, little realizing where it would lead.

I thought maybe I'd been forcing it with my entertainment for Letty's club. Maybe being in Newton's family home provided Vibrations. My mama had spoke highly of her Vibrations when she spoke at all. And then too, maybe my Gift was just coming of age along with the rest of me. A person goes through a lot of changes at that time of life.

Newton is not always the mama's boy his mama wishes him to be. She dresses him funny, which only makes him have to prove himself to the other boys in third grade. They all think it's a pastime to steal rides on the streetcar by clinging to the back end of it.

The Woodlawn Avenue car had just swung out of Lincoln Square downtown that afternoon, with Newton hanging off the back of it. Then he turned loose and lost his grip.

Right behind the trolley was coming Miss Dabney in her Pope-Detroit Electric. Most Bluff City people with automobiles have the gasoline or steam type. But Miss Dabney was said to be a nervous spinster with a terror of explosions, so she drove one of the only electric motorcars ever seen. It was as unusual as herself, in the shape of an Amish buggy with brass side lamps and snow-white tires. It would not go faster than a slow mule, and she steered it with a tiller instead of a wheel. Luckily, it was lightweight.

When Newton dropped backwards off the Woodlawn Avenue streetcar, Miss Dabney steered right over an arm and leg of his. Before she could get stopped, she'd passed over him and collapsed back in her seat, quite gray-faced.

All this I saw in a sudden revelation just before Mrs. Shambaugh let out her shriek. She pounded out of the house with all the Busy Fingers and me on her heels. We all fled down Fairview Avenue as from a burning house. Porch swings right down the block emptied as people stepped forward to see us pass.

"Where?" Mrs. Shambaugh screamed back at me, never breaking her stride.

"West Main Street just off the Square, near as I can figure," I yelled back at her. On we all sped, though it was better than five blocks. A person would not credit the speed Mrs. Shambaugh could put on, but then she is All Mother.

We were nearly the first on the scene. Newton Shambaugh

was stretched out in the gutter with tire tracks over two of his limbs. He only began to bawl when his mother was upon him, wailing, "Oh, what has happened to my poor baby boy? Is he crippled up for life?" et cetera.

Miss Gertrude Dabney was being helped down out of her Pope-Detroit by several men from the hotel barbershop. She looked shaky on her pins, but she surprised them all by whipping around and giving the Pope-Detroit Electric a good hard kick. "I will never drive in that thing again and will sell it for scrap. Oh, what have I done? I did not see that little critter until he dropped off the streetcar, and then I could not find my brake lever, and I steered *at* him instead of *away*. Though I could not have missed him anyhow. Oh, I feel worse than he does. Is he alive?" et cetera.

Newton was alive, though nearly smothered by his mother. He was soon on his feet and proving to all that his limbs were sound. "She run right over me, but I'm tough as old shoe leather," Newton crowed in his piping voice to the Busy Fingers. He'd suffered less harm than his sister had at Les Dawson's hands. Though all in all it had not been a good week for the Shambaughs.

Mrs. Shambaugh did not let fly at Miss Dabney as I expected. They're both ladies of a certain standing in the community and would not brawl in public. Besides, Newton capering around underfoot would have been a distraction. Miss Dabney had shown her regret by kicking the Pope-Detroit again and again. She kicked at the wheel once, got her foot tangled in the wire spokes, and nearly fell under the auto herself. And so after both being hysterical, each lady congratulated the other on her calmness.

When it finally penetrated to Mrs. Shambaugh that Newton caused the accident by jumping a free ride on the streetcar, she snatched him up and nearly did real damage to him.

The end of it was that the two ladies fell into a long and rambling conversation so tedious that all the crowd wandered back to the barbershop. "Was it not a lucky thing," Miss Dabney remarked, "that you happened to be so nearby when the accident occurred? I declare, I don't know what I'd have done if you'd had to be sent for. You might have been out paying calls, for I know you are very popular socially."

"Oh, but I was at home," Mrs. Shambaugh replied, only then remembering.

"But how . . .?"

I was standing close by, expecting my name might come up. And so it did. More confused than mystified, Mrs. Shambaugh tried to explain that I'd manifested Second Sight. If her head had been clearer, she might not have admitted it.

"The supernatural?" Miss Dabney said in an entirely more interested voice. "The Second Sight?" She is known to be eccentric, which only means that things surprising to others are no surprise to her. "But I thought you were a boy!" she said, bending over and looking at me through a hole in her motoring veil.

I don't consider myself eccentric, but here was a woman I could understand. She'd heard all about how Alexander Armsworth had once seen a ghost, and so she had the two of us confused. I put her straight. "Well, I call all this very interesting!" she declared. And then she gave Mrs. Shambaugh a ride home in her electric, though she'd sworn never to drive it again.

The Busy Fingers, under Letty's direction, straightaway abandoned me. I was left standing on the Square as alone as usual, and yet entirely changed. New Worlds were opening up. But even with the Second Sight I could not yet see them plain.

Drop a pebble in a pond, and the ripples will reach to far shores in every direction. That's the effect of that first Manifestation. There'd been witnesses aplenty, all talkative. And those who might see through that fibbing business about the United States geography tests could not explain my vision of Newton's mishap any more than I could.

I might soon be in the public eye, so I was anxious to practice my powers to see if I could get them working good. I didn't know but what Second Sight is like an unused muscle that needs limbering up and regular exercise to work right. As I was to find out, it's more of a sometime thing. Sometime working, sometime not. Sometime outdoing itself to an alarming degree.

As I couldn't practice in private in a two-room house, I imparted to my mama that I had the Gift. She come close to calling me a liar and then sulked. For many years Mama had claimed that the Gift ended with her, and so it was bad news to her that it hadn't. She was jealous and showed it. Still, she's a woman of few words, and we tend to go our separate ways.

At first, the more I concentrated, the more confusing my visions became. Oh, I'd have them, sure enough. But many were hard to decipher. I will mention one or two that I haven't deciphered yet and probably never will, just to show how little control I had.

I'd set out on our porch steps of a night, watching the streetcars pass and listening to the November wind rattle the leaves. This dry rustling and the far-off hum on the rails lulled my mind and led me onto unknown ground. On that very first evening I heard thunder again and saw the world lit suddenly blue. The fit was on me. Very nearly scared, I hid my eyes in my hands, and then of course my Second Sight took over completely.

I thought of a ship in an ice-strewn sea, sending out an unheeded message. But the scene shifted. And I saw the room under the Shambaughs' stairs where I'd met with the Busy Fingers that very afternoon. It was the same room, though changed, and the same group of girls, more changed still, and I was not among them.

They were old women. I barely recognized them. All had hair more blue than white except for Ione Williams, whose hair was sparse and the color of an apricot. In reality Ione's hair is thick and dark. Some were thinner and some fatter. Maisie Markham was enormous, overflowing a settee where Mr. Shambaugh's desk now stands. Each of them wore a wedding band rubbed thin with age. They were so old themselves that I was reminded of a coven of witches.

I could hear them cackling at something Letty was telling them, though I could not hear her at first. Her neck was drawn and crepey, and she wore the oddest pair of spectacles imaginable. They were of some shiny metal, set with little glittering stones.

But the two oddest things about this vision were these: All of the girls now grown old sat around in dresses like shifts that did not cover their knees, leaving their unfortunate-looking legs all bare. Though they wore flesh-colored stockings like pony girls in a circus. The other peculiar thing was that the odd bluish light that tinted the vision came from a metal box located where a potted fern now stands.

While Letty spoke on silently to the rest, bossy as ever, most of them kept one eye on the metal box. There was a moving picture in it, flickering, of a smiling young woman holding up a box of either cornmeal or baking powder. I don't know what else might come in such a box. The young woman smiled and nodded encouragingly to the Busy Fingers and seemed to be speaking too.

Then the vision faded. But I heard Letty's voice—cracked and old, speaking up clear as a bell. I only caught a few words. "Oh, lands," she was saying, "if only Les had lived, for a widow's lot is not an easy proposition. . . ." And all the old Busy Fingers seemed to agree.

And that's all I heard or saw of that first weird vision that haunted me long after.

Oh, there were other visions in those first days, though some were too vague to call to mind and some too outlandish to credit. Each seemed to start with a great ship laboring in winter seas, as if I was myself far off from solid ground. Once I even had a clear view of Indians tramping along the streetcar right of way, trudging by on foot, with the squaws bringing up the rear. They were all dressed in skins and carried bows instead of firearms. So I knew they were the redmen who'd used this trail long before the white man's day. They were traveling by night, lit by a moon that was not out in the real world. And I thought long about these people who'd lived across the land and left no mark and done no harm.

Oh, I had visions! I seemed to look in every direction, and the sights liked to drive me half silly. I'd have been a match for Miss Dabney if I'd told all I saw. Once I even saw faceless men in silver suits walking across rubble under a black sky. They bobbed like balloons or kids' toys. They were planting an American flag with too many stars on it in the gray ground. The flag was stiffened with wire, for there was no breeze nor any air. And where they were I could not tell, but it was unearthly. This vision dimmed quicker than most, for it was a dark night with clouds before the moon.

As I recollect now, I wonder if that wasn't the night I first saw the strange ghost boy. Him who was to loom so large in my life and drive out those other visions from my Second Sight. It seemed like he'd been deep in my dreams long before. When he began, I swear I don't know, though various people have quizzed me on this point.

But it may have been that night, or one soon after. Certainly I was on the porch, staring out into many a dim world. Over by the tracks I perceived a white form in utter darkness, no more than a blob, but glowing like Saint Elmo's fire. I tried to blink the whitish thing away, but it wouldn't go. Somewhere inside me came the sound of breaking glass and the startled cry of a child left alone in the night. The wind came up then, but not a tree branch moved. I was winter cold.

A boy lay huddled by the tracks not ten yards from the porch. It wasn't Alexander Armsworth, and it wasn't Newton Shambaugh. It was a stranger in parts strange to him, though how I knew this is anybody's guess.

I made no move in his direction; though it was not fear that held me back, for I knew he was there and not there. And I knew that while he was in great need, there was nothing I could do for him yet. He'd shown himself to me, and I knew we two would meet again.

He seemed pinned to the ground, and I saw his arms were bound to his sides. His head rose up and turned against the blackness of the Armsworths' barn. He was a curly-headed blond little fellow, younger than myself, if he had an age at all. I knew he was dead and undead and here and somewhere else. And he spoke an anguished message that I was still deaf to.

He melted like snow. The gravel beside the tracks continued to dazzle, and I thought of ice. Then the moon broke through and seemed to splinter the clouds into sharp lines of light. "Whiskers round the moon," I said to myself. And the brighter the moon beamed, the fewer traces of the boy I saw.

Another night I was returning from our privy when I heart the sound of great groaning. Not of a human voice or one that had once been human. This was the grinding of two great objects against one another—iron against ice, I thought, though why, I did not know. But I knew as sure as I was standing there that if I ventured around the house, I'd see my ghost boy laid bound up and all alone, living again through his dying moments.

All this made me wonder how I could put my powers to work. This entirely novel vision of the ghost boy was coming back on me, and it was not entertaining. Besides, to neglect the uses of a talent is not my way.

In the next days at school, it was clear that the Sunny Thoughts and Busy Fingers had closed their doors on me. Letty had sworn them all to secrecy, not wishing to give me credit. I know this for a fact because Tess or Bess whispered as much to me in the washroom. But fame in a school is very small potatoes to me. Besides, secrets a group will keep slip out in individual ways. And I later had the proof of that.

One afternoon when I was making my solitary way home from school, I heard a soft whir behind me and the sound of leaves being mashed in the gutter. A Pope-Detroit Electric brougham glided up. Miss Gertrude Dabney was erect at its tiller. She had her machine under control that day and rolled to a smooth stop.

There had been so much excitement at our first meeting that I hadn't taken in all of Miss Dabney. She had a reputation as the town character and lived up to it. Everything about her was unlike everybody else. They called her a recluse, which is something like a hermit. However, my notion of a hermit is not somebody who motors around town, running down small boys.

She lowered the side window by means of a strap and thrust her head out. Her motoring veil was pinned around a gray velvet toque that rose up from her head, giving her unnecessary height. From over one ear an egret feather rose even higher and curled in the air. She stared filmily at me through her veil. "Do you like my hat? I had it copied from a picture of Queen Mary."

"Yes, ma'am," I replied.

"Yes, what?"

"Yes, ma'am. I like your hat right well." This was not the first lie of my life, nor the last.

"I am only making conversation," Miss Dabney went on, "because I am in confusion. Are you or are you not the child who has the Second Sight? At a distance I thought so. Up close, I wonder."

This was understandable. I couldn't wear my Select Dry Goods outfit daily without wearing it out. So I only added parts of it to perk my other clothes. That day I had on the new coat with the bone buttons over an old striped flannel skirt and my regular black stockings. My hair was tied back with string. It was more disguise than outfit.

"I am the same."

"Ah, yes, I was quite sure. And your name is Hortense Miller?"

I began to see how Miss Dabney operated. She didn't like asking a straightforward question, but she liked a straightforward answer. "No, ma'am, my name's Blossom Culp, same as it was the other day."

"Are you sassy?" she inquired with her eyebrows high.

"No, ma'am."

"Witty, then. Would you like to come to tea?"

"Yes, ma'am." I knew that in the better houses tea was served with cakes. And since I was starved, I was ready to scramble right up into the Pope-Detroit.

"Tomorrow at four then," she said, drawing her head in

like a turtle. But she stuck it out again at once. "And you may bring a young friend. Children alone always feel outnumbered." Then the side window whistled up, and the Pope-Detroit slid soundlessly away. I watched it weave out onto the crown of the road on its motorcycle wheels and disappear into bonfire smoke.

My mind took a small leap forward and embraced Alexander Armsworth. As I've said before, a person does not like to be picked up and then dropped. It was high time me and him had words.

· 5 ·

EVERY MORNING at school just before the Pledge of Allegiance we have an inspection. Miss Spaulding takes volunteers, and I'd prepared myself that next day to be one.

"Who will serve as monitor for row five?" she sang out, and up shot my hand. "Very well, Blossom, front and center." I had on my complete new outfit and my plaid ribbon. In the cloakroom hung my tam-o'-shanter. I was ready to monitor and to take tea with Miss Dabney. I was also ready for Alexander Armsworth.

"Hands out for inspection, palms and backs." Miss Spaulding looked me up and down. "My, you have been thorough," she said in a lower voice. "You have nearly done some violence to those cuticles. Handkerchief?"

I whipped a clean one out of my shirtwaist front, folded with the ragged parts tucked in. "Very well, Blossom, work your row."

Letty was not in my row, and I was sorry about that. The

mortification of being inspected by me would have finished her off. There was a hole in the row where Les Dawson once sat, and behind was Alexander, trying not to notice me. "Handkerchief?"

He nodded.

"Well, let's see it," I said, twitching my shoulders like Letty.

He leaned forward in slow motion and drew out a handkerchief from his hip pocket.

"Comb?"

He nodded.

"Well, let's have a look at that too. I have a job to do, you know, Alexander." It like to drive him wild. His brows beetled, and he slapped a comb on the desk. "Hands, palms then backs."

I reached out and just touched his fingers. "Well, they look so-so to me." In truth they were scrubbed pink and smelled of Lewis Lye Soap. They jittered with anger.

"Move on, Blossom," he whispered, "or I'll black your eye."

"Meet me behind the ash pit at recess, or I'll tell Miss Spaulding where you was Halloween night, and I'll add to the story," I whispered back. Oh, I was ready for Alexander. My plans were laid. I moved on for a look at Harriet Hochhuth's hanky.

He made me wait behind the ash pit till recess was half over. I knew he would. He's broke out with pride. But he ambled up finally with his hands in his hip pockets, as if just happening by. "Don't think for a minute," he began, "that I didn't know it was you in Old Man Leverette's privy tricked out as a ghost. I was not fooled, though I lost my footing and fell."

"'Oh, a haunt! Oh, I am cursed!'" I quoted to remind him of what he'd said at the time.

"And now I hear tell you're going around saying you have the Gift and Second Sight and like as not can cure warts with the touch of your hand. You are busier than a one-armed paperhanger these days, Blossom. And all I want to know is, what business do you think you have with me?"

"If you would hush for one minute, you'd hear," I replied with some dignity.

"Well, hurry up. I haven't got all day."

"You have the same day as anybody else. And I'd think you could figure out the business me and you have." I waited while he played dumb and then continued. "Miss Spaulding grilled me good about that gang of yours doing all that Halloween mischief. You know she works hand in glove with the law. She'd as soon turn your name in down at the sheriff's as look at you. And even if she didn't, she'd whup the tar out of you for running with Les Dawson and them. She doesn't know you're falling in with that low-life bunch. And you notice she has throwed Les out of school already."

"He's better off," Alexander replied. "I wish I was out of this school."

"And what would your folks do to you if you got expelled?" I inquired. Alexander began to wilt. "You're one lucky kid," I went on, "to have a friend like me to save your good name. Hot tongs would not get me to rat on you. But of course I could."

"Unless," said Alexander.

"What do you mean by *unless?*" I asked.

"Unless I do something you want me to do." Alexander was picking up clinkers and throwing them against the schoolhouse wall, hard. Boys are always throwing things. It soothes their nerves. "You're nothing but a common blackmailer, Blossom. There's nothing too low for you to try."

"Well, I wouldn't stoop to pushing over privies," I replied. "I ain't sunk *that* low."

"If you keep harping about Halloween," Alexander warned, "I'll leave you where you stand and take my chances." So I saw I'd pushed him about far enough and went on to play my last card.

"What I want you to do is purely social. Miss Gertrude Dabney is having me to tea this afternoon and said I should bring a friend. I choose you."

"Choose again," said Alexander. "I don't go to tea parties."

"You'll go to this one."

"It's common knowledge that Miss Dabney is crazy as a coot."

"That may be," I said, "but she's having us to tea. There'll probably be cakes and cookies."

"You're just trying to get me alone," said Alexander, who can be very stuck on himself sometimes. "Miss Dabney doesn't know you from Adam's off ox."

"She knows me all right. And you know how. My Second Sight revealed how her auto run Newton Shambaugh down. That's common knowledge too. And if knowledge is common enough, even you hear it."

"And what if I won't go?" He stubbed at the ground with the toe of a boot.

"Then I turn you straight in to the principal. See if I don't."

"And I thought we were friends," he mumbled, harking back to an earlier time he'd planned to forget.

"We are. And Miss Dabney said to bring a friend."

Alexander gave this deep thought. Then as the bell rang, he said, "On two conditions. One: that we only stay a couple minutes. And two: that we don't have any talk about supernatural powers. I've put all that behind me. It only gets a person into trouble. And I don't want to hear any of your lies about powers of your own. Miss Dabney is weird enough without you adding to it."

"Anything you say, Alexander," I simpered, and skipped off.

But he yelled after me, "I'm not walking you to Miss Dabney's. I'll meet you in front of her house!"

"Four o'clock sharp!" I sang out over my shoulder.

No one passing Miss Dabney's house fails to mention her craziness, even though many of these people have little to go on. Besides, I've noticed that only a thin line divides the insane from the rest of the population.

Alexander joined me on the inside of Miss Dabney's neglected hedge, and we waded together through the leaves on the front walk. As we were going to a tea, I wore my tam-o'-shanter, though the band leaves a lasting groove across my forehead. I tried to take Alexander's arm, but it hung at his side, stiff as if broken.

Dead ferns drooped from hanging pots along the porch, and the railings were splintered. I rang the bell. Miss Dabney's shadow already loomed over us beyond the colored glass in the door. Alexander shuddered, and the door opened.

She towered over us like a silo. I believe Miss Dabney's the tallest woman I've ever seen. She stared down at us with alarm, like we'd come to take her away.

"I'm Blossom Culp," I reminded her, throwing my head well back, "and this here is Alexander Armsworth."

"Well, of course you are," said Miss Dabney, peering down her long nose.

As she was standing her ground, I said, "We're here for tea."

"I should only hope," she said, "as it is already set out." At that she gave way and walked off down a dim hallway past a cobwebbed grandfather's clock. There was a smell of wood rot and a biting chill to the place.

"You'll end up this way if you don't stop being so peculiar," Alexander muttered in my ear as we followed behind.

Every word Miss Dabney spoke confirmed Alexander in the notion that she was far gone in the head, but I caught a sparkle of mockery in her sharp eyes that spoke of sanity to me. I thought she might even have some clever secret plan up her long sleeve that had nothing to do with tea. She did.

We followed her trailing skirts into a back parlor where all the shutters were drawn, giving it a jailhouse effect. There were a dozen chairs, and Alexander picked one well away from me. He flopped down and commenced to pick at the crocheted doilies on his chair arms.

The room was so dark I could only see the glint of the silver teapot on a table before Miss Dabney. She was so tall and her sofa was so low that she nearly had to look at us through her knees. She wore a tea gown of old rose with bishop's sleeves. It showed a good deal of her neck and withered bosom, caked with Coty powder.

As my eyes adjusted, I saw the room was busy with ferns, bamboo stands, and marble busts. I was glad to see plates of iced bakery cakes beside the teapot. Just above Miss Dabney's head hung two large oval portraits in thick gilt frames. They were of a man and a woman, hand tinted, who looked so stiff I mistook them for kin of Miss Dabney. The man had a small pointed beard and wore a uniform heavy with gold braid. The woman was hard-faced, with pearls that wound round and round above a solid bust. She appeared to have a diamond crown on her head.

Alexander rolled his eyes at these portraits as if it was just like Miss Dabney's relations to go around in crowns and uniforms they weren't entitled to.

"I keep this room as cool as possible," Miss Dabney mentioned, making no move to the tea. "We live in a hot country, tropical by some standards, and I suffer from the heat." Alexander shot me a grim look. It was a nippy November day outside and freezing within. "All my tastes are English," Miss Dabney explained.

As there was nothing to say to that, she fixed on Alexander. "If you are the Armsworth boy, your family lives in that very large house on Pine Street. The one with the barn where you—"

"Yes, ma'am," Alexander interrupted.

"—discovered the ghost," finished Miss Dabney.

"Yes, ma'am. But I only knew that one ghost to speak to. Kind of like a fluke. And I no longer have any powers. I'd sooner not talk about the supernatural anyhow." Alexander sulked. "It's not natural."

"It is curious etiquette to announce what you will not discuss at a tea," Miss Dabney said. "But of course there are many topics we can touch on. Your sister is married to that bright young newspaperman, I believe?"

"Yes," Alexander said. "Lucille married Lowell Seaforth here a while back."

"And now she's in the family way," I blurted out suddenly, "with a little stranger due late next spring."

Alexander's face colored up something alarming, and Miss Dabney's eyebrows shot high. "Well, I don't know if children discussing such topics at a tea is quite etiquette either," she said, somewhat baffled.

"Listen, Blossom!" Alexander yelled at me, "don't tell lies about Lucille just to make yourself interesting. She isn't in the family way, or she'd have told us. Anyway, how could you—"

We all three of us seemed to know without me admitting anything. I wouldn't have any way of knowing except that as I sat in Miss Dabney's parlor, I had a sudden flash of my Second Sight. Not even thunder and lightning this time or any need to concentrate. When Miss Dabney referred to Alexander's big sister, my entire mind switched to Dr. Beasley's office downtown. He was sitting there in his white coat, with the metal reflector on his head. Lucille was fully dressed but blushing.

And Dr. Beasley was saying at that very moment, "Yes, yes, Mrs. Seaforth, a little stranger in late May, no question about it. And we must keep a sharp eye on the little mother-to-be and see that she stays in tiptop shape." All this I saw and heard as if I'd been there instead of where I was. Alexander's face was near purple with rage and shame.

I began to understand why he denied the Gift to himself. Seeing what others can't and knowing what's not yours to know leads to difficulties. I decided to blurt out less in the future, if I could get through this present situation.

Miss Dabney was fussing over the tea things. She was creating a diversion with food and trying hard to think of another topic that would be good etiquette, or at least safe.

"I beg your pardon," I said quite loud to Alexander. "Lucille is none of my business. I shouldn't have brought her up. And *you* figure out how I come by that particular piece of news, which you'll find out is true. But if you call me a liar one more time, I'll come up behind you sometime with a rock and knock you in the head. SPLATTER YOUR BRAINS ALL OVER THE SIDEWALK. AND I MEAN IT!" I screamed the last part.

"That is *much* better," Miss Dabney said, peering into the teapot. "I would far rather hear children quarreling than talking the way you two have been. I found it quite ... eccentric." Then she looked at us both, and even Alexander saw the mockery in her wise old eye. "Now, how do you take your tea?" she asked me.

"Oh, any old way," I replied, not knowing.

"No, no," she sighed. "That is not a proper reply. And this is proper English tea. Sent directly from Fortnum and Mason in London. There is no tea like it in Bluff City, and you must know how you take it.

"If you are unsure, say, 'Rather weak and just a little milk.' If you have a sweet tooth as I expect you have, say,

'One lump, if you please.' If you have exotic tastes, and I rather think you might, you could say, 'With lemon if you have it.' Some people take their tea with nothing at all in it, but that is rather austere.

"Now I shall begin again. Miss Culp, how will you have your tea?"

I swallowed hard and replied, "Three lumps and lemon. If you have it. Please."

"Not bad," Miss Dabney murmured. She held an ornate cup high. With little silver tongs she dropped three lumps, one at a time, into the cup. And I saw that lumps were sugar. Then with a tiny fork she lifted a thin lemon slice into the cup too. It was all dainty and interesting, and Alexander looked worried. Miss Dabney handed the cup to me. With her long arms she could reach halfway across the parlor.

As she did this, there came the first of several loud noises from the back of the house. It sounded like a hired girl had taken a hammer to the plumbing. Then there was the noise of a drawer being banged shut and knives rattling in it. Then heavy footsteps across linoleum, back and forth. An oven door banged shut. This continued and ceased. Then it would start up again, drowning out parts of our conversation.

"Oh dear," Miss Dabney mumbled to herself. "I wish she had a lighter touch.

"Now, Mr. Armsworth," she said, holding up another cup. Alexander gripped his chair arms, and no sound escaped him. "Allow me to fix your tea as most gentlemen like it. Not too sweet and with enough milk to fortify it. Will that do?"

"That will do me very well, Miss Dabney," he said, relieved. And I saw he was warming up to her within limits. His voice cracked as it often does. For many months now it's been changing, but not for the better.

"The cups you are drinking from are Rockingham china, and they are more than seventy years old. Rockingham was Queen Victoria's favorite china. Queen Victoria is dead, of course."

At that, the sound of the hired girl in the kitchen evidently attacking a milk separator with a potato masher filled the parlor. Me and Alexander watched Miss Dabney's lips moving; we couldn't hear everything she said because of the noise. ". . . and saucer are painted with different British castles. Notice the castles on your cups."

I was drinking from a cup with a gray castle painted on it, trimmed in gold. Underneath was the label: BALMORAL, A ROYAL RESIDENCE IN SCOTLAND.

"And what castle are you drinking from, Alexander Armsworth?" Miss Dabney asked.

"WINDSOR CASTLE HIGH ABOVE THE RIVER THAMES," Alexander read from his cup.

"Ah yes, Windsor," said Miss Dabney. "That is one of the homes of our friends portrayed on the wall above my head. The man in the naval uniform is King George the Fifth, Monarch of Great Britain. He is Queen Victoria's grandson. And the lady in the other portrait is his wife, Queen Mary, a handsome woman. Every afternoon I take my tea with the Royal Family."

Alexander shot me another look, grim again. This was to remind me that Miss Dabney was crazy after all, having tea with two pictures, and that common knowledge had been right about her.

"I am very proud of my Rockingham china." As she said this, there came the sound of breaking dishes from the kitchen. Miss Dabney looked pained.

She came to herself in a moment and passed around a Rockingham plate with small white sandwiches piled on Glamis Castle. These had been hidden behind the iced cakes and were scant temptation to me. "A proper English tea begins with bread and butter sandwiches and moves on to sweet pastries later," Miss Dabney explained.

During the bread and butter course, we listened to coal being shaken out of a scuttle. A sound of somebody battering the range with a poker followed.

Glancing at the closed door all this unnecessary noise came from, Miss Dabney passed the plate with the iced cakes. "Take one at a time," she instructed, "for I will keep passing them. An English tea is lavish but unhurried." I smiled into my cup, recalling how Alexander vowed to spend only two minutes on this visit.

"Now then, young Armsworth," Miss Dabney said, licking crumbs from the corner of her V-shaped mouth, "I wonder if they teach you any history at Horace Mann School."

"Plenty of it," Alexander replied. "Too much."

"Then perhaps you would care to tell me the worst disaster ever to have occurred on the North American continent."

I was glad she hadn't asked me that, for I had no notion. Alexander thought deeply and then said, "The shooting of President McKinley?"

"Wrong," said Miss Dabney. "Blossom, do you know?"

"The San Francisco earthquake?" I ventured. "My aunt foresaw it with her Second Sight."

"Nevertheless incorrect," said Miss Dabney, shaking her

head. "The worst disaster *by far* was the Revolutionary War of 1776!" She looked around the room in triumph, pleased at herself for knowing the right answer.

"But how can that be?" asked Alexander in a breaking voice. "We won!"

"Precisely!" said Miss Dabney as Alexander fell into her trap. At the mention of war there came the gunfire sound of spoons in a battalion of mixing bowls from the kitchen. But it died away. Miss Dabney waited and then continued. "The worst of all possible disasters was that ragtag of American Revolutionaries, who were nothing but trash, daring to defy the King of England. Why, if we had not won the Revolutionary War, we could be British today! In winning, we lost everything!" Miss Dabney's voice broke like Alexander's, but with emotion. "Just think," she said to him, "instead of being a young American boy, you might have been a young British gentleman." She shook her head sadly at this lost opportunity.

"And just what did we fight that war *for?*" she asked. "Tell me that!"

Alexander sank lower in his chair and mumbled. "Something about the Boston Tea Party." He blinked once and eyed his cup with sudden suspicion.

"A war over a tea party! That is rich indeed!" said Miss Dabney, and her voice dripped venom. "I wish *I* had lived in those times—in the reign of dear King George the Third. I would have taken up a musket and shot Paul Revere's horse out from under him! *One if by land and two if by sea,* my Aunt Fanny!" Miss Dabney got quite carried away and brushed crumbs from her front with a trembling hand.

Alexander balanced his cup on the chair arm, caught my attention, and tapped his forehead with one finger. This was to show that the evidence of Miss Dabney's craziness was piling up fast. I thought her ideas were interesting. We'd heard nothing like them at school. But I knew Alexander was getting restless, though there were plenty more tea cakes.

But in the next moment I suspected that all Miss Dabney's Revolutionary War talk was only to distract us. For in an innocent voice she said to me, "Oh, Blossom dear, do you know what a tea cozy is? I will tell you. It is a small quilted cap that fits over a teapot to keep it warm. I have left the tea cozy on the kitchen table. Without it the tea will go cold. Nip out to the kitchen and fetch it for me, if you please."

At that came the sound from the kitchen of two pie tins being clashed together like cymbals. Alexander's mouth gaped open, in relief that she wasn't sending him.

But there was nothing for me but to head off toward the noisy kitchen in search of a thing called a tea cozy. And from then on Miss Dabney's tea party took on an entirely different complexion.

· 6 ·

THE KITCHEN WAS at the end of a dark hall. I crept along with eyes peeled for a violent hired girl. Miss Dabney seemed afraid to ring for her own servant, and this made me somewhat shy.

Tan light filtered in through the breaks in drawn shades as I edged up to the kitchen. It looked to be empty. A door, half open, led to a shadowy pantry. But all was silent as a tomb except for water dripping into a pan under a modern icebox. The door to the back porch was bolted. The place was far too quiet after all we'd heard from the parlor. It was dusty and poorly kept, though there was no clutter, and the stove looked cold. The kitchen table stood out in the center of the room, and on it was a thing I took to be a tea cozy. It perched on top of a pile of linen napkins.

I kept one eye trained on the pantry door for fear a badtempered hired girl would swarm out, swinging a meat axe. She hadn't sounded like anybody who welcomed interruptions. Then I crackled across the linoleum on tiptoe and snatched up the quilted tea cozy.

Turning to take flight, I went blind for a flash, as I sometimes do. Lightning struck, and I looked back at the table. There sat a woman on the far side in a chair that wasn't there. She was realer than the room.

Her elbows were planted on the oilcloth. She was all angles and muscles, with thick wrists and red arms. Her hands cupped her cheeks, and she wept silently but copiously. The tears ran down her horse face and dripped from her lantern jaw. She was one plain woman, and wore an old-time over-all apron, never seen these days, and a starched cap. She was a pitiful looking thing, though powerful. I stood staring at her grief, not knowing which world I was in.

Neither did the hired girl, I knew in a moment. But I was rooted to the spot, though my feet itched to travel.

"Oh, whar am I to go? What am I to do?" moaned this big ghost in a countrified accent. "I'll be sent packin' and great will be my shame." She addressed the oilcloth now puddling with her tears. This was fearful but not noisy. "And my heart is broke beyond mendin'."

She let out a wail then, and the hair on my head prickled and rose up. But she was fading. I could see through her to the door beyond. And when she was all gauzy and then gone, I saw a coil of rope hanging from the doorknob. It had not been there before and worried me worse than the female form.

My mouth was dry from not swallowing. But my feet came alive. They hardly touched ground before I plunged back into the parlor. Luckily the tea cozy was in my hand, for I would not have gone back. From somewhere behind me came the sound of a kitchen chair dragging across linoleum.

"Ah," said Miss Dabney, entirely too calm, "you have found it." Our eyes met. "The tea cozy, I mean. Bring it here and many thanks." She kept her eyes on me. Oh, she was up to something all right. And the tea cozy was a flimsy excuse. We seemed to share a secret, and both of us glanced at Alexander. He was the picture of suspicion. *First me and next him,* I thought to myself as I settled back and took another cake. My heart was pounding from this first meeting with an actual ghost, not counting my ghost boy.

Miss Dabney played out her hand in leisurely fashion. She talked of this and that, mostly English topics. Every now and then she would shoot me sudden glances, trying to surprise my thoughts. The kitchen was unearthly quiet.

At last there were only crumbs on the cake plate, and Alexander was fidgeting. I knew he was eat up with curiosity about my trip to the kitchen. Just as it was time to go, Miss Dabney settled his hash.

Like a magician she whipped out a fresh plate of tea cakes from a small shelf under the tea table. "Oh, lands," said she, all astonishment, "an entire plate of cakes untouched! You two must divvy them up and take them along home with you." Alexander was half out of his chair. "Alexander Armsworth," Miss Dabney commanded, "nip out into the kitchen and fetch two linen napkins to wrap these cakes in. They are on the kitchen table." Far off in the back of the house a chair seemed to be kicked over. The sound was distinct.

Alexander's eyes bugged. But there was no denying Miss Dabney's tone. He glared at me, and his look urged me to go in his place. But I was busy crumbing my coat. He slunk off through the door to the kitchen hall. Miss Dabney gave me a long perky look that said, *Now we will see what we will see!*

We sat quietly, listening to Alexander's boots dragging slowly down the back hall. Then there was silence as he stood at the edge of the kitchen. Miss Dabney's mouth was drawn again into a sharp V.

The scream rang through the house, echoing upstairs and rattling the tea china. Miss Dabney bounced on her pillows. It was Alexander's screech, a blend of soprano and baritone. He exploded back into the parlor with the linen napkins fluttering in his grip like flags on a power boat. "BLOSSOM CULP," he screeched at me, not daring to take on Miss Dabney, "I WILL JERK A KNOT IN YOUR TAIL FOR THIS! NOW YOU'VE GONE TOO FAR!" Then he fetched up a long dry sob.

"Oh, heavens," Miss Dabney remarked mildly. "I see no justice in turning on Blossom. She returned composed from the kitchen and has sat with me ever since. Surely there was nothing for you to see in the kitchen, Alexander, as you have put all your powers behind you by your own admission. Besides, whatever you might have ... encountered was no more than Blossom saw."

But Miss Dabney was wrong there. Alexander saw a good deal more as it turned out, but he gibbered with fright and turned a nasty green before we got anything out of him. I wondered if he would throw up, for he was fuller of cakes than Maisie Markham.

Miss Dabney was eager to hear a clear account from both of us. I thought she might go over to Alexander and slap him sensible, but she waited till he pulled himself together.

Dabbing at the corners of her mouth, she said at last, "Perhaps if I begin with *my* side of the story. In matters occult I have had small experience and no extraordinary powers. The alarming noises from the kitchen we have all three heard have been quite audible to me for as long as I can remember, but, alas, they have also been audible to all my neighbors as well. Strange noises and the banging of the oven door at all hours have only added to my reputation for eccentricity. As for being able to entertain very much, I am in awkward circumstances. This too has condemned me as an eccentric, and so I live a rather solitary life. You cannot picture me entertaining the Women's Society of Christian Temperance to tea with that appalling racket coming from the kitchen. Some of the ladies might take fright and flee" —here she paused to glance at Alexander—"particularly as it is well known I don't have a hired girl. I doubt that any help I employed would be in my employ long.

"But, you see, I am not personally acquainted with— whatever that thing is in my kitchen. I *hear,* but I see nothing. I am not *frightened,* of course. Fear is not part of my make-up"—here she glanced at me—"but I am quite consumed with curiosity. And so I invited you, Blossom, to tea, and with every expectation that you would bring young Mr. Armsworth as your escort"—Alexander's grumbles interrupted her there, but she pressed on—"two such young persons as yourselves with extrasensory powers might get to the bottom of my little mystery. Tell me, Blossom, what you saw in my kitchen."

I explained about the raw-boned serving woman crying her eyes out at the table. I described her as well as I could, adding what she'd said about being shamed and sent away. I remembered the coil of rope and added that too. It shook me when Alexander turned on me again.

"Dadburn you, Blossom Culp, you're still lying. She wasn't sitting at any table. She wasn't crying her eyes out and talking. And you know it!"

"That's what I seen, Alexander," I replied.

"Alexander, calm yourself," Miss Dabney said. "Your time is coming." She made me tell my account all over again, taking in all the details and showing interest in the old-time apron.

Then it was Alexander's turn. "Well, it wasn't anything like Blossom says, of course," he began. "There was nobody at the kitchen table. As for the rope—well, I suppose I have to tell what I saw. But then I'm going home directly. Alone," he added, shooting me a poisonous glance.

"To be sure," said Miss Dabney.

"It was the same hired girl as Blossom says. A real ugly woman with big arms and feet. And the same apron."

"Yes, yes, quite," said Miss Dabney impatiently.

"But she was—" Alexander's face went gray. "She was strung up on a meat hook in the pantry with the chair kicked out from under her. There was a rope round her neck in a hangman's knot. And her tongue was out of her mouth, and her eyes were bugged out but dead. She'd strung herself up, and thank you very much for the tea but I got to be going."

"Not so fast," said Miss Dabney, lost in thought. "What you have both told rings a distant bell. I must ponder a moment. I am sure we are on to something."

Alexander gave her an injured look. It was true she didn't seem to take much pity on him for having seen such a fearful vision. Alexander's Second Sight was still stronger than mine, for he seemed to see the Unseen in moments of high drama. Then of course he got his wits scared out of him and showed fear. And there is nothing that a boy hates to show worse than fear.

I thought back about the sound of the chair dragging across the linoleum and then being kicked over. And I shuddered on Alexander's behalf.

"A large, raw-boned servant," Miss Dabney mused. "Oh, lands, that takes me way back. I wasn't more than four years old. We had a hired girl then, of course, my papa and I. My mother had died at my birth, and so Papa and I were on our own. I had a nurse too, but no, that goes too far back. There was a hired girl— And her name was Minerva. Yes, that was it, though how I remember I don't know, for Papa never mentioned her later."

Miss Dabney came suddenly back to earth. "Blossom, step into the front parlor and bring me that picture album on the table."

I fetched back an old leather volume heavy with tintypes. She paged through it past many portraits of a baby in long white clothes which I took to be herself. "Aha!" she said at one page, and her long finger jabbed out. "Draw closer, you two, and tell me if you have ever seen this face before."

We clustered around her, though Alexander was unwilling. He glanced at the picture out of the corner of his eye. It was a picture of a small girl with a large sash to her dress and long curls, possibly yellow. "That is my own childhood self," Miss Dabney announced.

Her childhood self was holding the hand of a tall, raw-boned, lantern-jawed woman who stared grimly into the camera. There were not two such faces on either side of the grave. "That's her," I said. Alexander made a strangled sound.

"Minerva," Miss Dabney said again, faintly. "Yes, of course. I remember the grownups whispering and strangers in the house. I was too young to understand, and they kept the news from me. Minerva hanged herself in the kitchen."

"She was afraid she'd be sent away," I mentioned, "in shame." I thought this deepened the mystery, but Miss Dabney nodded knowingly.

"Yes, and so poor Minerva might have been. It is clear as crystal now I'm put on the right track. Minerva would have been in love with my papa—a hopeless love for any number of reasons. But understandable. Any woman would have been in love with Papa, even the rawest country girl. But Papa could not have allowed anything unseemly. He would have sent her away before she made a fool of herself. Or him. He was very upright. I never married, myself. No man could have measured up to Papa."

Miss Dabney's eyes were damp. Alexander took advantage of her distraction by creeping toward the door. "Well, many thanks for the tea and the . . . entertainment," he croaked, fear in his eyes.

"Must you be going?" asked Miss Dabney.

"Yes, ma'am!" He hotfooted down the front hall. Miss Dabney and me followed along. By the time we were on the front porch, Alexander was passing swiftly through the gap in the hedge.

"Oh dear me," Miss Dabney said, resting a hand on my

shoulder, "your young friend has been unstrung by the afternoon's events."

"He's a bundle of nerves when it comes to the spirit world," I explained.

"You are fond of him," she said in a thoughtful voice. Alexander was only a blur in the distance then, and we watched him out of sight.

"I am not sweet on him," I said.

"Oh no, nothing so childish as that," she murmured. "But you are both getting past childhood. And you both have something in common, quite a rare quality."

I didn't point out to her that what Alexander and me had in common was far outweighed by what we didn't. But then her mind was tripping on ahead, following a trail of its own. Even this early in our association, I noticed that Miss Dabney lived mainly in recollections of the past and in future plans, tending to skimp the present. I, of course, live every minute as it comes. So the two of us were a good team.

Her voice floated above me as we stared out across the empty street. "If you had three wishes, Blossom, what would you wish for?"

Without thinking, I said at once, "Plenty to eat, at least enough." Her long fingers gripped my shoulder as she seemed to wince. Miss Dabney had never known hunger or how near her it lurked.

"And a chance to put my Second Sight to some use."

"Yes," she murmured, and her grip relaxed.

"And a chance to see the world," I went on, "for there is not a great deal going for me in Bluff City."

"Yes," she said again, "and what else?"

"I've used up my three wishes," I reminded her, wondering if she could count.

"So you have," she sighed. "I wonder why in storybooks only three wishes are offered, when in real life they are never enough." Then she came out of her reverie and handed over my napkin full of tea cakes. "Well, then, Blossom," she said in a commanding voice, "you are expected here again tomorrow at four. By then I shall have gathered my thoughts. After all, we must do something about poor Minerva."

And I headed off for home, wondering how a person would tackle the problem of poor Minerva.

· 7 ·

WHEN I GOT HOME that night, there was not much around in the way of supper. My mama had her feet propped up on the stove and was snapping a pan of frost-blighted runner beans that were not from our garden. After dark, Mama sometimes did her harvesting farther afield.

The grandeur of Miss Dabney's parlor was still on my mind. And the tea party on her Rockingham china lingered with me. There was nothing but bare rafters and unswept floors in our place, instead of Miss Dabney's heavy gold frames around Royalty, and tin mugs instead of Miss Dabney's silver and china. Still, I was under the spell of my first tea party and decided to re-create it with the napkin of cakes.

There was a spoonful of black tea in a can on the shelf. I shook that into a pot and put the kettle on the fire. When I began to fuss over the plank table, I felt my mama's dark eyes dart my way. When I glanced back, she was busy with her beans.

I turned up the coal-oil lamp. The table looked like a squirrel's nest. It was acrumble with broken shells where Mama had picked out walnut meats some days back. I swept them off and looked around for a tablecloth. There was nothing but a feed sack all washed for cutting up and making over, which I spread out on the table. Then I unwrapped the cakes, putting two on each side and the last one in the middle as a centerpiece. The pink rosebuds on the cakes made an odd match with their surroundings.

When the water boiled, I poured it into the pot. Then I peered in as Miss Dabney had done, though I only saw black leaves swirling in brown water. When they sank, I poured out the tea into a couple of tin mugs. "Well, come on, Mama," I said. "We're going to have us a regular tea party."

With only three teeth in her head, Mama does not speak distinct without effort. She muttered darkly. Her eyes fixed on the cakes, and she made for the table. I thought of asking her how she took her tea. But I did not want to be slapped silly for being uppity, and we had no sugar or lemon on the place anyhow.

It's unrewarding to serve tea to one who only wants to get to the bottom of the mug to read the leaves. But Mama made a meal out of the cakes. Her hands resemble claws, seamed with the topsoil off the runner beans. They snaked out twice, and she hastily gummed her cakes. Then she reached for the centerpiece and wolfed that down too.

I reflected on how fast a tea party will go when there is no conversation. The crosses in Mama's ears swung forward as she stared down into her empty mug to read her own tea leaves. She gave a disgusted grunt and flung the dregs out on the floor. Then she crooked a finger, which meant I was to hand over my mug.

She couldn't have seen to the bottom of it in that light, but she sloshed the tea around and squinted. She is a fearsome spectacle at her work. "Humph," she remarked, running her tongue around inside her collapsed cheeks. "Journeys over water."

How often had I heard her predicting journeys over water to her customers? It was one of her favorite prophecies, though few of her clients ever crossed much water except on the Mississippi bridge at Cape Girardeau.

"Two trips over water still in the future," she went on, "and one voyage already past, but interrupted . . . by death."

Then she gave me a squinting look, and her eyes bored a hole in me. She meant business, or seemed to. I listened against my will. "Two young folks," she rasped, "a boy and a young chit of a gal—you."

Oh, well, I thought, she's somehow figured out that Alexander and I went to Miss Dabney's.

"No," she said, more distinct, "you, but not that kid from the house. Another kid—dead now and tow-headed. His pore corpse trapped under a mountain of ice."

This rang a bell in my head. For this towhead sounded very like my ghost boy out by the tracks. He was never far from my mind. I gave Mama a hard look then, wondering if she'd seen him too and was building a tale around him. But she took my hard look for disbelief. Her hand whipped out and boxed one of my ears. This was like lightning striking, though it did not set off my Second Sight. Mama's was working in high gear.

"A beautiful woman, now living, of high degree—who's committed a wicked sin and a crime agin her own kid, the flesh of her flesh. And only you to bring her to justice, puny though yore powers be."

Even while one of my ears was ringing, I attended my mama. She'd never favored me with a reading. Prophecy is no parlor game to her. "Foreign parts," she concluded, upending the mug and dumping my future onto the floor. Soon after, she was sound asleep and snoring on her pallet. Any reading wears her out. She'll often sleep around the clock afterwards.

But I was kept wakeful by her message. Taking up my post out on the porch steps, I pondered in the dark. True or false, Mama's prophecies lack imagination as a rule. There is hardly ever any "pore corpse trapped under a mountain of ice" about her visions. Generally she sticks to future wealth and romance, with the occasional warning against dark men who limp. (My paw was once shot in the kneecap and staggers somewhat.)

As to the "beautiful woman, now living, of high degree— who's committed a wicked sin and a crime against her own kid," I was stumped. Miss Dabney is of high degree enough, as these things go in Bluff City. She is now living, though it would take more than imagination to call her beautiful. As to her ever having a kid she'd committed a sin against—that was completely out.

The "foreign parts" didn't signify at all. Still, Mama's been known to throw in a little something extra at the end to make her customers think they're getting a bargain.

No, I couldn't work it out and like to never get to sleep

that night. The tow-headed boy I'd seen who was dead as a mackerel and yet straining at the bonds tying him down on a bed of ice had me worried.

There is nothing like a parent's words to rile you up.

When I reported to Miss Dabney's house the next afternoon, she looked to have put in a restless night herself. She led me down the freezing hall to the parlor where the tea was laid out. There were cloths over the plates, and the cozy was on the pot. It was to be business first, a thing I can appreciate.

We were no sooner settled than there came the sound of a push-broom being worked over the kitchen floor. It thumped roughly against chair legs. Then followed the sound of a dustpan being knocked against the rim of a trash can. Minerva was working away in a fine old sweat. Since all this violent tidying seemed to leave the kitchen still dusty and ill kept, I thought it was a waste of Minerva's ghostly energy. But then I supposed she had nothing but time.

"She has been noisier than usual all day," Miss Dabney remarked. "I made haste to prepare this tea and thought the water would never boil. Of course *I* see nothing in the kitchen."

"Seeing isn't the same as doing anything about the situation," I pointed out, figuring Miss Dabney wanted me to rid her of Minerva. Most people would. But as I have mentioned, Miss Dabney is nothing like most people.

"Things cannot continue as they are," she said, worrying her back hair.

"Well, Alexander Armsworth might know how to get Minerva away to a quiet grave, but I don't see how I'll get him back in this house, even with threats."

"Minerva into a quiet grave?" said Miss Dabney, quite startled. "Oh, I doubt if she would like that. That would surely mean she had passed completely over to the Other Side, would it not?"

I said I figured it would.

"But how terrible for poor Minerva that would be!" Miss Dabney quivered on her cushions, and her nervous hands played all over her neck. "Don't you see, *Papa* is on the Other Side. He rejected her in this world and would surely do the same in the next. Papa was never known to change his mind. It is more than a girl like Minerva could be expected to endure. And besides, I'd be quite lost without her, particularly now that I know who she is. We've been together for so many years. Oh no, I'd hate to think of Minerva in a quiet grave. It gives me gooseflesh."

"But what—"

"Why you must simply have a word with her, child. She's far more likely to listen to *you*. I doubt she could even *hear* me. You will think of something to tell her that will calm her down and make her satisfied with her lot."

"But—"

"But of course you will. I have every faith in you. And there is no time like the present. Skip along to the kitchen. I will be right behind you."

What could I do but obey? Miss Dabney was already looming over me. She gathered up the skirts of her gray taffeta at-home gown to shoo me along like a chicken. I headed for the door to the back hall, but my heart wasn't in it. "I'd just as soon Minerva wouldn't be hanging by the neck in the pantry," I murmured.

"Oh, that's just showing off," Miss Dabney said. "Tell her

to be sensible. Be firm. One must be with servants."

"Maybe she's stepped out for a moment," I mentioned halfway along the hall. But as quick as I said that, there came the sound of a dipper crashing from a great height onto the drainboard.

The kitchen was as before, with the afternoon light falling in rays around the drawn shades. Dust in the air told of a recent sweeping, but the floor was gritty with old dirt.

I paused at the door. The only presence I felt at first was Miss Dabney on my heels. Then there was a ringing in my head, and the light went black for a moment. When I could focus on the room again, a shape stood in the far corner by the sink.

One large hand rested on a pump handle. There was a sense of expectation about the figure. Her outline was clear, and the details of her coarse features were lightly sketched in. But where the eyes should be there was only darkness. Her sleeves were turned back over large elbows, and I pitied her for spending eternity in such drudgery. Her vibrations seemed to tell me to state my business and be quick about it.

I cleared my throat and tried to look her in the eye, but it was like looking into the sun. Fuzzy darkness veiled her expression. The dipper turned over on the drainboard of its own accord. "Minerva?" I said, trembling somewhat.

She was motionless as a graven image, but the whole kitchen listened.

"Minerva, I've come to tell you something to your advantage." She waited. I was reminded of how a cat will freeze on a fence with one paw drawn up, to see if you are friend or foe. I was exploring new territory. The words welled up in me. "Minerva," I said, quite loud, "you will not be sent away in disgrace. This here is your home, and you are welcome to stay. Nobody wants to turn you out, and there is nothing shameful about you."

The ghost moved. One rough hand drew up to clutch the grooves on her rope-burned neck. My voice quivered, but I spoke on, high and clear like Miss Spaulding. "Mr. Dabney, he won't send you packing. He died . . . here a while back."

"In 1892," Miss Dabney whispered behind me.

"In 1892," I said aloud. Minerva's head turned slowly toward a wall calendar. It was last year's, but still late enough in history to give her something to think about. "And so you're to settle down and quit your fretting. Mr. Dabney's little girl—"

"Gertrude," Miss Dabney muttered.

"—Gertrude is all grown up now, and she would consider it a privilege to share her home with you."

"But tell her to be quieter, for Heaven's sake," Miss Dabney murmured.

"Say, listen, Minerva," I added, "if you could hold down the noise a tad, it would be much appreciated."

She stirred then, and I thought maybe I'd hurt her feelings, since she was clearly the sensitive type. But I saw that instead of grasping her ghastly neck, she was pointing to the rope marks on it. And now there were pinpoints of light where her eyes should be. They were looking into mine like a pair of beacons on a dark night. I nearly took fright.

"Oh, well, that hanging business," I said in some confusion. "You was . . . ah . . . overwrought at the time and did not know what you was doing. Let's just call that case closed. It was wrong, but you've reproached yourself enough. Besides, yesterday you scared Alexander Armsworth out of a year's growth with that stunt."

I didn't like to wind up negotiations on that note. And Minerva appeared hungry to hear more. After all, nobody had said a word to the poor soul in years. "Minerva," I said, "you were a good and faithful servant in your earthly life. You've earned some peace of mind."

At that the pinpoints of light swam and flickered with tears. Minerva's big head fell forward into her hands, and she wept soundlessly. But it was unlike her weeping and carrying on before. All the anger and misery seemed to seep out of her. She was still weeping with relief when she faded from my view. The dipper lay rocking on the drainboard, and the kitchen was silent.

Miss Dabney and I stood in the dark hallway for a time, hung up between two worlds. She said nothing to me, but her hand fell on my shoulder as it would often do in the future when she meant to show approval. After a while we made our way back to the parlor. Miss Dabney let out a startled cry before she'd taken a step into the room. The cloths were off the cakes. The cozy was off the pot. And the tea had already been thoughtfully poured out by an unseen hand. Minerva was settling down.

· 8 ·

THERE ARE very few people who'll do you a good turn, so don't expect anything. That's my motto, and I live by it. But here again, Miss Dabney was the exception. Name a rule, and she is the exception. It was her good intention to repay me for settling things in her kitchen. In my next visits to her place, I could just about see wheels turning in her mind.

She harks back to a time when well-to-do people felt like they should do something for the poor. But I was more independent than your average pauper. It also crossed her mind that she might make a young lady out of me. But here again I wasn't a likely candidate. My manners were not bad enough for correction, especially around her. Besides, to turn me ladylike might have rendered me useless and possibly ornamental. Then I would not be able to fend for myself.

As to giving me advice about the opposite sex, Miss Dabney was short on experience. She was in a muddle for several days before she got a bright idea for me.

I took to going to tea every afternoon at her house, and she made a square meal of it for me. I'd never eaten so good in my life, which was obvious. On my first visit after I'd had my chat with Minerva, there was sliced ham and pea salad prepared by Miss Dabney personally. We had fruit cake studded with sugar almonds, fresh baked, for dessert.

The smell of it hot from the oven greeted me at the door. "I am responsible for most of the tea," Miss Dabney whispered in the front hall, "but I found the cake done to a turn in the oven, though there had been no fire in the stove since morning. This is Minerva's little offering, as I see it, and I suppose it's fit to eat. Where she could have got the ingredients I do not like to think. But we had better sample it."

It was one of the better cakes I ever tasted. Miss Dabney and me were loud in our praise of it, in case Minerva might be floating behind the door, eavesdropping.

Later that week there were hot blueberry muffins and at a later date, English scones. Minerva was not as steady a worker as a mortal. Still, she would do a little ghostly baking now and then, and she was rarely noisy. "I really ought to pay her a wage, if I knew how," Miss Dabney would often say in a vague way.

Then one day Miss Dabney greeted me at the door with triumph in her eyes, and I knew she'd settled on something to do with me. In her hand was an advertising leaflet which she shook numerous times in the air. "You have wanted a way to put your powers to work, Blossom," she crowed, "and I have discovered the very thing!" She handed over the leaflet at last, which read as follows:

World   Renowned

PROFESSOR REGIS

Spiritualist   Medium   Scientist

An announcement of extraordinary interest to the good people of Bluff City. Any persons bereft of loved ones and wishing to make contact with the

SPIRIT WORLD

are invited to attend a series of seances

DAILY SESSIONS

at the Odd Fellows Hall above Nirider's Notions Store. Professor Regis, who has astonished the Crowned Heads of Europe, favors Bluff City with scientific explorations into

THE WORLD BEYOND

All up-to-date techniques used, including table-rapping, actual manifestations, and words from the GREAT UN-KNOWN spoken in English by a Control, who is an actual dead spirit in regular contact with Professor Regis.

* HEAR —Authentic messages from your Dear Departed

* SEE   —THE ACTUAL MESSAGE-BRINGER, lovely as dawn and trustworthy as the telephone

* FEEL —Her ghostly presence

which will banish all hints of trickery in your mind.

Now at last break down the age-old barrier between this life and the Next Crowned Heads of Europe and New York City persons alike swear by Professor Regis. Do not let this strictly scientific opportunity pass you by.

First week of December

No admission fee charged whatsoever

Skeptical persons invited, as well as the sincere

"Did you ever hear tell of such gibberish?" said Miss Dabney with her mouth pulled way down. "This sort of chicanery is all the rage. Common criminals roaming the countryside offering the snake oil of false promise to gullible people.

" 'Crowned Heads of Europe' indeed! Anybody who has performed for *them* will not be bringing his road show to Bluff City. The idea!"

What this had to do with her and me I did not know, but was soon to learn. "Why, child, you have the *true* Gift! You'll be able to see through this . . . humbug sorcerer with no trouble."

"But what if he's the real thing?" I asked, knowing such things are possible.

"Then I will eat my hat!" Miss Dabney said. I thought briefly of her hat before she went on. "You and I will attend one of these so-called seances, Blossom. Between us, I see no reason why we cannot rid Bluff City of a sham and a faker! We do not need any of these types from outside, as there are already enough shifty people right here in town and always were!"

There's no stopping Miss Dabney once her dander is up. We went to the first seance.

Riding in her Pope-Detroit Electric is an experience in itself. People will stop and stare, some in alarm. The passenger in a Pope-Detroit sits facing the driver. This requires Miss Dabney sitting behind the tiller to look around you to see the road. This she sometimes forgets to do, and we hit several curbs. What with these delays, we were the last two at the seance.

We climbed creaking stairs to the darkened Odd Fellows Hall, where the forms of fifteen or twenty people were barely visible, gathered into a horseshoe of chairs. At the far end stood a tall double-door cabinet, like an ordinary bedroom wardrobe. Before it stood a dwarfish, round man, already talking. His hands were planted on a bare wood table. Miss Dabney and I settled into chairs, though they were hard to see.

"That will be the so-called Professor Regis," Miss Dabney hissed loudly. "Keep your eye on him." Many people looked her way, but they couldn't have seen much more than her motoring veil and the egret feather high over her Queen Mary hat.

"As I was saying," Professor Regis said, "we must all release ourselves from the concerns and frippery of daily life to free our souls. Only an unfettered, unthinking soul will rise to the Astral Plane of the Spirit World. Be gone, Earthly Concerns! Be gone, Doubting Thoughts!"

You couldn't make out the Professor's features, but like many little men a booming voice made up for small stature.

"Some out-of-work Shakespearean actor, I suppose," remarked Miss Dabney.

"Hush up," said one of the forms near us.

"This world is full of Doubting Thomases," Professor Regis went on, "some of them of the female gender. But the Spirits come to us to dispel doubt and bring fond messages from them translated to a Better World. Let no one gathered here break the sacred flow of communication!"

"Horsefeathers," Miss Dabney said.

"Compose your souls in patient contemplation," Professor Regis urged. His voice lulled many in the room. People swayed. "Is anyone on the Other Side?" he asked in a hollow voice. There was dead silence. I have no doubt Miss Dabney could have crabbed his act with louder remarks, but she held her tongue.

A scent of incense curled up from the cabinet. The hall, which already smelled of cheap whisky coming from the Professor, took on a different atmosphere. "Draw nigh, Spirit of Mystery, Light-Bringer from a Better World!" Still, nothing happened.

"Is anybody there?" he thundered. "If you're in our midst, make a sign. Rap on this here table. One rap for *yes,* a couple for *no.*"

He held his little pudgy hands up, to demonstrate that he wouldn't be doing the rapping. At once there came a single rap like gunfire. A female voice cried out in the audience. It was Miss Dabney.

"Aha!" said the Professor. "Now we are moving in the Celestial Rhythms and mingling our fates with the Immortals!" He seemed to be rubbing his little hands together. "Tell me, who has come to lift the veils of darkness from our poor blind mortal eyes? Is it Cassandra of Fearful Prophecy?"

Two raps followed, making us all jump.

"I see. Well, then, is it the Oracle at Delphi?"

Two more raps, still nerve-racking.

"Well, then, it can only be her who favors me, Professor Regis, personally with her Unclouded Vision. Is it Little Sybil, whose untimely death generations ago has been conquered by her Great Gifts? Is it you, dear Little Sybil, Child of Two Worlds?"

It was Little Sybil all right, for one rap followed.

At this news Professor Regis threw up his arms. His billowing cape covered the cabinet doors behind him for a second. A ghostly presence rose up from somewhere. I was reminded of myself disguised as the Ghost in the Privy last Halloween night. The figure was small and white, wrapped in glowing gauze.

"Dare we to hope that you are here, dear Little Sybil?" The thing in white said nothing, but the table rapped once of its own accord. "Ah, then we are favored indeed," said the Professor, "for it is not at every seance that Little Sybil will materialize. Have you got a message for anyone here?" The table rapped yes, for Sybil seemed not to have a mouth.

"Then speak in whatever manner you choose and bring comfort to one in this company." The table rapped twice for no, and the Professor sighed. "You withhold your message because there are low-minded skeptics in this room who stifle your powers?" Yes, the table knocked. "Then dispel all doubt, dear Sybil!"

We'd all been concentrating on the Professor's words. For Little Sybil was suddenly standing at the back of the room, near us. She was certainly light on her feet, and many swore later they'd seen her flying overhead.

"Well, Sybil, have you found an earthling divided by death from a loved one?"

The table rapped once, and Sybil made her move. Sweeping a white veil, she seemed to float along behind the chairs, though she'd pop up and down behind people. Some spoke of hearing the rush of wings. Her long sleeves swept my arm. I noticed a white hand touch Miss Dabney's cheek. The plume on her hat jerked.

"Dear Sybil," the Professor sang out, "is there one here who's suffered a loss and a wound never healed?"

The table rapped yes, and Sybil came to rest behind Miss Dabney's chair. I could have reached out and touched her, but didn't. "And is this same member of our Sacred Circle a doubter of your powers and mine?" asked the Professor.

Yes, the table rapped, but softer.

"And is the doubt draining from her mind and heart?"

Yes, said the table quietly. A bluish-white finger reached out and explored Miss Dabney's hand, but was soon gone. Miss Dabney seemed not to be breathing right.

"And is this poor soul a distressed lady?"

Yes, the table replied.

"And is it her husband for whom she mourns?"

Two quick raps of the table denied this.

"Aha! I have it now, straight from your sweet spirit, Sybil. This lady mourns her dear papa, is it not so?"

One rap thundered through the hall, followed by deathly silence. Several people whimpered. The Professor listened to unspoken words. "And is there a sacred memento of the Dear Departed that this sad lady carries on her person or anywheres about her?"

The table replied in the affirmative.

"Hold up the memento, the souvenir of happier days, dear madam!"

Miss Dabney's fingers fiddled on the catch of her reticule, and I wondered if she knew what she was doing. She fumbled around and held something up. It appeared to be a man's watch and fob. A white hand appeared in the air and drew it out of her fingers.

"Oh, what a thing is a divine keepsake that binds two souls across the Great Divide!" the Professor intoned. His hands were outstretched. And then Miss Dabney's papa's gold watch was suddenly swinging in the Professor's grasp up at the front of the hall. Fleet-footed Sybil had vanished.

"And is there a message from the dear papa who lives eternally on Your Other Side, all-wise Sybil?"

Another single rap responded, but it was not the table talking. It came from inside the cabinet. Professor Regis whirled around, seeming astonished, and the gold watch winked once and vanished. "Then let this departed papa send word to his dear daughter, whose name swims before my face, but I can't see it clear. Is this devoted daughter named Ida?"

The cabinet knocked twice, after a pause.

"Might it be Maud?"

No, rapped the cabinet.

"Then it must be—"

"Gertrude!" shouted Miss Dabney, half out of her chair. "Oh, Papa, it is I, Gertrude!"

"Gertrude, of course," rasped Professor Regis in his whisky voice. "O Spirit of Gertrude's Papa, speak in the still, small childish voice of Dear Sybil, the Lasting Link!"

The cabinet began to speak in the hush that followed. Sybil had a whining voice, echoing and somewhat foreign. It would have given a heavyweight wrestler nightmares. "Oiuwwww, Gertrude, my little love, art...thou... happy?"

Miss Dabney wobbled in her chair, and her reticule skidded off her knees. "Oh, Papa!" she shrieked. "Yes, I am as well as can be expected. And hope you are the same!" Her whole body was as taut as a guitar string.

"All in these Blessed Isles are well and happy, dear Gertrude," came Sybil's distant voice. She was belting out her words somewheres inside the cabinet. "And remember, Gertrude, to show charity to them who's brought us together for this precious moment which is ... beyond ... price...." Sybil's voice died away, and more incense curled from the cabinet top.

"Praise his name!" said some in the audience, and others said, "Amen!"

Then there was a crash and a thump. Somebody called for the lights to be put up. But somebody else discovered all the bulbs were taken out of the sockets. By the light of several matches, we all saw what happened. Miss Dabney had passed out. She'd pitched out of her chair and lay flat on her face with her hat still on.

Many were convinced and converted by the sight of Miss Dabney measuring her length on the Odd Fellows floor. Professor Regis doubtless strolled back to his room at the Cornhusker Hotel well pleased with himself. It was clear why he charged no admission to his seances. He could make a good living from the items light-fingered Sybil lifted off the public. The pair of them had Miss Dabney's papa's watch off her with ease.

I was reminded of the murdering bridegroom Mama had fingered down home in Sikeston, the Bluebeard who killed several wives for their personal jewelry. There was no knowing the haul Professor Regis could make in Bluff City without even violence. If he was allowed to finish out his week.

Miss Dabney was taken home on the back of a buckboard, stunned. She come out of her swoon halfway there with me at her side. Her hat was over her ear, and she babbled about her papa all the way up the porch steps. I dealt with her like I would a child in getting her upstairs and into a night-gown. There was a glass of hot milk on her nightstand and a hot-water bottle in her bed. So Minerva had been quick to do what she could.

"Oh, I do not know what's come over me," Miss Dabney lamented repeatedly. "Where am I, and what is the hour? Look in my reticule for Papa's gold watch. I carry it every-where, for it keeps perfect time." I calmed her by making a guess at the time. Finally she drifted off, with her mouth working.

She looked old and shriveled there in her nightcap with a few gray strands of hair escaping. Her veined hands plucked at the counterpane long after she slept. This is often the way with strong-minded people. When they snap, they snap. While polishing off the last of the hot milk, I began to think of revenge on Miss Dabney's behalf. Professor Regis would not prey on any more susceptible people, or my name was not Blossom Culp.

At last I had my plan of attack pretty well worked out. I tiptoed out of the weird house. The courthouse bell had chimed one o'clock before I was standing on the grounds of the Armsworth mansion, under Alexander's window.

· 9 ·

I LIKED TO FREEZE before I raised Alexander. Whistles and soft calls did nothing. He must have a wondrous clear conscience to sleep that deep. A handful of gravel from the drive finally brought him around. His hair was on end when he threw up the sash and peered out. I'd scared the daylights out of him. Ever since he saw that ghost in his barn, he's been nervous of night sounds.

When he saw it was me, he started to shut the window. But I hauled off like I would throw more gravel. "Put on some clothes and come down because me and you have got some business." I yelled softly for fear of raising his mother, who is a terror.

Alexander took his time dressing, as I knew he would. Presently he stepped out of the back door in a mackinaw and knickers, with boots laced. I was glad he'd dressed warm, for I'd have had to send him back if he hadn't. "Well, Blossom, what now?" He swaggered over my way. "And make it snappy because tomorrow's a school day, and I need my rest."

I didn't dignify this greeting with an answer. I bided my time, for I was about to play on a weakness of Alexander's, one of several. There was no point asking him to stick up for the rights of a poor old lady like Miss Dabney. Chivalry is dead, and Alexander's the proof.

So I said, "You know how to drive an automobile or don't you?" I knew he once served a short apprenticeship at the Apex Garage. Consequently he thought he was the last word in auto mechanics, though he'd been sent away from the garage in disgrace.

"You get me out of a warm bed to ask fool questions? You'll go too far one of these days, Blossom."

"I will go far all right," I agreed, "but answer my question."

"I can drive anything on four wheels. My dad owns a Mercer, you know."

"I got no business with your paw. Can you drive an electric?"

"Miss Dabney's, you mean," he said, suddenly wise. "You aim on stealing it?"

"I aim to keep it from *getting* stolen. It's setting unprotected in front of the Odd Fellows Hall. And this town is full of thugs and lowlifes with no respect for property. The same type that pushes over privies on Halloween."

He let that pass. "Why doesn't Miss Dabney drive it home herself?"

"Because she's at death's door this minute, suffering a nasty shock."

"What could shock *her*?"

"I'll explain on our way down to the Odd Fellows Hall.

But only if you're sure you can drive an electric auto. I wouldn't want it turned over in a ditch."

"Come on," Alexander said importantly, "before we raise my folks with all this jabbering."

He paced along ahead of me. Still, I managed to tell him all about Professor Regis and the Spirit Sybil and what a fake seance was. He showed interest in how the Professor took valuable items off the public. He mentioned several times that if Miss Dabney and me had kept our minds off the Spirit World like he did, we wouldn't have got into this mess.

But he was listening all right. "What makes you so sure this Sybil you keep talking about *isn't* a ... genuine spirit?" he finally had to ask.

"Because I didn't need my Second Sight to see her. I seen her like everybody else with my regular eyes. People with the Gift like you and me, Alexander, can tell the difference easy." I paced along, a step nearer him, and he didn't seem to mind.

There's nothing darker than a town at two in the morning. When we drew nigh the hall, the Pope-Detroit parked out front looked like a big black parcel, cast in shadow.

"I'll have to spark it to start the thing," Alexander explained. "Then if the batteries aren't down, there'll be enough juice to drive it to Miss Dabney's."

I let him fiddle because I hadn't lured Alexander Armsworth out of bed just to take care of an automobile. I wanted him with me to scout around in the Odd Fellows Hall and to have a good look at that double-door cabinet. The auto was just an excuse I knew Alexander would fall for.

He had the lid off the battery box and was learning about

electric power as he went. Pretty soon I said, "You any good at forcing doors?"

Alexander's head rose up. "What kind of doors?"

"Oh, like that there door on the Odd Fellows Hall."

"Why would we want to do any such a fool thing as that? It's against the law."

"So is robbing the public at a seance."

I was another five minutes convincing Alexander to force the door with a tire iron from Miss Dabney's tool kit. I could have forced it myself, but if we were surprised by a night watchman, I saw no advantage in being the one holding a tire iron. Many's the farfetched appeal I had to make to Alexander's manhood before I convinced him we were going to climb dark stairs in a dark building in the darkest hour of night. If there'd been a hint of a real haunt around, you wouldn't have seen Alexander for dust.

But the notion of breaking and entering appealed to him. After much muttered backtalk, he took on the door of the hall with the tire iron. The sound of the padlock dropping on the step rang out. Everything's noisier at night.

As we felt our way up the stairs, Alexander remembered his manners and let me go first. It was dark as a pocket up there, but I was easy in my mind, thinking that we two were the only ones in the place.

There was a small vestibule at the top. Professor Regis had not thought to remove the bulb from the socket there. When I turned the switch, a wedge of light fell across the seance room. All the chairs stood around empty, like leggy spiders.

Light struck the cabinet beyond the table. Something held me back then. And I do not mean Alexander's cold hand plucking at my sleeve. On my own, I'd have retraced my steps, and I admit it.

But I tiptoed across the room, shadowed by Alexander. When we stood before the cabinet, I could all but hear Professor Regis's convincing voice calling for the spirit of Sybil. I tried to pull the doors open, but they were locked from inside. Running a hand over the smooth panels, I discovered a hairline break in the wood.

I applied pressure, and a small drawer sprang open. The old wood popped, and Alexander jumped. "Looky here," I whispered. "This is where the Professor dropped Miss Dabney's papa's watch. Then he jammed it shut, right in front of the public, though nobody noticed." The little drawer would spring open and shut at a touch. Alexander like to wear the gadget out, fooling with it.

I crept around the cabinet, to find there was no back on it. The bottom of the cabinet was heaped high with various items. The only light came from some gauzy stuff glowing with phosphorescent paint. It looked like Sybil's costume. In this dull gleam I made out sticks of incense and candle ends and a box of kitchen matches, which I reached for to cast more light on the subject.

Alexander had come around to hover behind me. Just as my hand closed on the matchbox, the pile of glowing gauze came alive and twitched. A terrible voice whined, " 'Ere! Take your 'ands orf me, you narsty old b—"

Alexander's high whistling shriek drowned all other sounds. Fear riveted him to the floor. Otherwise I'd have been left alone to face the talking gauze. The matchbox fell on my shoe, and the gauze thrashed around and rose up.

I kept my wits about me, but barely. Presently Little Sybil and me were eye-to-eye. There was blood in hers. It could only be Sybil, and she was earthly to a fault. I'd roused her from a deep sleep, for she blinked. Her forehead glowed with a dab of phosphorescent paint from her drapings. Her hair was the color of old snow. She looked bruised in the blue light, except for a black wet mouth. As she blinked slack-jawed at me, I saw she was snaggle-toothed. There was something of an old woman about her, but she was so scrawny and shapeless she couldn't have been older than twelve.

"Oooo might you be when you're at 'ome?" she inquired in her hollow voice. But it was too late to scare me, and she knew it.

Alexander's hushed voice came from over my shoulder, "O Lord in Heaven, I will be a good boy if only—"

"I'm Blossom Culp," I said, "and this hero behind me is Alexander Armsworth. We represent the law in Bluff City."

Sybil swept down for the matchbox, and struck a light to a candle nub. "Come orf it," she remarked in her odd accent. The letter *h* seemed to be missing from her vocabulary. "I've seen the law in my time, and you don't look nuffing like it."

"Be that as it may," I replied, "it's in your best interests to cooperate. If word gets out that you're human, the law won't be far behind. They'll have you in school before you know it." Sybil and me were nose-to-nose with only the candle flame between us.

"School!" said she, scandalized. "I never set foot in a school. You won't get me there! Besides, I'm sixteen."

"Eleven."

"Fifteen," she said, "nearly."

"Twelve."

"Mind your own business," she said.

"And what if I was to say they'd arrested your Professor Regis, found a certain gold watch on him, and locked him up?" I inquired.

"I'd call you a liar," spat Sybil. "Because the old b—"

"I got to be going now," Alexander said.

"—never was arrested in his life," finished Sybil. "With that 'oneyed tongue 'e can talk 'imself out of any tight place. Why, they found a pearl necklace, a silver cigar box, and forty-two dollars in cash on 'im in Vandalia, and 'e walked away from them. Nobody'll testify against 'im in court."

"And just where do you come in to all this?" I asked, seeing she was talkative.

"I don't," she said. "I sleep in this 'ere cabinet, and the Perfessor and I, we never ride in the same coach on the railway. Nobody can finger me, for I'm the Spirit Sybil. Nobody 'as laid a 'and on me during a seance, I'm that quick. Otherwise, I'm nowhere to be seen. We travel at night. I ain't seen daylight in two years."

"You look it," I remarked.

"You're no American Beauty Rose yourself," Sybil commented.

There's nothing like swapping insults to clear the air. I couldn't approve of her shady calling, but she had spunk, and I like that.

"Well, look here, Sybil, this is no life for a young kid such as yourself. You're in no better situation than a mole." Sybil blinked. In a way she was a mortal version of Minerva.

Nobody ever had occasion to give her a good talking to. "Just how do you live? When all this comes to light, it'll go better for you if you look like an innocent party—anyhow not quite the crook you are."

I thought she'd sulk, but she said, "Crikey! If you aren't the worst Nosy Parker I ever come up against! Orl right, if you must know, you must. Welcome to my 'appy 'ome." She managed to step out of all the gauze drapings and planted a bare foot on the floor. Alexander retreated a couple of steps. But he'd quit praying and was listening.

Sybil fixed the candle in a handy bracket on the cabinet wall. "'Ere I sleep," she said, pointing to a pile of rags on the cabinet floor I wouldn't put a dog down on. "And just there's my supper." She pointed out an empty can of pork and beans lodged in the corner. "There's the you-know-wot." She waved a hand at a china chamber pot. It looked to me like she slept with her head in the beans and her feet in the chamber pot. It was close quarters in that cabinet and anything but clean. There was a water jug, but no soap.

She warmed to the task of showing us around her narrow world. There was a flue in the top where the incense smoke rose up, and peepholes on various levels in the front doors. Sybil could scan the crowd out front well before she made her entrance. The whole cabinet was as busy as a Chinese puzzle and as clever. The entire contraption came apart for shipping.

There were other drawers and loose panels fitted to the inside, but Sybil passed over these. Only persuasion made her admit that the secret drawer on the front was where the Professor stashed items lifted from the clients. She showed us how she could gather this swag from the inside. What happened to the loot then she didn't say.

Oh, they had their routine all worked out. It was hard not to admire it. Alexander did.

But I needed to know more if I was to break up this act, which I meant to do, before the Professor and her caused more mischief. Sybil need be no match for me; she had no more supernatural powers than a hand-fed calf. Still, I had unanswered questions.

She was reluctant to give away all her trade secrets. So I appealed to her pride. There would be time later for threats outright. "Well, Sybil," says I, "I only hope this Professor Regis pays you a good wage. Looks to me like without you he don't have much of an act."

"Not 'arf," she replied, which I took to be agreement.

I could tell from the way she thrust her chin out that the Professor didn't pay her a thin dime. But I'd planted that seed and moved on. "I was in the audience yesterday myself," I said, "sitting next to a certain lady, well known in the community."

"The old party in the orful 'at," Sybil shot back. "The one that took a dive at the end."

"That's her. And it looked to me like you didn't pick her out of the crowd by chance."

Sybil smirked.

"Looked to me like she was a sitting duck for you and the Professor."

"That's right," Sybil preened.

"Did you know who she was ahead of time?"

"Didn't need to, did I?" said Sybil, swollen with pride.

"There's one like 'er at every seance and usually several. Sticks out like a sore thumb, even wivout the 'at. There's always some old maid 'ankering after 'er dear departed old dad. I seen 'er through the peep'ole before I manifested."

"But you took your time getting around to her."

"I'm that subtle," Sybil explained.

"And you knew she was an old—an unmarried lady."

"That's right. Reached down and touched 'er left 'and, where the wedding ring wasn't."

"And then you signaled across the room to the Professor."

"That's it. I 'old up one finger for yes, two for no. The Perfessor's brown-eyed. Blue-eyed people 'ave night blindness, but the Perfessor's got eyes like a barn owl."

"It's true about brown-eyed people seeing better in the dark," Alexander put in. "Champ Ferguson, he's brown-eyed, and we always depend on him when we're out at night."

I waited through this interruption and then said, "What makes you so sure she had some valuable object on her person, Sybil?"

"In this business," she said, "you can tell what people are worth in a glance." She gave me an up-and-down look. "And these old maids, they always carry around some keepsake or other. We take in cash money too. There's several ways of working things."

How true, I thought to myself.

"Well, that about tells the tale," I said carefully, "except for that nonsense about the table-rapping."

"That's the Perfessor's own invention, and 'e's that vain of it. There's a clapper under the table, and it works on a black thread running to the Perfessor's knee. Then at the end of the seance, 'e walks away from the table. The thread breaks, and Bob's your uncle!"

It was time to wind this up while Sybil was still halfway agreeable. She was the shifty type that could turn on you at any time. Still, for reasons of my own I needed to know a few personal things about her.

"Say, Sybil. You talk funny. Are you foreign?"

"What's that to you?"

I waited her out while she gave me a fishy-eyed look.

"Maybe I am, since you arsk," she said, shiftier than before. "My old mum, she as much as sold me to the Perfessor. I grew up in the Bermondsey Road—fast."

"Where's that?" asked Alexander. "St. Louis?"

"It's London, you chump," Sybil growled at him.

"London, England?" said Alexander, amazed.

"The same. Where else? And the Perfessor says I 'ave to do everything 'e says because I'm an illegal alien, the old b—"

"Then it's true he's astonished the Crowned Heads of Europe?" I asked.

"Crowned 'Eads! Don't make me larf! 'E never played north of Battersea Funfare the best day 'e lived. 'E worked for 'alfpennies in England and 'ad to come back to this ignorant country, where people will believe anything, they're that gullible!"

By then I'd had enough of Sybil. It'd be more trouble than it was worth to get out of her where the Professor hid all the stolen items. I figured what he picked up in one town he sold in the next. Anything left over was likely tucked away in the hidy-holes of the cabinet. He wouldn't carry it on himself. I knew enough to play Sybil's role at the Professor's last seance. But first I had to get rid of Sybil.

"Well, it's your life," says I, beginning mild. "But while the Professor is snug in his fine room down at the Cornhusker Hotel with a hot dinner in him, you eat straight from the can and sleep on rags in the dark."

"It's a 'ard life," Sybil agreed.

"And it's like to get harder for you. As I said, Alexander Armsworth and me, we represent the law in Bluff City. And they'll have you up on several counts. Being an illegal alien's a good start. Fraud and larceny is a couple more. Maybe nobody'll testify against the Professor out of shame at being bilked. But that won't keep the County Court from putting you away."

"Away?" muttered Sybil.

"In the Reformatory for Wayward Girls. You're a prize candidate if ever one was. They'll lock you up, throw away the key, and not look for it again till you're twenty-one."

"Crikey!" said Sybil, shrinking.

"There's just one way out for you." By then I had her eating out of my hand. Alexander too. He can never see a minute ahead. "You got any money?"

"I know where some is." Sybil's eyes slewed over to the cabinet wall.

"Take what cash you can find and leave everything else, including them . . . drapings. Clear out before daybreak. It's your only chance. Otherwise you'll be looking through bars with a number round your neck."

"Crikey," breathed Sybil again. "Wot if the Perfessor catches me? 'E'll 'ave me 'ead."

"Another good reason for getting an early start," said I.

"I don't know," whined Sybil.

"Run for your life. There's a milk train through here at five o'clock."

Then Alexander and me were gone, leaving the Spirit Sybil ankle-deep in her cabinet and lost in thought.

For a wonder, Alexander got Miss Dabney's Pope-Detroit started. I will say he steered it better than its owner. There was gray light in the east as we rolled along Fairview Avenue. Alexander was bright as a button over his new-found skill at steering. He was very brave on the subject of Sybil too, since I'd done all the negotiating and he hadn't been totally unmanned by fear.

Still, he thought of complaints. "Lookit here," he said, taking a curb close, "it's nearly daylight. How am I going to keep awake at school? Miss Spaulding, she'll snatch me baldheaded if I doze."

"There'll be no school for me and you today, Alexander," I explained. "We have a day's work getting ready for the Professor's last seance in Bluff City."

"Leave me out of whatever you've got in mind," he warned.

"You're already in it. It wouldn't do if word got out you'd spent a long night with me instead of at home in bed, where your folks think you are."

"Common blackmail, Blossom," he complained. "You know no other way."

"And another thing. Since your brother-in-law, Lowell Seaforth, is a newspaper reporter, it's up to you to get him to attend the seance. We'll want news coverage on this and plenty of it. I have no doubt Seaforth is always looking for a good story. And if he's anything like most cub reporters, he never knows where to find one. Have him there. It's as big a story as he's liable to stumble on around these parts."

"I don't see how there'll be a seance at all, without Sybil," Alexander said.

"Crikey!" said I in a hollow, foreign voice. "There'll be a Sybil there, orl right."

·10·

I WAS EVERYWHERE at once that next day, except at school. Not knowing when Professor Regis would turn up at the Odd Fellows Hall, I had to be there with time to spare, stowed away in the cabinet and already tricked out as Sybil. This part of the plan seemed foolproof because the Professor is a drinking man. And a drinking man is rarely alert early in the day.

Alexander's job was to hang out near the Cornhusker Hotel saloon. When Professor Regis issued forth, Alexander was to locate me posthaste. My first stop was at Miss Dabney's. Here I expected the worst. I'd left her raving and then knocked out by hot milk. I feared for her mind, but I reckoned without her grit.

She greeted me at the door, very grave. Her long face was stretched to record length. She looked like one suddenly sobered. A tragic heroine—Lady Macbeth or some such.

School days and hooky are nothing to her. Expecting I'd shortly be at her side, she'd laid out a breakfast in the parlor. There were hot English scones and herb tea. After I'd eaten my fill under her gaze, she intoned, "Well, Blossom, Bluff City has called me an eccentric old fool for many a long and weary year. Yesterday I fulfilled their fondest notions."

I shifted uncomfortably. The hall clock struck, and we both thought of her papa's missing pocket watch. "And a fine example I am to a young and impressionable girl such as yourself," she rambled on. "What could have come over me to be bamboozled by a transparent faker? I am mortified to my soul. I felt myself being drawn under the dastard's influence and was powerless in his grip. And the very idea of dear Papa speaking to me in that awful, shrill voice: 'Oiuwwww, Gertrude, my little love, art ... thou ... happy?' indeed!"

"Your sensibilities was being played on," I consoled. "The Professor and that Sybil knew you was faithful in your heart to your departed papa, and their whole low scheme depended on it."

"How true. My idiotic sentimentality clouded my judgment. I was nothing more than a—a—"

"Sitting duck," I said, and Miss Dabney agreed.

"You are a kindly and understanding child, Blossom." (Here I fidgeted under the weight of Miss Dabney's charity.) "But I daresay the seance room was full of gossips who will forget their own foolishness in remembering mine. I am nothing but a half-crazed, feather-headed ... old ... maid." The tears zigzagged down her face.

"Don't call yourself names," I said in a small voice. "We are a couple of ... unmarried ladies. And we have to stick together."

"Oh, Blossom," she moaned, and the tears flowed freely, some of them mine.

But it was not a time to give way. "We're not without our defenses," I piped up. Then I put Miss Dabney in the picture. I told her all about the nighttime raid Alexander and me made on the Odd Fellows Hall. I made it clear that Sybil was mightily mortal, though I left out about her being English. If Miss Dabney learned that, she might falter, but Sybil was not the sort of English that Miss Dabney held in high regard. Sybil was more chamber pot than Rockingham tea cup.

When I'd outlined my plan for the afternoon's seance, Miss Dabney's spirits revived. She needed no urging to play a small role in discrediting the Professor. "We will strike a great blow against this spiritualist quack!" she announced, and pounded her sofa cushions. Still, when I told her to leave off her usual hat so she'd pass unrecognized, she thought I was being overcautious.

We talked well into the afternoon before a pebble hit the parlor window. This was Alexander's sign that the Professor was heading to the scene of his daily crime. Chauffeured by Miss Dabney at the Pope-Detroit's top speed, I made it to the seance room with minutes to spare.

When I slunk into the back of the cabinet, I grinned in the gloom to find Sybil's evil-smelling nest empty and deserted. There was just time to explore every secret compartment and make a pile of the contraband I found. Not a nickel in ready money remained, but there was an accumulation of items from previous hauls. I slid back a final panel, and Miss Dabney's papa's watch and fob dropped into my hand.

I'd draped and veiled myself in Sybil's glowing gauze before I heard the Professor approach. He was humming a boozy tune. I nearly gave way to last-minute fright. Though

I didn't fear him, my plans would go haywire if he got a good look at me, for he'd find Sybil greatly changed.

He took a long route across the room and rapped sharply on the cabinet doors, right against my ear. "Well, Sweet Sybil, my little Cockney Immortal, art thou within, you little baggage?"

I rapped once on the inside of the door, meaning yes.

"Come now, my coy little sprite, let us reserve the rapping for the rubes. Answer nicely or I'll box your ears."

I spoke directly into the empty bean can for a hollow effect. "Oooiuw," I whined, "leave orf! I 'ardly 'ad a wink of sleep orl night. Leave me alone, or I'll be no good at the seance."

"A restless night, I daresay," the Professor replied. His furry voice had a dangerous edge on it. "The padlock on the downstairs door is twisted beyond mending. Am I to deduce that you flitted out for a breath of night air? You know the punishment for that!"

"Oooiuw," I whimpered, thinking fast, "a gang of rough boys pushed in 'ere. But I sent 'em packing wiv a flea in their ear. Scared 'em orf wiv my spirit act."

"Quite right," said the Professor. "You had nothing of a more . . . intimate nature to do with these boys, I trust?"

"Not likely," I whinnied.

"Are you coming down with something, Sybil?" he inquired. "Your voice sounds hoarse."

"As well it might!" I shot back. "There's damp in this cabinet, and this 'all is a regular tunnel of drafts. It's worse than . . . that place in Vandalia."

"Ah, Sybil, what a little ingrate you are. But for me, you'd be sleeping under a hedge somewhere. And don't speak lightly of Vandalia. We did well there. I'll see a tidy profit from our offerings in that village, even at pawnshop prices."

I watched him through a peephole as he donned his cape and ran a black thread from his knee joint to the table. But he hadn't finished his preaching.

"The conclusion of yesterday's seance was suitably... dramatic. Particularly for a first performance. It will draw the yokels. The old dame swooning added just the right conclusion—though I have learned at the hotel bar that she's a well-known local lunatic.

"But we must do better today than a single gold watch, my dear Sybil. I expect you to be on your toes, as it were. Let's pick this afternoon's pilgrims as clean as possible. Otherwise I will be forced to take it out of your hide."

I was spared more threats by voices at the bottom of the stairs. "Hark!" said the Professor. "The first of the suckers approach. Are you suitably attired, Sybil?"

I rapped once for yes.

A short while later he began his pitch. "Ah, ladies and gentlemen, welcome to the way station to a Better World! Enter this crepuscular chamber wherein the darkness will reveal more than the light of ordinary day!"

Crikey, I thought to myself and watched through the peephole. Between flutters from the Professor's cape, I could see the room filling with forms. Chairs bumped, and there was some nervous giggling, quickly stifled. I saw or heard nobody familiar, and I began to think of suitable revenge if Alexander failed to turn up with his brother-in-law, the reporter. I knew I could count on Miss Dabney, though I hoped she would not cave in again.

There was a good turnout, and the Professor's flowing words had them swaying in their seats at once. My hand went out to various items I'd pulled from the cabinet walls. I lit a match to make a quick inventory.

"Be gone, Worldly Concerns!" the Professor chanted. "Be gone, Doubting Thoughts!" I lost track of Miss Dabney's papa's watch. It'd slipped down behind the chamber pot, but I fished it out. "Draw nigh, Spirit of Mystery, Light-Bringer from the Blessed Isles of Forgetfulness."

I was alert just as he thundered, "IS ANYBODY THERE? If you're amongst us, make a sign. Rap on this here table, Ethereal Courier! One rap for *yes,* a couple for *no.*"

The table rapped once, and a gasp rose in the room. The Professor's cape flapped, and I lifted the catch on the doors. I also swept up the gold pocket watch. And then I was beside him, and if I seemed unlike Sybil, it was too late. For I was on the stage.

"Be still, my soul," Professor Regis boomed, "for we poor mortals gathered here are honored by a ghostly guest. Is it you, Little Sybil, who passed over centuries before yet return to lead us lest we fall down in darkness?"

I held my tongue while the table verified me.

"Then go forth to comfort one or more in this company. Preferably more."

My foot tangled in a trailing veil, so I did not float to the back of the hall with Sybil's grace. Still, I made it there, flatfooted. Several people were impressed enough to bury their faces in their hands. I moved along behind several tight collars and quivering hats, looking for my confederates.

Then I spotted Miss Dabney, though she was better disguised than I was. A black mantilla was pulled over her old head. Her idea of concealment was to forsake anything English. She seemed to be impersonating Queen Isabella of Spain. I waved a ghostly hand at the Professor over her head.

"Well, Sybil," he bellowed, "have you found an earthling divided by death from a loved one?" I raised one finger, and the table rapped once, right on cue.

"And has this poor soul suffered a loss and a wound never healed?" One of my fingers went up in reply, and the table rapped again. "And is there a sacred memento of the Departed this sad lady, wrapped in her mourning veil, carries on her person?" Up went my finger again, followed by a knee rap. Then I drew out the gold watch from my sleeve and held it, turning in the air, for all to see. Miss Dabney reached up for it, and it disappeared into her reticule.

"Oh, what a thing is a sacred keepsake!" chanted the Professor. He blinked in the dark, disbelieving that his game had been turned around on him. I floated up the center of the hall, making for the cabinet. At this particular seance, speed was my chief ally. As I brushed past the Professor, he reached out and grabbed my sleeve, but it came away in his hand. The crowd stirred, and I was soon back inside the cabinet.

In a strangling voice the Professor pressed on. "Dear Sybil, thou antic sprite!" His elbow thumped the cabinet doors. "Speak a message from the . . . ah . . . Great Beyond to prove your . . . extraordinary powers!"

"*Oiuwww,*" I began in Sybil's voice, "I'm the Ghost of Christmas Past!" As it was December, this was a timely, seasonal touch.

"What in the hell," groaned the Professor. Otherwise silence filled the hall.

"I'm the Ghost of Christmas Past," I insisted, "come back to distribute Sacred Mementos to the earthbound believers, 'ere in this sacred sanctuary, rubes, yokels, and suckers though they be."

With that I burst through the doors past the Professor, who was witless with shock. I was stocked with everything in his treasure trove. My bust had a new, irregular shape, for everything was stuffed down my middy blouse under Sybil's glowing costume.

Floating up to a farmerish-looking man in the nearest chair, I whipped out a solid silver cigar box and handed it over. "I hope you smoke," said I in a cheerful voice. Meaning to be a moving target if the Professor went into action, I flitted across to a shabbily dressed woman and dropped a garnet brooch in her lap. She made a grab for it. "A little something to remember me by," I said in my own voice.

Then I spied Alexander sitting beside his brother-in-law, who seemed to be writing blind on a note pad. "And have *you* been a good little boy this year?" I inquired of Alexander, tossing him a pair of tortoise-shell combs set with diamond chips.

By now several in the crowd were on their feet, and the seance mood was shattered. Some rough type yelled out, "Throw something my way, girly!" I pitched him a pair of cuff links in mother-of-pearl. And I let fly with a moonstone ring in the direction of another outstretched hand, looming up like a catcher's mitt. The air was full of the Professor's profits.

"Stop thief!" he shrieked. But the black thread connecting

him to the table seemed to chain him to the spot. "I am being robbed blind! Cut that out, Sybil!" And then again in a different tone . . . "Sybil?"

I had a double strand of pearls with a coral clasp still left in my front. I bore down on a slender lady in a heavily veiled hat, not stylish. "Here you go, sweetie," I said to her, very pert, "a small token of my esteem."

And great was my surprise when her hand shot out, locking around my wrist. The pearls rattled to the floor while the Professor sobbed in the background. The lady threw back her veil with her free hand. Even in that light I saw it was my teacher, Miss Mae Spaulding.

Somebody ripped the window blinds down, and light flooded in. People were standing on chairs. Others, unwilling to be seen at a seance, real or false, were ganging for the door. The cabinet was thrown open as pilferers rifled it for more treasure. Its unhinged doors smacked the floor, raising dust. The Professor punched the air with small fists, crying out for justice. The entire hall was a true beehive.

I meant to be out of my drapings and gone by then. But Miss Spaulding had me in one of her hammer locks. The sight of me in the grip of our teacher sent Alexander scurrying behind his brother-in-law. But of course in the long run there is no escaping Miss Spaulding.

Though the racket in the room was deafening, I heard her plain. "What a lot of explaining you have to do, Blossom," said she in an even tone.

· 11 ·

BEFORE LOWELL SEAFORTH'S STORY hit the next morning's newspaper, Professor Regis was long gone. He skipped directly from the Odd Fellows Hall to the depot with a mob behind him, half mean and half jeering. The public does not mind being cheated, but they like it to be convincing.

Alexander had seen fit to alert his gang, and they yapped at the Professor's heels like a pack of dogs. Les Dawson tried to shy a rock through a parlor-car window of *The City of Joliet*. It was reported that the Professor left the county cowering in the baggage car.

He went very short of baggage. His clever cabinet was kindling wood. He'd lost track of the Spirit Sybil. And his valise waits at the Cornhusker Hotel to this day.

None of this good work made me a heroine to Miss Spaulding. To her, tardiness is a misdemeanor, but truancy is a felony, and for every crime she has a punishment ready-made. Mine was to serve one hour detention after school every day till Christmas.

She dropped her net over Alexander on the same charge, but we served time in separate rooms. Alexander was not speaking to me anyhow, and said so. As we were being led away, he snarled, "I don't come near you, Blossom, but what I get up to my hips in trouble." Though *hips* was not the word he used.

When Miss Spaulding put me in her office that first afternoon, I meant to soften her up by satisfying her curiosity. She'd asked for explanations, and I had plenty. Thinking she had some Second Sight herself for knowing where to find me, I put a careful question. But she waved it away. "Rumors have been flying, Blossom, that you are dabbling in the occult these days. Doubtless this is just a phase you are going through. But when you and a certain other party did not show up at school on a day when a seance was advertised, I put two and two together." She was not talking of arithmetic.

Then she left me alone in her office to cool my heels and contemplate my crime. This brought back the earlier time I'd been carried in there half strangled by Les Dawson, which was a picnic compared to the present situation.

There's no outguessing Miss Spaulding. She returned with Alexander's brother-in-law, Seaforth. "Well, Blossom," she said, glittering at me through her pince-nez glasses, "though I am about half tired of your highjinks, I have given your case long thought. And I will review it to refresh your memory. You recall how you played the part of a ghost in a certain outbuilding Halloween night. Which ended in gunplay."

Lowell Seaforth scribbled quick notes, suddenly informed of earlier news items that got past him.

"And that event led to violence in this schoolyard, bringing matters under my jurisdiction."

I nodded, remembering Les attacking Letty and Miss Spaulding attacking Les.

"Then, if rumor can be credited, you found yourself in the company of a little club of girls, Blossom—the Busy Fingers or whatever. And you convinced them you had some sort of . . . supernatural powers. This led to an even odder association with an elderly lady given to . . . mental quirks."

"If you mean Miss Gertrude Dabney, she—"

"Silence, Blossom!" commanded Miss Spaulding. "You will have your day in court, in about two minutes. Somehow, by all this frenzied activity, you insinuated yourself into the shady machinations of an itinerant seance medium doubling as a confidence man."

Seaforth's pencil stumbled after Miss Spaulding's words. She's a very well-spoken, scholarly woman. I marveled at her nose for news. As a reporter she could wipe the floor with Seaforth.

"All this ended in your playing truant. It was inevitable," she said sadly. "And I mean to nip it in the bud. It is crystal clear to me, Blossom, that you are hungry for attention."

I was just plain hungry, but I said nothing and hung my head at a suitable angle.

"All my educational training has decided me on a solution to your case. As you hunger for attention, you are about to have it. Mr. Seaforth here, of the Bluff City *Pantagraph,* is going to interview you on this entire seance business. It is newsworthy in its way and thus not a waste of his time. And you may claim all the attention your story merits. In tomorrow's paper you will receive exactly the degree of acclaim you deserve. No more. No less. After you have this out of your system, I expect you to settle down to a quiet life and be a team player. And as Mr. Seaforth is kind enough to interview you, stick to the truth, Blossom, and nothing but the truth."

Lowell Seaforth is quite a good-looking fellow, with an Arrow Collar shirt and clean fingernails. What he ever saw in Alexander's big sister, Lucille, is the deepest mystery of this account.

I cleared my throat, ready to begin. "Take a chair," I told Seaforth, "and let me know if I go too fast for your note taking." Miss Spaulding's eyes rolled heavenward, and I began.

My detention hour was up and the sun was long down before I finished my story. I told it all just as it happened, with an occasional flourish. About how Professor Regis was immune to the law, since nobody would ever testify against him. And even if Miss Dabney took him to court over that watch and fob, nobody would believe her. So I naturally had to take the law into my own hands and dispense a certain rough justice of my own. I spoke a few words in Sybil's voice to show how I could take her place. And I gave Alexander just the amount of credit he deserved. No more. No less.

Seaforth took it all down, right back through Minerva to my vision of Newton Shambaugh falling off the streetcar. The only parts I omitted were the vague ones. I made no mention of the ghost boy I'd seen out by the car tracks by our house—the tow-headed kid strapped down on the ice. That would have been pushing my luck.

Miss Spaulding and Lowell Seaforth exchanged glances.

I was well pleased with my own account. Rumors wither in the presence of untarnished truth, as the poet says. But Miss Spaulding was far from satisfied. It stuck out all over her.

Sighing, she said, "Well, Blossom, I greatly fear you have overstepped yourself again. What you say about that re-pelling seance business has a factual ring about it, though there are some moral questions still outstanding there.

"But, Blossom, is it not enough to tell us of your many actual . . . activities . . . without fabricating?"

I opened my mouth to protest but closed it again.

"In short, Blossom, you may play at *being* a ghost, as you seem never to tire of, but you cannot *see* one. This flies in the face of science."

I'd sooner not fly in the face of science if it meant flying in the face of Miss Spaulding. So I sat swinging my feet and examining my boots, which were my old ones.

"And so, Blossom, for your own good and in the presence of the press, we must have one final confrontation with the truth. You have said that you have Second Sight, can see the Unseen, and have conversed with spirits. Is this true and will you go on record for it?"

I would and nodded.

"Very well, Blossom. Then prove it. Now."

I surely was between a rock and a hard place. Miss Spaul-ding turned her desk lamp full on my face. Lowell Sea-forth poised his pencil. This was no two-bit challenge from the likes of Letty Shambaugh. Miss Spaulding was out to settle my hash. I'd have gladly negotiated for a thrashing, but she doesn't make deals.

I sat there, swinging my feet and trying to invite one of

my fits. Squinting up my eyes, I thought hard about thunder and blue lightning. I'd have settled for another quick flash of Newton or a whiff of Minerva's gingerbread baking. Anything to get me going. But nothing came to mind. I thought this was a devil of a time for my Second Sight to quit on me.

Then I heard the first rumble. The sound I'd heard once before. The rasp of two great objects grinding together—iron against ice. It was deeper than thunder and at first farther off. But the roaring was soon in my ears and then in the room.

The office began to throb and pound, like engines in the earth running out of control. I had hold of the chair arms to keep from pitching out. If this was not the San Francisco earthquake, it was near kin of it.

The lamp with the green glass shade on Miss Spaulding's desk began to vibrate and then caper at the end of its cord. Books slid about, and a class picture swung out from the wall. Lowell Seaforth braced his boots on the floor where the boards popped and strained. Just before the desk lamp fell over, I saw Miss Spaulding's pince-nez glasses slip down her face. Her hand clamped over her mouth. The bulb in the lamp exploded. Lowell Seaforth's voice came up strong: "Damnation! What have we unleashed?"

And those were the last words I heard from that world for quite a time.

I was staring at a lamp bolted to a small nightstand, but it was not Miss Spaulding's lamp. It was still lit, swaying and throwing shadows in a strange small room. There was some comfort in this swift exit from the principal's office. But I didn't know where I was. Maybe out of my body, though I felt a chill, possibly of fear.

There is nothing more real than fear, fight it though you may. My mouth worked continually as in a nightmare, but I heard none of my words. Only later did I find out that I was telling Miss Spaulding and Seaforth everything as I saw and heard it. But I had left their world behind in time and space, and I was myself a kind of ghost in this foreign territory. I'd graduated to a whole new phase.

It was nothing like my quick glimpses into past and future and across town. My whole being was elsewhere. And nothing of this new place faded in and out as Minerva did. Never have I been in a realer spot, with every detail as clear as one small lamp could make it. I stood in the corner of an odd room with a slanting floor. A thing with padding and straps hung from a peg behind me. It put me in the mind of a straitjacket. This puffy object swept my cheek. I was half hidden by it, if I was visible at all.

This whole new world seemed set on the bias. A vase of dark velvet roses had already tipped over on a vanity table. The water fell in a silver line and ran off down the floor, darkening a rich carpet.

It was a fine room, though cramped, with wood panels and wine-colored silk on the walls. A door to another room was swaying open, casting a patch of light. A small clock set high in the wall told the time: It was just past midnight. But which midnight, it did not tell. Later I was to know. It was the earliest hour of April fifteenth, nineteen hundred and twelve. Just twenty months before the moment I'd suddenly departed from under Miss Spaulding's disapproving gaze. I'd slipped down through a crack in time, like a termite through a splintered floorboard.

Though I'd never been afloat in anything bigger than a rowboat, I knew I was on board a ship. The two windows in the room were round. One of these portholes, as they are called, had come open. The cold night air of long distances touched me to my marrow. A small pyramid of glittering ice had spilled in on the floor under the open porthole. Nothing moved except the shadows.

I'd known from the first that I wasn't alone in this place. But my eyes didn't hurry to survey the whole room. At last I looked in the far corner beyond the bedside lamp. A bunk bed was fitted there, and in it a small human form under a blanket was held down by a web belt.

We were on a great ship, this form and me. The whole room gave a lurch and a shudder. There was a sound of distant dynamos sighing to silence. The grinding sound had ceased. *Dead in the water,* I thought, as though these words could answer a puzzle. The sudden lurch explained the belt across the form in the bunk. Travelers on the sea have to be strapped in their bunks or they'll roll out.

The lampshade wavered once more, and I saw the blond curls of a tow-headed boy on the pillow. I knew I was meeting up at last with the boy I'd seen before, out by the trolley tracks. I knew him like a long-lost pal. Once, he'd come to me. Now I'd come to him. I waited to find out why.

He was fitful in his sleep. His small, pale hands worried the blanket drawn halfway over his head. I took a step out onto the carpet, looking down to see I was still in my old broken boots. The carpet was thick, but my feet didn't appear to sink into it. I feared that if I examined myself, I'd be transparent. *Oh, Minerva,* I mused, *I know just how you feel, you poor shade.* There was a lightness in my head like the beginning of influenza or something of the sort.

Along the porthole wall was an orderly pile of luggage, beside the pile of ice shavings. Each piece carried a shipping label. Printed on the labels were the words WHITE STAR LINE. And beneath was the name of the boy, who was still sleeping.

First Class Passenger MASTER JULIAN POINDEXTER travelling
with LADY BEATRIX and SIR CLIFFORD POINDEXTER.
This valise wanted on the voyage.
Southhampton–New York.

My hand rested on the top of this pile while I pondered. I could see through my fingernails to the smooth leather lid of the valise beneath. My whole hand looked like a spun-glass starfish. And then my gaze was drawn to the open porthole.

Outside it was a night both black and white. Julian Poindexter and me were far out to sea. There was the black line of a far horizon beneath a moon that beamed through icy rays. *Whiskers round the moon,* I whispered, knowing I'd once said that before. The vast ocean was calm beneath a silent sky. More sky and water than ever I'd seen in one place. I cried out at so much cold loneliness.

Julian Poindexter stirred in his bunk behind me. It was odd to read his name on his baggage, for I seemed to know it all along. He was only half asleep, as a kid often is. A distant door opened in the room—or cabin, as they call it at sea—connected to ours. People entered in there hurriedly. "Mother?" Julian said. But only I heard him.

I waited by the luggage while the sea air bit at my glass

fingertips, wondering if the people in the next cabin were Lady Beatrix and Sir Clifford; wondering if they were Julian's mama and paw; wondering if they would come in to check on him; and wondering if they'd see me if they did.

Then I quit wondering about these matters, for my hand was still on a label glued to a valise. And in the wobbling light I read something beneath Julian Poindexter's name I'd missed before. It was the name of the ship we were on. I knew where we were then, and why we were dead in the water. I knew why the engines were shut down and why there was ice on the cabin floor. For the label told that we were on the Royal Mail Steamship *Titanic*.

We were all at sea on a ship sunk many months ago. And even now it was sinking beneath us.

• 12 •

THE SINKING of the *Titanic* on its maiden voyage was a well-known disaster. Word of it had even reached Bluff City, and we studied it at school, here a year ago spring. Our teacher was Miss Botts, who said this famous event was a clear-cut example of mankind's destruction by his own vanity.

So I was well aware that the *Titanic* and quite a number of passengers and crew sank suddenly. At a rough estimate, 1635 souls perished. I had no doubt Julian Poindexter was among the doomed, for I'd already seen him in his death agonies out by the streetcar tracks.

If I feared for my own skin, cast adrift on the ill-fated *Titanic,* I disremember now. Though I didn't relish being an on-the-spot witness to Julian drowning in ice water.

But I felt a sense of mission in all this. Julian had shown himself to me, a person sensitive to the Spirit World. And these haunts only come forth when they have a tale to impart, and they'll go to any length to find an understanding ear. I glanced at the wall clock again and judged there was little time to get to the bottom of the story. We'd hit the iceberg an awful whack and were already riding out of the water. By my calculations there wasn't two hours left. I couldn't save Julian Poindexter, because nobody can rewrite history, but I hoped to learn how his roving spirit might find ease.

The noise from the cabin next door grew louder with a pair of wild voices. I barely grazed the carpet in crossing it for a glance into the next cabin. There I saw a man and a woman grappling with each other.

The woman had the look of a famous beauty. Her hair was drawn up high on her head. Her shoulders and arms were naked but for a quantity of diamonds and rubies. She wore a red satin gown and was screaming. I took her to be Lady Beatrix Poindexter. As she was called *Lady* on her luggage label, I figured she was English.

The man with her was clearly Sir Clifford. He had a heavy, drooping mustache and wore black and white clothes. There was the look of a thin walrus about him.

They both shouted at once and by turns. Sir Clifford had Lady Beatrix by her wrists, which burned with rubies. But he couldn't do a thing with her and was himself white as a—ghost.

"We are going to die!" shrieked Lady Beatrix, with some reason. "I know it! I feel it! Oh, I cannot set foot in a life-boat. It will break up like an eggshell on these seas. And you know how I suffer with the cold!"

"Shut up, Beatrix!" the man replied, clinging to her wrists.

"Oh yes! It is all very well for you!" she spat. "Women and children to the lifeboats, while you men linger here on deck, smoking cigars in perfect comfort!"

"Have some sense, Beatrix!" the man bawled. "If the ship is sinking, there will be scant comfort for me on the deck!"

"I should never have come on this ship with you. You have never had a good idea in all your life! Making a new start in America—ha! How very like you to think up a scheme that will kill us both! I should have stayed behind in England and endured my poverty!"

"Poverty forsooth! You're hanging in jewels!" the man barked, outraged.

"Yes," Lady Beatrix hissed back, "every penny I possess is sunk in this jewelry. Oh, sunk! Why did I say that? I am beside myself! And much good my poor bits of jewels will do me when I am dying of exposure in that lifeboat. *If* the lower classes do not murder us before we can get to the deck! No, no, no. I see it all now. I should have lived on in poverty until Julian comes of age and into money of his own. Then I might have thrown myself on his mercy. Certainly *you* have not turned out to be much of a provider. My mother was right about you from the start!"

"Oh leave off, Beatrix!" Sir Clifford remarked loudly. "This is all disastrous enough without bringing your mother into it!"

There was an explosion of light outside that flashed at the portholes. Lady Beatrix screamed again. "Ice and now fire!" she pealed. "We are dead twice over!"

"Shut up, I tell you!" Sir Clifford flung her wrists down and dashed to a porthole. "It is only a flare they've sent up, signaling for a rescue!"

"And who would come to the aid of a ship widely advertised as unsinkable? Answer me that! I abandon all hope!" Lady Beatrix whirled about the cabin, pulling down a fur cape and turning out all the drawers.

"Is there no ready money? Give me all you've got! What if I am saved and you are not? When have you *ever* thought of me?" She shrieked on in higher and higher key while reducing the room to a shambles.

The two were in the last stages of panic, running up against each other in their haste. They were nothing like I pictured upper-crust English people. Even if I'd been visible, I doubt they'd have noticed me. They exited at last through a doorway to a long corridor, attempting to pass through at the same time. This was not easy, for both wore life jackets. Lady Beatrix threw hers on over her fur cape. Her shrieks echoed away down a long passage.

The cabin lights blazed upon the confusion left behind. Only a moment later, the door to the corridor opened slowly again. Sir Clifford, all alone, stepped back inside, the picture of stealth. He went over to a cupboard and pulled out one of Lady Beatrix's long cloaks. Rummaging on a shelf above, he jerked down a bandbox, tore off the lid, and took out a large feathered hat with veils.

Imagine my amazement when he planted this female hat on his own head, drew down the veil, and threw the long cloak over his shoulders and life jacket. He crept to the door, flipped off the lights, and peered out. Then he slipped away, pulling the door shut behind him. But not before I saw his wild eyes. They stared blind with fear between his mustache and his wife's hat brim.

I stood there between the two cabins, trying to digest this. Nothing we'd learned in Miss Botts's class seemed to bear on this scene. Then I recollected the ancient law of the sea in such circumstances—women and children to the lifeboats first.

As a result, very few men survived the sinking, for the *Titanic* was sailing short on lifeboats. It broke upon me what I'd witnessed. Sir Clifford had returned to disguise himself in his wife's clothes. With any luck at all, he could slip into a lifeboat and nestle in among the women. I trusted he had the sense not to get in the same boat with his wife, who would surely set to screaming again and give him away. I thought how disappointed Miss Dabney would be in titled English people acting this way.

Then, just behind me, Julian cried out. I stepped back into his cabin, and my filmy hand hung near his pillow. "Mother?" he said again, looking through me to the far room. "Father? Why have we stopped? Are we at New York? Is it morning?"

I reached out to take his hands, which were still plucking at the blanket, but I could give him no comfort, nor even get a grasp on him. He whimpered like any child left alone in the night. None of the loud-mouthed carrying on between his folks had stirred him; he was probably used to that. Yet he was half aware of danger in a groggy way.

With no thought of anything but themselves, his own flesh and blood had left poor Julian for fish bait. This was low, but I recalled more against these villains. It may have been all too easy for his mama to leave him behind if she inherited his money. Miss Botts had hit it on the button. This disaster was a clear example of mankind's destruction by its own vanity. Poor Julian was left behind as a human sacrifice to greed and selfishness. No wonder he couldn't rest easy in his wet grave. Who could? If this was an instance of English child care, I for one would settle for Bluff City and my mama.

Running feet pounded above our heads. Machinery creaked as the lifeboats were lowered. Julian had sobbed himself back to sleep. His thumb drifted up to his lips, though he was somewhat old for this habit. Some people actually go to their graves sucking their thumbs, which is a pathetic thought, but sobering.

There's no fighting fate, or changing what's over and done with. Still, I struggled to wake Julian and send him flying for the lifeboats. I yanked on his blanket, but my poor transparent fingers poked right through it. I darted over to where his life jacket hung on the peg, but my hands scooped through it like a fork into whipped cream. I couldn't have lifted a matchstick, let alone a life jacket, for I was a ghost, haunting the past. History can be very cruel.

I wrung my starfish hands and hung over Julian's bunk. But my hollering was heard only by Miss Spaulding and Lowell Seaforth back in some future world. *Oh, Julian, Julian,* I wailed, *why have you conjured me up when I can't do a durn thing to save you?*

Then I was by the porthole again, staring out. I could move about that cabin with no more effort than a goldfish twitching its tail. Lifeboats were in the water, lit by the spiky moon, which only made the sea bigger and emptier. The women and children were calling back to their menfolk. Some stood in the small boats clutching their heads. Others seemed to be rowing like men. I was viewing a scene few had lived to tell. There would shortly be frozen bodies bobbing in that unforgiving water, awash in a sea of deck chairs.

I skinned my eyes for Lady Beatrix or the shameful Sir Clifford, but the lifeboats were fanning out from the dying ship, and the calls grew faint. The *Titanic* moaned in reply, and there was the sound of breaking glass and thunder from the boilers. Spookiest of all, a pleasant string orchestra above me was playing a church hymn, "Lead Kindly Light." The notes warbled on the water and played across the pathway of the moon.

Then the first bodies hurtled past the porthole, as people dropped into the sea. I tumbled back across the cabin and threw my weightless body across Julian. His head was higher than his feet as the *Titanic* began its final slide. He woke and struggled against the band that held him fast. His mouth was a startled circle. And in that moment I know he saw me. Working one hand free, he reached for where my face was, and his fist closed in the air.

The electric lamp failed, and water roared through both portholes under heavy pressure. In the last second I found I could clasp Julian's small hand. He clung tight. This was a miracle, but we were soon parted. A ton of numbing water knocked the bunk from under me. The walls splintered, and the room closed like a lady's fan. What wasn't drowned was crushed. I seemed to glimpse the green bottom of the sea, five miles below.

The floor I hit was polished pine, bone dry except for the spatters of sea water from my drenched hair. Miss Spaulding's desk lamp lay shattered. But the overhead light was on, casting a hard glare. I was rolling on the floor of the principal's office, and I was sopping wet.

Thrashing around on the level floor, I called out for Julian. But it was Lowell Seaforth who stood me on my feet. My poor old boots gushed ice water, and my teeth rattled in my head.

Across the desk Miss Spaulding stood with her hand still clamped over her mouth. As I was set on my feet, something wet and heavy fell from my shoulders to collapse on the floor. Miss Spaulding muffled a shriek. Learned woman that she is, words failed her.

I was coming to myself fast and glad to be back. Still, bubbles that seemed to be Julian's last strangulations broke in my brain. I heard the sudden silence of a string orchestra quickly cut off in the clatter of collapsing music stands. I stood, shedding water on the heavy thing at my feet.

"Was I here the whole time?" I inquired, hearing my voice at last.

Lowell Seaforth stared at me with immense respect. "Yes . . ." he said, ". . . and no."

He bent down and dragged up a wool blanket heavy with sea water. His jaw tightened as he unfurled it for Miss Spaulding to see. Her hand shifted from her mouth to cover her eyes. "Oh no," she sobbed, "this cannot be! This goes against everything!"

The blanket that Seaforth held high was from Julian's bunk. I'd snatched at it when I rolled away from him and the water closed over us.

Miss Spaulding crumpled into her chair. There were white

letters woven into the center of the blanket. They spelled out:

ROYAL MAIL STEAMSHIP *TITANIC*

I was not surprised to see them. No more than my mama would have been in my place. She'd prophesied all this on the day she read my tea leaves.

· 13 ·

Once you are famous, your fate falls into other hands. This I learned shortly after the busiest hours of my life up to that point. I refer to the afternoon when I broke up Professor Regis's criminal seance and rounded off the evening by sinking on the *Titanic*.

Miss Spaulding was out of school for two days, victim of the first sick headache of her life, so we were all crowded in with Miss Winkler's seventh-grade bunch.

Lowell Seaforth seemed to go underground, as writers will when they have a lot of raw material to get down on paper. His first effort was to publish in the *Pantagraph* the news of how I broke up the seance. This filled four columns under a headline reading:

SUPRIOUS SPIRITUALIST ROUTED BY LOCAL LASS

It ended with an all-points bulletin inquiring into the whereabouts of a wayward girl, only known name being Sybil. Miss Winkler dealt with this article in Current Events but did not call on me.

I'd thought Miss Dabney would be very interested in me

leaving my body to experience the *Titanic* sinking. It touched on two topics popular with her: the unearthly and the English. I paid her a call the first chance I got, when the salt water from the Atlantic Ocean was still damp in my hair. But she could scarcely attend me; she was entirely too excited by the busting up of the fake seance and so pleased to have her papa's watch back that she'd fixed it to a ribbon depending from her bosom.

She was still draped in the black mantilla from the seance, and crowed considerably at the role she'd played herself. Pouring out cocoa from her Rockingham pot, she urged corn muffins on me. I suspected they were from Minerva's unseen hands and passed them up, having had enough spectral doings for one day. Miss Dabney also warned me about going out in winter weather so soon after a shampoo, so I gave up trying to tell her anything.

On the third day after the event, we were back under Miss Spaulding's jurisdiction. Each time she looked my way, she seemed ready to break down and bawl, but this was only a combination of nasty shock and deep confusion. After all, I'd flown in the face of science, which is her creed. She was soon to suffer more irritation.

Shortly after morning recess, which Letty Shambaugh and her club spent by plotting against me, the door banged open and a disorderly gang of men marched on Miss Spaulding.

"Here now!" she cried, but found herself outnumbered.

Several wore the checkered vests and high-polished yellowish shoes that marked them as St. Louis men. Two carried cameras, and some apprentice types lugged in tripods. They were all newspapermen and insistent.

As any interruption to education is always welcome, everybody in the class, particularly Les Dawson and Alexander, milled around. Miss Spaulding was backed up to the blackboard by several reporters, demanding to have me pointed out. One brandished a St. Louis newspaper with a headline that screamed:

HUMBLE SMALLTOWN GIRL CONDEMNED IN TRANCE
TO RELIVE DREADFUL RECKONING OF CRUEL SEA
WICKED HOAX OR PSYCHIC BREAKTHROUGH?

Lowell Seaforth had released my tale of Death at Sea to all the St. Louis papers, a move sure to advance his career. He entered our classroom on the heels of the out-of-towners. Under his arm was the fatal blanket, folded and dry. "Mr. Seaforth!" wailed Miss Spaulding. "Are you the author of this outrage?"

He made a small bow, and there was calculation in his eyes. "Oh dear," Miss Spaulding whimpered, "do not let them set up those cameras. This is a place of learning." She grasped a blackboard pointer to her chest and took on the posture of a trapped rat.

"My dear Miss Spaulding," Seaforth said, "there is much for children to learn about the workings of a free press in a free country. These journalists have made a long trip for a look at Blossom. I've set down the . . . facts of her case in black and white. But what you and I have witnessed as unassailable truth, these . . . gentlemen are inclined to regard as . . . human interest, at best, or a childish prank."

"Who could blame them?" Miss Spaulding murmured.

"And so the burden rests with you and me, Miss Spaulding. We know our evidence will vindicate Blossom. But I am only an untried small-town reporter. Your word as an educational leader is the only thing that will save Blossom from being thrown to the wolves, as it were. In the interest of truth, you will surely not let that happen."

I sat with folded hands at my desk. Miss Spaulding darted me a hooded glance. It was plain that she was considering throwing me to the wolves in the interest of peace and quiet.

"We don't have a prayer of explaining Blossom's powers to these hardbitten skeptics," Seaforth continued smoothly. "But to borrow a phrase from yourself, she deserves her day in court. They will want to take photos of Blossom and the blanket. And they'll just naturally want her teacher in the picture."

"I?" asked Miss Spaulding faintly.

"It is only right," said Seaforth.

"Will the Bluff City *Pantagraph* run pictures too?"

"It is only a matter of time," Seaforth replied. Miss Spaulding's hand crept up to arrange her back hair.

She and I were shortly posed before her desk, holding the blanket between us to display the legend: ROYAL MAIL STEAM-SHIP *TITANIC*. The air was yellow with flash powder as the cameras shot away at us from every angle. I was not so blinded that I missed seeing Letty at the back of the room, working her hands in hopeless rage. The rest of the Busy Fingers gaped at me. I could have taken over the entire club at that moment and run it to my own satisfaction. But new worlds were opening up to me. This is often the way with life.

Directly after the picture-taking, Miss Spaulding rounded

on the reporters. She'd sized them up, as I had. They tended to snicker and poke each other with elbows. Some looked capable of spitting tobacco juice on the floor. And their language was not good.

She dropped her end of the blanket and expanded. "And now, gentlemen," she announced, "I will remind you that this is a public-school classroom, not a Roman orgy. You will find yourselves seats at any available student desk. Be seated at once. It is a teacher who presides in a classroom, as any of you who may have gone to school will know."

Several of the reporters looked like they'd been slapped. We all watched ten or twelve grown men trying to fit themselves behind the desks.

Miss Spaulding took up her blackboard pointer. "You have broken into a busy school day to track down a story you have already judged as a laugh and a lie. But I wonder," she mused, fingering the pointer tip, "if you have contemplated the amount of research this story entails. You have come to point the finger of scorn at fantasy. I wonder how you will handle hard facts." There was grumbling from the invaders, quickly stilled by a flash from the pince-nez glasses.

Miss Spaulding held up a corner of Julian's blanket. "You see a blanket emblazoned with the *Titanic* name. Is this well-made throw from a prominent English mill a fake? Surely a young girl in Bluff City did not weave it on a home loom to perpetrate a fraud. I trust you mean to contact a responsible official of the White Star Line to verify this piece of hard evidence."

There were furtive looks among the St. Louis men, who'd

not considered doing any such thing. Even Seaforth swallowed hard, though he was in the clear.

"We move on to other matters," Miss Spaulding said. "During Blossom's . . . experience . . . she called out the names of passengers on the *Titanic*'s sad maiden voyage: the Poindexter party. I wonder how many of you have checked this name against a passenger list of the ship. Such a list is a matter of public record."

There were several hung heads among the St. Louis crowd. "No, I thought not," she said. "Blossom, stand up and stand tall!"

I leapt from my seat, forgetting all about my stake in this matter. I was not wearing my Select Dry Goods outfit, so was in my natural state.

"Gaze again, gentlemen of the press, upon the young girl who has piqued your idle curiosity. Is this a child who has moved sufficiently in the elevated society of England to describe its manners and its members? Supernatural forces alone would have placed her in such circles.

"Is this a child who contrived to drench herself in salt water in the presence of her teacher to pass herself off as a shipwreck victim far out to sea?"

"Blossom's never been anywhere in her life!" Letty piped up, and all the Busy Fingers agreed.

"Letty, see me after school!" Miss Spaulding barked.

"Gentlemen," she concluded, "you are dismissed. You have a good deal of homework to do. Doubtless a story beyond your capacities can be adequately dealt with by such as the *Chicago Tribune* and the *Milwaukee Journal*.

Horror was written across the faces of the St. Louis men

at the mention of these superior newspapers. They struggled from their desks and filed out. "Do not replace your hats until you have left the building!" was Miss Spaulding's parting shot.

The class burst into applause in admiration, but she walloped the desk with her pointer and canceled recess.

The next day Lowell Seaforth broke the story in the *Pantagraph*. He had a picture off one of the photographers that showed me and Miss Spaulding and the blanket. The article took up most of page one, under a headline reading:

LOCAL EDUCATOR ROUTS ST. LOUIS PRESS CORPS

OVER THE SUPERNATURAL STORY OF THE CENTURY

My mama saw the picture, and so I had to read the whole story out to her. Then she whupped the tar out of me for giving away a story I could just as well have charged money for. But there was a gleam in her eye, and I knew she saw future possibilities. She was not the only one.

· 14 ·

By the early spring of 1914 a person would not have recognized Bluff City. The Cornhusker Hotel was raising a four-story wing to lodge the visitors come to spot ghosts, expose the whole business, have religious experiences, inquire into relatives lost at sea in various ships, have warts cured, locate missing house pets, get their palms read by Mama, and take pictures of me at recess.

Anybody wishing a full account of all this activity will have to thumb through back issues of the *Pantagraph*.

I'd passed the winter granting interviews, only telling the unvarnished truth. The truth is too much for some people and too little for others. But they all fazed me very little. The world is hungry for novelty.

At first I took care to dress in my best. But I soon learned that the tackier I looked, the better they liked me. Miss Spaulding brought these interviews to a halt. She claimed they were cutting into my education. She also said if ever

I felt a fit of the Second Sight coming on during a school day, I was to get out of her sight and her classroom.

One of our winter visitors was an official from the White Star steamship line, come all the way from Southampton, England, to verify the blanket. He pronounced it authentic and then tried to make off with it. But it was impounded by the Bluff City Chamber of Commerce. They hung it in the window of their office on the Square behind a picture of me, blown up to life size. It was blurry but a fair likeness. Beneath, a notice in ornamental print said:

> BLOSSOM CULP—PINT-SIZE PROPHETESS
> HER SPIRIT IS KNOWN TO ROAM
> BUT SHE CALLS BLUFF CITY HOME

The Select Dry Goods Company sold authentic copies of Julian's blanket, handwoven, in a full selection from crib size to double-bed. And there was a new sign down at the depot to greet newcomers.

> WELCOME TO BLUFF CITY
> 1100 MILES FROM THE ATLANTIC OCEAN
> BUT THE LAST SPOT THE TITANIC WAS SIGHTED

Schoolchildren contributed pennies for a combined monument and souvenir stand to be raised to Julian Poindexter in the Greenwood Cemetery. The paved road to Pittsfield was renamed the Titanic Turnpike. And the football team over at the high school called themselves The Invincible Icebergs. A local poet, name of Manfred Eams Davenport, wrote a poem honoring me which he recited with gestures in church halls. It went like this:

> *Down, down into the ice-strewn sea*
> * Great Titan plunged with boilers burst,*
> *With all its wealth and majesty,*
> * A vessel vaunted and then curs't;*
>
> *And few to mark its watery grave*
> * Except a bit of floating flotsam,*
> *And many passed beneath the wave,*
> * But not, thank God, our wondrous Blossom.*

Miss Spaulding read it in class, without gestures, and pronounced it "sickening."

Certain citizens, unhappy at the turn Bluff City was taking, wrote to the *Pantagraph* suggesting I be put in a foster home out of town or a reform school until my majority. While these soreheads were far outweighed by others cashing in on the town's new progress, I inclined to caution and determined to lay low until much of this blew over.

My fame was not merely local. A firm out in Fort Lee, New Jersey, was making a moving-picture show of my experience, though they were taking liberties with the facts. I was to be spectral, but adult, and Julian was to be revised as a grownup too. The pair of us were to be lovers defying time, but we were to die at the end of the picture, locked in embrace on a facsimile of the ship. The well-known actress playing me was to be Miss Dorothy Gish. A tribe of Arizona Indians was said to be raising a totem pole in my likeness somewhere on the outskirts of Tucson.

I was offered a free trip to a girls' college called Radcliffe, in Massachusetts state, where a professor was writing a book on me. I already knew there were colleges for girls who could not get their educations on their own, but there's a difference between studying and being studied. I turned the offer down, though that professor is writing the book anyhow, probably from newspaper clippings.

Every newspaper in the United States seemed to discover the names of the Poindexters on the *Titanic*'s passenger list. Lady Beatrix was reported saved and brought to safety on the steamship *Carpathia*. Julian and his paw were pronounced lost at sea. I dreamt several nights of Sir Clifford dropping from deck to water. He fell past Julian's porthole in a large feathered hat and lady's flapping cloak. But I had no actual vision of this spectacle.

In fact, all the notoriety seemed to run my Second Sight completely off. Despite repeated urgings and a cash offer from the Louisville *Courier-Journal,* I was indifferent to more dabbling in other worlds. Who knew but what I might have to live through any number of disasters, past and future. History is jammed with them.

Besides, there was a missing part to my *Titanic* journey. The beautiful woman of high degree who'd committed a sin and a crime against her own kid was Lady Beatrix, much as Mama had read in my tea leaves. But it looked to me like Lady Beatrix, wherever she was, got off scot-free. I half thought I'd see Julian again as before, out by the trolley tracks, dying again. I'd been able to do little on his behalf, and he was a determined little critter, even in death.

All this I mentioned to Alexander Armsworth, who I was on speaking terms with again. He'd taken to walking me home from school. And there were two or three of his sex he'd beaten up for the privilege.

The shortcut home is through the Armsworth property, as I've pointed out before. One day Alexander strolled me right past the bay window of his family's mansion. When I wondered aloud what his mama would think of him keeping company with me, he said I seemed to be okay in her books. This was progress indeed.

Mrs. Armsworth's a woman very hungry for a notable place in society, which money alone has never given her. I guess my fame raised me a notch in her opinion. Besides, it was due to my experience that her son-in-law, Seaforth, was promoted to Night Editor of the *Pantagraph,* with offers from other papers too. A woman of finer fiber would have me up to the house for a visit is what I thought. But in this life you take what people are willing to give. No more. No less.

Alexander always walked me right to my door before we parted. There were generally several strangers hanging around outside, often wanting me to bless small medals and suchlike. Alexander grew expert at waving them away. Even the streetcar made a brief stop opposite our porch to point out this landmark.

It was worth a look. Our tumbledown shack had undergone an awesome change. With money in her mattress and credit at the bank, my mama had the place rebuilt, and was showing a profit inside.

A thatched roof covered the old tin one. The siding, once featuring flattened-out oil drums, was now covered in shingles strangely like gingerbread cookies. The porch, which had often fallen down in the past, was now held up by pillars painted to represent candy canes. And the sheet-metal flue was newly encased in a tall chimney of pink brick oozing mortar, set at the angle of the Leaning Tower of Pisa. The whole place was worked over to recall Hansel and Gretel. Though my taste was still largely unformed, I knew this was bad.

A sign outside shaped like a descending ocean liner announced Mama as a "Seeress" and "Spiritualist Advisor, Cash in Advance." She was working three shifts a day and charging whatever she felt like. She insisted on being addressed as Madame Culp, even by me.

That one particular day, me and Alexander lingered on the front path, newly paved in colorful stones. A gang of gardeners from an expensive nursery had plowed the yard, which was once swept dirt. They were putting in a flower bed shaped like a White Star Line life preserver. The round border was going to be white tulips, and the name TITANIC was being spelled out in blue crocuses. That day they'd got as far as TIT.

Our front door, freshly painted with Dutch hex signs, was ajar. The sweeping skirts of someone I took to be a client of Mama's had just passed inside. I figured this was another sucker about to be relieved of a dollar or so on the strength of my reputation.

Mama was still at the door. Even Alexander lingered for a look at her. She wore a new long purple gown of washable velveteen embroidered in cloth-of-gold stars and crescent moons. Her black hair coursed down the shoulders of this shroud, but was held flat on top by a metal tiara set with glass stones. Circles of rouge flanked her nose. The only feature recalling Mama's earlier self was her collapsed cheeks. Even with income, she had not bought dentures. Though her speech remained muffled, I was just as glad, for she would surely have taken on the look of a grinning skull, though she never grins.

She hitched a thumb at me, summoning me inside. Alexander cut out. On my way in, Mama gave my arm a painful pinch, to remind me to watch my p's and q's during whatever was to follow.

There's no room in this account to describe the changes inside our place. Mama had not run electricity in, but candles in branching holders replaced the coal-oil lamps. Incense smoldered from brass pots hung from the rafters. And the walls were swagged with cloth in pagan patterns, draped back by tasseled ropes. The effect was of a permanent tent.

Mama worked her jaws in her usual silence while dragging me to the center of the room. Two chairs were drawn up to a card table. Mama's tarot cards were there too, but not laid out. A lady occupied one of the chairs. Sunlight no longer saw the place, so I was practically nose-to-nose with Miss Dabney before I recognized her.

The egret feather on her Queen Mary hat curled upward, reaching for an incense pot. I was mortified to find her here and suspected plotting behind my back. I also figured money would change hands, and Mama would not be the poorer for it.

There'd been many sudden changes in Bluff City, as I have said, but they did not alter Miss Dabney's reputation for craziness. Though Lowell Seaforth had dealt kindly with her and Minerva in his write-up, others had not. A young girl such as myself who, among other feats, can skate back in history and return with evidence is a universal wonder. But a crazy old lady with her pantry haunted is another matter. Certain citizens who had once chuckled behind her back would now laugh in her face if she showed it.

Tourists peeled souvenir pickets off her porch. Lower types, likely local, left small dead animals on her threshold. She'd had the law out one time to discourage a cameraman from the Indianapolis *Star* who'd taken a picture of her kitchen through a back window. But the picture was printed anyhow, and there was no proof of Minerva in it. Near neighbors were organizing to have her sent off to the Eastern Star Old Ladies' Home.

She'd let the battery on her Pope-Detroit Electric run down and went nowhere. So imagine my surprise to find her planted in the middle of our place. Whenever I'd called on her through the winter, she sat folded in one corner of her sofa in a flannel nightgown, looking wan. But on this particular day she was her old self and then some.

After an awkward pause she said, "Well, Blossom, I thought to return a call, as you have favored me with so many." She tried to park her bony elbows easily on the table, but one slipped off. She was clearly keyed up. Her voice wobbled and trailed away.

I thought of making tea, but knew that Mama would only read it. So I waited the two of them out. Miss Dabney's papa's watch danced at her bosom. She was having palpitations, and I didn't like her coloring beneath the face powder.

Mama muttered something, but it was neither clear nor polite.

Miss Dabney rummaged in her sleeve for a handkerchief she couldn't find and then gave out a shuddering sigh.

"Truthfully, Blossom, this is not a social call. I do not make them, as you know. It regards a...matter...that surpasses everything so far for pure wonder. Nothing supernatural! Oh no!" She put up a gloved hand as if to stop traffic. "We've surely had enough of that, no offense meant, dear. Something else has occurred. Something beyond my . . . wildest dreams."

Even Mama paused to consider just how wild Miss Dabney's dreams might be.

"Your mother—Madame Culp—visited me earlier in the day."

I goggled at this. Mama had changed considerably, but not to the point of paying calls. She'd be taking on Alexander Armsworth's mama next, I thought, and my flesh crept.

Miss Dabney warmed to her topic. "Madame . . . Culp is a very intuitive wom— lady, of course. And when she received a certain letter—by sea mail—from England, she brought it straight to me."

"Well, Mama is no hand at reading," I mentioned. Mama's foot in a new shoe shot out and kicked me hard on the ankle.

Miss Dabney coughed delicately. "As Madame Culp knew that you and I are friends, she was kind enough to ask me to have a look at this letter. My interest in things English is well known." Miss Dabney's eyes had an unnatural shine to them. I still feared she might be having a stroke.

Stepping out of the range of Mama's foot, I said, "But Madame Culp here can't even read the word *England*, so how'd she know where the letter was mailed?"

"Ah, she did not need to read a word," said Miss Dabney in a voice of gathering grandeur. Then she rummaged in her reticule, drawing out a square envelope of heavy cream paper. "The coat of arms upon this missive told the tale!" The envelope trembled in her grip. She couldn't bear to part with it, though I saw at a distance it was addressed to me.

I stepped around behind Miss Dabney to see what a coat of arms is.

On the envelope flap a lion and a unicorn both on their hind legs were tussling together in a forest of curlicues above a Latin motto. Making no sense of this, I finally said, "Well, that is real artistic, no doubt about it."

"Oh, Blossom," said Miss Dabney, "poor benighted child, do you not know who this letter is from?" The feather fluttered on her hat like it had never left the bird. "It is from Queen Mary."

And so it was.

I won't disclose the exact contents, as the letter was personal to me. The truth was that it didn't come straight from Queen Mary's own hand. It was written under her command by one of her secretaries.

The wording was so dignified and English that Miss Dabney had to interpret most of it. Besides, the ink was badly blurred. She'd evidently read it over many times and wept tears of excitement all over the page.

The gist of it was this. In one of her castles Queen Mary had picked up an English newspaper that carried an account of my psychic experience. All England still mourned the loss of the great *Titanic,* so anything to do with it made news.

The Queen had been somewhat consoled that several high-placed persons of her acquaintance had been rescued. But this comfort turned to ashes in her mouth when she learned that Lady Beatrix Poindexter had saved herself, not to mention her jewelry, while leaving her own son on the Atlantic floor without a backward look, so to speak. Lady Beatrix had returned to England, puddling with hypocritical tears the whole way. And this same Lady Beatrix was a Lady in Waiting to Queen Mary!

I didn't know if this was an astonishing coincidence or not. It might be that all the titled people in England know each other, something like the Odd Fellows club. Later I was to find out that this is somewhat true.

Queen Mary was "grieved and appalled" (I quote) that a lady holding such a favored position with herself was "so lacking in parental feelings and selflessness." (I quote again.)

Evidently she challenged Lady Beatrix as to the particulars of my experience. Lady Beatrix denied everything and then screamed that she was cursed and damned to Hell, threw herself at the Queen's feet, and carried on. The letter didn't spell this out, but the meaning came through.

Queen Mary wound up by commending me as "an instrument of divine providence sent by an Agency not to be questioned, to rectify a great wrong." My celebrity was well earned, Queen Mary declared, for I'd cared more for a small lost boy than his own "heartless maternal parent." The Queen referred to me as a "young American friend of the British Way," and said if ever I was to be anywhere near

England, I would be welcome. King George sent his regards too.

Miss Dabney fell back in the chair. The reading took everything out of her. All she could add were disjointed phrases, like "Queen Mary, the Dear Soul of Goodness" and "To think I have lived to hold word of Royalty in my hand" and "This almost makes up for all I've been put through," et cetera.

Mama was growing restless, always a dangerous sign. I wondered how we could wind up this visit. I wanted to get Miss Dabney home before one of her sinking spells. "Well," said I, "it was civil of the Queen to drop me a line. I hope she kicked that Lady Beatrix down a long flight of stairs."

"Blossom, Blossom, you do not grasp the meaning of this letter."

I thought I had mastered the main points of it, and said so.

"No, no. This is an invitation from the Royal Family. The very personages who hang in my back parlor. Blossom, think! A Royal invitation is a Royal command!"

Between Miss Spaulding and my mama, I figured I'd been commanded royally all my days. If the Queen of England was going to start on me, I wondered if life was worth living.

Miss Dabney's mouth was pulled into its former foxy V shape, and she beamed at me through the incense smoke. In a voice from Grand Opera, she said, "You are going to England to visit the Royal Family. You, Blossom! A young American girl who has not had any"—her eye darted hastily around Mama's murky tent, and she changed her tack—"has not had any such opportunity is going to make her curtsy like a proper English girl. Blossom, think!"

Her voice cracked in all directions like old pottery. "You are going to be presented at Court! And of course I shall accompany you and cover the expenses."

This last information was mainly for Mama's ears. But my mind was elsewhere. I wasn't completely sure that the letter meant anything quite that definite. But Miss Dabney's mind was speeding ahead like the *Wabash Cannonball*.

Mama slapped a hand with many rings on it down on the table. In a slurred snarl she said, "I can't spare the kid. She's good for business."

"I beg your pardon?" said Miss Dabney, with her eyebrows at their highest.

"You heard me," muttered Mama.

"I am confident we can come to an arrangement," breathed Miss Dabney, horrified that this opportunity might slip away.

And I'm sure they did, though I never heard the exact figure.

Miss Dabney staggered to her feet. Her reticule and other small items rained down from her tall form. "Oh, Blossom, *England!* You have brought my fondest dream to fruition. I will die happy!"

I sincerely hoped she wouldn't die on the spot. "So much to do. The planning! The steamship tickets! We must make haste! Punctuality is the courtesy of Kings. That is a well-known English saying, and they live by it!" et cetera.

She said more before reaching the door. But she didn't pass through it before Mama called out in a voice as clear as a public orator. "That'll be a buck and a half for this here one-time session."

· 15 ·

THE BLUFF CITY *Pantagraph* carried a full account of this latest bombshell. It drove everything but the hog-market report off the front page. A true copy of the Royal letter ran, flanked by a lion and a unicorn. American flags and Union Jacks flowed into four oval portraits. One was of Queen Mary, crowned. One was King George in his uniform. Beneath him was a shot of me far from flattering; it was a candid shot on a frizzy day for my hair. Underneath Queen Mary was a view of Miss Dabney. She sat for it in a new hat inspired by the lady above her. They were as alike as a pair of slippers.

Beneath my likeness was written:

LOCAL PSYCHIC WONDER CHILD SUMMONED TO EUROPEAN COURT

Under Miss Dabney's was:

PROMINENT OLD SETTLER TO CHAPERONE CULP PRODIGY

ON GRAND TOUR

Lowell Seaforth wrote the main article, exercising good taste throughout. Any reading between the lines was strictly up to the individual *Pantagraph* subscriber.

Miss Blossom Culp, Horace Mann schoolgirl acclaimed for her psychic inclinations, will sail shortly from the port of New York for Europe. The daughter of Madame Culp, local clairvoyant, will embark on the RMS *Olympic,* sister ship of the ill-starred *Titanic,* source of Miss Culp's repute.

Accompanying her will be Miss Gertrude Dabney, retiring member of local society. "For purposes of the journey," Miss Dabney told this reporter, "Blossom will travel as my ward. This is something like an honorary niece. It is an English custom, one of several with which I am familiar."

Completing the traveling party will be Alexander Armsworth, son of the prominent Joe Armsworths of Pine Street and brother of Lucille Armsworth Seaforth. His mother told this reporter, "An ocean voyage and travel in foreign parts will augment my boy's education. Mixing with persons of a social rank far above any in Bluff City will knock some of the rough edges off him. Miss Dabney has been gracious enough to include him in the sailing party, at our expense, naturally."

In London, England, the party will put up at Brown's Hotel to await further Royal word. Mrs. Joe Armsworth begs to inform any who may wish to transmit marconigrams or other messages of bon voyage to the travelers that they will make the ocean crossing in First Class accommodations.

Being Seaforth's mother-in-law, Mrs. Armsworth heard tell of the famous Queen Mary letter before the *Pantagraph* set it in type. She hastened to batter down Miss Dabney's door to get Alexander in on our England trip. This is the same woman who'd always been loudest in branding Miss Dabney "crazy as a coot." But now she was eating crow.

I doubt she had much trouble getting her way. It was an entertainment of Miss Dabney's to promote a romance between me and Alexander, though she only mentioned to me that he'd be useful in hauling luggage around.

Late in her life Miss Dabney was discovered by all the ladies of Bluff City's upper crust. She was suddenly invited to join the Daughters of the American Revolution club. This "turned her stomach," she said. The Daughters seemed not to know that she still rooted for the English to win in that particular war.

Mrs. Shambaugh left a calling card on her. Alexander's mama left several notes pleading to give her, me, and Alexander a bon voyage party to see us off.

"I suppose we must let the Armsworth person have her party, though she is almost unbearably pushy," sighed Miss Dabney. "Only mention Royalty to American backwoods types, and they are on their knees. The irony of this is intense.

"But remember, Blossom, if you grow up to marry young Alexander, you will have that Armsworth woman as a mother-in-law. Consider carefully before you commit yourself." Her eyes narrowed with mischief, as if she'd like to throw a wrench into Mrs. Armsworth's party. Alexander's mama's parties are not hard to ruin. They're disasters to start with.

Miss Dabney turned to other concerns. She'd sent off to Nugent's Department Store in St. Louis to outfit us for our trip. For herself she ordered several English tweed suits, for strolling on boat decks. She also sent for a gnarled cane "for country walks." This stumped me because I thought

London was quite a built-up area. She also laid in several Mosher skirts, Gibson blouses, and quite an impressive turn-out in Utrecht cut velvet to wear at the Royal Court. If we never made it as far as the Royal Court, I feared for her sanity. "I hope Queen Mary will not be in powder blue, for I will be," she remarked. She returned to humming the British national anthem.

For me she ordered six changes, some nautical, and others with flounces enough to stun Letty Shambaugh. She also had Nugent's send me a Princess dress. This number had whale-bone running up the spine, forcing its wearer to assume a regal posture, sitting or standing. "Though you may be tempted to slump," she said, "your dress won't be."

The day our tickets came by mail from the White Star Line at number 9 Broadway in New York City, Miss Dabney was sick to her stomach with joy. We passed several happy afternoons in her back parlor in a swamp of Nugent's tissue paper. The sight of her excited as a child made even such a practical person as myself sentimental.

Alexander was half off his head at the prospect of crossing the Atlantic on the biggest steamship still afloat. Not to mention missing all the school time.

Miss Spaulding had had about enough of me for one school year and nearly said so when she gave me her blessing for taking the time off. She loaded Alexander and me down with a ream of homework to do on shipboard. This was wishful thinking, and she knew it.

As for me, I was ready for a change of scene as I usually am. There's roaming in my blood, from both sides of the family. Besides, I'd tired of being a public monument in a small place like Bluff City. It had taken away such innocent pleasures of the past as tricking myself out as the ghost in Old Man Leverette's privy. I sometimes thought I'd been robbed of my youth.

We were to leave directly from the bon voyage party. The night train connected at Mattoon for the through train to New York on the Pennsylvania Line. By the evening of our leave-taking, I was worn to a frazzle from anticipation and keeping watch over Mama. She eyed my new clothes with calculation. She was now far too well-off to think of selling them, but old habits die hard. I kept my new steamer trunk locked and slept with the key on a chain around my neck. The purpose of my journey seemed to mean nothing to Mama. The only kings and queens that cut any ice with her are in a deck of cards.

I was to wear my new Princess dress to the Armsworths' party, to give it a rehearsal. Just at twilight the men came to take my trunk to the depot. I set out soon after in all my new elegance for the walk up to the Armsworths' mansion. Mama didn't so much as bid me good-bye. But that is Mama to a T.

As I stepped over the trolley tracks in my new gun-metal-gray kid shoes with pearl buttons to the ankle, I recollected earlier times such as back when I'd come home daily across these selfsame tracks in a pair of cardboard boots with the heels down to nubs. And of course I thought of Julian, whose death brought on these many changes.

I lingered on the very spot where I'd first seen him. In the old days I might have kicked around in the gravel to look for evidence left from his manifestation. But now my shoes were worth keeping nice. They pinched my toes as I limped on up the hill to where the Armsworth mansion glowed from every window against a starlit evening.

As will happen at the Armsworths' parties, only a minority of the invited showed up. Still, a good turnout came to see how an ugly duckling like myself might be turned into a swan suitable for floating in a Royal moat. And they came to gawk at Miss Dabney, who was usually observed only from a distance.

Lowell Seaforth was there. So was Alexander's big sister, Lucille. She swayed and waddled from room to room, since the Little Stranger she was expecting was drawing nigh and no longer little.

Mrs. Armsworth swept down and led me in a grip of steel about the rooms. She proclaimed to all that I was "the wonderful little neighbor girl who all the Armsworths had been so fond of these many years." Alexander's paw stood by a bank of hothouse flowers gazing sadly down into a glass of ice-cream punch. Alexander kept his distance from me through most of the evening. "I will see enough of you on board ship," he muttered in passing.

The Shambaughs came, bringing Letty. She simpered up to me. Her eyes summed up the lace tippets on my Princess dress and the wide taffeta sash that was cutting me in half.

"Well, Blossom, just look at you!" she said in her mother's own grown-up voice. "I have always said a good dress will cover up any flaw."

"Then you had better get one like it," I replied.

Soon after, Miss Dabney made her entrance. People stood back and stared up at her. This formed a solid wall of humanity which she took to be a receiving line. She started down it, offering her hand. A flush of excitement put roses in her cheeks. Over her powder-blue velvet she wore a cape lined in enough fox skins to stagger a trapper.

The Hacketts and the Markhams and the Beasleys and several other worthies followed in Miss Dabney's wake. The rooms filled up with guests working hard to avoid the hostess. Alexander lurked around the walls in a blue serge knicker suit with brass navy buttons. He looked like a high-class stowaway.

At last the Armsworths' hired girl bore in a large cake. It was baked in the shape of the steamship *Olympic* and rode on waves of blue icing. Everybody said they'd seen nothing like it.

Mrs. Armsworth directed Alexander to serve me. Off a dainty plate I ate a small lifeboat and part of the smokestack. The refreshments reminded me of former times when my mama hired out to work in the kitchen for the Armsworth parties. She'd piled many a finger sandwich onto trays, though she'd never been allowed nearer society than the pantry. I was not puffed up with pride for waltzing in where Mama had never trod. That was just as well considering what happened next.

The kitchen door banged open again directly, and the hired girl burst through it. Her hair stood on end, and her eyes bugged out. I hoped she hadn't seen a ghost, for I had enough on my mind. She made a beeline for Mrs. Armsworth, who already sensed trouble from afar. There was much frantic whispering between these two, all too late.

There in the door from the pantry stood my mama.

I barely knew her. She was dressed in her notion of what

ladies wear to evening parties. The outfit was new and unfamiliar to me. It was stuck all over with green sequins and cut very low at the bosom. I hadn't seen so much of Mama since I was weaned. Forks stopped in midair. There was instant silence throughout the house—possibly the entire town.

Mama's well-oiled hair was braided high atop her head, entwined with orange silk poppies that fought with her dress. Her crusted elbows above long wrinkled gloves stood out from her sides. Gold-colored chains hung to her waist. Below, chiffon in four colors looped to hobble her skirts.

The circles of rouge on her cheekbones were enlarged, reaching around to her ears. Her eyelashes seemed clogged with soot. Where her mouth had been was a gash of red paint, folded into her sunken gums.

Mrs. Armsworth ceased breathing.

Mama crashing a party was not my chief worry. I searched her over to see if she brought her tarot cards or any of her fortune-telling paraphernalia. I feared she meant to turn a profit at this prosperous gathering. But she showed nothing on her person except a nearly clean lace hanky stuck in a yellow belt. Where Mama assembled this getup from, I will go to my grave wondering.

I wondered too if she meant to hold me hostage at the last moment. But when I searched her small black eyes, I saw no dollar signs in them. I saw something else that had never been there before.

It was Miss Dabney who revived first. She flowed toward Mama through a sea of human statues holding cake plates. In a powerful voice she inquired politely, "It is Madame Culp, is it not?"

"Is it?" said Alexander's paw in wonderment.

"Oh, what have I ever done to deserve this?" his wife replied.

Miss Dabney stretched out her long hand and shook Mama's. I doubt if anybody ever shook hands with Mama before. By then the whole party had flocked into the dining room, watchful and waiting. Miss Dabney turned to face them, and her velvet skirts made a graceful arc. She linked an arm around Mama's, and the two stood there facing the party, as unlikely a pairing as Bluff City ever witnessed.

Miss Dabney tall as a crane. Mama beside her like a shrunken, highly colored parrot. Miss Dabney delicate as a historic painting of an ancient duchess. And Mama... quite opposite.

Mrs. Shambaugh announced from behind a potted palm, "This intrusion has torn the entire fabric of polite society!"

But Miss Dabney was deaf to this and led Mama forward into the enemy ranks. It was slow going. Mama shuffled unwillingly, and her claw dug into Miss Dabney's white glove at the wrist. And I knew Mama was afraid for the first time in her life.

Her who'd gazed on severed heads down in Sikeston. Her who'd more than once picked up my paw insensible with drink and flung him off the porch. Her who'd showed courage in various situations I won't go into.

Miss Dabney pulled her pleasantly around the dining-room table. Mama's many colors seemed to run together as she grew smaller and smaller. Skirts whispered in the crowd as many drew back from her. Those who'd scorned her from afar grew uncertain up close. I'd feared her myself on occasion, not without cause. But this was not the woman I'd feared.

I'd entered the Armsworth mansion for the first time myself. But I'd been invited. Mama in a getup that would knock a canary off its perch was the only one in these fine rooms who'd braved them unbidden. But she didn't shame me, and I meant to show them all that. Lady Beatrix might forsake her own flesh and blood. But I was Blossom, not Beatrix.

I stepped from the crowd, creaking in my dress. Mama appeared not to know me. Using her elbow for a handle, I tugged her up to Mrs. Armsworth, who was being held erect mainly by her corsetry.

"Mama," I shouted, "let me make you acquainted with Alexander's maw, who has been our good neighbor these many years!" Both ladies flinched.

Mrs. Armsworth had turned into a pillar of salt or some such inanimate object. It was Alexander's paw who stepped around his wife and stuck out the hand of friendship. "Mrs. Culp," he said, very civil, "it is right nice you could make it to this little gathering."

Mama's black eyes took him in, showing terror when he made a small bow. And then Mama spoke, in her muffled way. "My gal here—Blossom . . . I figured I might see her off . . . this bein' a special time and all . . . she's a willful little . . . thing . . . but she ain't give me too much grief."

I understood all this lengthy speech, and various other guests caught parts of it. Alexander's paw seemed to understand completely. "We are all right proud of Blossom," he boomed. "She's put our town on the map. Why, your little gal—daughter has been good for Bluff City business!"

"She ain't been bad for mine either," Mama replied, less muffled than before.

"Let me make you acquainted with the family," Mr. Armsworth said. "You know my wife." He gestured toward Alexander's maw propped against a door frame. "My son-in-law, Lowell." He snapped his fingers, and Seaforth stepped up. "My daughter, Lucille." She waddled forth and pumped Mama's hand, glittering at her own maw to show her daring.

The party seemed to draw breath again as Alexander's paw led Mama away through a crowd warming to the novelty of her. The orange poppies in Mama's black hair quivered as the mob swallowed her up. I grew very pensive at this taste of society Mama was getting. She must have wanted it bad. It only goes to show how a parent can surprise you. I reckoned that from then on she'd take on the traits of other mothers. It was a sorry moment to see our old life erased in a single stroke.

Miss Dabney's hand dropped to my shoulder for a comforting pat. Then she spoke in a voice meant for Alexander's mama, who still slumped stricken nearby. "*Mr.* Armsworth is indeed a gracious host to a guest who had every right to be invited. We will not see more noble hospitality at the Royal Court!" And then she favored Alexander's mama with a pitiless stare.

"This is the worst night of my life," Mrs. Armsworth said, her eyes filling.

"But a welcome relief for your long-suffering guests," Miss Dabney shot back. And she wasn't wrong. Mama was the life of the party. In the gang of guests her voice rang out as clear as it ever gets. She was making a hearty reply to her new acquaintances. "Aw pshaw!" said she, not a bit shy. "I wouldn't take no money to tell yore fortunes at a social occasion. Gimme yore palms, and I'll read 'em for all you-uns!"

They were lined up with their palms out when Miss Dabney gathered me and Alexander up. As the guests of honor we'd been forgotten in favor of Mama. This was just as well, for we could make a quick departure.

Miss Dabney shooed me and Alexander out a side door. I took his arm as we departed for London, England, and he let me.

· 16 ·

MOST OF THE INFORMATION about steamship travel in this account comes from Alexander. I will keep it to a minimum, as it is almost all tedious.

After our train journey we passed a night in New York City before embarking on the high seas. We saw very little of the town, which was plenty. It's a place where everybody has their hands out for your money. What you will not give freely they take by force.

We put in a restless night at the new Astor Hotel, which has a thousand rooms and an orchestra on the roof. Miss Dabney and me occupied one room, and Alexander had the one adjacent. Between the pair of them I liked to never get a wink of sleep. Miss Dabney burned the midnight oil to practice a Royal curtsy before the mirror. Alexander sat up late reading the White Star Line literature and piped in facts about the steamship *Olympic* through the keyhole.

"If you stood the *Olympic* on end," said the keyhole, "it'd be higher than this here hotel, being eight hundred and eighty-three feet from stem to stern."

The idea of the *Olympic* being stood on end made my blood run cold.

By first dawn we were off in a motor taxi behind the wagon carrying our trunks to the dock. Alexander fidgeted and trod on our toes the whole trip. He's getting ganglier by the minute and was worse than a sackful of squirrels. "They had to build the wharf ninety feet farther out into the Hudson River to accommodate the *Olympic*," he explained. "And still her stern sticks out into the waterway, a dangerous hazard to river shipping." I wished in my heart he'd sunk on the *Titanic* once to see how it feels.

At the wharf the great ship towered above the freight wagons. It reduced burly men with trunks on their backs to nothing more than ants. "She's as high as a six-story building from water line to bridge," Alexander informed us, with his head lolling out the taxi window.

It looked higher than that to me, and its long nose was like a giant knife ready to strike. Far below it, you couldn't see the cobblestones for the crowds, excited and happy as if none of these big ships ever sunk with all hands.

"She'll consume three thousand, five hundred and forty tons of coal on the crossing," Alexander recited.

Tiring of all this information, Miss Dabney replied, "You will not be called upon to stoke the furnaces, Alexander."

Once we were up the gangplank and in the ship, I was calmed by its immense size. It went against nature that anything this large could be flimsy enough to sink. We followed our luggage through the lounge, which shamed the Astor Hotel lobby in every way. "True elegance, English elegance," Miss Dabney breathed as we passed oil paintings on a stairway beneath a cut-glass dome.

"There's a separate smoking room reserved strictly for gentlemen travelers," Alexander noted.

"You will not be doing any smoking on this voyage, Alexander," Miss Dabney remarked in reply.

The *Olympic* seemed to wait until we were in our suite before she sounded her horn. An awful blast tinkled the chandelier and made the mirror ripple over our own private fireplace. The very ship shuddered at her own bass voice. Why they call boats *she* when they have such deep voices is beyond me. I quaked somewhat on entering the stateroom for Miss Dabney and me. It was the mate to Julian's, with the same silk walls and the familiar White Star Line blankets folded at the feet of our brocaded beds. Alexander's cabin was equally fine. Sparing no expense, Miss Dabney had reserved the "Regence" suite, meaning much goldwork on mahogany and ancient tapestries on the chairs.

She told me to leave my luggage be, as there were maids to deal with that. Then she directed me and Alexander to be seated in our sitting room. There she meant to advise us about conducting ourselves.

Though we were at home, so to speak, she never removed her hat. "We are in the Great World now, children. And this dictates a grand manner. I do not expect you two to return to Bluff City spoiled and uppity. However, while we are on shipboard and abroad, we must all comport ourselves to the Manner Born."

Alexander looked ready to rebel. His spotty forehead wrinkled, and he clenched his large hands together. Miss Dabney had seated us before the fireplace, where a big basket of assorted flowers covered in cellophane stood on the hearth. He stared into them, wild to be out exploring the ship. "Alexander!" said Miss Dabney. "Are you attending me?"

"No, ma'am."

"I supposed not. Where are your thoughts?"

"Up on deck," he replied promptly. "It's one-third of a mile around."

"Then leave us at once and pace it off. I despair for that Miss Spaulding, as it must be uphill work to teach you anything."

"Yes, ma'am!" Alexander agreed, tipping over a chair in his haste to be gone.

"Boys," Miss Dabney pondered as Alexander vanished. "What if I had married and had some? Life is full of pitfalls. Where was I?"

"Comporting ourselves to the Manner Born," I reminded her.

"Yes. You see those flowers, Blossom?"

They were hard to miss, as the basket stood five feet high.

"It is customary for friends to send passengers such gifts as fruit and flowers on sailing day. Since Bluff City people are ignorant of this nicety, I had the flowers sent to myself from the hotel florist. This is an example of keeping up the right appearances. Do you follow me?"

I nodded.

"Very good. Now look around you. We are in the finest quarters on the ship. There are three classes. We are in First Class. Obviously all three classes arrive in England at the same time, but persons answering a Royal command have no choice but to travel in high style." Here she drew herself up to her greatest height. "*Noblesse oblige,*" she quoted in the French tongue.

"Even the ship is a mark of social standing. The White Star Line sends several over this route, but the *Olympic* carries a special prestige. Traveling on an American ship is naturally out of the question. We are not a seafaring nation, and it shows up in the service."

Miss Dabney dropped her voice suddenly. "It is as well Alexander is out of the way, for I turn now to a more personal matter. Your ... fame has not yet found you out thus far in our travels, Blossom. This is just as well. Who knows what unfortunate attention this might draw to us? Never think I am ungrateful to your ... ah ... supernatural powers. After all, we would hardly be en route to the English Court without them. And I have not forgotten your good works regarding Minerva.

"But people such as our fellow travelers in First Class might take you as a ... curiosity, if they knew ... everything. I have outfitted you as a fashionable young girl traveling as my ward in the best tradition." Here Miss Dabney eyed me. My traveling coat from Nugent's was too long in the sleeve. And neither me or Miss Dabney is handy with a needle. Only my fingertips showed at the cuffs.

"Do I look to the Manner Born?" This was preying on my mind.

Miss Dabney fingered her furs thoughtfully. "Near enough, I think. If you are ... ah ... discreet in your demeanor."

This meant I should keep my mouth shut or I'd disgrace us all. But coming from her, I took this kindly. Besides, at the time I didn't think I knew anybody on the *Olympic* to talk to anyhow.

"As the trip progresses," Miss Dabney went on, "I shall point out other—"

Another horn blast interrupted her lesson. The ship began to slide backwards. There were farewell cries from the deck and band music. Confetti and tickertape snowed past our portholes. A strange look came into Miss Dabney's eyes and played all over her face. I recognized the expression. It was the same as came over Mama the night she crashed the Armsworths' party. Miss Dabney's dream of the Great World was coming true. But her face told a different tale. You want to be careful what you wish for in this life, in case it may come true.

Ask Alexander and he will tell you that the *Olympic* crosses the Atlantic in five days, sixteen hours, and forty-five minutes. I don't know how it manages without his assistance. From our first hour out, he was all over the ship and seemed to know everything and everybody. When he wasn't in the boiler room or the gym or some such place, he undertook to show me around.

Alexander got the hang of ship travel right off, but Miss Dabney never did. She was continually confused by the *Olympic*'s great size. Meaning to do much strolling on the decks in her new tweed outfits, she often made a wrong turn and ended up in the Turkish bath. She was forever asking somebody the way to the ocean.

That first evening the three of us had our dinner in the A La Carte Restaurant. The meal took three hours and five forks. Miss Dabney presided at our table in a high pearl collar. And while many of our fellow travelers stared at her, they'd speak to Alexander and call him by name when they passed our table.

"We will make five hundred and fifteen miles a day," he explained that night when him and me ducked into the gentlemen's smoking lounge for a look around.

"I'm in no hurry," I told him. For the closer we got to England, the more I worried that Miss Dabney was in for a letdown. It didn't stand to reason that Queen Mary would meet us at the dock. We passed the library, where Miss Dabney sat in her evening gown at a desk, writing on the ship's stationery.

"Who in the devil's she writing to?" Alexander asked me. "*Minerva?*"

"She's keeping up appearances," I explained, but this went over his head.

We'd have passed the five-odd days without untoward event, except that two things happened, both noteworthy.

That first night I dreamt of Julian, who called out my name over and over. I dreamt the *Olympic* was passing like a whale directly above his bones, scummy with green slime. It was the regular kind of dream anybody can have, and went on so long that I overslept. When I woke up, Miss Dabney was dressed and gone, likely in search of the ocean. But I wasn't alone in the stateroom.

A scrawny servant was bearing in my breakfast on a silver tray. The door slammed to on her skinny behind and nearly sent her flying across the cabin. This I saw through bleary eyes. I sat up with my hair standing out like the nest of a large rat. Even with riches, I wouldn't keep servants. They rob you of privacy.

"You're to 'ave your breakfast in bed, miss," said the weedy maid. "The old party in the funny tweeds ordered it, so 'ere it is." As she plunked the tray on my bed, I jerked fully awake. Hovering over me was none other than Sybil.

"Crikey!" we both cried, nose-to-nose once more. It could only be Sybil, with her stringy body lost in her uniform, and her crafty face. "It carn't be!" she gasped, blinking at me. "Luvaduck! You don't 'arf get around, do you?"

"Likewise, I'm sure," I replied, wondering at what a small place the Atlantic Ocean is. Sybil poured out the tea. She was expert in her duties. But then I figured she'd always been a quick learner.

"Wot brings you on the 'igh seas? I thought you and that other kid was the law in—wot was the name of that place where you sent me packin'?"

"Bluff City."

"That's it. But never mind the story of your life. I 'aven't the time to 'ear it. Work you like a galley slave on this tub is wot they do. Not a minute to myself. Still, the eats is better than wiv that Perfessor Regis." She lifted the cover off a plate of small fish stretched out in a row, all staring up at us.

"What's them?" I inquired, drawing back.

"Kippers, you chump," explained Sybil. "This 'ere's a proper English breakfast!"

"Well, Sybil, since them fish still have their heads and tails on, fling them back in the sea. They deserve a chance like anybody else."

"Regular music-'all comedian, aren't you?" said Sybil, settling down on my bed to eat my kippers—eyes and all.

"Excuse my fingers," she said. "I never got the 'ang of a knife and fork."

There was nothing left but cold toast and tea for me after she'd taken the edge off her appetite. A full stomach seemed to perk her up no end. "I don't 'old it against you, pokin' your nose into my business and ruinin' my career as the Spirit Sybil. You done me a good turn if you but knew it. I 'ope you done in the Perfessor while you was about it, the old b—"

"He won't work Bluff City again in a hurry," I assured her.

"Never mind. There's plenty more Bluff Cities on 'is map of the world. 'E'll be orl right. But I'm glad enough to be out of 'is clutches. Goin' 'ome to the Bermondsey Road, I am, thanks to you. I won't be any illegal alien there. Though you give me some 'ard times—not that I bear grudges." Sybil wiped her greasy paws on my sheet. " 'Ad to 'op freight trains orl the way to New York to get this job."

"How'd the *Olympic* happen to take you on?" If this was the kind of help they hired, we'd be better off on an American ship is what I thought.

"I'm that subtle," said she. " 'Ung around the docks in New York makin' careful inquiries. Seems they was short of 'elp due to several staff bein' laid up wiv the flu. Narsty climate in America, no good for civilized people. I marched up the gangplank on sailin' day, sayin' I was sent by an employment agency. They 'ad to take me on, they was that desperate. Oh I can make my way in the world, orl right. Not like you 'oo's spent 'er 'ole life lollin' around between silk sheets. Some people 'ave an easy time of it and no mistake."

Sybil might have lectured on and on about my easy life if Alexander hadn't set to banging on my door. "Come on up topside, Blossom," he yelled, very excited. "You wouldn't credit what's happening up there! Aren't you up? I been up two hours!"

At first I figured we were sinking. But then I remembered that any little thing will excite Alexander.

"No, I'm not up!" I yelled back. "Lemme alone. This boat is worse than the Astor Hotel. A person can't get any rest!"

But Alexander babbled on through the keyhole, making no sense. "There's going to be an aeroplane," he said at one point. And then something about "Mr. Birdsall's eyeglasses."

"I don't know no Mr. Birdsall," I yelled back.

"I do. Hurry up or you'll miss everything."

In a low voice Sybil said, "Is that the kid wiv you the night you run me orf?"

"That's 'im—him."

"Wot's 'e goin' on about? Aeroplanes and Mr. Birdsall's eyeglasses? Is 'e orf 'is 'ead?"

"No, that's normal for him," I said, my mind elsewhere. An idea was coming to me that might liven up the proceedings. Now that I thought of it, Alexander'd been getting too big for his britches. I wondered if I couldn't give him a minute or two of excitement without the aeroplanes. "Say, listen, Sybil. How'd you like to go into your Spirit act," I whispered, "just for old time's sake?"

"I wouldn't say no." Sybil smirked a snaggle-toothed grin. Though she's of a criminal nature, we were thinking along similar lines.

"Too bad you don't have any veils left from your old

act," I mentioned. "Still, you're a fright even in your natural state."

"A bath towel might work," she said, moving to a cupboard. "Keep 'im talkin' while I make meself ready."

It's no trick to keep Alexander talking. Finally, pulling up the greasy sheet, I called out, "I can't hear you worth a darn, Alexander. You better come in. I'm decent."

He burst through the door. "Come on, Blossom! You going to sleep the day awa—"

Sybil had taken up her post in a shadowy corner. A towel longer than she was hung from her chin to the floor, glowing white. Above it her waxy face and old-snow-colored hair was drained of all color. She sucked in her cheeks, and her jaw hung slack. She won't look worse in death.

"Oooo," she moaned. "I am a Spirit, returned from the grave to punish evil deeds and narsty thoughts. Look on me and despairrrrr."

Alexander went whiter than Sybil. The hair stirred on his head, and his large knees buckled within his knickers. "Oh no!" he shrieked up and down an octave. "My Second Sight's come back on me. It'll run me crazy! Save me, somebody!" et cetera.

"What's wrong, Alexander?" I inquired. "I don't see nothing."

He raised a trembling finger. "Right there in that corner. It's a haunt and . . . Wait a minute. That looks like . . . Naw, it couldn't be."

Sybil dropped her towel and stepped forth in her misshapen maid's outfit. "Sybil 'erself in the flesh. 'Ow's it goin', mate?"

"Not bad . . . Sybil. I guess it's too much to ask how you come to be in Blossom Culp's stateroom, out here in the Atlantic Ocean."

"Well let's put it this way, mate. I got more business in 'ere than wot you 'ave, if we 'appened to be found out by the old party wiv the walkin' stick and the fur piece."

Alexander got his color back and then some. It came to me that he was growing somewhat less susceptible to the spirit world and somewhat more to the opposite sex. Of which I am a member.

He banged the foot of my bed. "Blossom, you'll go too far one day with these vaudeville tricks of yours." But he didn't speak with his old vigor. He was too busy regaining his dignity. "And don't blame me if you miss your only chance in a lifetime to see an aeroplane."

Then he straightened his tie, squared his shoulders, and marched out.

Sybil collapsed on Miss Dabney's bed, and we had a good laugh. I nearly regretted having to run her out of Bluff City so quick. She was not bad company. " 'E's a good-lookin' cove in 'is way," she commented upon Alexander. "A bit gawky, but that'll pass."

I was inclined to agree. But I didn't have all day to gossip with Sybil. If I was ever going to see an aeroplane, I thought I'd better get up and go look at one.

· 17 ·

THE DECK WAS THRONGED with all the First Class passengers, muffled against a stiff breeze. The wind thrashed the feathers on the ladies' hats, and put out the men's cigars. Miss Dabney was likely in their midst, as she was anxious to make friends. And Alexander was doubtless at the forefront of the action.

In my new plaid coat with the cape attached, I seemed to blend in with the well-dressed crowd. In dribs and drabs I overheard what was exciting them. The particulars I picked up were these.

An American gent, name of W. Atlee Birdsall, was traveling in our class. He was very short-sighted in more ways than one. He'd left home without his eyeglasses. Lacking them, he was all but blind. So he sent a marconigram back to the Wanamaker stores in New York City to mail new spectacles on the next ship out. He meant to wait for them at his English address.

The Wanamaker stores saw in this request a chance for

advertising. They cabled back to the *Olympic* the sensational news that Mr. Birdsall's glasses would be delivered to him on board ship. To do this, they hired the famous aviator T. M. Sopwith to fly out and drop the spectacles in a well-padded box on the *Olympic*'s deck. Nothing like this had ever been attempted, and many people remarked on the novelty of it.

I worked my way through the mob to where the widest part of the deck was roped off. On my way I noticed Miss Dabney in the throng. She leaned heavily on her walking stick, trying to make conversation with a lady near her, without success.

Being agile, I was soon up to the rope. Well beyond it three figures stood waiting in the open for the aeroplane. A talkative gent I'd elbowed aside pointed them out. "The fellow with all the gold braid is the ship's captain himself, Commander H. J. Haddock."

The small elderly man in a derby hat who stared around unseeing I took to be W. Atlee Birdsall. "And who's that third fellow with them?" I asked, though I knew already.

"Oh," said the talkative gent, "that's young Alexander Armsworth."

"It would be," I replied.

The faint sputtering of an engine soon came from the clouds. The *Olympic* set her own decks shivering with a blast from the horn. The crowd went wild as the first aeroplane of my experience broke through a low cloud and swept over us. "And that fellow up there," said the talkative gent waving a cane above him, "will be T. M. Sopwith, the greatest air ace still living!"

The aeroplane looked like a bird's skeleton as it made a figure eight above us, waggling its brittle wings. The *Olympic* returned the salute with another blast. Ladies waved hankies up at T. M. Sopwith. He turned again in the air and flew well out ahead of the ship, dropping down near the choppy waves. It was a sight to turn your stomach giddy.

"And now he'll drop the parcel, see if he doesn't!" said the talkative gent.

The plane made straight for us. Its double wings wobbled and then held firm, and I fancied I saw T. M. Sopwith's goggles through the whirring propeller.

"Little lady," said the talkative gent, poking me, "you are witnessing the Modern Age in action!"

T. M. Sopwith's aeroplane drowned out the cheering crowd as it roared over us. A brown package was already falling out of the sky, end over end. All eyes except Mr. Birdsall's followed it down. The package dropped several yards off the bow into the ocean.

"Well, that's a black eye for the Wanamaker stores!" declared the talkative gent, just like he'd predicted it. The aeroplane sputtered off, but no one waved.

Alexander seemed to be breaking the bad news to Mr. Birdsall, for the little man wagged his head in dismay. This would have ended the incident except for Alexander. He'd taken to being very pushy in a social way. This trait he probably inherited from his mama.

That evening Miss Dabney very nearly had a seizure when she found an invitation under our door to dine at Captain

Haddock's table. "You cannot comprehend the honor of this invitation, Blossom! We dine with the captain! At last we are recognized! All eyes will be upon us! What shall I wear?" et cetera. This was all understandable as nobody had spoken a word to her the better part of two days. However, I suspected we were riding to this particular social occasion on Alexander's coattails.

This was true. Miss Dabney made a grand entrance into the main dining room with her head held so high she appeared to be all chin. She wore a necklace of old garnets over a rustling gown and trailed her furs.

But after Captain Haddock had blinked in surprise at the sight of her and then bowed, he clapped Alexander on the shoulder like an old chum. The male sex can be very hearty and sudden in their friendships.

Rounding out the captain's table was Mr. Birdsall. This stood to reason, since the captain was consoling him on the loss of his spectacles. As we were a somewhat unlikely gathering, Miss Dabney was right—all the eyes in the dining room were upon us.

She sat between the captain and Mr. Birdsall. Her garnets flashed as she inclined her long head first toward one gentleman and then the other. "And what takes you to Europe, madam," inquired the captain, "pleasure entirely?"

"No, indeed." Miss Dabney preened. "A Royal Command!" She expanded on this, invoking Queen Mary's name. The captain looked both startled and baffled.

As to Mr. Birdsall, I never have heard his voice. He's a very soft-spoken man and of a retiring nature, much like Miss Dabney when she's acting normal. But she agreed to everything he seemed to murmur, and he gazed up at her in admiration. I squinted my eyes, trying to learn how she'd appear to one half blind. But Alexander kicked me under the table when he noticed. You can carry the Grand Manner too far, and Alexander did.

At the end of the dinner when the orchestra began to play dance tunes, the two gentlemen took glasses of brandy, and Miss Dabney agreed to just a thimbleful. "We have learned a valuable lesson today," said Captain Haddock, "though at Mr. Birdsall's expense. There is much irresponsible talk going about that aeroplanes will be the scourge of the skies in the event of war."

Something trembled deep within me, and my sight flickered.

"But today we have undeniable proof that an aeroplane cannot hit the largest ship afloat with a parcel, let alone a bomb! This news should silence those prophets of doom who rule out the Navy in future wars!"

Miss Dabney grasped her bosom in alarm. "Wars? Doom? Bombs?"

"Steady on, madam," said the captain. "Nothing like that on the horizon. No one is ready for war—England, America, France, Germany. Quite out of the question."

The captain's voice faded, and the white tablecloth went blue. I heard the roll of thunder I alone had heard before. Lightning nobody noticed played over the brandy glasses, and the fit was on me. I remembered how Miss Spaulding once said to leave the room if my Second Sight struck me sudden. "Fresh air," I muttered to Alexander beside me, and sped to the open deck.

The wind cut my eyes while I clung to the railing. Anybody passing would have taken me for a seasickness victim, for I blinked and swallowed hard, trying to fend off my fit. I knew it was to be fearful. Worse than the black lonely ocean far below, and worse than my former visions.

Music drifted out from the dining room. "Under the Bamboo Tree" was being softly rendered. But this tune sank beneath the awful sounds of bombs and battle, and I fell into my trance. It was a vision of the future, where I ventured without taking a step. And it aged me.

It was several minutes as long as years before I come to myself again. I still clung to the railing, and the wet wind had wrought havoc with my hair. But I'd been chilled by worse than wind. Somebody had fetched my coat, for it was over my shoulders. I could see the present world again. The ship glowed over me, and the four smokestacks were pale against the night. Alexander stood beside me.

"Your mind leave your body like it did . . . other times?" he asked quietly. I nodded.

"Was it real bad this time? Worse than ever?"

I nodded again.

"Well," said Alexander very kindly, "let's us walk around the deck. It will calm you. It's a third of a mile around."

We'd passed the lifeboats and were rounding the stern when Alexander said, "Maybe you ought to tell me what you . . . saw. Otherwise, it will prey on your mind."

"Only you, Alexander. I wouldn't tell nobody else. It's too ugly, and people won't believe what they don't want to. It's human nature."

So I told Alexander and only him. I knew he'd keep it

to himself without taking any childish oath. And this was nothing childish. Captain Haddock had set me off with his talk of no war and no bombs. I'd seen a vision of the future.

I saw men, young men burrowing in trenches like moles. I saw the loops of barbed wire and the flash and fire of explosions. Beams of light searched the clouds and found aeroplanes—dozens of them, flying in patterns. The guns fired and recoiled and fired again. The aeroplanes fell through the lights, whining like beasts. But still the bombs rained out of the skies, and the young men died in a swamp of mud. And I knew they were English and American and French and German and others too. Captain Haddock was right in one particular: They weren't ready. But they died anyway. Millions. And they broke open like ruined toys.

Or they tore at their throats when the air went yellow with gas. And then these young men fell too, and the tears streamed from their dead eyes. They died in the mud. And others died adrift in life rafts on this very sea, which burned in sheets of oil as great warships turned over in the water. And still the bombs rained down from the dragonfly aeroplanes.

I wept for them all. Mama once called my powers puny. And she was right, for I could only see. I could no more change the future than the past. I hadn't even been able to save one small boy—Julian.

Alexander heard me out, never breaking in. We paced on quite a distance before he spoke again. "Soon?"

"Very soon," I said. "And then again. And again. And on and on."

"They'll tear up the world," he said. "These wars will. And what will they fight over?"

"I don't know," I said. "Even the dead won't know."

There were few on the deck, for it was a bitter night. We passed only one couple, a tall lady and a small man. But they seemed lost in one another's company and didn't notice the cold or us.

"That was Miss Dabney and Mr. Birdsall," Alexander murmured.

I'd taken the two figures for lovers, and so this surprise brought me back from the future somewhat.

"They have everything in common," Alexander declared. "All Mr. Birdsall's tastes are English too. He lives over there part-time in a country cottage and reads Shakespeare."

"Then I expect he knows how he likes to take his tea," I mentioned. Freshly returned from bombs and death, I was talking of a tea party. It seemed strange and wrong at first. But then I thought that in a savage world we have to cling to whatever small pleasures and niceties we can devise. Maybe Miss Dabney had learned that early in life.

Alexander took my hand as we strolled on, and I let him.

·18·

LONDON IS CALLED the finest city on earth. Maybe so, but it's a backward place. Smoke from a million chimneys brings on early evenings and blackens the stonework. Much beer is drunk in murky saloons, and they eat fried potatoes off greasy newspapers in the streets. All manner of goods is sold door to door. And the vendors' cries begin long before dawn. You wouldn't credit it, but in this Center of Empire, sheep are driven through the parks to graze, like open country, though a railroad tunneling underground throbs beneath their hooves.

It's a gray city wrapped in yellow fog. And the street lamps burn all day long. But it's a big place, indifferent to a small troop of Americans washed up at its door.

We put up at Brown's Hotel to await a Royal summons. We'd likely be waiting there yet if it wasn't for an idea Alexander put me onto. In her Promised Land Miss Dabney seemed overcome by her old shyness. She couldn't dash off a letter to announce us to Queen Mary. And she couldn't call in the press, as Miss Spaulding might do. So she holed up in Brown's Hotel, baffled.

Brown's was no bigger than the Cornhusker Hotel back home, and less modern. I'd expected something more like the Astor Hotel than these poky, dim rooms. It looked like a boarding house done over. "Lord Byron's valet founded this hotel," Miss Dabney repeated. And "Mr. Theodore Roosevelt honeymooned here, though I do not recall with which wife." And "It is the correct address for refined guests who abhor making a vulgar show."

Maybe so. Though my travels had accustomed me to such things as bathtubs and hot water. Come to find out, the English do very little bathing.

They do a good deal of sitting though. The Brown's Hotel parlors were ranked with a clientele who'd come long distances to remain stationary in chairs. Several sat asleep all day before the fire, hogging the heat.

Here Miss Dabney made herself at home. It wasn't etiquette to speak to the other guests, who stared at the London *Times* or simply into space. In this silence she was safe from snubs. England is a nation of recluses, so Miss Dabney fit in, lapsing into her Bluff City ways.

Mr. Birdsall called on her twice daily. Mornings for coffee and afternoons for tea. In her Queen Mary hat she poured for him in a corner sofa, unwilling to stir far from it. But each evening when me and Alexander returned from our exploring, she quizzed us about all the London sights, stroking her cheek in wonder.

What she and Mr. Birdsall discussed all day in the parlor, I never heard. Only their tweeds were loud. But whenever he was nigh, Miss Dabney grew as skittish as a young girl. She took on the look of a startled flamingo—blushing pinkish. It had been a shipboard romance, but they seemed not to notice they were now on dry land.

When Mr. Birdsall returned to his club in the evenings, Miss Dabney began to look haggard and careworn. She'd soon admit defeat and confess she'd led us all halfway round the world on a fool's errand. I saw this coming and wondered how to forestall it. As I've said, Alexander stumbled onto the solution, though of course he didn't know what he was doing. Armed with a guidebook, me and him marched forth each morning to do the town.

It's my way to go right to the heart of the matter. I inquired of the hotel porter where Queen Mary and King George put up when they're in town and learned it is Buckingham Palace. This is an easy walk across the park from Brown's. Alexander was willing to go as he wanted to see the Changing of the Guard. They change every morning at eleven-thirty.

The Palace stands in quite a good neighborhood behind an oversized statue of Queen Victoria. Alexander turns out to be the kind of traveler whose nose is never out of the guidebook. " 'Queen Victoria,' " he read aloud, " 'is carved from a solid block of marble. On the sides of her pedestal are groupings representing Justice, Truth, and Motherhood.' "

"Come on," I said, "let's get closer to the Palace." We didn't get much closer. Tall ironwork fenced off the front yard. The Palace rose behind it, grim and gray. Across the yard the Grenadier Guards in scarlet capbands pounded the paving in precision marching.

" 'If the Royal flag is flying, this signifies that the Family is in residence,' " Alexander read. It was snapping in the breeze, so this was one favorable sign.

A Guardsman in a tall fur hat with a tight chin strap stood outside the fence. His sentry box was the image of Old Man Leverette's privy. I first took it for a public convenience, though it lacked a door. I approached him at once, but could not catch his eye.

Counting his tall hat, he rose up seven feet. The chin strap drew all his features together into furrows. "Say listen," I said up to him. "How does a person go about dropping in on Queen Mary?"

This civil question merited no answer. Thinking he was deaf, I repeated myself louder. Still, nothing.

My third try brought a response, though it was rude. " 'Op it, kid," he growled, though his mouth seemed not to move. As he was armed, I gave up on him. For all I knew, a simple question might well be a capital offense in England.

So near and yet so far, I mourned, gazing up at the blank windows. If it wasn't for Miss Dabney, I'd have written Royalty off. A person knows when she's not wanted, particularly me.

"Come on," Alexander said. "There's plenty more to see." And as regards London, he was right. Since I have no patience with a guidebook, I was at his mercy, and a boy's taste in sightseeing wouldn't suit everybody.

Alexander was inclined to museums, and there are several in London. They are places where things are kept that would otherwise be thrown out.

We went to the Victoria and Albert Museum by riding the Piccadilly Underground Line, a train in a smoky tunnel. We were in search of a thing called Tipu's Tiger.

At last we found it, pointless though it was. It wasn't a real tiger at all, but a kind of large mechanical toy an eccentric Englishman brought back from India in 1795. This large wooden beast is mauling the figure of a small, surprised wooden man in a top hat. If you push a button, the mauled man lets out a strange and tinny squeal. This gives an accurate idea of Alexander's taste in points of interest.

Another time we rode on an omnibus to the British Museum. As I was getting the hang of such places, I was for taking it room by room. There were many fine statues of the old Greeks. And a blue and white glass urn called the Portland Vase which a madman had shattered in 1845. This was entirely reassembled very artfully.

"We've come here for the mummies," Alexander said, dragging me on. These dead bodies were kept in the Egyptian Rooms. On the way are large paintings from the original tombs. One shows a man being judged in the Hereafter. They are weighing his heart on a scale, balanced with a feather. Standing by is a hippopotamus, waiting to eat the man if he fails the test.

The mummies were nearby. When I was younger, I'd have taken to them with more zeal. Now this deathly place made me queasy. Coffins littered the floor. "One of these mummies is unwrapped to show his excellent state of preservation," said Alexander, darting from corpse to corpse. "Here it is!"

We both stared down on a being dead now 5500 years. If this was an excellent state of preservation, may I never see decay. " 'The hot sands of Egypt have completed the preservative process,'" Alexander read in a hushed voice. The mummy's nose bone was nearly naked of skin, and there were no eyeballs beneath the lids. His leather chest had the look of an old saddle. Breaking through the cracked hide were tufts of brittle hair. I turned away from this ancient.

But behind me were other mummies, wrapped like small packages in an eternal post office. There was a mummified cat, with chipped ears, and one of her kittens as small and as flat as my hand. Only a little scrap of life that had drawn breath for a few days and then lingered on in this state for fifty-five centuries. There was a dog's mummy too, and a gazelle and a jackal. But I remembered the kitten most, though as a rule I'm not sentimental about house pets.

When Alexander had looked his fill, we left the British Museum. I was burdened by the litter of centuries, left around to be stared at by us modern strangers. I wondered what would be left to speak for our twentieth century after all its bombs and wars. "Isn't there a thing to this town but museums?" I inquired of Alexander as we made off down Great Russell Street. "Look in that book and find something different."

"One more museum," Alexander said. "But it's the best one, so I'm saving it for last."

It was the best, though weirder than all the rest. And Alexander and me set aside an entire day for it. Madame Tussaud's, it's called, composed entirely of waxwork figures. All the famous and notorious persons of past and present are fashioned in wax as real as living flesh. And they're in their own clothes or realistic costumes. Moreover, most are situated in settings called tableaux that tell of their lives.

Many of the earlier figures, all victims of the French

Revolution, were carved and outfitted by Madame Tussaud herself, though she's now dead. When we entered the museum lobby, it became weird at once. A small, withered lady in a long black gown of old-fashioned cut stood by the ticket-takers. She wore wire-framed spectacles and an out-of-date frilled cap much like Minerva's. A small smile played around her old lips, and she clasped blue-veined hands before her modestly.

"Who's the old party?" I asked Alexander.

"That's Madame Tussaud," he replied.

"I thought you said she was dead."

"She is. That's a waxwork of her."

"Then why are we whispering in her presence?" I inquired, but Alexander only shrugged.

I was for starting with the historic tableaux, as they'd be something educational to tell Miss Spaulding. After all, we'd done none of our schoolwork and had no intention of doing any. But Alexander was hellbent for the Chamber of Horrors, which is down the cellar. Later we got to the tableaux, such as the beheading of the Queen of Scotland and the most famous one, called Sleeping Beauty. But I'll mention the latter one now, as it is interesting.

When Madame Tussaud was locked up in a dungeon with French Royalty during the Revolution, she made a waxwork of Madame Du Barry while she slept. Madame Du Barry was shortly to meet a bad end, but her waxwork is enjoying a long life. She was a woman famed for her beauty, and her image lay on a rough prison bed behind a velvet rope. Her lovely hair streamed down the coarse pillow, and the promise of impending doom showed in her sleeping face.

But the best thing about her is this. A small motor is imbedded in her bosom, causing it to rise and fall, like breathing. This completed the realism. As mechanical devices go, it was far more clever than Tipu's Tiger.

Following signs for the Chamber of Horrors, Alexander dragged me through the main-floor rooms, past Abraham Lincoln and any number of worthy people. At last we found the Chamber's entrance down a long dark flight. As this is popular, the stairs were crowded with people tittering nervously at the sight of dungeon doors below. Above us through barred prison windows were the wax faces and clutching hands of crazed convicts. All this was exactly Alexander's cup of tea.

The Chamber itself was a series of low-vaulted rooms lit by torches. The blood-stained bathtub of a mass murderer who'd killed many of his wives while they soaked was the centerpiece of one room. Several dozen methods of torture were shown, including an Iron Maiden which opened and closed on a body spiked through with red holes. Jack the Ripper was also there, lurking in a corner.

One exhibit was covered by leather curtains. A sign before it read:

NORTH AFRICAN RITUAL EXECUTION
VIEWING RESERVED STRICTLY FOR
PATRONS OVER THE AGE OF 18 YEARS

We waited patiently till the coast was clear. Then Alexander drew back the curtain. At close range a life-sized dead man was hanging from a big meathook. The hook entered his stomach and emerged just below his ribs. His arms and legs dangled well above the floor. Realistic horseflies encrusted his contorted face. Alexander dropped the curtain, and we returned in haste to the upper rooms.

On our way to the tableaux I stopped short and reined up Alexander. There in a far room beneath a massive chandelier stood Queen Mary. I knew her well from the portrait in Miss Dabney's parlor.

We entered what Madame Tussaud calls The Throne Room, and were struck blind by the crystal and gilt. There stood all the images of the Royal Family in a room copied from Buckingham Palace. Queen Mary was proud as a partridge with her roped pearls and royal crown. Her glass eyes looked out over the heads of human observers. She had a certain strong beauty, though she didn't measure up to Madame Du Barry, and as the Queen is now living, the wax workers may have flattered her some.

Beside her stood King George. He was a handsome man, though not tall. Around them stood their children. Featured among them was the young Prince of Wales, barely twenty years old and already a heartthrob to the young women of all countries.

The Family stood among much gold furniture. "Well, this is as close as we'll get to the real thing," I mentioned to Alexander. Even these big dolls awed me, good American though I am.

"Maybe we could bring Miss Dabney here," Alexander offered. "And just let her *think* she's being received at Court. After all, the guests at Brown's Hotel don't do any more moving around than this bunch."

"She'd never fall for that, you chump," I replied. Still. Alexander's impractical notion set me thinking.

After we'd done the Queen of Scotland being beheaded and the Battle of Trafalgar, we just about had our fill of wax figures. I nearly missed a special announcement lettered on a sign. But it stopped me dead.

LATEST TABLEAU

RECENTLY UNVEILED

Madame Tussaud's announces with pride its most current and striking tableau. A re-creation of a tragic moment during the sinking of the White Star Liner

TITANIC

Look upon the last moments of young Julian Poindexter, scandalously abandoned to his fate in eerie loneliness.

This tableau precedes the London opening of the American cinematograph on the subject. The forthcoming moving picture is based on the account of an obscure American girl who claims to have shared young Poindexter's death agonies through Spiritual Translation. One flight up.

I clutched Alexander's arm. Then we shot away, one flight up. The tableau was in a room faintly lit in watery green. Shadows danced to suggest the roll of a ship dead in the water. We worked our way through the crowd gazing on. Suddenly I was standing almost where I'd stood before. Beyond a rope the tableau's floor was pitched at the angle of the *Titanic* just before it took its dive.

It was Julian's very cabin, down to details. The clock had just struck midnight. Beyond the portholes stretched an oil painting of the night sea. And in the far corner, dimly lit, a waxen figure of Julian in a nightshirt seemed to struggle up from the bedclothes. They'd captured his tow head and sleepy eyes to perfection. And just his look of frozen, gathering fear. I could nearly hear him call for his mama, and I went numb again from the iceberg night.

Alexander commenced poking me. "But you're not in it, Blossom! He's all by himself."

This was true. Though the longer you looked, the better you saw a shadow cast on the floor and up over Julian's blanket. It seemed to outline the presence of a young girl, though not of my shape and nothing distinct. Madame Tussaud's was playing it safe.

The whole thing was too much like one of my trances. I remember very little till we were out in the street again, lost in thought. "It doesn't seem right to me," Alexander said. "Them leaving you out entirely when if it wasn't for you, they wouldn't have enough facts to flesh out a tableau."

I basked a little, as it's unusual for Alexander to take my side in anything. He had more to say. "And then when that moving-picture show comes out, they'll have some lady playing you who's completely grown up and filled out." He glanced once at my somewhat straight shape and shook his head. "It's not right," he claimed.

I said nothing.

"They ought to at least pay you something," Alexander mumbled. "It was your story. They often pay money for stories that aren't even true."

"I wouldn't take no money," I said. "That'd be like dancing on Julian's grave." But my mind was elsewhere.

We'd walked nearly back to Brown's Hotel. An omnibus rumbled by, plastered all over with ads for Whitbread's Ales and Pear's Soap and the London Palladium. On the back of the omnibus a plain white sign lettered in black read IT PAYS TO ADVERTISE.

And so it does, I thought. A scheme was forming in my mind. At the worst, it could only get us arrested. But if everything went just right, we might get famous enough to send Miss Dabney sailing straight into Buckingham Palace. I'd been famous before. I could be again. My method was somewhat vulgar by Miss Dabney's high standards, but if it brought her to Queen Mary, she would surely not mind. And neither would Julian if he knew.

"Still," said Alexander, "Madame Tussaud's was the best museum."

"I'm glad you liked it," I told him, "for we'll be going back tomorrow early. Let's just find us a stationery store where we can buy a big piece of cardboard and some ink. I'll do the lettering on the sign myself."

"What sign?" asked Alexander.

"And I think I'll wear my nightdress. It'll be more dramatic than regular clothes."

"What nightdress?"

"And you'll be in charge of putting in a call to the London *Times* and various newspapers, as we'll want the publicity."

"What publicity?" asked Alexander, completely buffaloed. He can never see a minute ahead.

· 19 ·

Though we meant to be back at Madame Tussaud's before the press got there the next morning, Alexander and me had breakfast with Miss Dabney. It wouldn't do if she got wind of our scheme too soon. Vague though she was and growing vaguer, she smelled a rat. I hoped to put her off the scent.

Alexander had failed to bring his guidebook to the table, not needing it. Miss Dabney noted this. "And where are you children off to today?"

"Westminster Abbey," I replied. "The Tower of London," Alexander said at the same time.

"An ambitious plan," she remarked, her brows arching. "And, Blossom, may one inquire why you have worn your coat to breakfast, buttoned to the neck?"

The reason was that I had on my nightdress under it, the skirts hitched up in my bloomers. "It's colder than a witch's —it's cold as ice in this dining room," I explained.

Fortunately the waiter bore in our breakfasts: stone-cold masses of clotted baked beans on fried bread. This is an example of how the English start their day.

"You are looking very smart this morning, Alexander," Miss Dabney said. "I have not seen you in your best knicker suit since the evening we dined at Captain Haddock's table."

"Thank you, ma'am," Alexander replied, his voice breaking again for the first time in weeks. He fidgeted throughout breakfast, earning us an early escape. Miss Dabney sent us packing. We snatched up the large sign Alexander had left with the porter, and I fitted it around him under his overcoat. We were soon racing along Dover Street.

The doors of Madame Tussaud's were just opening, and we were the first two inside. I wondered if Alexander had made it clear to the various newspapers the sensational quality of what we were about to pull off. It's hard to get your message across on an English telephone, and I saw no newspapermen around.

We sped past the waxen image of the founder and beyond. Then we hung around the notice pointing the way to the *Titanic* tableau. With nobody about, I peeled my new sign off Alexander. I'd done the lettering myself, which I'm expert at. It fit neatly over the other sign and read as follows:

LATEST TABLEAU
RECENTLY REVISED

Madame Tussaud's begs to inform the public that its most current and striking tableau has been greatly improved: a re-creation of a tragic moment during the sinking of the White Star Liner

TITANIC

Now look upon the last moments of young Julian Poindexter, comforted on his deathbed by the image of Miss Blossom Culp of Bluff City, U.S.A.

Her who was translated back to the Great Disaster and wondrously returned to tell the tale. Miss Culp is Madame Tussaud's crowning achievement, being absolutely lifelike due to a new secret process.

If you have not seen the tableau today, you have not seen the tableau atall. One flight up.

Nobody was in the *Titanic* room when we got there. So there was time to stow our coats in a dark corner. I flipped the skirt-tails of my nightdress out of my bloomers.

The tableau was lit in its wavering green. And Julian's bedside lamp illuminated his sad, motionless features. I stood there communing with his image. But his spirit was elsewhere, for I felt nothing unlikely except the biting chill of that night far out to sea.

Ducking under the rope, I stepped cautiously down the slanting floor. Where the shadow was cast across his blanket I cast myself, kneeling by his bunk. My nightdress fanned out upon the carpet. Up close, Julian's wax image lost none of its realism. Each blond eyelash was separately set. Peach fuzz on his cheeks gave way to shades of gray beneath his haunted eyes.

I reached out for his hand as I'd done in our last moments, but it was not easy. In a way he was more worrisome than the mummy, being more lifelike. And of course I had not died with the mummy, and hope I never do.

Seeming to hear the creak of lowering lifeboats, I lightly

grasped Julian's hand. I hoped none of his fingers would come off. Then I practiced remaining as still as a statue. Immobility is not my way.

"Turn your head a little this direction," Alexander muttered. "Your hair hides your face. That's better. Hold it right there." It was easy for him to say, fidgeting out there beyond the rope. I locked eyes with Julian's glass ones just as the first museum visitors entered the room.

Voices came from the darkness outside the tableau. "Oh, do look, Papa," came a childish one, "she's breathing!"

I had little choice there. And after all, Madame Du Barry breathes and is well known for it. The room seemed to fill with the awed and curious, and I was reminded of one of Professor Regis's seances.

It's a strange thing about the public. They'll believe anything written on a sign. And they'll see exactly what they expect to see. No more. No less.

I must have been there on my knees at Julian's side for an hour. Long enough to know that baked beans had been a poor choice for breakfast. Voices rose at the rear of the crowd. Over these I heard Alexander, seeming to speak to someone near him but sending me a clear message. "It must be reporters from the London papers come to cover this new, improved tableau," he sung out.

"I can assure you all, gentlemen," said an official voice at the door, "that Madame Tussaud's has not altered the *Titanic* tableau in the least particular. Some crank has posted a mendacious sign over the real one. And no doubt the same crank has issued false reports to the press. Our tableau depicts only the lad, Julian P—"

At that moment the museum official caught his first sight of me. He said a word that surprised men often use. And I seemed to hear the steady scratching of reporters taking quick notes.

"That waxwork is an impostor!" announced the museum man. The velvet rope quivered in his grasp. And the crowd laughed merrily. I breathed on, very lightly, and my eyes comforted Julian's image. "This exhibit is closed to the public! Step along smartly, please! Everyone out!" But the museum man's own voice only drew more gawkers. The room seemed full to overflowing.

I knew a way of clearing it at once.

My hand slid away from Julian's. And my head turned slowly to the crowd. I rolled my eyes half up under the lids as if they'd been set in rather hurriedly. And then I stood up very slowly, letting the folds of my nightdress fall out.

The English are said to be a very calm and emotionless people. This is an outright lie. They will scream and grow faint and knock each other down to get out of a room just like any American.

The newspapermen drew back, but they were still with us. The museum official seemed turned to wax himself. Alexander was in complete possession of himself, of course. "Gentlemen of the press," he said, "this here is the real Miss Blossom Culp, who will gladly entertain any questions you may care to put to her."

Well, the rest is history, as the poet says. There are few reporters in Great Britain who do not claim to have been there the day I come to life at Madame Tussaud's. Some raked me over the coals for desecrating a museum exhibit. Others gave me full marks for displaying "a pert and antic ingenuity that is purely American." But they all wrote me up in lengthy articles, many claiming to be exclusive interviews.

The response to this was heavy in a nation easily swayed by the supernatural. But I'd been famous before and will doubtless be again. So I bore it all with modest patience. Even later when Madame Tussaud's asked me to sit for the sculpting of a waxwork of myself to be added to the tableau. I'd given them more free advertising than they're ever like to see again. And I will say this: After their first shock, they treated me right. I was never threatened with imprisonment after the first hour or so.

It was unnecessary to confess anything to Miss Dabney. When Alexander and me finally got away from the museum on the day of my unveiling, we stormed into the hotel parlors breathless. She and Mr. Birdsall occupied their corner sofa, swapping favorite lines from Shakespeare. He had his new spectacles on, giving him a froglike look. But still he gazed up at Miss Dabney with the same admiration.

She sat with an early-evening edition of a newspaper screaming my name on her lap. But she only pulled her mouth down in a sharp V, saying, "It could have been much worse. The pair of you were so shifty-eyed at breakfast this morning that I feared for the Crown Jewels."

We were all nearly put out of Brown's Hotel though, for the number of bouquets of waxen lilies and other tributes I received from leading British spiritualists. I had many odd callers too, but the hotel doorman turned them away.

Brown's never savored the publicity like Madame Tussaud's did.

It was another week of relentless acclaim before we heard from Buckingham Palace. Evidently Queen Mary kept up on her newspaper reading, for a footman or some such delivered an envelope to the hotel, bearing the Royal coat of arms.

A hotel servant brought it into the parlors on a silver tray, causing Miss Dabney to leap up, shrieking, "I am vindicated! I am justified! We have not come this distance to be turned back at the gates! I do hope Queen Mary will not be in powder blue, for I will!" et cetera.

This sudden noise created a worse scandal in Brown's parlors than any of my highjinks. Sleepers woke suddenly, thinking war had broken out.

The Royal letter was much like the first one I'd had from the Queen. It expressed profound pleasure to learn that I and my party were in London. Surprise and shock at what I'd been up to played no part in the letter, as Royalty is above all that. The letter signed off by inviting Miss Dabney and me to an occasion called a Drawing Room. This is a simple party during the day. Miss Dabney wrung her hands in ecstasy, and Mr. Birdsall goggled at her with complete understanding.

As a Drawing Room is for ladies only, Alexander was out of the picture. On the day of the party Mr. Birdsall took him to his club for lunch, which Alexander reported as being white fish in a gray sauce surrounded by brown peas.

All Miss Dabney's uncertainties fell away as we prepared for the Drawing Room. She was neither skittish nor withdrawn. When she strode out of Brown's to get into the hired limousine, I'd never seen her looking finer. An entire spray of egret feathers rose from her Queen Mary hat, which wound round and round her powdered forehead in satin bands. Her papa's watch swung from her bosom like a military medal, nestled in much fur.

I won't comment on my own appearance out of modesty. I wore my first wide-brimmed hat. And my Princess dress, previously noted, is now on my image at Madame Tussaud's, where you can have a look at it yourself if you're ever there.

As our high black limousine drove through the gates at Buckingham Palace, a small crowd always at the fence sent up a cheer. Miss Dabney raised her hand in a small gesture. It did them no harm to think they'd caught a glimpse of the Queen herself.

Since the Palace is never open to the public, we were shortly beyond the limits of Alexander's guidebook. Well-dressed flunkies ushered us along with a gaggle of other fashionable ladies down many marble halls.

Expecting the Queen to pop out from behind any pillar, I craned my neck. But this was rushing my fences. We were shown into a paneled room for a lesson in how to behave.

Our instructress was a lady-in-waiting, doubtless a replacement for Lady Beatrix. She was as well spoken in her way as Miss Spaulding, though highly placed English people whinny their speech strangely through the nose. She seemed to smile. At least her lip curled back over brown teeth.

"Ladies," she drawled, "though I am sure that most amongst you are accustomed to Court usages, permit me a review of certain points, for the sake of any who may be unfamiliar with them." Here her milky eye drifted over Miss Dabney's feather and rested on me.

"In addressing the Queen, 'Your Majesty' is to be used initially and 'Ma'am' thereafter. Take care to pronounce 'Ma'am' to rhyme with 'calm' as I do, rather than with 'jam.'

"Referring to the Queen as 'you' is not done. It should be, 'Did Your Majesty enjoy a pleasant day?' And never, 'Did *you* enjoy a pleasant day?'

"However, it is Royalty that initiates conversations, and so the selection of a suitable topic does not rest with the visitor.

"Upon meeting or taking leave of the Queen, ladies are expected to curtsy. The occasion of turning your back on Her Majesty should not arise. And above all, do not *shake* the Queen's hand. Permit it to rest gently in your own, and briefly."

"She is completely right," Miss Dabney whispered to me, "down to the last detail."

We were next shown into a room well known to me. It was the same as the copy at Madame Tussaud's, though shabbier. Beyond great windows small Royal dogs romped in a private park. A tall door opened, and in stepped Queen Mary in a procession of more ladies-in-waiting. Miss Dabney sighed in relief, for the Queen was in mint green and not powder blue.

We were all lined up in some sort of order. The duchesses seemed to be farther ahead, bobbing and simpering. I followed Miss Dabney, who moved well above the floor. A different lady-in-waiting announced us. "Your Majesty, Miss Gertrude Dabney, a visitor from America."

Seen together, the two didn't look as much alike as I expected. Miss Dabney had a few years on the Queen, and even when her curtsy was at its lowest, she still towered over Royalty. Queen Mary offered her hand and gave Miss Dabney a veiled once-over. Though her eyes told nothing, she searched her Royal mind for a pleasantry. At last it came to her. "We like your hat."

"How kind, Your Majesty," Miss Dabney breathed.

And then the fondest moment of her life passed, and it was my turn. "Miss Blossom Culp, Ma'am," announced the lady-in-waiting, "of whom Your Majesty has heard."

My knee crooked unbidden, and I bobbed, staring straight into a bosom bejeweled and fortified.

"Ah—of course," said Queen Mary. "The Miss Culp who has both edified us with her goodness and won our hearts with her witty ways. Tell us, Miss Culp, how does it feel to be a footnote to history?"

My tongue swelled in my mouth. I seemed bewitched, for I spoke in Mama's coarse voice, and all other training went out the window. "Aw pshaw, Your Highness, it wasn't nothing," I warbled. "You know yourself how them reporters blow an event up just to sell papers. And I'm switched if I don't think your English papers is worse than ours back home!" Then I gave her hand a good pumping.

The lady-in-waiting looked faint. "Lady Winstanton," she announced quickly, "and her daughter, the Honorable..."

Well, that's what a Drawing Room is like, for the benefit of those who never went to one. I could have done better, and I might have done worse. But that's true of life in general. Miss Dabney didn't correct my etiquette. She drifted in a dream long after the event.

We sailed on the next boat home. I spent our last night in England clipping out newspaper articles regarding myself, as documents for use in this present account. On the reverse side of a photo of me sitting for my waxwork was a classified ad which drew my eye.

FORTUNES AND FUTURES SKILFULLY TOLD
Palms read and dead loved ones contacted
Seance sittings in a refined atmosphere
Four shillings with this advertisement
See Sybil of the Bermondsey Road.

Later, on the boat home, Miss Dabney and I settled into deck chairs while Alexander paced off the deck. She reviewed everything tirelessly. "It was very wonderful," she said of our Drawing Room day. "It is ritual that gives shape to life." And I suppose that's the role that Royalty plays. There are many kinds of wisdom in this world, and Miss Dabney is very wise in her way.

"But it will be good to get away to a quiet village and a home of one's own," she said, sighing.

"I won't be sorry to see Bluff City again myself," I said.

"Bluff City?" Miss Dabney rose up from her deck chair. "Oh, Blossom," said she, all astonishment, "I am only seeing you and Alexander safely home. Then I shall dispose of my properties there. Mr. Birdsall has been good enough to ask for my hand in marriage. And as dear Papa is gone, I shall give it myself. Atlee—Mr. Birdsall—and I will live in England in a small cottage he keeps on the verge of the River Avon."

She spoke like this was common knowledge. But her eyes were upon me, and they had the shy gleam of a young bride's. I wondered what Minerva would do with herself in an empty house. But I said nothing. Minerva was part of the past, and Miss Dabney was looking to the future.

During our homeward voyage we dined again at Captain Haddock's table. We toasted Miss Dabney's future wedding, and I was allowed a full glass of Madeira wine. Strong drink is a mocker, as the poet says, but this particular glassful only knocked me out as quick as I went to my bunk. And I dreamt till dawn.

It was one of those busy dreams with everybody you ever knew crowding in. Newton Shambaugh fell off the back end of a large cake baked to resemble the *Olympic*. All Letty's Busy Fingers girls wrung their hands until Sybil appeared wearing Miss Spaulding's pince-nez glasses. She pronounced them all chumps.

Old Man Leverette stepped forth from his privy nearby and fired off both rounds of his shotgun. The air filled with white bursting stars like the egret feathers on Miss Dabney's hat.

Mama was there in her getup too, pouring a Rockingham cup of tea leaves over Professor Regis's head. And then they all ganged into a Pope-Detroit Electric auto and drove away on the crown of the road into a haze of autumn smoke, arguing among themselves.

Then the scene cleared, and I saw Julian. Not as green and scummy bones being nibbled at by sea creatures. Nor as his waxy figure in Madame Tussaud's. In the dream he scampered across flowered fields beneath a pale and watery sun. It may have been England. It may have been somewhere much farther off. I stood deep in daisies, watching him away into the distance. Alexander was there too, standing beside me.

Time warp

Lightning split the air, traveling down the rods on the roof. It clamped my hand to the doorknob. I couldn't turn loose or turn back now. My skin sizzled, and the door blew in, jerking me half out of my boots.

Inside, the light like a white fog peeled my eyeballs and took me prisoner. The sounds I'd heard in the distance were clearer and nearer: the pyongs and the beeps alike. They were no noise of nature or the human voice. . . .

———◄(◦)►———

"Comedy is a strong point. . . . Scenes will have readers laughing out loud." —*Booklist*

BOOKS BY RICHARD PECK

Amanda/Miranda
Are You in the House Alone?
The Dreadful Future of Blossom Culp
Father Figure
The Great Interactive Dream Machine
The Ghost Belonged to Me
Ghosts I Have Been
A Long Way from Chicago
Lost in Cyberspace
Strays Like Us
A Year Down Yonder

The Dreadful Future

of Blossom Culp

RICHARD PECK

PUFFIN BOOKS

PUFFIN BOOKS

Published by the Penguin Group

Penguin Putnam Books for Young Readers,
345 Hudson Street, New York 10014, U.S.A.
Penguin Books Ltd, 27 Wrights Lane, London W8 5TZ, England
Penguin Books Australia Ltd, Ringwood, Victoria, Australia
Penguin Books Canada Ltd, 10 Alcorn Avenue, Toronto, Ontario, Canada M4V 3B2
Penguin Books (N.Z.) Ltd, 182-190 Wairau Road, Auckland 10, New Zealand
Penguin Books Ltd, Registered Offices: Harmondsworth, Middlesex, England

First published in the United States of America by Delacorte Press,
Dell Publishing Co., Inc., 1983
Published by Puffin Books,
a division of Penguin Putnam Books for Young Readers, 2001

1 3 5 7 9 10 8 6 4 2

LIBRARY OF CONGRESS CATALOGING-IN-PUBLICATION DATA
Peck, Richard, date
The dreadful future of Blossom Culp / Richard Peck.
p. cm.
Summary: Blossom, not the most popular member of her freshman class in 1914,
travels ahead seventy years, and returns in time to make Halloween
a memorable night for her classmates and teachers.
ISBN 0-14-131094-4
[1. Time travel—Fiction. 2. Schools—Fiction. 3. Psychic ability—Fiction.] I. Title.
PZ7.P335 Dq 2001 [Fic]—dc21 00-062668

For Patsy and Ron Perritt, in friendship

1

UNLESS YOU NEVER GOT OUT OF GRADE SCHOOL, you'll have noticed how life keeps making you start over.

In the year of 1914 my class went from being eighth graders at Horace Mann School to being freshmen at Bluff City High School, which is just across the road. Being the youngest and newcomers over there, we were all regarded as lower than a snake's belly. I don't know who sets such rules. My name is Blossom Culp, and I live by rules of my own.

I've been looked down on before, plenty, so turning into a freshman didn't hit me as hard as some I could mention. Letty Shambaugh liked to die of shame. She's lived all her fourteen-plus years with her nose in the air, her paw being the owner of the Select Dry Goods Company.

On the other hand, the last time my paw showed his face in Bluff City, my mama run him out of town. Above her head Mama waved an empty blended whiskey bottle, the blended whiskey itself being in Paw. Though she could outrun him sober, she kept just at his heels to the city limits.

I only mention this to show the difference between me and Letty Shambaugh. Her mama can keep her paw in line with one hand while running the Daughters of the American Revolution with the other.

Letty lives in the lap of luxury in a large all-brick house on Fairview Avenue, famous far and wide for its good taste. My mama and me occupy a two-room dwelling by the streetcar tracks just behind the Armsworths' barn. Though Mama and me have made improvements on it, every election year some candidate or other promises the voters he'll have our place demolished in the interest of progress.

Never mind. The world is full of Letty Shambaughs, and this includes the high school. But there is only one Blossom Culp, and I am her.

That's more or less what Miss Mae Spaulding said to me on the last day of school. Miss Spaulding is both eighth-grade teacher and principal of Horace Mann, being not only a very learned woman but well organized.

When Miss Spaulding called me into her office, Letty Shambaugh and all her little club of girls pointed their fingers at me and hooted.

Letty, looking shapeless in her shell-pink graduation dress with a big corsage stuck to her shoulder, twitched her elbows and said, "I expect Miss Spaulding has bad news for Blossom. I have an idea Blossom is to be held back."

All the girls in her club, which is called the Sunny

Thoughts and Busy Fingers Sisterhood, agreed with her, like they're supposed to.

I didn't dignify this charge with a reply. There was no earthly reason I'd be held back to repeat eighth grade. Nobody would. It was clear that Miss Spaulding had had enough of all of us, which is more or less what she said to me.

If you've ever been summoned to a principal's office, you know the feeling. Decorating Miss Spaulding's wall are a bust of the poet Longfellow, a portrait of President Woodrow Wilson, and a well-worn paddle. I'd been in there before, and there's nothing homelike about it.

Though Miss Spaulding has no more figure than a runner bean, she makes up for it with posture. But on that day she was somewhat bent, as teachers get toward the end of a school year.

It had been a busy afternoon. We'd had the handing out of diplomas, several speeches, and the traditional maypole dance. Then we said the Pledge of Allegiance one last time and called it a day.

It had all tired Miss Spaulding worse than regular routine, and I hadn't seen much point to it myself. She settled into her desk chair and seemed to wilt.

"Well, Blossom, we have lived to see this graduation day."

"Yes, ma'am."

"You and I have had our little differences over the years, have we not?"

I nodded, recalling several.

"Without checking the records," she said, "I believe I saw you first in this office in fourth grade."

"Yes, ma'am. That was the year me and my mama moved up here from Sikeston. And naming no names, a bunch of girls dragged me into the rest room and pretty nearly took me apart."

Miss Spaulding sighed. "I am afraid, Blossom, it was something you must have said that . . . excited their curiosity."

"Oh, well, shoot," I said. "Any little thing will set them off."

"Then along about sixth grade," she continued, "there was that blue racer snake that Maisie Markham found in her lunch bucket. The poor child actually put her hand on that thing, thinking it was liverwurst sausage. You will recall how the experience affected her digestion."

I remembered clearly. Anybody would. "She's gained all that weight back since and then some."

"The culprit, however, has never been brought to justice."

"It wasn't me," I said.

"It wasn't *I*," Miss Spaulding said.

"I never thought it was."

She sighed deeper. "What is past is past, I suppose. But I wonder if much progress has been made. I refer to the maypole dance today."

She was closing in on me fast. But this is America, so I hoped to have a chance to defend myself.

"I am not referring to your dress, Blossom. Never think it."

Letty Shambaugh had decreed that all the girls should wear shell-pink, made up of yardage purchased at her paw's Select Dry Goods store. I was hanged if I'd go along with that. I wore my gray princess dress, which there is still some wear in. On my chest I planted my spelling medal. I'm a champion speller, which comes in handy in the writing of this true account.

I even perked up my outfit with a new purple sash, which was as far as I'd go. There was nothing to be done about my hair, which kinks in this weather.

"I am referring to the maypole dance itself," Miss Spaulding said, "after all those rehearsals that went so well. How long did we rehearse our dance, Blossom?"

"Every dadburned night for a week," says I, "weaving them ribbons around that pole, with Letty Shambaugh bossing us all like she was—"

"It would have been a lovely spectacle," Miss Spaulding said, "so graceful with all the ribbons making pretty patterns. But it was not to be, was it?"

"Fate moves in mysterious ways," I said.

"Who, Blossom, do you suppose went to all the work of digging around the maypole in the dead of last night and undermined its foundations? Who so unbalanced the pole that one sharp tug on a ribbon would bring the whole pole crashing down, barely missing Ione Williams's head and grazing Letty's corsage? Who, for that matter, gave a ribbon the

sharp tug? I grant you, it made all the boys laugh, if that was the intention."

"Anything will make a boy laugh," I said. It was a regular scandal how the finger of blame always pointed my way when any little thing went wrong.

"But we must let bygones be bygones." Miss Spaulding sighed. She'd waved me into a chair, and there I sat, swinging my legs, waiting for her to come to her main point, which she always does.

"Next September, Blossom, you will be across the road at the high school. This is a first-rate opportunity, if you will but take it, to make a fresh start with a clean slate. You will find high school very different. It would be fortunate if high school did not find you so . . . different. Do you follow me?"

I thought I did. "Lay low and keep my nose clean?"

Miss Spaulding looked pained. "In so many words, yes. Blossom, you are growing up and beginning to become a young . . . lady. Anytime now your . . . form may begin to fill out."

She looked down at her own form, which never has, and cleared her throat. "You will develop . . . new interests, such as your personal appearance and daintier habits."

I wiped my nose on my sleeve and wished she'd come to her point without going all around Robin Hood's barn. She can be very plainspoken if she tries.

"In short, Blossom, I think it would be better for you and the community at large if you put some of

your old habits to rest. There are better ways of getting attention than dabbling in the . . . occult."

"If you mean my Second Sight," I said, "it's no prank, like the snake in Maisie's lunch or the maypole—whoever pulled them stunts. It's a Gift, and it's in the blood. I get it from my mama, who is seven-eighths Gypsy. Mama could take a squint at your tea leaves, Miss Spaulding, and read your whole future like a book."

"That won't be necessary," she replied. "I know my future."

"You do?"

She nodded. "Once you are across the road at the high school, my future will be smooth sailing. I look forward to some much deserved peace and quiet."

"Mama could give you a closer reading than that," I said. "Mama could pinpoint the hour of your death to a minute!"

Miss Spaulding flinched. "Blossom, there are people who do not want the hour of their deaths . . . pinpointed. There are people who think all this . . . spiritualism is hogwash."

"They're ignorant."

"Nevertheless"—Miss Spaulding straightened several small items on her desk—"it's high time you learned how to get along in *this* world without worrying about . . . other locations."

"When the fit comes over me and I get my Vibrations, seems like I don't have much say in the matter. You remember yourself, Miss Spaulding, that time right here in this office when I had one of my

spells. I was here and elsewhere all at once. You sat right there and watched my spirit wander back in time until I found myself aboard the steamship *Titanic* just when it took its fatal—"

"Please, Blossom." Miss Spaulding put out her hand like a crossing guard. "You need not refresh my memory. The event is still vivid in my mind. I have given your . . . experiences long thought, and I have come to the only possible conclusion, a scientific conclusion."

She paused. "You will have heard the term 'puberty,' Blossom?"

The term rang a bell with me, but I couldn't exactly put my finger on it. Miss Spaulding's face had gone beet-red. She cleared her throat a number of times, rapid-fire.

"Puberty is that time of life when a young girl begins to become . . . an older girl. It is a time of considerable . . . upheaval to body and brain alike. I have concluded that your . . . psychic episodes were purely a temporary condition. Do you comprehend my meaning?"

"I can see ghosts, too," I told her.

Miss Spaulding wilted more till her chin was on her chest. You never saw a tireder woman. Trying to help her out, I said, "You mean, I was going through a stage and now I'm beginning to outgrow it?"

She perked up. "Precisely, Blossom! Put your past behind you and all your . . . exploits. Over at the high school they like team players. I'm sure you can

settle down and be one if you put your mind to it."

"I guess I could try," I said.

"Try, and you will succeed!" Miss Spaulding sang out. "Do not be tempted, Blossom. If you begin to ... Vibrate, or whatever it is you do, or if some thoughtless classmate goads you into showing off, turn a deaf ear!"

She heaved herself up from her desk. "Mind over matter, Blossom. Let that be the motto for your future!"

*

Throughout the summer of 1914 I thought over Miss Spaulding's advice. I supposed it was possible that I was outgrowing my Second Sight. Mama always says my Powers are puny compared to hers, though she's the jealous type. I even thought it might be just as well if I was more like other people. I was about half-willing to lay my Powers to rest.

But that's where Fate stepped in. I was to learn it isn't possible to turn away from my talents. A Gift is a curse if you don't put it to work.

As a freshman at Bluff City High School I was often to recall with a wry smile how Miss Spaulding had warned me to look to my future. For I was to set foot into a future world beyond all Miss Spaulding's scientific conclusions, even beyond the imaginings of any person now living.

I was to see the Dreadful Future firsthand for myself, and as plain as the nose on your face.

2

ON A WARM SEPTEMBER MORNING my route to high school took me around the Armsworth family barn and across their property. My mama economizes on breakfasts, kicking me out of the house early, so on my way I'm always greeted by the smell of frying bacon coming from the Armsworth mansion.

Alexander Armsworth, a kid of my acquaintance, lives there. He can't help but know me since we're near neighbors. However, Alexander managed to avoid me all that summer like I had the typhoid fever.

Him and me have reason to be friends, though a boy rarely listens to reason. We're the only two people in Bluff City with the Second Sight, except for my mama. I get my Gift from her. Where Alexander gets his is anybody's guess.

Seems like all he does is deny he has it. One time he saw a ghost right there in the loft of the Armsworth barn. Locally that outbuilding is still known as the Ghost Barn because of this famous hap-

pening. But it took wild horses to drag a confession out of Alexander.

Let him catch one glimpse of a haunt or some poor restless soul in search of a decent grave, and he turns tail. A boy hates to show fear worse than poison, and when it comes to the Spirit World, Alexander Armsworth is scared of his own shadow. He is girl-shy, too, or at least shy of me.

But he is not bad-looking. I lingered along that morning under the bay window of the Armsworth dining room, hearing the clink of knife and fork and Alexander's mama whining. But there was no reason to linger, though I kicked a certain amount of gravel. If Alexander spied me from the bay window, he'd take to the cellar till I was off the place. He treats me worse than a ghost.

I slowed again when the high school hove into view. As Bluff City is an up-and-coming place with better than twenty-two hundred inhabitants, they have a first-rate high school.

It was larger than I remembered, and the entire student body was milling around outside, many of them as big as grown-ups. Nearly all the female sex was in long skirts. The boys parted their hair in the middle and gummed it down with grease. Everybody was trying to look like everybody else with much success.

Some that I took to be juniors and seniors were arriving in autos—roadsters and touring cars and such—and the country ones were coming in by the

wagonload. The football team showed off by tackling each other on the field out back. It was a sight.

Everybody seemed well acquainted with everybody else, calling out greetings. Though I'm used to going it alone, I wouldn't have minded knowing someone to call out a greeting to. But the only familiar faces I saw were Letty Shambaugh and her club of girls. They'd congregated around Letty for mutual protection under a shade tree. She seemed to be getting them organized. I don't look for friendship or even common decency from Letty, so I was willing to pass them by.

But Letty hollered out, "You there, Blossom Culp! I want a word with you." At that her whole club turned my way.

Ione Williams was there, and Harriet Hochhuth and the Beasley twins, Tess and Bess, who are identical, and Maisie Markham, who stands out a mile.

Letty has the sweetest little face you ever saw until you come to her mouth, which is mean. She bustled up and began to speak. Then her eyes popped when she saw the spelling medal I wore depending from my front.

"Well, if that doesn't about take the cake!" she exclaimed. "Wearing that old grade school spelling medal to high school!"

"Did you ever?" said several of her club.

"They are not going to be interested in your so-called past achievements here at the high school," Letty continued. "Take my advice and throw that thing away."

I made a silent vow right then to wear that spelling medal on my chest until it fell off.

"But never mind about that," Letty said. "What I want to say to you is this, Blossom. You will find here at the high school they have such a thing as school spirit. The freshman class must pull together, and as Miss Spaulding used to say, 'A chain is only as strong as its weakest link.'"

Letty left no doubt as to who the weakest link was, and all her club looked right at me.

"We don't have any intention in this world of being dragged down or embarrassed to death by you, Blossom. Let this be a warning." Her eyes narrowed to slits.

"Is that a fact," I remarked.

She patted her hair bow. "You cannot help your background, Blossom, or do much about your looks. But I hope in my heart you won't make a jackass of us all by telling tall tales and poking your nose into other people's business and claiming you are some kind of a witch or whatever, which are three of your bad habits."

There are times in life when it's better to remain silent and let your fists do the talking. I was winding up to knock the socks off Letty Shambaugh when I caught a glimpse of Alexander Armsworth in the distance, which distracted me.

He was wandering into the schoolyard in a new belted knicker suit with his eyes peeled for two high school cronies of his, Bub Timmons and Champ Ferguson.

Then from within the schoolhouse a bell rang, the first of many. Everybody ganged toward the entrance. Alexander was claimed by Bub and Champ, and Letty surged ahead with all her club. I was left to face high school alone, keeping Alexander Armsworth in the corner of my eye.

I suppose high school is educational, though very little of it is to my taste. The teachers can teach only one subject, so you spend half the day traipsing from one classroom to the next, herded along like hogs in a chute.

To keep us freshmen in our place, we all had to wear what they call beanies, which are little orange and black skullcaps with the number 18 on them, as we are to be the graduating class of 1918. I had to anchor my beanie on my unruly hair with a hatpin.

As headgear they are not flattering, though Letty wore hers like a crown of jewels. On Maisie Markham's big head, the beanie looked like a covered button. But if you turned up without one, some sophomore had the privilege of wiping the floor with you.

Our days began with a thing they call homeroom. Here attendance is taken and announcements are made. All the freshmen are stuck in the same homeroom, so it was no better than being in Horace Mann School. In the first week we had class elections. Letty was made president of the class, and Alexander was made vice-president. My name didn't come up.

Our homeroom teacher was an ancient person, name of Miss Blankenship. We returned to her later

each day for English literature, where she was driving us with a whip through a play called *Hamlet*. Every day she put a new quotation from this play on the blackboard, such as:

SOMETHING IS ROTTEN IN THE STATE OF DENMARK

Act I

which was written out in her quavering hand. Until Miss Blankenship, I hadn't known that a woman can go bald, too. But she wasn't blind. One false step and she nailed you.

Though I could put up with most of high school, I nearly drew the line at what they call Girls' Gym. I get all the exercise I need, and I'm not in the habit of taking off my clothes in public. Still, we all had to take it except for Maisie Markham, who was excused on the grounds of weight.

I'd expected the gym teacher to be a big, beefy woman, like a heavyweight wrestler in bloomers. But here I was proved wrong.

Her name was Miss Fuller, and she was more willowy than muscular. She wore a bandeau of flowered silk tight across her forehead and artistic drapings in several colors hanging down over her bloomers. Satin ribbons that attached to her gym shoes crisscrossed to the knee over her cotton stockings. She had a wan face and sad spaniel eyes with a suspicion of rouge dotting both her prominent cheekbones.

Under her direction, we ran relays and swung In-

dian clubs, but she favored what she called Artistic Expression. She'd crank up an Edison Victrola and play a song called "Pale Hands I Love Beside the Shalimar." To this accompaniment we were to turn ourselves into fields of waving wheat or sometimes flowers sprouting and putting out foliage.

She was a great one for graceful movement, and I'd often fall down, as I found it hard to maneuver in bloomers and rubber shoes. I wouldn't have minded it much except for the locker room. Here we had to strip down and shower together in a big galvanized metal enclosure.

Every now and then me and Mama drag a washtub in from the porch at home and have a bath before the fire. But we take turns.

In Girls' Gym we all had to splash around under the spigots together. This was not natural to me, particularly as Letty Shambaugh took it for an opportunity to make remarks about my person.

Her person, which I glimpsed through the steam and soapsuds, was pink and dimpled all over. I could only hope this bathing business wouldn't continue on into cold weather, which is not good for your health.

From Girls' Gym we went daily to the study of history. It was taught by a new teacher, name of Mr. Ambrose Lacy. Many of the sillier girls had crushes on him. Because Letty Shambaugh sat across the aisle from me, I happened to notice she'd written Mr. Lacy's name on her notebook cover, encircled it with a heart, and lettered in the following poem:

If you love me as I love you,
No knife can cut our love in two.

Sickening though this was, Mr. Lacy took it in his stride, seeming to have a long history of being admired. He was a handsome man and knew it, with regular features and a cleft in his chin. His hair was yellow and wavy, and all his neckties and pocket handkerchiefs matched. As high school teachers go, he was about average, but he struck so many vain poses that I personally thought he'd have done better on the stage.

He was fond of the sound of his own voice. One time early in the semester he clasped his hands in the small of his back and proclaimed: "Rome is dead, and the once-great British Empire is on its knees. But Bluff City is in her prime! Where else on earth do the tracks of the Wabash Railroad and the Illinois Central cross, creating prosperity and a topnotch daily wage for those willing to work?

"Boys and girls, we had better search the history of Bluff City to learn why we're sitting so pretty. What is history but mankind's record where we look for guidance? We search the past for wisdom because the future is the Great Unknown!"

"I'm not so sure about that," I said, speaking out before I thought.

Mr. Lacy looked down at me, startled. He'd been as cranked up as Miss Fuller's Victrola before my interruption. "You aren't?"

"Well, no," I said. "An aunt of mine foresaw the

future, so it wasn't the Great Unknown to her. Here awhile back she had a vision of the San Francisco earthquake a week ahead of the actual event."

Across the aisle Letty Shambaugh threw herself onto her desktop and began drumming it with her little fists. "Oh, no. Blossom's going to tell more lies about her trashy family. I could just die. Somebody stop her." Et cetera.

But Mr. Lacy paid her no heed. He hadn't noticed me before, but now he did. "Did your aunt make this—ah—prophecy known?"

"Shoot, yes," I explained. "She was living right there in San Francisco at the time, in a rooming house on Mission Street. She preached the earthquake's coming from the street corners and notified all the newspapers."

"I see," said Mr. Lacy, staring at me like a cat had spoken.

"It didn't do her any good, though, as it turned out."

Letty moaned. "Oh, don't let Blossom finish the story. Her endings are always simply awful. Somebody stuff something in her mouth." Et cetera.

"Nobody likes hearing bad news," I said, "so my aunt was widely ignored. She began to lose faith and to disbelieve her Powers, and that led to a regular tragedy."

"It did?" said Mr. Lacy. The whole classroom had gone quiet except for Letty moaning.

I nodded. "My aunt failed to save herself. Her

vision foretold that the entire south end of the city would collapse into its own cellars. But on the night before the great quake she just went to bed like anybody else. Of course, when it struck at dawn and she was throwed across her room and felt the floor give under her, she was proved right.

"But it was too late to get out. Down she crashed and ended up pinned under half a house. Alive though she was, she'd have been left to rot except that one of her arms was poked through the wreckage and stretched exposed on the sidewalk."

Mr. Lacy shuddered, but all the boys were attentive. Ahead of me, Alexander was listening. He wouldn't turn around, but I saw how red his ears were getting.

"There my aunt was," I said, "like a rat in a trap all day with only her hand and arm free out there on the public pavement."

I dropped my voice as I came to the terrible part of this true story. "On that hand my aunt wore a diamond ring. Imagine her horror and dismay when some looter came along on the sidewalk outside and all but trod on her helpless hand. Then he looked down and saw it.

"This looter fellow hunkered down and took hold of her hand, which my aunt tried to jerk away. Then he saw it wasn't a dismembered limb or lifeless. By then he'd noticed the diamond sparkling on one of her fingers.

"He took her hand in his rough grasp and com-

menced to twist at her ring, determined to take it from her. But it was a tight fit and wouldn't work loose.

"Well, sir, the looter rubbed my aunt's finger raw, but he couldn't pull that doggoned diamond ring over her knuckle. All this time she was screaming from under the house, unheeded."

I fell silent then to give everybody time to picture this awful scene and to figure out what was coming next if they had any imagination.

"Then my ill-fated aunt knew the worst when her hand was raised to the looter's stubbled face. She felt the hot wetness and sharp teeth when his mouth closed over her ring finger."

The classroom was tomb-silent. Mr. Lacy, who is naturally pale, went paler. "You don't mean," he began, "that—"

"You bet your boots," I said. "The damnable looter chewed my aunt's finger off and bit the bone in two. Then he made away with her ring. The fire department didn't dig her out till nightfall. They never located her diamond ring, though her finger was found in a gutter nearby just where the looter had spat it out."

The room remained hushed except for the pounding sound of Maisie Markham's feet as she galloped to the door with both her hands clamped over her mouth. Maisie doesn't have the stomach for a good story.

3

I SAT BACK PRETTY WELL SATISFIED at this true story of my nine-fingered aunt.

Besides, it was history, being about the San Francisco earthquake, and this was history class. But across the aisle Letty was clutching her forehead. Up ahead Alexander sat slouched in his seat, his ears burning with embarrassment. A person knows when her efforts to contribute aren't appreciated. I got no better from Mr. Lacy.

He swallowed heavily and said, "Blossom, since you're responsible for this upset, you'd better skin on down to Miss Fuller's locker room and see that Maisie is all right. The child may need to stretch out on the cot down there until she's better."

"I'll need a pass," I said, reminding him of one of the many rules around this place.

"Just go, Blossom," he barked, so I went, making a dignified exit.

Any moment of freedom in a school day is worth its weight in gold, so I took my sweet time getting down to the locker room on my errand of mercy.

Since high school teachers don't work a full day, they have such a thing as a free period. Miss Fuller was having hers when I finally sauntered into her office at one end of the lockers.

She was at her desk busy with paper work. But Maisie was nowhere in sight, and she's hard to miss. When I explained that I'd been sent down on her behalf, Miss Fuller recounted how Maisie had lost her lunch on the way here but had recovered enough to be sent home.

"She has a weak stomach," I remarked. "She stuffs her face with candy the livelong day—licorice and suchlike."

"A very unhealthy habit," Miss Fuller noted.

"And nasty," I added.

As I had no place to be, I lingered at Miss Fuller's desk, noticing that she was extra wan-looking today. Behind the horn-rimmed reading spectacles, her magnified eyes were more soulful than usual. Though she'd seemed intent upon her paper work, her mind was drifting. This is the sort of thing I can often tell about people, don't ask me how.

I expected to be sent on my way, but Miss Fuller's thoughts were off gathering wool. I thought of taking a peek at her gradebook, but who cares about a gym grade? Then my eyes fell upon a fatal document.

It was a note on the desk. There was a page of writing that ended with numerous X's, representing kisses. I knew that handwriting even upside down.

My eyes popped, but I kept a poker face. It was a letter from Mr. Lacy.

Miss Fuller seemed to notice me again. "What class did Maisie get sick in?" When I told her, she only said, "Ah." But her hand fluttered up to the back of her neck. "Ambrose—Mr. Lacy is quite a good teacher, I believe?"

So-so, I nearly said, but I was on my guard now. "He is right good," I remarked, "and many of the girls are sweet on him."

"Indeed?" she said.

Naming no names, I quoted to her the poem Letty Shambaugh had written to Mr. Lacy on her notebook cover. I hoped to share a good laugh with Miss Fuller, but I was in for another surprise.

" 'No knife can cut our love in two,' " she echoed. "That is a real beautiful sentiment."

It was about the worst corn-fed sentiment I'd ever run up against. But something was dawning on me fast. Love had come to Miss Fuller. She had it bad for Mr. Lacy, and being a gym teacher, she didn't know a good poem from drivel.

She sighed and returned to her work, but she was watching me on the sly. Since I often do the same, I can tell when it's being done to me. Miss Fuller's hand skated over the papers on her desk, concealing Mr. Lacy's note and picking up another page.

She stroked the artistic knot of hair that rode high above her bandeau. "Speaking of poetry," she remarked, "how does this strike you?"

She read aloud in a mournful voice like the coo
of a mating dove:

> "Thoughts are bluebirds high above,
>   Winging toward you with my love;
> Soaring over oak and pine,
>   They bring the news that I am thine."

I like to have gagged. This poem was more sickening than Letty's. Miss Fuller had no doubt
cribbed it off a two-cent valentine.

"What do you think?" she asked, and waited for a
reply.

My head whirled. Not only was Miss Fuller stuck
on Mr. Lacy, but she was writing slop to him like a
young girl. It shook my faith in grown-ups.

"I have heard worse," I said cautiously, though I
never had.

Miss Fuller sighed again and plucked at the tails
of her bandeau. "Don't be kind," she sighed. "My
poor words are unworthy. For me, Artistic Expression is limited to the dance. With poetry, I seem to
strike out."

She'd get no argument from me on that score.

"I don't suppose you know any . . . suitable poetry, Blossom?"

I could see the woman was desperate, so I racked
my brain. Then suitable poetry came to me. It was
Miss Blankenship's daily words from *Hamlet*, which
had seeped into my head.

"How about this?" I said.

"Doubt thou the stars are fire;
     Doubt that the sun doth move;
Doubt truth to be a liar;
     But never doubt I love."

Miss Fuller blinked at me from behind her horn-rims. Her hand stole up to her long cheek. "That has a nice ring to it," she said. "Did you write it?"

"No, but Shakespeare did," I explained, "in *Hamlet*, Act Two."

"Nevertheless," she said, "it seems to hit the nail right on the head." She pushed paper and an ink pen across the desk at me. "I'll be much obliged if you'd just copy out those words. I would like them for . . . my scrapbook of Beautiful Thoughts."

She grew shifty-eyed then as people will when they're lying.

The bell rang just as I finished my copy work. I was ready to scoot, but Miss Fuller looked up in a dreamy way, saying, "You are a strange child, Blossom, and not a promising physical specimen. Still, you are somehow sympathetic."

"Many thanks," I told her, as these were the first halfway civil words I'd heard in high school. Then I cut out.

The schoolyard was emptying when I stepped out into the afternoon sunshine. There, at the foot of the steps, stubbing his toe in the earth, was Alexander Armsworth. Reminding myself how Miss Fuller could make a fool of herself over the male sex, I

meant to breeze past him in case he had no greeting for me. But he did.

"Well, Blossom, you've put your foot in it again with that tall tale about your so-called aunt getting her ring finger gnawed off."

With so much on my mind, I'd nearly forgotten history class until this rude reminder. Alexander smoothed the front of his argyle sweater and expanded his chest to its limit.

"Now that we're in high school," he said, "we're not kids who'll swallow everything we're told."

"Is that a fact?" I retorted. His voice had changed some more over the summer, and he clearly liked the sound of it. I lit into him.

"Alexander, I've had it up to here with lectures. You're sounding more like Letty Shambaugh every minute, and it'll be a cold day in you-know-where when I need advice from either one of you."

I felt my face heat up, though I'd meant to keep calm. A person can take only so much.

"I'm only speaking for your own good, Blossom. And of course, on behalf of the freshman class." He pointed to his beanie. Being provoked, I scanned the ground for a rock big enough to lay across the side of his head. But there's never one when you need it.

"Some friend you turned out to be, Alexander," I said, more in sorrow than in anger. "Here I am just coming out of Miss Fuller's locker room with some real interesting news I might be willing to share. But all you can do is carp and complain. I suppose you were hanging around just to put me in my place."

Alexander cast his eyes to the sky. "Don't flatter yourself, Blossom. I'm hanging around because we're going to have a meeting of freshman class officers."

"You and Letty are getting too thick to stir," I remarked.

Alexander spoke then of what he called "the entire slate of officers." Letty had appointed Harriet Hochhuth secretary, Ione Williams treasurer, and Tess and Bess Beasley sergeants at arms.

"Trust Letty to make officers out of her whole club," I said. "And what business do you have to conduct anyhow?"

Alexander drew himself up importantly. "One item of business is the Halloween Festival, when each class holds a fund-raising event. Us officers have got to come up with a crackerjack event for Halloween night to show the entire school there are no flies on the freshman class."

"Is that a fact?" I replied, as this was the first I'd heard of the so-called Halloween Festival. "It sounds to me like the school's trying to keep us busy on Halloween night so certain parties I could name won't get up to mischief and outright vandalism."

"That kind of Halloweening is kid stuff, Blossom." Alexander spoke in his deepest voice.

"Then you've come a long way from last Halloween, when you and Bub Timmons and Champ Ferguson and Les Dawson came to considerable grief when you tried to turn over Old Man Leverette's privy."

Alexander's ears went pink. He pushed right past me up the steps to his freshman officers' meeting. But at the top he turned to fire a parting shot.

"And, Blossom," he said, "take my advice and stop wearing that old grade school spelling medal. Nobody gives a hoot in high school." Then he vanished.

There I stood, without a friend in the world and eight months to go in the school year. Though I can generally manage to keep my sunny side up, my spirits were low on that October afternoon.

But it is always darkest before the dawn. I was to find a friend sooner than I knew, and in quite an unexpected place.

4

WHETHER IT'S DUE TO MY SECOND SIGHT OR NOT, I've always been drawn to people—even the living —who are lonely or troubled in their thoughts. It seems to be my fate. Possibly Miss Fuller pining for love of Mr. Lacy at her desk in the locker room is an example. A better example than her cropped up in the following week.

For reasons of his own, Mr. Lacy formed the habit of sending me off on various errands during history class. As this gave me freedom and a relief from history, it suited us both.

One afternoon I was killing time after I'd delivered the attendance slip to the main office. As is my habit, I dropped into the girls' rest room down in the cellar of the school.

Mama and me don't have running water piped in at home, so the sight of all that white tile and rushing water at your beck and call is a comfort. Moreover, the conveniences are all in little cubbyholes with doors on them. I believe people deserve their privacy, especially me.

The girls' rest room is strictly modern with rolls of paper where you'd expect to find pages from the Sears, Roebuck catalogue. I was sitting at my ease in one of the cubbyholes that afternoon when something came over me that seemed supernatural. Though I didn't Vibrate, my flesh crawled as I sensed I wasn't alone.

With the thought came a low sob from the next cubbyhole. Glancing down, I saw under the half wall between us a foot planted there in a broken boot. Another sob followed the first. When I heard paper tearing from the roll, I figured my neighbor was of the living. Still, you never know.

Settling my skirts, I stole out to investigate, but my squeaking door gave me away. The next door over was yanked open from within, and there I stood, staring straight inside at a girl still sitting.

She had a pinched face and a slack jaw. Slumped there with her skirttails hitched up, she was blowing her nose with a square of the paper they provide. Her nappy old flannel jacket and a feed sack skirt made me a regular fashion plate by contrast. From her general condition I took her to be one of the kids in from the country. Her hair was arranged roughly into pigtails, and there was more than mud on her boots.

It's not my way to stand around chatting to people in these circumstances. But the girl gazed up at me with eyes as sad as Miss Fuller's, set in a face far sadder.

"You didn't see me," she said in a country drawl. "Bear that in mind."

"If I wasn't to see you, why did you open your door?"

"I get lonesome," she whined, sniffing a red nose. "I reckon I'd have opened up even if you'd been one of them teachers. It's a sight how lonesome you can get in a big, busy place like Bluff City."

It was neither big nor busy there in her cubbyhole, but I let that pass.

"You a freshman?" I asked, just making small talk.

"I reckon," she replied.

"Then where's your beanie?" I pointed to my own, bristling with a hatpin on my head.

"Is that what them things mean?" she said. "I wondered."

Country children are slow to catch on to our ways, but this example was slower than most. I began to have suspicions.

"Say, listen, if you're a freshman, how come you aren't in Miss Blankenship's homeroom?"

"Who?" The girl drew back. "What?"

I had her cornered, and she saw that, so I changed my tack. "My name's Blossom Culp. What's yours?"

She didn't like giving out her name. But finally she said, "Daisy-Rae," looking like she might try to climb her wall.

"Pleased to meet you, Daisy-Rae. Why don't you come on out of . . . there? This isn't any way to

carry on a conversation." I strolled away to the sinks to give her time to pull herself together.

"Well, all right," came her voice from the cubbyhole, "but just for a minute."

The plumbing at the high school is first-rate, but I'd never run across anybody so fond of it before. My suspicions deepened as they often do. Something was definitely rotten in the state of Denmark.

A chain was pulled from within. Water flushed, and Daisy-Rae edged out. She was a tall and gawky type, putting me in the mind of a wild turkey. Her pigtails were tied up with binder twine, and her elbows were out of her flannel shirt sleeves.

"You in from the country?"

"How'd you know?" said Daisy-Rae.

*

That's how I found a new friend. Unless you're slower than I thought, you'll have figured out what I saw at once. Daisy-Rae was a stowaway here at Bluff City High School. She'd never signed herself up on the rollbook, and she'd never darkened the homeroom door. Daisy-Rae had been down here in a cubbyhole of the girls' rest room since Labor Day, sitting her life away.

I confronted her with the facts of her case just to clear the air.

She turned a ghastly green. "How do you know so much?" She glanced toward the door, but it was too late to run.

"Oh, I have my ways," I said. "For one thing, I'm

Gifted with the Second Sight. I can see the Unseen and the Living Dead, which is about what you are, hanging out down here day in and day out."

"Oh," said Daisy-Rae, kind of goggle-eyed, "I thought we just run into one another by accident."

"Well, in this case we did," I admitted. "But what I can't figure is this: How come you don't go to class like everybody else?"

Daisy-Rae rammed one big toe against the other. She was one awkward girl. "Well, I *meant* to," she said. "I come to school that first day, but all them faces in that big schoolyard was just a blur. I says to myself, *Daisy-Rae, you're nothin' but a girl from the backwoods and the hollers. A place like this could chew you up and spit you out.*"

I nodded in sympathy, knowing the feeling.

"Then a bell rung, like they do," Daisy-Rae went on, "and everybody ganged into the schoolhouse. When I got inside, nobody said boo to me, and I didn't know which way to turn. I come across this indoor outhouse, so I just went in one of them little horse stalls, banged the door shut, and flopped down."

"Well, I never," I declared. "And you been here ever since!"

"I go home at night," Daisy-Rae said. "You can leave after they ring that bell the sixteenth time."

And I thought I'd heard everything.

"Of course, this place fills up with girls at lunch and in them short spaces between the bells."

"Them—those short spaces between the bells is

when we're going from one class to another," I explained.

"Is that right?" says Daisy-Rae. "That's interesting."

"What do you do when the other girls come in here?"

"I just pop out of my stall and mill around with them at the sinks. None of these girls notice me. Seems like they can't focus on anybody they don't already know."

That's about the size of it.

"At lunch I go out in the schoolyard and climb that shade tree out there."

"I never noticed you," I said.

"Well, that's the point, ain't it? They wouldn't know one country kid from another anyhow. The teachers ain't no different."

Bad though her grammar is, Daisy-Rae rattled on, being starved for company. I didn't mind, as I found her story interesting. She was rawboned as a new colt, but she had her wits about her. I admire that.

"Beats me why you go to all the work of coming to school at all. Your paw and maw make you?"

Daisy-Rae flapped a bony hand in the air. "Aw, naw," she said. "Paw's dead, and Maw's up in Michigan, pickin' fruit. I come to town on account of Roderick. He's my little brother. That one-room school out in the country wasn't doin' him no good. So I brought him in here and signed him up at the Horace Mann School across the road. I thought I'd

come over to the high school and pick up some education for myself till I thought better of it."

"Your brother . . . Roderick . . . was he too smart for a country school?"

Daisy-Rae pondered, scratching her head with a long finger.

"To tell you the truth, they couldn't do nothin' with him there. He's medium simple."

"How's he doing at Horace Mann?"

"Oh, right well," she said. "In town it seems like they take a long time to catch up with you."

She had a point there. I could have named her several numskulls of my acquaintance who got passed from grade to grade eventually.

"Roderick don't mind it," Daisy-Rae said. "Of course, he'd just as soon be one place as another."

This world is full of wonders. Daisy-Rae was one, and I had no doubt that Roderick was another. "If you'll take my advice," I told her, "you'll turn yourself in and start going to classes. I grant you, it's like a stretch in jail, but at least it's not solitary confinement." I made a meaningful gesture to her stall.

"Well, I wasn't lookin' for advice exactly," Daisy-Rae said in a thoughtful way. Then fear entered her watery eyes. "You wouldn't turn me in, would you?"

"Who me?" I replied. "A friend wouldn't do that, and you can count me as a friend."

My words seemed to work magic. Daisy-Rae was pitifully snaggle-toothed, but her smile shone with a rare beauty then. It was a cautious smile to begin

with. Then she beamed at me, and her eyes brimmed with tears.

The bell rang, rattling the window grates.

"That's old number sixteen," Daisy-Rae noted. "Another day, another dollar, as the sayin' goes. I reckon we can all go on home now."

5

Just when I'd been feeling extra-friendless, now I had me a Secret Pal. In the weeks that followed, I'd nip down to the rest room after my errands and pass the time of day with Daisy-Rae. We both looked forward to it. Once in a while, during biology or *Hamlet* or the shower room, I even envied Daisy-Rae her quiet life.

Still, her situation worried me. "I know you got to wait around till your brother gets out of school every day," I said to her, "but why don't you get out and walk around the town or something?"

She waved this well-meant suggestion away. "I'm nothin' but a country girl, and I'd get lost in a big place like Bluff City. Besides, I'll need a warm spot like this, come winter."

"You're a truant, you know," I informed her.

"I thought a truant was one who don't come to school," she replied. "I come to school."

She had me there.

Out in the schoolyard at lunch, she stayed up her tree. But she could talk the gold out of your teeth

when we were on our own down in the rest room. In worldly ways she was backward. But there were no flies on her when it came to noticing things.

"That towheaded boy in the fancy sweater," she said to me one time, "you got a soft spot for him?"

I like to have dropped my teeth. "If you mean Alexander Armsworth," I said, "I don't know what you're talking about."

Daisy-Rae smirked. "I seen the way you look at him out there in the yard. He's standoffish, though, ain't he?"

"Alexander goes his way, and I go mine," I said, somewhat prissy. But you don't stay on your high horse long around Daisy-Rae.

"That Alexander," she remarked, "he's runnin' in bad company."

There was more truth than poetry to that observation. "You mean those two big galoots, Bub Timmons and Champ Ferguson," I said. "Alexander's a very well-brought-up boy, and he's trying to live it down. I've told him myself he ought to stay clear of Bub and Champ. Bub's spent five semesters in the sophomore year, and Champ's old enough to get married."

"Don't I know it," Daisy-Rae said, smirking again. I suspected she knew more than she was letting on.

"What do you know?" says I.

She reached down under her skirts and scratched at a flea bite through a hole in her stocking. "When nobody notices you're there, you hear things. Besides, Roderick and me, we live out just past Lever-

ette's Woods. We cut through on our way home. You know that swimmin' hole out there with the big rope hangin' down?"

"I heard tell of it," I said.

"Well, them three—that Bub and Champ and yore Alexander—they mosey out there about every afternoon these warm days to swim. That's where they do their big talkin' and smokin' and makin' plans for Halloween. It's a sight. Me and Roderick, we spy on 'em."

"Smoking?" says I. "If Alexander's mama gets wind of him smoking, she'll wear him out. And as to Halloween, what are you talking about, Daisy-Rae? Alexander's on the committee for the Halloween Festival. He's left Halloween pranks and stunts behind him, to hear him tell it."

Again Daisy-Rae smirked.

*

That's how I happened to pay a visit out to Leverette's Woods myself one mild October afternoon, guided there by Daisy-Rae and her little brother, Roderick. Whatever Alexander was up to, I meant to get to the bottom of it.

Old Man Leverette once owned all that territory out past the streetcar trestle over Snake Creek. He owned the woods that bear his name, with a well-known Lovers' Lane winding through it and the swimming hole. He also once occupied a large frame farmhouse just beyond the woods, now going to rack and ruin. Come to find out, Daisy-Rae and her

brother occupied a chicken coop behind the old abandoned Leverette farmhouse.

Old Man Leverette himself has retired into Bluff City. However, since he's a lover of peace and quiet, he'd have done better to keep to the countryside.

I met Daisy-Rae under the shade tree after school. She knew how to blend in with the crowd. I never saw her coming till she was right there beside me.

She wasn't easy in her mind till we'd crossed the road to where her brother, Roderick, sat waiting on the steps of Horace Mann School. He was a pathetic little gnome of about nine, and there was no doubt that him and Daisy-Rae were blood kin. Like her, he was slack-jawed, with a face far older than the rest of him.

As his only garment, he wore a small pair of bib overalls. His bare shoulders had no more meat on them than a coat hanger. He shambled toward us. His posture was bad, and since he was clutching his middle, I figured he had the bellyache.

But Daisy-Rae, being a big sister, summed up the situation. "Now what have you got?" she inquired, taking him by an ear and giving him a good shake.

Roderick's teeth rattled, but he said nothing.

"Come on." Daisy-Rae turned his ear inside out. "Let's see what it is this time." She reached down inside the bib of his overalls and felt around in there. Presently she drew up a long tail with a gray mouse struggling at the end of it.

I'm not nervous of vermin, but the idea of carry-

ing around a live mouse with those scratchy little claws down the front of your overalls gave me the willies. Daisy-Rae swung the mouse by the tail over her head and let fly with it. The mouse lit running.

"I swan," she said to me, "I have to shake him down every blessed day, and you wouldn't credit what I find on him."

She got a good grip on his hand, and off the three of us strolled, out past the sidewalks and into open country.

"You can call me Blossom," I said, just to put Roderick at his ease.

But Daisy-Rae said, "He won't call you nothin'. He don't have a lot to say."

When we got out past the trestle bridge and onto dirt road, I noticed that Daisy-Rae was less gawky. Even Roderick, who had a tendency to drool, drooled less. When we reached the wire fence around Leverette's Woods, they both vaulted right over it with easy grace. I had to take it in stages.

In the woods they followed a faint trail like a pair of Indian scouts. Not knowing the territory, I tended to crash through the underbrush. At length Daisy-Rae drew me up short, whispering, "When we get to the swimmin' hole, we'll skin up that big elm tree. I have an idee we won't have long to wait." Roderick had already slipped on ahead of us, quiet as a . . . mouse.

The swimming hole's a quarter of a mile back into Leverette's Woods. When we came to the elm tree beside it, I'd have given up if I hadn't been set

on getting the goods on Alexander and his chums. I'm no squirrel for climbing trees. I gazed up the elm's tall trunk. There high in the foliage was Roderick's face, peering down already like a somewhat dim-witted owl.

Daisy-Rae boosted me from behind, but I'll never know how I shinnied up the ten feet to the first branch. I was about to give out when Roderick's small, grimy hand shot out of the greenery and guided me onto a branch. There I settled while Daisy-Rae swarmed up behind me and eased onto a nearby limb.

Roderick settled on a perch of his own above us. They were both as natural up a tree as a pair of bats. I was giddy looking down until I got my bearings. Through the leaves I had a fine view of the swimming hole and a patch of tall grass directly below.

"Hark at that," Daisy-Rae murmured before I heard them coming. She had ears on her like a librarian. "Sit real still, and don't swing yore legs nor nothin', and they'll never know."

Not a minute later, following the sound of small bushes being tramped down, Bub Timmons and Champ Ferguson stepped out of the woods right under me. With them was Alexander.

"Whooeee," remarks Bub, "won't that water feel good."

"Last one in," says Champ, "sucks eggs."

Alexander said nothing but threw himself in the weeds and commenced wrenching his shoes off. Durned if they didn't all three start shucking off

their clothes. Somehow I hadn't thought this far. The grass was soon littered with shoes and shirts and Alexander's argyle sweater and boys' union-suit underwear. Quicker than tongue can tell, Bub, Champ, and Alexander were all naked as jaybirds.

"Well, I never," I whispered to Daisy-Rae.

"You have now," Daisy-Rae whispered back.

They were soon all neck-deep in the water, but not before I had an eyeful. They splashed and ducked one another as boys will, playing the fool. Then Alexander heaved out of the pond on the far side and pulled himself up a tree where the big rope swing hung down.

What a sight Alexander was, clambering up that tree as naked as the day he was born. He looked for all the world like a plucked chicken. Then he edged out on the branch where the rope was.

Pounding his chest with both hands like Tarzan of the Apes, he roars out in his deepest voice:

"O, WHAT A ROGUE AND
PEASANT SLAVE AM I!"

which made Bub and Champ in the water hoot and catcall.

"What kind of talk would that be?" Daisy-Rae whispered to me. I explained it was just Alexander showing off with lines from Miss Blankenship's *Hamlet*, which, of course, meant nothing to Daisy-Rae.

Nearly overbalancing, Alexander dragged up the knot end of the rope and swung out over the swim-

ming hole. He swung right at me, his legs high and wide. I sat real still, taking in the view before he turned loose and hit the water.

By and by the three of them dragged themselves out to dry off in the last rays of the sun. They flopped down in the weeds beneath us and commenced to brag, describing what kind of tattoos they'd all get once they were grown and free of Bluff City.

Bub declared he was going to have a big heart tattooed on his shoulder with a place left blank for lettering in the name of his sweetheart when he was ready to settle down. Champ favored a Chinese dragon with a tail wrapping his arm from elbow to wrist. Trying to keep up, Alexander said he wanted the American eagle tattooed completely across his chest. But Champ remarked that on Alexander's chest there wouldn't hardly be room for a wren.

They all laughed like hyenas and wrestled around in the weeds till Bub pulled out a tobacco pouch and papers and rolled three cigarettes. The air was soon foul and blue from their puffing. Alexander had a job to keep his lighted. He was going green around the gills, though the rest of him was white as chalk. He barely got the thing smoked, and then if he didn't say, "I'll have me another of those coffin nails, Bub, if you don't mind."

I rolled my eyes at Daisy-Rae, and she rolled hers back from her branch.

Halloween soon came up in their conversation. I

was all ears to hear Alexander say, "I won't be available on Halloween night itself, what with the Halloween Festival that I am in charge of." It was something to hear how important he could make himself without a stitch on.

Bub and Champ pointed out that it was fair and square to Halloween any night around the end of October. Indeed, to do all the damage they proposed, it would take them most of a month. And since boys rarely come up with any new ideas, their plot turned upon Old Man Leverette. They're out to get him every year.

I found myself leaning far forward to hear their disgusting plan to plague Old Man Leverette. They could hardly get it discussed for rolling around in the weeds, helpless with laughter and anticipation. It was a nastier plan than turning over his privy, and I about had to give them some credit for originality.

I had no time for anything else because disaster struck right about then. I heard what seemed the crack of a nearby rifle. Daisy-Rae gave out with a little gasp, and above me Roderick drew up his bare feet.

Then the world went topsy-turvy. The rifle crack was, in fact, my branch breaking. It held my weight for an instant more. Then suddenly I was dropping through the air in a blizzard of whipping leaves, following my big branch to the ground.

I had only time to think that if I wasn't killed, I might finish off anybody I lit on. There were startled

yelps from the boys below as the sky seemed to fall on them. I believe they began to crawl different ways, but they didn't get far.

I rode that thing like a bucking bronco, leaving Daisy-Rae and Roderick far above me. It seemed to take forever before I crashed to earth, jarring my eyeteeth. Where there'd been weeds and naked boys, now there was a jungle of leafy branches and quivering twigs. I nestled, somewhat stunned, in the midst of it.

Very near me I heard bad language from the surprised Bub. Champ muttered, too, and then I heard Alexander's voice.

"Oh, no, lightning must have struck. Where is my underwear? I can't go home like this, and I'd better be going." Et cetera.

I had the sense to keep quiet. Let them all think lightning had struck, and it would be far better for me. I began to crawl backward along the limb, trying to slip away unnoticed while the boys untangled themselves.

Chancing a look up in the tree, I saw Daisy-Rae's boots still dangling from her branch and all but invisible. Roderick remained up there, too, looking down at me, almost interested. Then I stole away in a low crouch, bruised all over.

I'd have made a clean getaway, but my toe snagged in a root, and I went sprawling. Glancing back, I saw Alexander's head popping up, wearing a sort of wreath of elm leaves. He could see me, too, unless he was dazed. I had no intention of hanging

around to find out. Boys are modest to a fault. I lit out like a jackrabbit.

Through the woods I sprinted until I got a stitch in my side and slowed to a walk. There was nothing to hear but birdsong. The evening shadows were growing long on the ground. Getting my breath back, I began to slip along, practicing Daisy-Rae's and Roderick's quiet way in the woods. With a pair of moccasins in place of my boots, I wouldn't have made a bad Indian.

Having had enough excitement for one day, I took my time finding a way out of the woods. But there was more to come.

Sharpening my senses, I seemed to hear murmuring somewhere through the brush ahead. I thought of cooing doves before the sound became a man's baritone voice.

Bending double, I made my careful way along behind a screen of elderberry bushes. More like a frontierswoman with every stealthy step, I sensed open country ahead of me. The man's voice droned on, nearer now. One false step would betray me, so I worked along extra-careful.

Still, I almost blundered onto them. Ahead of me were open fields and Old Man Leverette's abandoned farmhouse outlined against the sunset. Nearer, just within the woods, was the Lovers' Lane, winding its way. Beside the gate into the Leverette pasture a pair of lovers stood beneath a weeping willow tree.

Luck was with me. I was still a good five yards

away with an elderberry bush between me and them.
I hunkered down quick, barely breathing. In that
position I was to suffer several nasty shocks.

The lovers were locked in embrace. I couldn't see
the lady, she being in the arms of a broad-shoul-
dered swain in a blue serge suit. He seemed to be
reciting poetry to her. He turned his profile aside
and proclaimed these well-known lines:

> "Doubt thou the stars are fire;
>   Doubt that the sun doth move;
>   Doubt truth to be a liar;
>   But never doubt I love."

It was Mr. Lacy. The sunset played across his
yellow hair. While he paused for a moment of
dramatic silence, the lady emitted sighs. I was all
ears.

"Oh, how perfectly lovely, Ambrose," says the
lady in a familiar voice. "It is like you to choose
lines from Shakespeare, knowing how fond I am of
all his works."

Surely my ears deceived me. But no. Mr. Lacy
bowed to cover the lady's hand with kisses, and I
saw her face plain. It was Miss Mae Spaulding,
principal and eighth-grade teacher of Horace Mann
School.

My heart was in my throat at horror and dismay
to find my old grade school principal in the embrace
of Mr. Lacy. You're never too late for love, I suppose, but what of Miss Fuller, the deceived gym
teacher?

While Miss Fuller was languishing in her locker room, here her beloved stood, quoting the same Shakespeare I'd provided her with to another woman. You talk about a snake in the grass.

They fell to kissing again, Miss Spaulding firmly under his spell. I'd thought she had better sense, but then I'd only seen her during a school day. The spectacles she always wears on a chain had fallen off her nose and were swinging free. Her hair was escaping from its bun, and Mr. Lacy was all over her. Before I could recover from this shock, I got another one, quite a lot worse.

Staring intently through the bush at these so-called lovers, I failed to protect my backside. Maybe I heard a twig snap behind me, maybe not.

A hand closed like a claw on my shoulder. Another thorny hand, scarcely human, clapped over my mouth. My breath was cut off, and my heart hollered. Pinned though I was behind the elderberry bush, I wrenched my head around.

I was staring up into a fearful face with eyes sharp as black diamonds boring into mine. Then I was scared for sure. There aren't two faces like that anywhere in North America. It was my mama.

6

ANY SCENE WITH MAMA IN IT is always painful to recall. Though I could have walked, she dragged me clear back to town by the scruff of the neck. Over her humped shoulder was a sack of hickory nuts. Mama is a fortune-teller by trade, but in the fall we add to our income by nut gathering. We also do a certain amount of gardening, often in other people's gardens.

On our homeward trip we paused once for her to cut a switch off a bush for my legs. Mama isn't up-to-date on child raising and is liable to whup the tar out of me over any little matter.

At home she flung me into a chair and eased the sack onto the floor, saying, "Ooph'll larn youoph to fool arounph in theph timber, youoph little—"

"Mama," I said, "put your teeth in if you're going to talk." I can understand her anyhow but hoped to distract her. She won't wear her teeth much, a good artificial pair, and will leave them around most any-place. Luck wasn't with me, as they were right there on the table between a pack of playing cards and her

crystal ball. She popped them in, which fills out her face no end, and turned on me.

"Now listen, Mama," I said, talking fast. "I only went out to the woods to learn what a bunch of boys were going to pull on Halloween. You know yourself what damage they can do if some responsible person such as myself doesn't put a stop to it."

Mama's snaky eyes narrowed. She thrust her terrible face closer to mine, and her earrings swayed. They were a pair of gambler's dice hanging from her lobes, which is an example of Mama's taste in jewelry. I talked faster.

"I didn't set out to spy on Mr. Lacy, my history teacher, who's two-timing Miss Fuller, the gym teacher with Miss Mae—"

"Shut up," Mama remarked, taking up the switch. Her mean gaze fell on my legs.

"It was an accident, pure and simple. I just chanced onto that Lovers' Lane, where—"

"You was creepin' up on that house. I caught you at it." Mama lashed the air with her switch, testing it. I tried not to notice.

"What house?" I inquired.

Thwack went the switch on the tabletop with a dreadful sound. "The old Leverette place, don't play goody-goody with me."

It's remarkable how plain Mama can speak with her teeth in. They grinned at me, but she didn't.

"The old Leverette place?" I echoed. Mama seemed to be off on one of her tangents.

Thwack on the table again. "You heard me. You

don't go near that place. I tell you one time, you listen." *Thwack* yet again.

"I don't have any business in Old Man Leverette's tumbledown place."

"You can say that agin," Mama mocked, but she'd turned loose of the switch. It rested on the table as a stern reminder. There was something going on in Mama's mind.

"You keep clear of that place," she advised, "or I'll slap you to sleep."

"Why, Mama?"

She grunted, somehow pleased. "I knowed you hadn't figured it out. Ain't I told you time and agin your Powers is puny compared to mine? I won't have you dabblin' in things you can't handle. I got my reputation to consider."

It began to dawn on me. "You mean the place is haunted?"

"I know what I know." Her teeth clacked in some satisfaction. "You don't know nothin'."

Nobody likes to be talked down to that way, especially by a mother. I tried to reason the situation out. "It couldn't be haunted by Old Man Leverette. He's alive and kicking right here in Bluff City."

Though she was still looming over me, Mama drew out a pouch of Bull Durham chewing tobacco from the black folds of her shroud. She pulled off a plug and popped it into her mouth. While she jawed it down to size, I gave the matter more thought.

"Was there a halo about the place?" I asked her. Mama can occasionally tell if a place is haunted if

she sees a mystical halo arching over its roof. It's one of her better ways.

"If you had any Powers whatsoever," she responded rudely, "you'd know that for yourself."

At least she seemed to forget the switch. A plug of Bull Durham will soothe Mama every time. "It ain't that kind of a haunting," she offered, just to show her superior knowledge.

I sighed. There isn't much you can do with Mama. Her temper was cooling, though. She ambled around the table and sat down. She can strike a kitchen match with one flick of her thumbnail. She did so now, lighting up a coal oil lamp. We're not wired for electricity because of the expense and because Mama says the fad for it won't last.

"Draw up your chair, and I'll give you a readin'," she says in quite a civil manner, like I'm a customer. There is no charting Mama's moods.

She swept up her pack of cards. There's nobody like Mama for handling a deck. She can shuffle in the air and cut them one-handed. "Take a card, any card," she said, fanning them out on the table.

I turned over the two of clubs, having no doubt she'd give the same reading to any card I happened to draw. There's a lot of show business in Mama.

"Hmmmmm." She squinted at it, then up at me. "That's real interesting, that is," she said, gargling tobacco juice.

"Well, Mama, let's have it. Am I going to make a long journey and meet a handsome stranger?"

Mama doesn't take any sass. "If it's yore fortune

you want to hear, I can give it to you in a nutshell: You won't set down for a week if I catch you near the Old Leverette place. But I ain't doin' a reading on you. That there two of clubs is sending a message. If you don't clam up, I ain't tellin' you what it is."

Between Daisy-Rae and Mama it's a wonder I have any grammar left. Her head began to bob and weave. Her eyes rolled back in her head, which is not a pretty sight.

"Oh, yeah," she muttered, "I hear it clear. Here comes the message from the Great Beyond. Lay it on me!"

I waited patiently, having no choice. At last in a far-off voice she spoke: *"Not all the Unliving are dead!"*

Then she jerked awake. "Where am I? What time is it? What'd I say?"

I sighed. "You said, 'Not all the Unliving are dead!'"

"Did I? Ain't that interesting!"

"If you say so, Mama. Is that the entire message?"

Her eyes squinched to glittering slits. "It's more than enough to them with the Second Sight, which you ain't got much of." She parked her Bull Durham up in her cheek in a final way, so I figured the reading was over.

"Gittin' about suppertime, ain't it?" She glanced over to a bare cupboard and a cold stove. "How does a nice fried chicken sound to you?"

Reaching down on the floor, she fished up a bur-

lap sack and tossed it across the table at me. My heart sank.

"Git a nice plump one," she ordered, "and don't take all night about it."

I took up the sack with a heavy heart. I don't mind doing chores, but I hate rifling around in other people's henhouses every time Mama gets a taste for fried chicken.

"One of these fine nights," I mumbled at the door, "I'll get my head blowed off."

"Keep yore head down," Mama advised. Then, just as I was crossing the threshold, she added, "Who'd you say them two lovebirds was, carryin' on in the woods?"

"That was Miss Mae Spaulding, my old grade—"

"Never mind about her," Mama said. "Who was the dude?"

"Oh, him, he's my history teacher, name of Mr. Ambrose Lacy, and a regular snake in the—"

"I thought I knowed him!" Mama nodded wisely. "He's trouble with a capital *T* and always was!"

Over my shoulder I saw Mama's gaze shoot to her crystal ball to make me think she'd read some special knowledge there. I doubted that, but how she knew of Mr. Lacy I couldn't tell. Mama is not exactly a member of the PTA.

There was no time to ponder this point. "You stick to yore own business," Mama said, sending a jet of brown tobacco juice onto the floor. "Curiosity killed the cat."

But satisfaction brought that cat back, I remarked

to myself as I followed Mama's long, crooked finger pointing out into the night.

An open-sided streetcar, all lit up, clattered past on the tracks outside our house. I followed along in its wake, walking a rail with my sack over my shoulder.

There on the far side of the Armsworth barn, I supposed, Alexander and all the Armsworths were tucking into a good roast beef and mashed potato dinner. Some people have all the luck.

Hoping to make quick work of my chore, I planned to pay a call on the first henhouse I came to. When you're borrowing chickens, it's best to work the other end of town. But I was half-starved, and Mama's temper is short.

As luck would have it, I came up on the back lot of Old Man Leverette's town property. There, beyond a row of dry hollyhocks, was the Leverette privy, and there, at an angle across his punkin patch, the Leverette henhouse.

A light glowed from the window in the kitchen door, but it seemed locked up for the night. I waited a moment in the privy's shadow and then drifted with care across the punkin patch.

Working along a woven-wire fence, I found the gate into the chicken yard and made my way across hen grit and worse. Then I eased open the crude latch on the henhouse door. From within came the little sighs and flutterings of chickens gone to roost.

Nothing you can name smells worse than the in-

side of a henhouse on a windless night. I slipped inside and waited for my eyes to adjust to the gloom. The Rhode Island Reds were all but invisible on their perches, but the white breeds glowed dimly.

I took a careful step on the slick floor, and a large hen stirred by my ear. The bead of her eye observed me, and I froze. She tucked her head under a wing again. My watchful eye scanned down the row to find one of her sisters less alert.

Chickens aren't the brightest of birds, but easily flustered.

I found a likely specimen, well feathered out. Her beak was tucked beneath her wing, and her neck curved plumply. My hand moved out, fingers itching. In a sudden gesture I had her by the throat, shutting off her wind.

Then things went seriously wrong.

From behind me the henhouse door was nearly wrenched from its hinges. Night air gusted in, and every hen in the place rose up and screamed bloody murder. I turned my particular fowl loose, and she flapped, squawking, away to the rafters.

There's nothing louder than surprised chickens, and the air was white with feathers. I have no doubt they all laid eggs at once. I could have laid one myself.

"REACH FOR THE SKY," a voice roared. "I GOT YOU COVERED." I dropped my sack. It was one of those days.

"TURN AROUND SLOW AND EASY."

As I turned, I saw a great bear-shaped shadow filling the henhouse door. I was also staring into both barrels of a shotgun. "Hold your fire." I sighed. "I am unarmed."

The barrels twitched. "ARE YOU A BOY OR A DWARF?"

"Neither," I answered, somewhat discouraged.

As there's no back way out of a henhouse, I was soon in the open air, which cleared my head, though both barrels were still trained on me.

"Why, there you are, Old—Mr. Leverette," I said quite politely. "I been looking all over the place for you."

"I'LL BET," Old Man Leverette thundered. A rising moon played on his thatch of white hair and whiskers. He's an immense old person, but spry. He squinted at me down his gun barrels. "Durned if you aren't a girl!"

"That's right," I replied, "come to pay you a neighborly call. If you recollect, I dropped in on you last Halloween."

"How many chickens did it cost me that time?" he asked in a threatening voice.

"It was a visit in your best interests. So is this one. Last year I saved your privy from being knocked over. This is your lucky day, as I'm back to do you another good turn."

"If you ain't cool as a cucumber!" Old Man Leverette marveled. His barrels lowered. "Seems like I do recollect a young gal hanging around my privy. What did you say your name was?"

"Letty Shambaugh," I answered, since I always give Letty's name whenever I'm in a tight corner.

He rested his shotgun in the crook of his arm. "Well, Letty, I was just setting to my supper, so talk fast and make it good."

I meant to do my best. "It's like this. Purely by chance I happened to overhear three boys from the high school laying plans to make a regular mess of your front porch and do you an injury the night before Halloween."

"Do tell," Old Man Leverette said. "Who'd you say these boys is?"

"I didn't. Kindly don't interrupt. They mean to set a paper sack of fresh horse manure on the porch floor in front of your door. They're going to ring your bell and set the sack of horse manure afire. Then they'll hide in your shrubbery and watch you run out and stomp on that sack to put the fire out. It could burn your feet and set your nightshirt afire. You could also slip in that mess and break your hip. At your age a broken hip is no joke. Of course, that won't happen now that you've been warned by a responsible person such as myself." I paused to catch my breath.

Old Man Leverette uttered an oath and tugged on his chin whiskers. "The old horse manure stunt," he said in a remembering voice. "We used to pull that one when I was a kid."

"Boys will be boys," I observed, "unless somebody stops them."

"Oh, we'll fix their hash, Letty." A devilish grin lit

up his craggy face. "I suppose you are free the night before Halloween to give me a hand?"

"I can make myself available," I replied, always willing to help out.

"Good." Old Man Leverette then outlined a plan that he devised right there on the spot. It seemed a sure cure for Halloween mischief, and I could see nothing wrong with it.

At that we shook hands on this still-secret plan. I was ready to slip away, but my hand remained locked in Old Man Leverette's big grasp. "If you'll kindly turn me loose," I said, "I'll be on my way."

"You and me has some unfinished business," he rumbled. I felt a sudden chill in the night air. "Chickens."

"Chickens?" I squawked.

Old Man Leverette dragged me out of the henhouse yard and up to his back door. I set my heels, but he was two hundred pounds over my weight.

"Let's us discuss this in a neighborly fashion," I piped. But we'd crossed the threshold into an old-fashioned kitchen. The table was set for one, and the large frying pan on the stovetop was red-hot.

He dragged me to a drainboard. There sat a plump fryer, cut up and rolled in cracker crumbs and ready for the pan. It was even salted and peppered. With his free hand Old Man Leverette reached into a Hoosier cabinet and drew out a checkered napkin.

Then he freed me, saying, "One good turn deserves another. Leave me a drumstick and a thigh,

and you can take the rest home in that napkin."

With a pounding heart, I scooped up chicken parts, making short work of this. I was just sailing through the back door when Old Man Leverette raised his voice.

"I bid you good night, Letty, and the next time I catch you anywheres near my henhouse, YOU'LL BE PICKING ROCK SALT OUT OF YOUR BACK END TILL THE DAY OF JUDGMENT."

I cut and ran.

*

At home I found Mama dozing in her chair. Before her, the cards were laid out in a pattern on the table. She'd been telling herself her own fortune, which puts her to sleep every time. She jerked awake in her usual sudden way.

"You took yore sweet time," she snarled. "A person could have died of starvation and bin cool enough to bury."

Her sharp eye fell on the checkered-napkin parcel swinging in my hand. "What in tarnation do you call that?"

"Supper," I replied briefly.

"That ain't no chicken! Let me remind you a chicken's got claws and feathers and a comb and two little beady eyes. Girl, sometimes I wonder if you got good sense."

I unfolded the napkin on the table with a small flourish.

Mama's eyes widened, and her jaw dropped.

"Well, I'll be a . . . It's cut up and ready for the pan. It's even salted and peppered! Girl, how'd you work that?"

"Powers, Mama." I smiled sweetly. "I got wonderful Powers."

7

ON MY WAY TO SCHOOL the following day I had much on my mind, as I often do.

There was that son of a gun Mr. Lacy, horsing around with two respectable women of the community. Somebody ought to fix his hash.

There was Alexander Armsworth, who was liable to be shocked senseless by Old Man Leverette's plan to foil the vandalism of his front porch. Unless Alexander was given a timely warning.

There was Mama, as there always is. Her sly hints that something was seriously amiss with the old abandoned Leverette farmhouse nagged at me. If I didn't get to the bottom of that for myself, I'd begin to question my Second Sight.

There was even the freshman fund raiser for the Halloween Festival to plague me. I seemed to have no part in planning it whatsoever. A person doesn't like being left out, especially me.

I decided to tackle Alexander first. As Daisy-Rae says, he's standoffish and getting worse. But I figured I owed him a debt. If I hadn't informed Old

Man Leverette about what him and Bub and Champ were planning, then Alexander wouldn't be about to get the daylights scared out of him.

Besides, after I'd saved him from making a jackass of himself, he'd be the one to owe me a debt. I liked the sound of that.

But when we all filed into homeroom that morning, his desk stood empty. Old baldy-headed Miss Blankenship was just closing her door to latecomers when Alexander slipped in.

He darted up the aisle with his head scrunched down between his shoulders and his eyes on the floor. You talk about sheepish. When he slipped into the seat ahead of me, his ears looked on fire.

He'd have looked different to me anyhow since he had his clothes on. But with so much on my mind, I couldn't think why he was looking hangdog and embarrassed to death.

While roll was being taken, I poked him once between the shoulder blades. "Say there, Alexander," I whispered into his red ear, "I got some real important information for you regarding Old Man—"

"Lemme alone, Blossom," he hissed hatefully out of the side of his mouth. "You and me are not on speaking terms, and that's permanent. Keep out of my way, or I won't be responsible for the consequences. I could wring your scrawny neck, and you know why!"

I blinked at these cruel words. From the corner of

my eye I noticed Letty Shambaugh smiling snidely from her seat.

This is no way to start a day. I drooped through till afternoon, lonely as a cloud. Without Daisy-Rae to call on, I'd have considered quitting school. During history class I drifted down to the girls' rest room.

"It's me, Daisy-Rae," I said in that echoing place. The door of her stall edged open. While I propped myself up at the sinks, she eased out of her hiding place when she was sure the coast was clear.

"If you don't look like somethun the cat drug in," she remarked. "Why such a long face?"

Daisy-Rae's face is at least as long on her best day, but I let that pass. "If you'd heard how Alexander Armsworth lit into me this morning, you'd know," I told her.

"Well, what can you expect?" Daisy-Rae said. "After he seen you was spyin' on him buck-naked."

"He seen—saw me?"

Daisy-Rae folded her bony arms across her front and nodded. "Wasn't me and Roderick still hidin' up that tree? Yore Alexander caught sight of you scattin' away through the timber. He had no more sense than to tell that Champ and Bub.

"They both blamed Alexander for the whole thing, sayin' you're sweet on him and foller him wherever he goes."

"That's a dad-burned lie," I said.

"I'm only tellin' you what they said," Daisy-Rae replied. "Say, listen, you wouldn't have nothin' on you to eat, would you? I brought me an apple for lunch, but it didn't stick with me."

As it happened, I'd brought a chicken leg, but I'd been too low in my mind to eat it at lunch. I pulled it out of my pocket and handed it over. Daisy-Rae commenced gnawing on it, lint and all. Soon she was chicken fat from ear to ear.

Watching her work over that drumstick reminded me of Old Man Leverette, so I told her all about his plan and my part in it. "Alexander will have to take his chances," I said with some satisfaction, "now that he won't let me warn him."

Daisy-Rae is a good listener, particularly if you feed her. To the sound of her gnawing, I told her all about how Mr. Lacy was two-timing Miss Fuller with Miss Spaulding. Getting more off my chest, I added, "And I don't have a Chinaman's chance of taking part in the Halloween Festival. Seems like Alexander and Letty have got that all sewed up."

"That ain't all they're up to," Daisy-Rae said, throwing the polished bone reluctantly away. "I eavesdropped on them lollygaggin' in the schoolyard at lunch. Yore Alexander and that Letty's going out tonight to one of them moving picture shows."

I bristled. "Well, if that don't—doesn't take the cake!" I said. "She's set her cap for Alexander, and she's using her position as freshman class president to win him. That snake in the weeds Mr. Lacy could take lessons from Letty!"

And Daisy-Rae agreed, which is what friends are for.

*

That's how me and Daisy-Rae and Roderick happened to attend the moving picture show ourselves that very same Friday night.

If rumor had it that I followed Alexander everywhere he went, then so be it. Besides, I wanted to see for myself how that little simp Letty was playing up to him. Being a boy, Alexander is gullible. Some responsible person might have to save him from Letty's clutches.

Moving pictures are the coming thing, and since Bluff City is a progressive place, we have the Bijou Picture Show, which is downtown on the square.

You'd think two country children such as Daisy-Rae and Roderick would be hard up for novelty. But I had to talk fast to persuade her. She swore she'd get lost in town at night and all the bright lights would strike her blind. You talk about back-woodsy.

In the end I had to meet them in the schoolyard at dusk and lead them downtown. When we got there, though, Daisy-Rae's eyes were big as cartwheels at all the lighted-up shopwindows. When we came to Shambaugh's Select Dry Goods Company, she threw on her brakes.

"Would you look at that?" she said, giving me a nudge. "Ladies' housedresses at ninety-eight cents! Prices is going through the roof. And looky here, a

buck and a quarter for shoes." She hitched up her patched skirt and examined her boot, which was tied to her foot with baling wire. "Lucky for me I still got plenty wear left in this pair."

Roderick pressed his nose against the shopwindow and took everything in, though I doubt he can read prices.

When we got to the square, we hung around in the shadow of the courthouse across from the Bijou. Soon Alexander arrived with Letty on his arm. He paid her way, and into the show they went. Us three followed unnoticed.

In former times I've snuck into the Bijou free at the stage door. But I had three nickels laid back for a rainy day, which this was. So I treated Daisy-Rae and Roderick. Up over the Bijou entrance was a name written in electric lights:

MISS PEARL WHITE

Daisy-Rae nudged me. "Who might she be?"

"Miss Pearl White? Shoot, Daisy-Rae, she's the most famous moving picture star in North America."

"Well, I ain't never been in one of these places before." Dragging Roderick along, she followed me inside.

The lights were dimming for the organ recital. We lingered at the back till we saw Letty and Alexander in two on the aisle up near the screen. Luck was with us, as the row behind them was empty.

"Easy does it," I muttered to Daisy-Rae. Like two Indian scouts—three, if you count Roderick—we

skulked down the aisle and settled silently into seats behind them.

Letty was twitching her little shoulders in a taffeta blouse. Alexander's arm was snaking around her.

"Oh, Alexander, you better not," simpers Letty, "at least till the lights go off."

Daisy-Rae pretended to run her finger down her throat at this sickening scene.

I strained to hear their conversation but only caught snatches. The organ music was swelling up, playing variations on the popular "When You Wore a Tulip and I Wore a Big Red Rose." Still, I heard the odd word or two.

". . . If I do say so myself," Letty remarked, "it is a first-rate idea that nobody but myself would have thought of."

Alexander, who'll agree to anything, nodded. "A Haunted House will show the whole high school there are no flies on the freshman class."

"We can charge a dime admission fee as a fund raiser," smug Letty said. "It will be the best event in the Halloween Festival."

The organ music swelled up to several crescendos, so I was fighting to hear every word there for a while.

". . . A dungeon, naturally," said Letty, ". . . with rubber hose for snakes. A skeleton for one of the closets would be a nice touch. . . ." Et cetera.

Then while I could hear nothing but organ music, they began to elbow one another.

". . . Absolutely not," Letty whined. "You will

have to talk her into it, Alexander. She positively turns my stomach."

"Count me out," said Alexander firmly. "I've dropped Blossom like a bad habit. I'm not speaking to her again. Ever."

But Letty worked her little shoulder nearer Alexander. She reached up and tickled his ear, which went its reddest. "You must make the sacrifice," she said, "in the name of freshman class unity. It's your duty, Alexander, though heaven knows I realize how repulsive and pushy Blossom is."

Next to me Daisy-Rae was making a nasty gesture at Letty's back with one of her fingers. Even Roderick's drooling mouth seemed especially turned down in disgust.

I was spared more of this insulting conversation as the lights went out and the picture began.

At first a public notice was flashed up on the screen:

IF YOU EXPECT TO RATE AS A GENTLEMAN
YOU WILL NOT EXPECTORATE
ON THE FLOOR

Behind us a camera began to grind. Onto the screen flickered the next message:

MISS PEARL WHITE
in the ninth episode of
THE PERILS OF PAULINE

Daisy-Rae nudged me hard. "Which is her name, Pearl or Pauline?"

"Just hush up a minute," I whispered, "and you'll get the hang of it."

"Quiet behind, please," spoke Alexander from the seat ahead.

The whole civilized world knows that in each episode of *The Perils of Pauline*, Pearl White as Pauline defies death and lives to tell the tale. They even flash words on the screen to explain the story, though that's of little use to Roderick.

In Episode Nine, Pauline is fleeing from cannibals down a beach. They're gaining on her, and poor Pauline is about winded. She looks back a lot and runs to beat the band.

Daisy-Rae's fingers closed tight on my arm. Roderick was on the edge of his seat.

The words

PAULINE FLEES INTO THE SURF

flashed on the screen.

She's knee-deep in ocean waves, and the cannibals' spears are flying all around her. Daisy-Rae flinched, and Roderick bobbed and weaved. "She's a goner for sure," Daisy-Rae whispered. But Alexander up ahead didn't shush her this time. Now his arm was creeping around Letty's little shoulders.

Up on the screen Pauline is searching the sea, looking for help.

HELP IS ON THE WAY

Sure enough, out of the sky swoops a hydroplane, a double-winged job skimming the waves.

"Where'd that thing come from?" breathes Daisy-Rae.

Pauline plunges into deep water and begins swimming like a fish. Roderick seemed to be swimming in his seat, throwing his arms around.

A SAFE HAVEN, OR IS IT?

Though the cannibal spears are still whizzing around her, Pauline makes it to the hydroplane and pulls herself up on the wing.

As she staggers into the rear seat, the pilot raises his goggles and grins evilly back at her. He has a slick little mustache and mean eyes.

"I wouldn't trust that dude for a minute," Daisy-Rae remarks, "but I reckon Pauline don't have much choice."

The hydroplane soars into the air, leaving the cannibals behind. Roderick swoops in his seat, turning his arms into hydroplane wings. Alexander begins to nuzzle Letty's neck.

Of course, the hydroplane pilot is Pauline's worst enemy, a two-timer who has deceived her in love.

Since she has already resisted his advances in Episode Eight . . .

HE TAKES HIS REVENGE

The two-timing pilot lights up a cigarette and flicks away the match, which lands on one of the wings.

"Watch out," Daisy-Rae warns. Roderick is all eyes.

The wing smolders and bursts into flames. Pauline sees and clutches her throat. So does Daisy-Rae. The hydroplane begins to wobble. Roderick falls out of his seat but climbs right back into it.

The cowardly pilot stands up, and lo and behold, he's wearing a parachute. In a single bound he jumps from the blazing plane, leaving Pauline defenseless.

CAN PAULINE ESCAPE HER FATE?

"I don't see how!" roars out Daisy-Rae, answering the screen. Roderick is up on the arm of his chair now, riding it like a horse and drooling overtime.

"What a noisy bunch of rough types behind us," Letty remarks to Alexander. "Somebody ought to call the usher and have them thrown out."

The hydroplane goes into a dive. Pauline is trapped in the back seat without a parachute. For some reason, she's now wearing a chiffon scarf, which is blowing far out behind her.

The organ swells up with the sound of a screaming hydroplane, more or less. The ocean looms near as Pauline and her plane go into a spin.

It's too much for Daisy-Rae. There's no point in trying to tell her it's only a show and not real. She comes up out of her seat, shrieking, "THERE AIN'T A MINUTE TO LOSE. SOMEBODY DO SOMETHUN TO HELP THAT PORE GIRL."

Daisy-Rae's flailing elbows accidentally clip the back of Letty's little curly head a nasty whack.

Knocked half out of her seat, Letty says, "This is too much. Alert the usher, Alexander."

He begins to look back—my way. Things are happening so fast now I can hardly think. Besides, Daisy-Rae is hysterical beside me, which is distracting.

As it happens, Roderick, who's brighter than he looks, goes into action.

Just before Alexander turns and sees me behind him, Roderick reaches down into the bib of his little overalls. He draws up one of his mice. A nice plump one with a long gray tail and white whiskers.

Quick as a wink, he reaches forward and drops the rodent down the back of Letty's blouse.

"Oh, Alexander!" she says, striking out at him coyly. "Stop that this minute!"

Alexander throws up both his hands innocently. Then he notices the lump in Letty's blouse. Trapped under that taffeta, the mouse is trying to make its way over Letty's shoulder to freedom. Alexander's eyes grow wide at this moving lump climbing around under Letty's cap sleeve.

Continuing its trip, the mouse seems to lose its footing and falls forward, tumbling into Letty's small bosom.

She looks down, but all I see are the little quivering curls on the back of her head. Then she looks up at Alexander's two free hands. Then the mouse must have started clawing around down in her front.

Letty's plump little fists reach for the sky and grab air. She goes off like a Roman candle.

"SOMEBODY SAVE ME," she whoops. "I AM IN-FESTED." She flies straight out of her chair, clears the row ahead of her, and lands in a heap by the movie screen.

There she does a kind of native dance on her back. Both her hands are jammed down her neckline, and the buttons on her blouse are popping like corn. The audience comes to its feet for a better view, and several applaud.

The organ swells up with variations on "Oh! You Beautiful Doll," and on the screen it says:

RETURN TO THIS THEATER NEXT WEEK
For the THRILLING CONCLUSION

"Let's git while we can." I elbow Daisy-Rae into action. Us three scramble out of our seats and up the aisle.

But I chance a backward glance, and my heart sinks. There's Alexander standing in his row with his hands on his hips in a disgusted pose, looking daggers right at me.

8

NEXT WEEK AT THE HIGH SCHOOL, word of the upcoming Halloween Festival was on every tongue. The halls were decorated with orange and black streamers and twisted crepe paper. All in all, the mood of the place was more festive than my own.

You could learn of each fund raiser class project by reading the various bulletin boards down the main hall, which I did. The seniors were giving a costume ball with a live band at the hotel downtown. The juniors, trying to copy the seniors, were also giving a dance, but in the gym. The sophomores were planning a wienie roast and hayride.

I came at last to a ladder with Tess and Bess, the Beasley twins, on it. They were tacking up the freshman fund raiser poster. I supposed this was their job as sergeants at arms.

The poster, decorated with several jack-o'-lanterns and black cats, read:

FRESHMAN CLASS HAUNTED HOUSE
Enter If You Dare

and
Have the Living Daylights Scared Out of You

❋

Experience: the dank dungeon and the
bat-filled attic

❋

Hear: clanking chains and unexplained sobs

❋

See and Touch: the ghastly remains of former
victims

❋

Also: spiders, snakes, and other attractions
Many Will Enter, but Few Will Survive
Admission 10¢ as a charitable contribution
signed, Letty Shambaugh,
Freshman Class President

While I was reading this corn-fed poster, Tess and
Bess with tack hammers in their hands looked down
from their ladder.

"Why, good morning, Blossom honey," they said
in chorus. They often try to speak together like a
tuneless duet. I looked up in surprise, as I'm not
used to being spoken to by members of Letty's club.

"Isn't a Haunted House the cleverest idea you
ever heard of?" said Tess or Bess.

"We'll be scared to death, literally," the other one
said.

That would be no great loss, I thought. Wandering on, I smelled a rat, as I often do.

As I entered homeroom, Miss Blankenship was

lettering her daily message from *Hamlet* on the board:

TO BE OR NOT TO BE:
THAT IS THE QUESTION
Act III

Halloween or not, Miss Blankenship is always business as usual. Letty was absent. It was Wednesday, and she'd been absent all week, no doubt suffering the lingering effects of mouse infestation.

But Alexander soon entered. He strode down the aisle with shoulders squared. His ears were hardly pink, and his hair was slicked down with Vitalis hair preparation. As I have mentioned, he is not a bad-looking kid.

"Good morning, Blossom." He nodded civilly.

I flinched. Alexander slipped into his desk chair, arranging his pens and setting out his schoolbooks in neat order.

Something is rotten, I thought, *in the state of*—

"Say, listen, Blossom." His head swiveled to me. "What is your opinion of our Haunted House class project?"

"It will prove without doubt that there are no flies on the freshmen," I mocked.

He blinked. "That's what I thought, too." He turned away, but not for long. "By the way, Blossom—"

"I thought you and me weren't speaking, Alexander."

"Oh, that," he said. "I'm not one to carry grudges

and hope you are the same. We have the unity of the freshman class to consider."

"Is that a fact."

Alexander nodded, making a full turn. "How would you like to take part in running the Haunted House?"

I shot him a dangerous look. "How would you like to—"

But the first bell sounded then, and Miss Blankenship turned on us.

"Meet me under the shade tree in the schoolyard at lunch," Alexander whispered importantly. "We'll discuss the matter."

Like Hamlet himself, I could hardly make up my mind all morning. As I was not born yesterday, I knew Alexander was playing up to me only under Letty's orders. For reasons of her own, she'd decided I was to be in on the class fund raiser. I decided to play along just to see what they were up to.

At lunch I awaited Alexander under the shade tree. Daisy-Rae's broken boots were dangling down from a branch, so at least I'd have a witness.

Alexander strolled up. "Well, Blossom, here is the deal. Letty—several of us officers have decided on the various attractions for our Haunted House. Tess and Bess, dressed up as bats, will flit around in the attic. Ione and Harriet and several others will jump out of closets at people. And we're going to dress Champ Ferguson up as a monster, and—"

"Champ Ferguson isn't a freshman," I reminded him.

"I know, but he's almost six foot tall, and we need a monster that size. Nobody'll know him when we get him disguised."

"And what part are you playing in this, Alexander?"

He drew himself up. "I'm in charge of the dungeon, which is in the cellar. I'll be leading customers around in the dark down there and letting them feel the deadman's remains. We'll have a couple of peeled grapes for his eyes and a wet sponge for his brain and some warm spaghetti for his guts and—"

"Hold it," I said. "I've heard enough. Where do I come in on this deal?"

"You'll be the star attraction," he said, "sort of."

"Is that a fact."

"Sure. You're to dress up like a witch—you can borrow some of your mama's clothes—and tell people's fortunes. We'll charge them an extra nickel for the reading."

I gave this some thought. Considering the other corn-fed plans they had for their so-called Haunted House, they could use a star attraction. And they knew it, too. It's a sight how agreeable people can be when they want something out of you.

"Of course," Alexander said, "you can just fake the fortune-telling part."

I bristled. "Fake it? What for? I'll remind you, Alexander, I got Powers and the Second Sight, same as you. You know yourself me and you can see the Unseen and glimpse Other Worlds if we put our minds to it."

"Well, just hush up about that," Alexander said, glancing nervously around. "I have left all that kind of thing behind me, and I don't care to discuss it. Besides, I don't think we have those powers anymore." He cleared his throat. "I haven't been troubled in that way for quite a spell now. I expect it was just a stage that we have outgrown."

"Is that a fact," I replied. "Gimme your hand."

He thrust both his hands into his pockets.

"Gimme your hand, and be quick about it." When I got him to stretch out a hand, I turned it palm up and ran my fingers lightly over it, squinting hard.

"Hmmmmm," says I, "that's real interesting, that is."

"Knock it off, Blossom."

"Oh, yes, I see it clear now." I pointed at random to a little line running across his palm. "Danger lurks in your immediate future."

"Cut it out, Blossom."

"No question about it," I said. "I see . . . I see a dark and windswept night. Not Halloween. No. Sooner than that." Alexander's hand quivered in mine. "I see two—no, three shadowy figures. And . . . what's this? A porch! That's it, a porch. I see these three figures carrying something . . . a sack. PEEE-YEW," I said. "It stinks. I see these three figures carrying this smelly sack up onto the porch."

I checked Alexander's face to see how he was taking this. His eyes were growing wary and dark.

"I see these three figures touching a match to this

nasty sack . . . in front of the door. They're laughing like fools and punching each other on the arms. They're ringing the doorbell now and scampering off the porch. But lo and behold! Something they didn't expect is about to—"

Alexander grabbed his hand away. His ears were burning bright, and his friendly mood was forgotten.

"Very funny, Blossom," he sneered. "As if I didn't know where you came by that information."

"It's all there in your hand, Alexander. As you can see, I'm a first-rate fortune-teller. I could tell more if I felt like it, which I don't."

"You're a first-rate snoop, Blossom. You've snooped on me at the . . . swimming hole, and you've snooped on me at the Bijou Picture Show. My life is hardly worth living, you spidery-legged little—"

"Hold it right there, Alexander." I spoke sternly. "If you get on the wrong side of me, where will you be with Letty? Me and you both know she sent you to sweet-talk me into telling fortunes. It has taken you quite a while to get up your nerve, too, and it's Wednesday already. We are but two days from Halloween, and if you fail in your mission, your name will be mud with Letty. Give it some thought!"

He did.

"For two cents," he muttered, "I'd resign as vice-president. It's not worth the grief."

"Never mind," I said. "This is your lucky day, as I'm willing to overlook your foul temper. I reckon I can make myself available as fortune-teller. Where

are you setting up this so-called Haunted House anyway?"

Looking relieved, Alexander said, "Oh, it's ready-made, and we're decorating it real good. We're using the old abandoned Leverette farmhouse out in the country."

My eyes no doubt popped. "How's that again, Alexander?"

"The old broken-down farmhouse," he explained, "out past the—ah—swimming hole."

I swallowed. "I see. Well now, that puts a new light on things."

Alexander eyed me. "You can't back out now, Blossom. You gave your word."

"Maybe so, but I also gave my word to Mama that I'd never go near that place."

"I will grant you," Alexander said, "that your mama is crazy as a loon and mean as a weasel, but what has she got against that old falling-down house?"

"Don't you know, Alexander?"

"No," he said, but he was looking shifty.

"Mama says that place is haunted or something. I mean, *really* haunted."

"There you go again, Blossom, telling tall tales and lying through your teeth."

"I didn't say a word about it, Alexander. I don't know what particular problem the old Leverette farmhouse suffers from. But I tell you one thing: It suffers from *something*. Mama doesn't kid around."

"In that case," he said, "why don't you just sneak off on Halloween night and don't tell your mama where you're going? The whole town knows you've done that type thing before."

"I might and I might not," I replied. "But I know one thing, Alexander. I'm going to find out what ails that place. It would be a rich joke indeed if the freshman class tried to run a fake Haunted House in a real one. Before I commit myself to telling any fortunes in that place, I mean to find out the truth."

"You do that." Alexander jittered. "You check it out and let me know your decision." He turned then, ready to cut out.

"Not so fast, Alexander. Me and you are going out to the old Leverette place tonight—after dark. With our particular Powers, we ought to be able to plumb its deepest mysteries."

Alexander was shaking his head briskly. "No, you don't, Blossom. You don't drag me into one of your harebrained schemes. You've made up this whole thing to get me alone somewheres. Count me out, and that's final!"

"Very well, Alexander, and maybe you can get Letty Shambaugh to tell fortunes on Halloween night, as I will not be available."

And that's how me and Alexander Armsworth happened to pay a visit in the dead of that very night out to the old Leverette farmhouse beyond Leverette's Woods, to learn for ourselves if that strange place concealed some eerie mystery beneath its sagging roof.

9

I T WAS A DARK AND WINDSWEPT NIGHT, and Alexander was in one of his sulks. He slouched along the country road with a railroad lantern in the crook of his arm and took long strides, trying to outdistance me. Our shadows were long on the road in the light of the bobbing lantern. His only conversation was grunts.

By and by we came along past Leverette's Woods, where the wind was thrashing the treetops. "The entrance to Lovers' Lane is right around here somewheres," I pointed out.

"Oh, no, you don't," Alexander said. "You won't get me into any Lovers' Lane. We'll go around by the pasture." So we were soon waist-high in unmown grass, proceeding across the pasture Indianfile. I had a job to keep up. Alexander wouldn't have minded giving me the slip.

He slowed when the sloping roof of the old Leverette place loomed ahead of us. Then he dropped down in the weeds so quick I nearly fell over him.

"I tripped over a stone," he said, though I didn't see one.

"We better keep moving," I said. "It's cold, and besides, you're going to set the grass afire with that lantern if you're not careful."

"Nag, nag, nag," said Alexander. "I twisted my ankle."

Across the moon an owl flew with some small creature in its claws. The lightning rods on the roof of the old house pointed like daggers at the black sky. From beyond the place came the sighing of a wind pump turning in the breeze. I smelled rain in the air and sensed a storm.

I heard something else then, I swear I did. Clear on the night air, it was a peculiar *pyong, pyong, pyong* with the occasional *beep*. Coming and going, it sent some strange signal.

But I couldn't place it. It was nothing I knew or quite earthly. From the corner of my eye I checked Alexander to see if he'd heard it, too. But it was dark in the weeds, and the lantern seemed to burn lower.

"I think my ankle's swelling. My sock feels tight."

"You'd better give that ankle some exercise," I said, starting up. But as I took my next step toward the house, I froze in my tracks.

All of the many windows in the old abandoned Leverette place were like dead eyes. Except for a window upstairs beneath the drooping drainpipe. From a single room came a dim blue light, flickering, pulsing.

Pyong, I heard distantly. *Pyong, pyong, beep*. A sudden wind went through me, or something did. The racing clouds cleared the moon, and I saw something on the roof among the lightning rods. It was some strange arrangement of rods and sticks stuck up on a small pole. But it faded while I watched.

Then, just for an instant, the whole place glowed. From every window in the house white light poured, throwing pale shapes on the untended yard.

It was electric light, but of course, the old Leverette place had never been wired for electricity. Old Man Leverette doesn't even have electricity in his residence in Bluff City. I blinked, and the house went black again. Maybe a little blue sparked from the upstairs window again, then utter darkness.

I settled back in the weeds beside Alexander. He was bent low, examining his ankle. Or hiding his eyes. I decided to wait until he'd gathered what courage he had.

The old wind pump sighed again. Dry leaves scudded out in swirls from the woods. Just to liven up Alexander a little, I spoke the following lines in a spooky voice, right in his ear:

" 'Tis now the very witching time of night,
When churchyards yawn and hell itself breathes out
Contagion to this world. . . ."

All of Alexander's hair seemed to stand up on his head. Even his beanie quivered. "Would you shut up with that kind of talk. Where'd you get it anyhow?"

"It's *Hamlet*," I explained, "Act Three. Don't you ever read the blackboard?"

"This isn't English class," he snapped, "so cut it out. It's getting late, and I'd better be getting—"

"You're right," I said fast. "We'd better conduct our investigation. We wouldn't want midnight to find us in *that* place."

I jumped up and headed for the house, as brave as possible under the circumstances. Alexander had no choice but to follow. Thunder rolled out of the distance, following a lightning flash.

At the top of a flight of wooden steps the porch was in deep shadow. Dead autumn leaves crunched beneath our boots, and Alexander tried to take charge. He held the lantern aloft at the front door. Over it a sign had recently been tacked up. It was orange cardboard with squiggly black letters that read:

REPENT WHAT'S PAST;
AVOID WHAT IS TO COME

"Tess and Bess did that sign for the entrance," Alexander explained. "It's a nice, scary motto."

"It's from *Hamlet*," I said, "also Act Three." We stepped inside, Alexander politely letting me go first.

In the front hall the lantern threw red light across curling wallpaper and up a long stairway. "Here's where we'll collect the admission fees," Alexander said in a breaking voice. "We'll have a couple jack-o'-lanterns around for light. The cobwebs are real."

I touched his sleeve to quiet him. We stood in that

shadowy place while I listened to the house. If I started Vibrating and picking up messages with my inner ear and my special Powers, I wanted to be close to the front door. But I heard nothing except the wind in the eaves and a spatter of rain in the gutters. Far off, a loose shutter clapped against the house.

"Quit listening," Alexander muttered. "You're just asking for trouble."

Never a step ahead of me, he gave us a tour. The dining room was bare except for trash and an old-fashioned gasolier fixture hanging down from the ceiling.

"Harriet Hochhuth is going to hang in that china closet over there. We're going to string her up with wires as an artificial corpse."

Alexander scooted through a door, taking the lantern and leaving me in darkness. "This here's the kitchen," he hollered. I skipped on into the so-called kitchen, which was a filthy mess.

"We're going to stretch Champ Ferguson out on this drainboard," Alexander explained, "and disguise him as a monster, which we're sewing together from spare parts found in a graveyard. There'll be a big bucket of grape juice for blood. That's one of my own crackerjack ideas."

"And over there"—Alexander pointed—"are the stairs to the cellar, where we're setting up the deadman's dungeon and model torture chamber." He turned his back on the black cellar stairs, making it clear he wasn't going down there tonight.

"Where am I to tell my fortunes?" I asked. "I wouldn't mind a well-aired spot. This kitchen smells like a bear's breath."

"You'll be upstairs in one of the bedrooms," Alexander said in an offhand way. "We don't have time to wander around up there."

He was more than ready to leave right then.

"Listen, Alexander," I said, "we've come out here to give this house a thorough investigation. We aren't going to learn a thing with a quick look around a couple of rooms."

He sulked.

"It's all right if you're afraid to go upstairs with me," I said. "I understand."

I had him there. He wasn't about to hang around down here all by his lonesome. His imagination was already working overtime.

We were in the dining room again as Alexander edged toward the front door. He knew he was going to have to go upstairs with me, but he was putting it off. Setting the lantern on the floor, he reached down to rub his so-called twisted ankle.

Suddenly, right behind him, I saw a small wink of light, bright in the lantern glow. I'd like to have turned to stone. My mouth fell open. Alexander happened to notice my bugging eyes.

Slowly, slowly he turned to look behind himself, his face as white as this page. The brass knob on the china closet door was winking in the light and turning.

My boots seemed nailed to the floor, and Alex-

ander began to sway. Still the knob kept turning, all by itself.

Squeaking on its hinges, the door opened upon the blackness of a tomb within. Peering from inside was a frightful sight, a face not quite human in the flickering lantern flame. It appeared to be an ungrinning skull.

"Oh, I will be a good boy for the rest of my life," Alexander moaned, "if only this isn't happening!"

He sagged, but he couldn't run any more than I could. The ghastly little face looked up into Alexander's tear-filled eyes. The terrible little mouth drooled. It was Roderick.

He stepped out of the china closet in his small pair of bib overalls.

"What say, Roderick?" I greeted him, though my mouth was dry. Roderick looked us over but said nothing.

"Who," moaned Alexander, "who in the—"

But the kitchen door banged open then, sending a shudder through the house. Footsteps stalked, and another fearful apparition appeared in the dining room door. Alexander's head swiveled toward this new horror. He grabbed his throat.

Daisy-Rae marched in. "There you are, you little rascal!" She was wearing a feed sack nightgown and a nightcap of faded flannelette. Sweeping Alexander aside, she made a grab for Roderick and hooked him by the ear.

"Ain't I told you time and agin not to slip off? It's a-way past your bedtime!"

Alexander's eyes were like saucers, and in truth, Daisy-Rae in her night togs is a sight. He managed to stand clear of her flailing elbows as she nearly shook Roderick loose from his ear.

"Who," Alexander moaned again, "who in the—"

"Hey there, Blossom," Daisy-Rae said, nodding her wan face at me.

"Hey there, Daisy-Rae," I replied.

"Be glad you ain't got any little brothers," she said. "They are a continual worry. It's my own fault. I had no more sense than to tell Roderick here that you and yore Alexander was coming over tonight to check over this place for haunts. Naturally the little scamp had to spy on you. You know how he is." Roderick's neck seemed permanently bent, but she never turned him loose.

Out of the room she marched, quick as she'd come. Roderick scampered by her side, trying to keep up with his ear. The back door banged behind them as off they went to their chicken coop home.

After a long pause Alexander spoke. "Don't tell me. I don't even want to know."

❖

Delay it though he would, it was time to explore upstairs. The thought of those throbbing blue lights in the upper window skated past my mind. But I planted a firm foot on the stairs, keeping Alexander by me. Thunder crashed above the attic. Lantern light wobbled on the treads as we climbed up through the house. The things that live in walls skit-

tered, seeming to warn one another. Cobwebs swept our beanies and caressed our ears.

Where the stairs curved at the top, I dropped back a little just to see how far ahead of me Alexander would go. The ceiling had fallen up there, so he crunched along a step or two over broken plaster, holding his lantern high.

Alexander opened the first door he came to and banged it shut again. Making a strangled sound, he took flight and shot into the next room he saw. After a moment he spoke in a hollow voice. "Now here is a good room for your fortune-telling, Blossom. Yes, this will do very well."

I was standing in the upstairs hall. Even without the lantern I could still see. My gaze fell to the door Alexander had opened and closed so quick. There was a line of light under it, bright across the dusty hall floor.

It glowed like daylight but whiter. To save my soul I couldn't walk past that door. I looked back down the curving stairs into blackness.

"Get in here, Blossom!" Alexander called out from a far room. "Don't go near that door! You hear me? There's something there. I don't know what, but . . . something."

I hardly heard him. Everything faded except for the light beneath the mystery door. All by itself my hand reached for the knob.

10

LIGHTNING SPLIT THE AIR, traveling down the rods on the roof. It clamped my hand to the doorknob. I couldn't turn loose or turn back now. My skin sizzled, and the door blew in, jerking me half out of my boots.

Inside, the light like a white fog peeled my eyeballs and took me prisoner. The sounds I'd heard in the distance were clearer and nearer: the *pyongs* and the *beeps* alike. They were no noise of nature or the human voice.

Suddenly I was free of the electrified doorknob, so I threw up my hands, thinking I'd be burned by the light. But it was cold. Then I was drawn like an autumn leaf into a funnel of brightness. I swam in this spiral, never trying to breathe. My kinky hair flattened against my skull as I gathered speed. My spelling medal flapped like a loose shutter against my chest.

I seemed to shriek, though no one heard, not even me. But my thoughts cried out. *Oh, Mama, you were right. I never should have come near this place. . . .*

But it was too late. Whatever was to befall me now was happening already.

I traveled in a great void past thunder and beyond lightning. But I wasn't alone, far from it. Looming up from every side were creatures far worse than any in Alexander's dungeon or model torture chamber. There were circular monsters that were all mouth. There were creatures with lights for eyes and steel for skin who wielded long glowing tubes of light for swords. Their dreadful jaws snapped at me in passing, and those bright swords of light tried to snag me. But I hurtled on.

Then, don't ask me how, I was swimming up through dry waters. Square ahead of me stretched a glassy skin like the ice on a pond as seen by a fish. I rocketed nearer this cruel barrier, expecting to batter out my brains.

In an explosion of ice or glass, I burst through. Gasping with my first breath, I did a neat somersault in real air and fell flat on my back on a carpeted floor. My eyeteeth were all jarred loose. Though I was as dizzy as a swung cat, I tried to raise up on my elbows.

Looking toward a door, I saw I was still in the old Leverette place. The bedroom door was painted now, but I knew the knob. Though I saw where I was, I'd fallen out of my time. Or I'd been pushed.

"Oh, wow," said a voice quite near me. "I've pushed DELETE and RETURN. What more can I do?"

*

My beanie was over my ear, but my mind was clearing. Cautiously I scanned the bright room. A bookshelf without books held long rows of narrow boxes in bright colors.

Beside them was a sight that made me shrink. It was a creature nearly my height. I'd seen it not moments before, or a near cousin to it, hurtling through space. It had a cast-iron face and a long tube of glowing light that it brandished for a sword.

I chanced another look at this specimen. It was only a large, air-filled doll. The wicked iron face was painted onto a slick skin that may have been rubber. It was a monster-shaped toy or perhaps a work of art. There is no accounting for taste.

My shifting glance fell upon a wall calendar. It was decorated with more monsters conducting warfare in tin airships. But it was the date on the calendar that burned my brain.

I raised a trembling hand to count on my fingers. Arithmetic is not my best subject, but from the year on the calendar I saw I'd slipped ahead near enough . . . seventy years.

My eyes dropped to the floor. There was someone in the room with me. I'd known that right along. I was stretched out beside a table and chair. There were several legs, two of them human.

Planted on the carpet were two things of white rubber and colored canvas. Figuring they were shoes, I took a closer look. Written on these so-called shoes were little words:

ADIDAS

I chanced a look up the legs. They weren't long and were covered by ordinary blue denim work pants, somewhat farmerish. Well worn, too. I craned my neck to read a small announcement stitched to the seat:

SEARS TOUGHSKINS

Still, nothing moved but me. Above the pants was a plain cotton shirt stretched over a boy's torso. It was short-sleeved of the undershirt variety. I was up on my knees now beside the occupied chair. This undershirt was lettered boldly across the chest:

PAC-MAN FEVER

I looked up into the face of a boy.

He was a kid of thirteen or so—eighth grade, tops. Except he would not be born for many years. I knew that much. His cheeks were freckled, and a shock of red hair hung on his forehead. Propped on his nose were spectacles that gave him a learned look.

He sat at a desk before the keyboard of a thing like a typewriting machine. There were other buttons and a lever before him and a variety of metal boxes. One of them contained a window with a small curl of gray smoke rising out of the shattered pane. That was where I'd entered this particular world.

The boy looked worried. My nose was near his thigh, since I'd been reading his outfit. Being a boy, he was trying to be brave. Still, his elbow edged away from me, though he seemed rooted to his chair.

"Oh, wow," he said again. "And they call this model state-of-the-art." Somewhat disgusted, he smacked the keyboard of his machine with the heel of his hand. "I guess I could try the CLEAR key or maybe GOTO. They promised open-ended options, but this is ridiculous."

"You can say that again," I remarked.

That moved him. He jerked up his Adidas feet and grabbed himself. "You can *talk*," he gasped.

"And what's more, I can make sense," I replied, "which is more than you're doing."

"Wow," he pondered, "I didn't think even Atari had the chips for speech yet. I hadn't counted on a voice option. I can't seem to get a fix on this model." He gave the keyboard another thump.

"It's an off brand," he went on, "a loaner from off the showroom floor. Its hardware is fairly primitive, and I can't say much for its peripherals. I traded in my Atari 2600 VCS, which is somewhere between obsolescent and obsolete. Now I'm waiting to take delivery on the 5200, which is basically a teen toy and actually reasonably sophisticated for adult games. I'm in the Gifted Program myself."

"Is that a fact," I said. "You speak any English?"

He blinked at me in wonder and rubbed his chin in thought. "I guess I sort of . . . made you happen," he remarked. "In the Career Discovery module at

school I'm already locked into Systems Analysis as a life's work, but now I wonder. With you, I guess I sort of looped when I should have branched. Where'd you come from?"

"Bluff City," I answered cautiously.

He nodded. "You do look sort of inner-city. But what I meant was, what *game* are you from?"

One of his fingers edged out to press a key on his board. He seemed to think he had to push certain buttons to make me talk sense.

"I mean, like, are you from Berzerk or Demons to Diamonds or Donkey Kong or Chopper Command or what?"

"Listen, bud," I replied, "this is getting us nowhere."

"Let me put it this way," he said. "We can always erase if we aren't achieving interface. Are you composed of electronic impulses, or are you just a bug in my flow chart?" He slapped his machines again. "I'm going to have to know where to store you. In this model I've only got sixteen K of RAM."

"RAM?" I inquired.

He blinked again. "Random Access Memory."

"Let's look at this whole thing another way," I said. "And hold off on that talk about erasing me. I've been through enough already. Where I came from, we were having an electrical storm. Thunder, lightning—you follow me?"

"We were having a storm, too," he said, "but it's clearing off now." He jerked his head toward a window, but I dared not yet look outdoors into more

of his world. "Maybe it was the same storm?" He rubbed his chin in thought once more.

"Maybe," I said, more cautious than before.

Through the round spectacles his eyes searched me. "What's that thing on top of your . . . hair?"

I reached up slowly. A steel helmet with horns and a flashing light wouldn't have surprised me. But it was only my beanie, hanging by a hatpin.

He squinted at me. "You sure you're not a game component? You know, an animation. Your . . . hat has numbers on it. What does eighteen stand for? That doesn't compute with me."

Well, of course, there were numbers on my beanie, same as any other freshman's. "That's our graduation year," I said without thinking. "We graduate from Bluff City High School in 1918." My mouth clamped shut on this information. It seemed to seal my fate.

"Oh, wow," the boy breathed, and thunder rolled over distant hills. The metal box before him emitted a single *pyong* and then a solitary *beep*.

*

There was nothing simple about my situation, but it boiled down to this. My Second Sight and the lightning and maybe something else had ganged up on me. I'd slipped through time into the distant decade of the 1980s without leaving this upstairs room of the old abandoned Leverette farmhouse.

But in this future world the farmhouse was abandoned no longer. Somebody had remodeled the old

place, making it strictly modern and then some. This upstairs bedroom was now occupied by a boy named Jeremy. Though he managed to introduce himself, he was still halfway convinced that he'd created me in his machines, "programmed me," as he kept saying. He even made me acquainted with his equipment, his "power supply transformer" and his "television interface box," his "joystick" and his "paddles." You never heard such gibberish.

When I could get a word in, I said, "You can call me Blossom."

"Outrageous," he replied. "You got to be kidding. That's better than Tron." He slapped a knee and chortled.

"Listen, buster—Jeremy, this is no laughing matter. What we have here is a serious problem. I happen to have considerable Powers of the occult type and have wandered out of my time before. But never this far."

Jeremy waved a hand. "Oh, I got that figured. My black box has been malfunctioning all evening. The electrical storm—maybe two storms, one at your end and one at mine—messed up my computer's head. It picked up on you. Due to a long shot circuitry-wise, you basically just slipped into a time warp."

"A what?"

"It's a well-known phenomenon," Jeremy replied. "You're definitely not up on your Ursula Le Guin, your Isaac Asimov, or your Madeleine L'Engle, are you?"

"Not entirely," I muttered, figuring these three probably hadn't been born yet.

"The time warp is in all the sci-fi literature as a distinct potential, so it stands to reason, doesn't it?" He spoke confidently, but his eyes weren't so sure.

I creaked up from the carpet, bruised both fore and aft. Tripping through a time warp is similar to falling out of a tree. My gray princess dress, which I wear for every day now, and an old coat of Mama's with a ratty fur collar were half wrenched off my body.

Jeremy gave my togs an interested stare. "Funky," he remarked. "Is your gear recycled?"

But I'd turned from where he sat to the door with the familiar knob. Hoping against hope, I thought that beyond the door I might find myself again in the plaster-strewn hall of the old abandoned Leverette place. Just maybe Alexander might be out there, holding his lantern aloft in the dark, waiting for me.

Limping across the room, I peered around the door. The hallway was brightly lit. The floor was smooth with polish. High on the opposite wall was a round device with a small red light in it. Written on this object was a motto:

SMOKE ALERT

I glanced down the curving stairs. On the window at the landing was another motto, glued to the glass:

THIS HOUSE PROTECTED
BY ELECTRONIC SURVEILLANCE

I banged the door shut. All escape was cut off.

Not far from panic, I raced back across the room to the dreaded window. Sweeping curtains aside, I stared out into the night. Icy fingers of fear gripped my vitals.

"The wind pump," I whispered, "it's gone. And right about there should be the chicken coop where Daisy-Rae lives with her little brother, Roderick."

"Who?" said Jeremy softly.

"And the woods. They ought to be right over there, with the little gate to Lovers' Lane. Why, me and Mama have all but lived off them woods in lean times, what with the hickory nuts and squirrel stew."

"Squirrel what?" asked Jeremy.

But where all these familiar landmarks should be was a blanket of twinkling lights as far as the eye could see. Just where the gate to the woods should be two paved streets crossed.

Above them was an electrified lantern, sending out a beam of green light. As I watched, it was joined briefly by a yellow light. Then they blew out, and on came a red one. I shivered at this strange signal.

There was a house on every corner, glowing with white light. On each roof was an elaborate lightning rod or something very like one. In the distance beyond the ruined woods where the swimming hole should be were two brightly lighted golden arches and a sign blazing white fire that read:

McDonald's
40 Billion Sold

Clutching my forehead, I turned to the boy.

"Don't tell me Bluff City's grown all the way out here, Jeremy. Why, we're a couple of miles from the Courthouse Square!"

"Bluff City?" he said. "Oh, we never go there. There's not much to Bluff City except parking lots and urban renewal. Where we are is Bluffleigh Heights, basically one of your better upper-middle-class suburbs."

"I see," I said untruthfully. "Then I take it you don't go to Horace Mann School?"

"Where?" said Jeremy. "I'm in eighth grade at Bluffleigh Heights Magnet Middle School. I'm in the Gifted Program."

"So you said," I remarked. "And what does the Gifted Program mean . . . basically?"

"It means we're all reading at or near grade level and pretty heavy into computer math."

I gave this some thought. "You mean you can do your homework on that . . . computer thing?" I jerked a thumb at his machines.

"How else?" Jeremy gave his black box a small pat. "Homework, of course," he said, "and video games."

"Games?"

"I've got them all: Yar's Revenge, The Empire Strikes Back, Kaboom, Star Strike, Night Stalker,

Moon Master, Defender, Atlantis, you name it. Here I've got real arcade action, you know?

"I was up to here with coin-op games. Now I don't even have to leave the house except to go to school. And we're hoping for a breakthrough even there. I foresee the time when we can hook into a master control and attend classes without even getting out of bed. You could completely Betamax your absenteeism, you know?

"I mean the technology's there already. It's just a matter of breaking through an entrenched bureaucracy and knocking out the power of the athletic department that wants you actually there up in the stands, supporting the teams. Basically it's just a question of time before—"

It was no good. I had no doubt Jeremy was making sense in his way, but I was only catching every other word. At least he was a human being and not a monster with a metal face or that big blown-up dummy that stood under his calendar.

I noticed something else in Jeremy, too, for figuring out people is one of my Gifts. He was a lonesome boy up in his room surrounded by his machines and creatures. It was a lonely place, this future.

The thought brought a couple of rare tears to my eyes. I'd never had a favored position even in my own world of 1914. But I missed it now. The homesickness for my vanished place flooded through me and spilled out at my eyes.

"I've got to get back, Jeremy. I'm needed elsewhere. I've got to get back to teach Alexander and Bub and Champ a lesson when they pull that prank on Old Man Leverette's porch tomorrow night. I've got to get back and straighten out that two-timing Mr. Lacy, who's sparking Miss Spaulding and Miss Fuller all at once. I've got to get back and tell fortunes at our freshman class Haunted House. Halloween's the day after tomorrow!"

Jeremy blinked at me through his round spectacles, as I pointed out into the night. I have a long and bony forefinger which I inherited from Mama. I pointed it out into the dreadful, glittering night of Bluffleigh Heights.

"Home . . ." I moaned in a strangled voice.

Jeremy rubbed his chin, deep in thought. His gaze dropped to a small white instrument among the other machines on his desk. It had a curly cord and a small barbell arrangement resting on a stand with small numbered buttons. "I don't suppose you could . . . phone . . ." he mumbled.

Then far down in the house a door banged. Heavy footsteps stamped up the stairs.

Jeremy quivered, and his gaze darted to the door. "Oh, wow," he said.

11

"With any luck," Jeremy said in a low voice, "it'll be Mom, home from her Parents Without Partners meeting."

"And without any luck?" I wondered.

"It'll be my sister." He spoke in a grave voice and wrung his hands. "What am I going to *do* with you?"

He sized me up again, though he'd been staring holes in me ever since I . . . arrived. "Quick," he said, "get over by my Darth Vader."

"Your what?"

"That plastic thing." He pointed at the artificial monster. "Stand over by it, and don't move. Hold your pose. *Freeze.*"

Just as the doorknob rattled, I lifted my skirts and took a giant leap, landing next to the Darth doll. It was staring out at the room, and suddenly so was I. Me and it stood cheek to cheek. The door banged back.

Somehow Jeremy made it to his chair. Looking up with a casual air, he said, "Hi, Tiffany. What are you doing home? Did the mall close?"

An overfed girl of sixteen or so shambled into the room. Without shifting my eyeballs, I caught a terrifying glimpse of her.

She'd cut her skirt in two, for it hit her well above two large and naked knees. Over her big chest she wore a flimsy shirt with some small animal stitched to the left side, possibly an alligator.

Her face was made up for some dreadful stage drama, purple at the lips and green along the lids. But her hair was worse. It was plucked half out of her head and chopped off. Wisps at the side were dyed pink. She wore earphones like a telephone company operator.

"HEY, TIFFANY," Jeremy roared, "HOW ABOUT GETTING OUT OF MY ROOM?"

She was a slow girl and possibly deaf. She pulled the plug from one of her ears. Like my mama, she pierced her ears. But . . . Tiffany had pierced hers three times on each side. Gaudy bangles hung down from her lobes.

"Just shut up for like one minute, you little space cadet," she remarked to Jeremy. "I'm totally into Billy Joel's 'The Nylon Curtain.' " She was tapping one large foot in a rhythm, and so she may have been getting music from out of her earplugs, or thought she was. " 'Combat Rock' with Clash is coming up."

"Just . . . get . . . outta . . . my . . . room, okay?" Jeremy said to her. "Please."

"Chill out, nerd," she responded. "Have a Dorito."

She slouched across the room and offered a cellophane sack of something to Jeremy. I could have reached out and touched her, but I never moved. She smelled unpleasantly of perfume and tobacco, both stale.

"Did I get any calls?"

Jeremy shook his head.

"I can't handle it," Tiffany said. "Mom home yet?"

Again Jeremy shook his head and pretended to press several keys on his machine.

"Awesome," she remarked. "Then I'm like the boss here, you know? Hey, look!" Her hand swept out to point at the broken window on Jeremy's machine, scattering the Dorito things all over. "You totaled your screen, you little airhead. Like don't even *consider* borrowing my Sony."

The very thought of anybody borrowing her . . . Sony seemed to turn Tiffany into a raging beast. She whirled my way and punched Darth Vader beside me. It hit the wall and bounced back. If she had another punch to deliver, I'd take it full in the face. Still, I never moved or even blinked.

"Like, aren't you a little old for dolls?" she sneered at Jeremy. "Ew, these are super skanky." She gestured at me and Darth. "Like Barf City. Gross me out. Totally."

"Just . . . get . . . outta . . . my room, Tiffany," Jeremy said hopelessly.

"Who needs you, honker?" Tiffany slumped from

the room and banged the door behind her. I'd never heard tell of a girl named for a lamp before, though this one was none too bright.

Jeremy wiped small beads of sweat off his forehead. He blinked at me like I might not come to life again. I blinked back, glad for the chance, and stepped out of my pose.

"That is one bad-tempered girl," I remarked. "What's put her in such a mean mood?"

"Tiffany?" Jeremy said. "Oh, that's as good as she gets. Basically I guess it's because we're from a broken home."

I scanned the room again. It looked all right to me. "The roof fell in on me and Mama once," I said. "And the porch has fallen off the house a couple times."

Jeremy stared. "Not that kind of broken home," he explained. "I mean our mom and dad don't live together anymore. Dad's living in a singles condo complex out on the Airport Highway."

"Oh, well, shoot," I responded. "I'm in a similar situation myself. The last time we saw my paw, he was hopping a freight for Centralia."

Jeremy poked his spectacles higher on his nose. "You mean in olden times you people had divorce?"

"Well, I don't know about divorce," I said. "That sounds expensive."

"I thought that all you did was pop corn and bake bread and sit around the fire telling stories and laughing a lot. It's on all the Christmas cards."

I decided not to try to explain to him about Mama.

*

I spent a restless night, though it gave me time to ponder. There were a couple of beds, one stacked upon the other. Jeremy sent me up a ladder to the top one. I was to sleep up there flat against the wall where nobody could see me.

I may have dozed, for I seemed to dream of pages fluttering off a calendar decorated with rocket ships. I dreamed, too, of Alexander Armsworth holding his lantern aloft in the immense distance. Waking once, I sensed some newcomer in the room. It must have been Jeremy's mama. Light from the hall slanted across the room, and a figure approached to check on him. But when she went away, she eased the door shut with care, so it couldn't have been Tiffany.

Toward morning I was awake again. "Jeremy?" I said quietly.

"Yes?" He was as awake as me.

"I've been giving this entire mess some thought. It couldn't have been the storm and your machines that brought me here. Not entirely. My particular Gift works in a different way. Seems like I'm drawn out of my time to those in need."

There was silence in the bed below.

"Do you follow this line of thought?" I inquired.

"Yes," he said. "Need. I'm going to need some replacement parts. The screen, of course, and all the

circuitry governing the editing function and error detection. We're talking in the neighborhood of a couple hundred bucks over the warranty just to get even. But I can cover it."

I sighed. "If you're talking about your machines, Jeremy, that's not quite the kind of need I meant."

*

Then, while I was resting my eyes, it was suddenly daylight in the room. A shock of red hair and two eyes appeared by my pillow. Jeremy hooked his spectacles over his ears and gave me more close looks. We were about nose to nose, but still he stared. He even studied Mama's old fur piece around my neck like it might be growing on me.

"You're still . . . here," he said quietly. "I guess we better consider your . . . bodily functions."

"Whoa!" says I. "Listen, where I come from we don't discuss that type thing in mixed company."

"Well, my bathroom's right through that door if you need it, and . . . do you eat?"

What did he take me for? I gave him a disgusted look, and he decided to check out the house, darting for the door in a pair of pajamas printed all over with moons and airships.

As I was climbing down the ladder from my so-called bed, Jeremy ran into his sister in the hall outside. I froze to hear her greet him in her rude way. She called him both nerd and honker and invited him to bag his face. Then she lumbered off down the

stairs. The house rocked as Tiffany banged out the front door.

Jeremy popped back into the room. "The coast is clear," he announced. "I heard Mom's Trans Am tool out of the garage before I got up. She's an interior decorator."

Though this meant little to me, it seemed to calm him. "Come on," he said. "Let's find some breakfast."

I hung back, not scared exactly, but a little uncertain.

"It's okay," he said, but still, I was far from sure. He walked over to where I stood, digging my toe into the carpet. "Don't worry." A little shy himself, he put out a hand and took mine.

It was quiet then, but for the cheeping of a bird or two outside the window. *At least they haven't done away with birds,* I thought.

Jeremy peered at me in his thoughtful way. "I guess you'd be a real old lady now if you . . . I mean, you know what I mean."

I nodded. "I guess I'd be a real old lady or . . . out of the picture entirely." I pointed to the ceiling. In the mornings I tend to be moody.

"Well, anyway," said Jeremy, "come on. We can't hang around up here all day. I don't have a chance of sending you back till I can give my equipment a little TLC. We've got to go to school."

I hadn't thought of that.

"School? I'm a fugitive from 1914, Jeremy.

They'd drop a net over me and put me in a side-show!"

"Oh, just chill out on that, Blossom," he said. "I got that part all programmed. You can leave that to me."

So having little choice, I followed him out into his world, though my spirits were not high. There was more trouble ahead. It stood to reason.

12

As far as I could see, every corner of the old Leverette farmhouse had been brought up-to-date. Though it was not to my taste, it was all strictly modern.

In my opinion, the kitchen went too far. It was one machine after another, each with its own name: Cuisinart and Frigidaire and Hotpoint and Whirlpool. It was all microwave this and radar control that.

I looked for the drainboard where Alexander was going to stretch out Champ Ferguson for a monster. In its place were big double sinks and a drain that chopped up the garbage and ate it.

When Jeremy showed me how this so-called garbage disposal worked, I remarked, "You don't leave much for the hogs."

He shook his head. "It's against the zoning to keep livestock in Bluffleigh Heights. I guess you people in the olden times kept a lot of hogs and chickens around."

"I have handled no hogs," I replied, "but I've kept a chicken or two."

We were to eat our breakfast on high stools drawn up to a slick counter. Jeremy slid a bowl before me. "This is basically a high-fiber whole-grain product with dried fruit and wheat germ additives and minimal preservatives."

"It looks like fodder to me," I said suspiciously. "What's fodder?"

"It's what you'd find in the nose bag of a horse," I said. "Tastes like it, too."

We washed this mess down with a couple glasses of what Jeremy called a vitamin C concentrate. I've personally had better grub out of Mama's kitchen, which is only a cookstove and a cupboard, basically.

The little clock on the counter flashed the time in red numbers. Jeremy noticed and said, "Just stay here, Blossom. I'll be right back. Then you'll see how we're going to pull off going to school together. It'll be a real scam. Trust me." He charged out of the kitchen in his airship pajamas.

What could I do? I was a stranger in strange parts. I sat waiting as the high-fiber whole-grain product settled like a brick in the pit of my stomach. The clever little so-called clock flashed 8:07, then 8:08.

I wondered how I was to pass unnoticed in Jeremy's magnet middle school. I thought of Daisy-Rae holed up in her stall of the rest room and wondered if that was a possibility for me. Away my mind wandered.

It'd been a hard night, and my guard was down. Maybe I heard a noise outside the house, maybe not.

Suddenly footsteps sounded on the back porch. I about jumped out of my skin and fell off the stool.

A key fumbled for the back door lock. There I sprawled in a heap on the kitchen floor, and in the wrong decade altogether. The key turned. I'd never make it to the dining room. There was a big double-door electrified icebox nearby. With any luck, I might squeeze in between it and the wall. I made one of my giant leaps.

Planting one boot in the little space, I was knocked nearly senseless by a collection of brooms and mops that keeled out on my head. There was hardly room for them, and none for me. When the kitchen door opened, I was standing right by it in full view.

A woman entered. She carried a ring of keys and a large paper bag of supplies. It hid her face from me and mine from her. She wore pants like a man and high-heeled shoes, which is one odd combination. Staggering under her load, she brushed past me.

I never moved, though I slewed my eyes around to the door. If I budged, she'd notice. But I might make a clean getaway. Still, I didn't like leaving the house on my own, never knowing what new threat might wait for me outside.

The woman eased her bag onto the counter and began taking various grocery items out of it. She had Jeremy's red hair, and I figured she was his mama. I was about to surrender myself to her and hope for the best, though it's always difficult to

explain anything to a mother. I took one brave step forward and began to clear my throat.

At that moment she reached into her grocery bag and hefted out a cardboard container, labeled "LIGHTLY LUSCIOUS LOW-FAT MILK." She jerked open a door on the icebox, and it caught me square in the face. I slammed back into the corner by the brooms. My nose seemed mashed level with my cheeks, and it hurt too bad to cry.

The woman continued with her tasks, jamming various items into cupboards. She reached up and turned the knob of a small device sitting on a high shelf.

Though my nose was throbbing, I gaped in wonder. In the window of this gadget a tiny man appeared. The kitchen filled with the sound of his piping voice. It was some kind of improvement on the Bijou Picture Show moving pictures, with color and noise added. The cheerful little man on the screen was doing exercises to music, much as Miss Fuller operates in Girls' Gym. The midget man danced about like a cunning monkey. He had a head of hair as frizzy as my own.

"Well, now I've seen everything!" I exclaimed, but Jeremy's mama never heard me. Her hands were busy with her chores, and her eyes were glued on the little exercise man. But she was about to get a shock. And so was I.

A fearful figure entered from the dining room. Though the creature was not tall, it filled up the door from side to side. Its skin was silver, and its

arms and legs were ringed like thick snakes. Its knees were large shiny circles, and its boots were of tremendous size. Something like a fishbowl served for its head. It grunted.

I was speechless, but Jeremy's mama took one look and let rip an almighty scream. In her hand had been a box labeled "FRUIT LOOPS." This object went soaring through the air, narrowly missing me.

Her hands clapped over her heart, and she slumped. "Oh, Jeremy," she said, "what are you doing in that thing, and why aren't you in school?"

His voice came from far off inside the fishbowl.

"Hi, Mom. We're wearing costumes today. It's the school Halloween party. I'm just leaving."

By squinting, I could make out his face blurred behind curved glass. It was Jeremy's voice, too, more or less. His eyes shifted to me, and he sized up the situation. I saw he was going to keep his mama talking while we got out of there somehow.

"Did Tiffany wear a costume to school?" she asked.

"Mom, you know those high school kids think they're too grown-up for that. Besides, Tiffany looks like Halloween all year long."

"Now, Jeremy." His mama sighed. "And what are you supposed to represent?" She planted a hand on her hip and examined his outfit.

"I'm a Citizen of the Galaxy, of course," Jeremy said in a hollow voice. "You're definitely not up on your Robert Heinlein, Mom. I made my knees out of hubcaps. What do you think?"

"They're . . . tubular. And what did you do with the goldfish?" she asked, staring him in the globe.

"They're in the powder room sink," he said, waving a kind of flipper. "They'll be fine."

His mama stood between us, but he still had her full attention. "If you don't scoot," she said, "you'll be late. Maybe I ought to drive you, but I've got six window treatments to finalize this morning and a designer sheet luncheon."

"No sweat," Jeremy said quickly, swinging his large legs and taking two steps toward me and the back door. "Plenty of time."

Not able to look back because of his glass head, Jeremy made steady strides. At the last moment he grabbed my hand, and we issued out the back door.

"Have a nice day, honey," his mama called out, absorbed once more in the little exercise man inside the moving picture box.

*

There were no sidewalks in Bluffleigh Heights, and all the paved streets curved, seeming to go nowhere. Me and Jeremy made our way along in the ditch while he learned to walk in his costume. He soon got the hang of it, throwing one padded leg around the other.

There'd been progress of a sort in automobiles. They had glass in all their windows now and strictly modern headlamps. They could get up high speeds, too, though many slowed at sight of me and Jeremy.

"I begin to see your scam," I told him as we

ambled on. "I'm to change into your Citizen of the Galaxy outfit and wear it to school, as nobody will see my face clear in that bowl. But what are you going to wear?"

He blinked like a fish wearing spectacles.

"Actually," he said, "I'm going to wear this, and . . . you're sort of in costume already. If you see what I mean."

I looked down at myself: at Mama's old fur piece with the fox face and bent ears. At my tarnished spelling medal. At my old patched princess dress that lapped down over my everyday boots. I saw what he meant.

"What about my face?" I asked. "I don't have a mask."

Even through the bowl, I met Jeremy's gaze. I saw what he meant.

*

The way I figured it, a school is a school, through-out history.

But when Bluffleigh Heights Magnet Middle School hove into view, I couldn't make head or tail of it. It was a low, flat-roofed structure crouching in a bald yard. There was no architecture to it. Miss Mae Spaulding, principal of Horace Mann, wouldn't have run a worm farm in the place. But the usual crowd churned around outside, showing off. Most were in Halloween costumes, though in the 1980s it's hard to tell.

Jeremy began to drag his feet. The costume was a

burden to him, and his bowl was fogged up from heavy breathing. "This is the part I hate," he mumbled.

"If you're worried about me," I told him, "I can always nip down to the rest   m for the day. This girl I know, name of Daisy-Rae, spends half her life in—"

He shook his bowl. "I didn't mean you. I'm glad you're here, Blossom. It's . . . just going to school I hate." His voice rang sorrowfully.

"That's only natural," I pointed out. "But shoot, Jeremy, you're a right bright kid—Gifted, I mean."

"It's not the schoolwork," he said faintly. "There's nothing to that. It's . . . everything else."

I should have known right then why I'd found my way through time to Jeremy. The evidence had been piling up from the first moment. But it was too simple to see.

Many in the crowd stared our way and laughed like hyenas. One girl was dressed up as a pig in a picture hat. She was the durnedest-looking thing I ever saw. Pointing right at me, she remarked at the top of her lungs that I was so grody she couldn't handle it.

As far as I could tell, we fitted right in. One of the boys had painted his face green and wore a cape with a stake through his heart. Some of them hardly wore enough to cover their shame, and I personally counted seven Darth Vaders. The smallest kid in the bunch, wearing a neat white suit, did nothing but

run in circles, proclaiming, "Da plane come, boss. Da plane come."

It was a sight.

I'd decided to lay low and keep my mouth shut, always a good plan. But a rough type stepped into my path. "Awright," he barked. "Take off your mask, so we can like see who you are." He made a grab for my nose.

"Bag your face, honker," I replied with dignity.

This could have led to fisticuffs; but a bell rang within the so-called school, and we were carried along with the tide. Jeremy reminded me of Alexander Armsworth, as he was never a step ahead of me. I began to wonder who was looking after who. Through the schoolhouse doors we swept, though I personally had little hope for the place.

13

IT WAS A MADHOUSE all morning long, and little learning took place. Every class period was a Halloween party, though I doubt things were much better on a regular day. As for decoration, they had no orange and black crepe paper. Instead, all the walls were brightened up with a thing called graffiti, much of it poorly spelled.

Before the first class, which may have been English, I mumbled to Jeremy in alarm, "I'll be one too many when they take attendance."

"Take what?" Jeremy asked, and into the room we ganged. There was much milling around in there, and I swear to this day I never spied the teacher. If this was the Gifted bunch, may I never see the slow ones.

But I soon saw a sight all too familiar to me: a gang of stuck-up girls sitting in a tight clump. Remembering the Sunny Thoughts and Busy Fingers Sisterhood, I meant to give this bunch all the free air they could breathe. When I settled into a desk, Jeremy drifted away. This being eighth grade, everybody steered clear of the opposite sex.

One stuck-up girl spotted me at once. She was pretty to a fault and wore a ballerina costume with a sickeningly pink tutu. In her hand she carried a wand with a glittering little star at the end of it. She waved it around in sweeping gestures.

"Oh, you guys," she said to the girls, "like, look!" She waved her wand at me. "That is *so* grisly, like I am *sure*."

"Ew," said all her group, looking my way. "Gross us out," they said in a chorus.

"That is so *ill*," said the pig girl in the picture hat. "Gag me with a spoon. Really. Is that makeup or a mask? And what does the eighteen mean on her . . . hat?"

"Oh, I know what that means," said the ballerina, wielding her wand. "On an Ugly Scale of one to fifteen, she's an eighteen."

The whole group rocked with laughter, like they were supposed to.

I had the durnedest feeling I'd been through all this before.

"But who *is* she?" wondered the pig girl.

At that the ballerina, quick to take charge, jumped up and began counting the noses of her bunch with the wand: "Melissa, Kelly, April, Chrissy, Michelle, Hilary, Heidi." She sighed with relief. "*We're* all here." Then she flopped down, and the group closed ranks around her, losing all interest in me.

But I hadn't lost all interest in them. I edged out of my desk and made my way across the littered

room to where they clustered like birds of bright plumage.

"Ew, get away," said several.

"Like, no way is she going to sit with us," said the pig person.

"For sure," came a chorus, and they all looked to the ballerina for leadership.

Arranging my fur piece, I marched up to her.

She tapped her wand nervously on the desk, as all eyes were upon her, including my beady black ones. "Say, sister," I said, "what's your name?"

They all gasped in shock.

"That's *Heather*," said several, amazed at my ignorance.

"Is that a fact?" I remarked, taking a closer look. I had the odd notion I knew her.

"You must be like really new in town. Really," breathed the pig. "Like a foreigner or something."

"Oh, no," I answered. "I'm an . . . old settler in these parts." I grinned at them in Mama's evil way. "Sort of the Spirit of Halloween Past." They shrank.

"In fact," I said, warming up, "I'm planning to tell fortunes and give readings and bring messages from various worlds to customers at a certain Halloween Festival . . . tomorrow night."

I had them listening now. But Heather drew in her cheeks and said, "I'm sure," in a mocking way.

"In fact, I feel one of my trances coming on right now." I swayed slightly and let my eyes roll back in my head like Mama does.

I had them in the palm of my hand now, though

many threatened to rolf on the floor. "Barf City," said the pig.

I swayed some more and let my long, bony finger reach out, drawing a bead on Heather's forehead.

"She is so zeeked out," said Heather uncertainly, "like, forget it, okay?"

By now my eyes were staring at the back of my skull. "*I have a message for a girl name of Heather that comes to her from the Great Beyond,*" I moaned in a truly hideous voice. "*This is your grandmother speaking, Heather, honey,*" I continued, squeaking like an old lady.

"I am *so* sure," Heather said to her group. "How could she know my family, she's so scruff. Besides, Grandma isn't in the Great Beyond. She's down in Sun City, Arizona."

"*It is I, Heather, honey,*" I squeaked hollowly, "*Grandma, down here in—ah—Sun City. Just wanted to say hello and . . . stay as sweet as you are, precious.*"

"Wig me out," said Heather, scratching at her little golden curls with her wand. "If you're so smart," she said to me, "what's my grandma's name?"

I had her there.

"*Why, Heather, honey,*" I answered in a real far-off voice, "*you know my name as well as your own. We were always one of the First Families of Bluff City. Silly child, I am the former* LETTY SHAMBAUGH."

Heather's wand clattered to the floor. "*Grandma!*" she shrieked, both wigging and zeeking right out. Even her tutu collapsed in a quivering pink mass.

As her group closed around her pale and trembling form, the pig girl rose up, shouting, "Somebody go for a guidance counselor for Heather!" The pig straightened her picture hat in a businesslike way, ready to assume command of the group.

I withdrew.

＊

That was the only bright spot in a dismal morning. We moved from Halloween party to Halloween party, all at the taxpayers' expense. After my run-in with Heather's bunch nobody would come near me. Several whispered remarks, though, and pointed my way.

I noticed Jeremy wasn't doing much better. In every class there was a bunch of boys in a tighter clump than the girls. But Jeremy was never one of them.

He sat forlorn and friendless at a desk while the others entertained themselves by pouring Halloween punch from paper cups on one another. Occasionally one of them would come over to drum on Jeremy's bowl with a pencil. Otherwise, he seemed to be a perfect outcast.

I supposed Jeremy, being right smart, didn't fit in. The dumb ones always make the best followers. Still, he was one lonesome kid. I know the feeling.

By noon I was up to here with Bluffleigh Heights Magnet Middle School. We all were following an evil cooking smell to a place called the cafeteria

when I remarked to Jeremy, "How's about you and me playing hooky?"

"Playing what?" he said, stumping along on his big silver legs.

"It's a rotten shame to waste the day in a place like this," I said. "Besides, I've got to start thinking about getting back you-know-where. Tonight's the night I'm to report to Old Man Leverette when those boys are going to make a mess of his front porch. I just naturally have to be there to teach—"

"Oh, I don't think you can get back that quick, Blossom." He spoke in a rush, like he didn't want me to go. "But we can cut out of school if you want to. How about checking out the mall? We could always cruise past Radio Shack and have a look at their components."

It didn't sound like my kind of place. We made a sharp turn just before the cafeteria and slipped outside through a fire door. A person couldn't hear herself think in that school.

"Now where?" Jeremy wondered.

"Bluff City." I spoke firmly. He reminded me of Daisy-Rae and Roderick. It was uphill work to get them into town, too. "There's got to be something left of the town I knew, and I mean to find it, Jeremy. I know curiosity killed the cat. But satisfaction brought that cat back."

"It's a long way," he said, "and this costume is pretty heavy."

I thought he might slip back home and change

into his regular clothes. I had no doubt he could pull
this off, as his mama was not a noticing kind of
woman. Besides, she'd be at her . . . designer sheet
luncheon. But he pointed out that since I was going
dressed as I was, he'd better stick to his costume.

Away we labored over the curving streets of
Bluffleigh Heights on a brisk autumn afternoon seventy years hence.

Jeremy was a good companion, though mostly
quiet inside his fogbound bowl. We walked for a
quarter of an hour, and still I could see nothing
familiar. It's a sight how homesick a person can get
this near home.

What looked like pastureland in Old Man Leverette's south forty turned out to be something called
the Little League field. When we came to where the
old streetcar trestle spanned Snake Creek, there was
only a wide highway bridge choked with automobiles speeding past a 7-Eleven store at the far end.

A lump was fast forming in my throat. Being a
sensitive type, Jeremy noticed. His spectacles were
steamed up, and his bowl was blurry; but he didn't
miss much. "Tell me what it was like, Blossom. The
olden days, I mean."

Since he seemed to know no history whatsoever, I
told him various true stories.

One of them was how I happened to borrow a
chicken from Old Man Leverette. That just naturally brought up the swimming hole in Leverette's
Woods and how I chanced to observe Alexander

Armsworth and his cronies swimming and smoking in the altogether.

I went on to tell him about Mr. Ambrose Lacy, who had both Miss Spaulding and Miss Fuller on the string. I told him about Letty Shambaugh and her club and how Alexander took her to the moving pictures. And that brought up Daisy-Rae and Roderick. I worked in pretty nearly everybody.

I even mentioned how my mama's occult Powers had warned her of the old abandoned Leverette farmhouse and its eerie Vibrations.

"She was plugging into my malfunctioning electronic impulses," Jeremy observed. "There are people who can pick up shortwave radio on their hearing aids and false teeth. Your mom is probably a natural transistor."

"Wouldn't surprise me a bit," I said.

All this conversation carried us right into town. There beside a busy street was a sign that read:

WELCOME TO BLUFF CITY
68,002

"Sixty-eight thousand and two what?"

Jeremy blinked. "People."

"Well, I'll be a ring-tailed monkey!" I exclaimed.

On we went, deeper into this swollen Bluff City. Then, with minds of their own, my feet swerved away from the sidewalk. We took off across a vacant lot and down an alley.

Jeremy had to struggle along in his Galaxy boots

over ruts and a number of objects labeled NO
DEPOSIT, NO RETURN. "Where are we heading?"
He peered anxiously at the backs of various build-
ings.

"I'm switched if I know," I said. "It just feels
right."

It wasn't a minute more before I saw a familiar
sight against the sky. It was the roof and bell tower
of Horace Mann School. The bell tower was
boarded up, and there were missing shingles on the
roof; but my eyes misted over at sight of the old
place.

Dragging Jeremy along, I said, "Well, of course.
It's all crystal clear to me now. This route we've
been following down back alleys was once the
streetcar right-of-way. Many's the time I've walked
the rails along here."

Grunting to keep up, Jeremy followed my skip-
ping form into the old schoolyard.

"And here's where we had our graduation day
maypole dance last—"

A sign above the schoolhouse door caught my
eye. It was a new one, and it read:

MAE SPAULDING MEMORIAL
MEDIA CENTER

Substance Abuse Counseling Available

I blinked. This was more information than I
could . . . program. Instead, I grabbed Jeremy's
puffy sleeve. "And right across the road is Bluff City
High—"

But across the paved street was no such thing. My old high school had been leveled. In its place was a large, rude structure topped by a gaudy sign:

INTOWN MOTEL
* DAY RATES * WATER BEDS * CABLE TV *
* ICE MACHINES *

My heart sank. They had erased my world.

14

A MOMENT PASSED before I felt Jeremy's hand patting my arm.

"I'm sorry, Blossom." He spoke in a small, kindly voice.

"What happened to my world? There's nothing left. It just as well never have existed."

"It's a . . . rotten shame," he said.

"I'm grossed out, Jeremy," I whimpered.

But it's always darkest before the dawn, as I've often said. I gathered up my courage, ready to scout out more hopeful landmarks than these.

> "There is nothing either good or bad,
>   but thinking makes it so,"

I said to him.

"That's a good attitude," Jeremy remarked.

"It's *Hamlet*. Act Two."

On we went where the streetcar tracks had been until we came to a paved yard with rows of little mechanical hitching posts. A sign read:

METERED PARKING

I knew where we were now. Our path was crossing Fairview Avenue, the proud street lined with the
all-brick homes of the well-to-do. "Letty Shambaugh
lived in that very house." I pointed to the large and
tasteful residence.

But her porch had been hacked off. A shutter or
two hung from a single hinge. The houses on either
side were gone, like missing teeth. "Must have been
a fire," I remarked.

"Several," Jeremy said. "This neighborhood hasn't
hit bottom yet, but it's on the way down."

Overshadowing the entire street was a tremendous building with blank sides and skylights in the
roof. We detoured from our path to read a sign over
the entrance:

FULLER MEMORIAL RECREATIONAL
FACILITY
* JOGGING TRACK * HANDBALL COURTS *
* SENSIBLE WEIGHT REDUCTION *
* INTERPRETIVE DANCE *

"Eureka!" I exclaimed, smacking my forehead.
"Don't you get it, Jeremy?"

He didn't seem to.

"This here recreational facility is named in memory
of Miss Fuller, the Girls' Gym teacher. It's bound
to be!"

Jeremy rubbed the bowl near his chin.

"And that media center back yonder is named
in memory of Miss Spaulding."

Jeremy nodded.

"*Miss* Spaulding," I explained, "and *Miss* Fuller. They kept their maiden names right to the grave!"

"And that was good?" he pondered.

"Shoot, yes. It means that neither one of them fell into the clutches of Mr. Ambrose Lacy and married that two-timing polecat."

"Oh."

"I bet you *I* had something to do with that." I grinned evilly. "In fact, I ought to be getting back to 1914 this very minute, and—"

"Come on, Blossom." Jeremy caught up my hand and pulled me along back toward the streetcar right-of-way. "Let's see some more. This is interesting. Really."

And of course it was. And about to get more so.

As we threaded our way along through the alleys, I knew we'd soon come to the place where me and Mama lived. Jeremy knew, too, as I'd told him how me and her occupied a property hard by the tracks right behind Alexander Armsworth's barn.

As we trudged along, Jeremy said, "You won't be too disappointed if—"

"Not me. Our place was fixing to fall down even back then. If Letty's big house hasn't held up, I can't expect too much from our old dump."

Which was just as well. When we came to the home of my youth, there was nothing there but smoothly mowed grass and a tremendous big horse

tank with soft sides of a bright blue color. It was brimming with water, but not a horse in sight.

"Well, that's where me and Mama lived," I said, just lightly stroking her fur piece. "But what in the Sam Hill do you call that big soft horse tank?"

"That's an aboveground swimming pool," Jeremy said. "But look, Blossom, that barn you told me about is still here."

And so it was. I chanced a look at it from the corner of my eye. The barn on the old Armsworth property stood where it always had, in good repair, too.

I shrank then and felt the chill winds of autumn around my heart. Oh, I didn't fear that barn because it had once been haunted. It wasn't the past that worried me. It was this future.

His globe glancing everywhere, Jeremy waddled to the far side of the barn while I remained rooted to the spot. He waved a padded arm for me to follow, but I wouldn't. I still felt the chill.

Presently I saw his silver form returning around the corner of the barn. "It's still there, Blossom," he said, loud inside his bowl. "A great big old house with fancy porches and turrets and a lot of colored glass over the doors. It's nice."

"Well," I said thoughtfully, "it was always one of the better addresses."

"And guess what, Blossom. It's still being lived in. They haven't turned it into a media center or a recreational facility or a free clinic or anything. There

are curtains at all the windows and pots of flowers on the sills. There's a power mower on the lawn, and they've even got all their leaves bagged. There's a Buick Century in the driveway. Come on, let's check the place out. We can always pull the old trick-or-treat number on them." Jeremy bounced in his space boots and reached for my hand.

But I drew it back.

I thought of the Armsworth mansion as I'd known it. I smelled bacon frying and thought of the Armsworths having their breakfast every morning as I made my way to school across their property. I thought of Alexander Armsworth. And not just as the kid I'd known. I thought of myself, too, as I was and as I would be.

"No, Jeremy," I said. "I better not find out who those people are up in the house now. There's some things about the future a person ought not to know. I think we should turn back now."

"Back?" Jeremy said faintly. His hand was still out for mine.

"Back to Bluffleigh Heights, and then I think we better say our good-byes."

There was a small lump in my throat, for many reasons, and a small lump in Jeremy's, too. I noticed it just under the rim of his bowl.

15

WE HAD NO TROUBLE getting past Jeremy's mama and back up to his room. It was just evening, and we had the shadowy upstairs to ourselves. Tiffany wasn't home. The mall hadn't closed.

The dark corners made the place more like the old abandoned Leverette farmhouse. Once in his room with the door closed behind us, Jeremy reached for the light switch, but I drew his hand away.

"I might get back better in the dark," I said.

He turned away from me and eased the fishbowl off his head. "Oh, wow. I'm glad to get out of that thing. I guess this is about my last year for Halloween, the costume part at least."

His head of hair was faintly red in the failing light. It stood up in peaks. He slipped off his hubcaps and massaged his knees. Then he took off his spectacles and breathed on them. He was only playing for time.

"I've had a real nice visit, Jeremy. Many thanks."

"My pleasure," he said politely. I reckon his voice

was changing, for it cracked then. "Come back any
. . . time."

"Well, I don't know about that," I said. "But I
guess I can figure how I happened to pay this particular call."

"There were the electrical storms," he said, "one
at my end and one at—"

"I doubt it was the weather, Jeremy. I figure
maybe you needed a friend."

He wasn't sure. "Looks like you came a really
long way just to spend a little time with me."

"Well, there's nothing more important than friendship," I said. "I get a little lonesome now and again
myself. Maybe I came for us both."

"Seems like you just got here, and now you're
leaving."

"Well, that's me all over," I told him. "Busy every
minute. Tonight I'll be at Old Man Leverette's town
residence, teaching Alexander's bunch a lesson.
Then tomorrow night I'll be right here in this very
house, telling fortunes.

"Did I tell you we of the freshman class are running your place as a Haunted House? We're going
to stretch Champ Ferguson out on the drainboard as
a monster and run a crackerjack dungeon and model
torture chamber in your cellar. We're going to have
ghosts in your corners and bats in your belfry. We're
going to charge ten cents."

"It sounds great," Jeremy said with his head
down. "Wish I could come along."

But he couldn't, and he knew it.

"You can be there in . . . spirit," I said. "You can think of us tomorrow night seventy years ago. I could even tell my fortunes right here in your room. Shall I?"

He nodded. His eyes were glistening. Maybe mine were, too.

"Blossom, since you've got to be going, I guess I can tell you this." Jeremy rubbed one of his padded legs with his big boot. "I haven't had too much experience with knowing girls. But I really like you, a lot. Of course, you're . . . different."

"Oh, well, shoot," I said, my face a little warm, "I've been called different even in my own time."

Jeremy smiled a little and scratched his red thatch. "I guess what I'm trying to say is, if I was Alexander Armsworth, it wouldn't be Letty Shambaugh I was taking to the . . . moving pictures."

The last light left the room then. There was nobody to see, and with any luck I'd soon be gone. So I thought: *Oh, well, shoot.* Then I stepped forward and gave Jeremy a little kiss good-bye.

He took it real well. Then he said, "Blossom, when you're gone, how will I know you were ever really here? I see you're real now, but later I might wonder."

"Like I was only a stage you were going through?" I asked him. "And later you outgrew it?"

"Like that," he said, "basically."

I chanced to glance down at my spelling medal then. It was hanging by a thread from Mama's old ratty coat. I'd sworn to wear that medal till it fell off me. I gave it a little tug, and it came loose in my hand.

"Here." I held it out to him. "I was the champion speller of Horace Mann School. This medal was at one time my most prized possession. Take it to remember me by. It will always remind you that you have a friend, a good old friend."

Jeremy reached out and pulled back. "Tell you what, Blossom. Take it along with you on your trip and hide it somewhere in this house, somewhere I can find it later on if I begin to forget. Sometime when I'm lonesome again, like I was before you came."

"Let me see," I pondered. "Where'd be a place safe for seventy years?" Then it came to me. "You know that china closet down in your dining room? Roderick hid in there one time and liked to scare the wits out of Alexander Armsworth, though it didn't faze me."

"China closet?" Jeremy said. "Oh, yes, we keep the stereo components in there."

"First time you get lonesome, check around in there. You'll find this spelling medal of mine under a loose floorboard. That'll be a sign I'm thinking of you."

"Is there a loose floorboard?"

"There will be."

It was time to go then, and we both knew it.

Jeremy drifted over to his machines. They looked dead as doornails to me, and I don't suppose he could get a beep out of them. But he said, "I could try a little patching and looping to . . . help you off the launching pad."

But I told him I'd better try to do it my way. It was almost night then, and we were two dark shapes in the room—three if you count Darth Vader. I fastened my beanie tight with the hatpin and arranged Mama's fur piece so it wouldn't strangle me if I got up speed.

"This is the part I'm never sure about," I admitted. "I have to give it my all."

It grew darker then, dark as a pocket. I heard a distant sighing sound. It was the wind pump out past the chicken coop on the old abandoned Leverette farm. I cocked my ears to hear it clearer and let my brain go blank. I commenced to Vibrate, and I felt my mysterious Powers take charge.

Wind blew through Jeremy's window, for there was no glass in it now. A whirlwind circled my form and gave me goosebumps. There was a shower of sparks, but cold and white as snow. Or maybe these were the white pages torn from seventy calendars. Whatever they were, they gusted into a tremendous cyclone.

I never moved, and I traveled like the wind.

*

It was a gentle landing as these things go. There was no carpet on the floor now. The heels of my

boots bumped on bare boards. They were gritty with plaster dust.

I'd kept my eyes tight shut, though not from fear exactly. When I looked around me, I was in the empty, ruined upstairs room of the old abandoned Leverette farmhouse. Pale moonlight fell through the broken window. My spelling medal was in my hand.

I walked toward the moonlight right through the emptiness where Jeremy's machines had been— would be. Torn wallpaper hung down in curls, and I smelled the smells of an empty old house far from town: the mildew and wood rot and dead field mice in the walls.

I chanced a look out the window. There I saw the black branches of Leverette's Woods beyond the gate to Lovers' Lane. The wind pump was back too, singing and turning in the night breeze. There was the chicken coop, right where it should be. In one of its windows was a coal oil lamp. The lamp burned low, for it was past Roderick's bedtime.

I looked for the blanket of glittering lights as far as the eye could see. I looked for the golden arches and "40 BILLION SOLD." But they weren't there, not yet. It was the night before Halloween. And it was 1914. My next thought was of Mama.

I cut and ran for home.

❖

"Girl, where you bin?"
Before I could get across the threshold, she came

down on me like the Johnstown flood. I was out of breath from . . . much traveling, and I sagged somewhat in the doorframe.

Mama's teeth were out, but she was speaking clear. "You was gone all night and all day, too! I'll larn youoph."

She reached for Paw's razor strop that hangs over the pitcher and bowl. She saves this back for special occasions. Believe it or not, I was glad to see her.

"Well, Mama," I said, hoping to distract her, "have you had your supper?"

"Of course I ain't! And I see you come back empty-handed. I couldn't eat a bite anyhow." At least she seemed to forget the strop. The dice dangling down from her ears danced, and her flinty eyes bored into me.

"Why, Mama, I think you were worried about me," I said, pushing my luck.

"Worried you wouldn't come back?" she asked. "Or worried you would!"

She regarded me slyly. "Where you bin anyhow? You look like three sheets to the wind and somethun the cat drug in."

Still, I hoped to distract her. "I'm half-starved myself," I remarked. "I haven't had a thing to eat all day but whole-grain high-fiber product and a chaser of vitamin C concentrate."

"Talk sense," Mama said.

She dragged me to the table and dropped me in a chair. When she turned up the flame on the lamp, its reflection flared in her crystal ball.

"Now then." She settled into a chair opposite. "I asked where you bin one time. I won't ask agin." She pointed at Paw's strop. "I'll let that thing do the talkin'."

"Much as I'd like to chew the fat with you all evening, Mama, I have a busy night ahead of me and no time."

She squinted at me over the crystal ball. "You got all the time I say you got." Reaching into her shroud, she pulled out a plug of Bull Durham and commenced to jaw it at her leisure. "Start at the beginnin'."

"Well . . . it's like this, Mama. Last night I nipped back to the high school to get some homework I'd left in my desk. And lo and behold, if the janitor didn't come along and lock up all the doors! I was stuck in that high school all night, Mama. Why, I had to sleep under Miss Blankenship's desk. I overslept as it turned out, and the first thing I knew, it was morning. Miss Blankenship was taking attendance! So of course, all I could do was go through the regular school day as usual. That's about what happened . . . basically."

There was a disturbing pause before Mama said, "That ain't even close." She made a point of staring into her crystal ball like she could read the truth in it. "Try agin."

I fetched up a sigh. It's always difficult to explain anything to a mother, as I've often said. "The truth is, Mama, I did something you told me not to do."

"That don't come as a shock to me," she remarked, drumming her long fingers on Paw's strop.

"I went out to the old abandoned Leverette farmhouse last night."

Mama's eyes flashed, but she looked deep into her crystal ball. "And what did you find out?" she said cautiously. She was staring hard at the ball, but she was seeing nothing. She was all ears.

I thought of a way to flatter her somewhat. "I found out you were right, Mama. Remember that time you went into one of your trances and said, 'Not all the Unliving are dead'? You hit the nail on the head that time."

Mama folded her arms across her front and made a satisfied sound. "I'm never wrong," she remarked. "What did I mean exactly?"

"You meant that while some of the Unliving are dead, the rest of the Unliving haven't been born yet. They're the people of the future."

Mama gave this some thought. "That's real interesting, ain't it? Them trances of mine is a marvel. I don't know how I do it."

"Me either, Mama. When it comes to Powers, you don't know your own strength."

Mama almost beamed. I figured this was as good a time as any to make my exit. "However, even with my puny Powers," I told her, "I can read your mind this minute."

She froze. "Git outta my head, girl."

"Oh, yes, Mama, I read you like a book. You just

as well hand over that gunnysack at your feet. You know yourself you're fixing to send me out into the night to borrow a nice, plump frying chicken."

Mama looked uncertain, but hungry. She could all but smell that chicken frying now, though she had unfinished business with me.

I had unfinished business with her, too. If she lived to be a hundred, she'd never tell me how strong her Powers are. She'd half known the old abandoned Leverette farmhouse was haunted by the future, so to speak. But I bet you a nickel my Powers are stronger. I can't picture Mama traveling through a time warp. Not to mention what they'd think of her if she turned up in Bluffleigh Heights. I am no oil painting, but Mama would scare a bulldog off a meat wagon.

Mama had stood at the door of the Dreadful Future. There was no doubt in my mind about that. But I had crossed the fatal threshold!

She fished up the sack and scooted it across the table to me. When I reached out for it, I palmed her set of false teeth that were resting by the crystal ball. I slipped her teeth into my pocket and said, "I'll be off now to pay a call on Old Man L—"

"*Hush yore mouth*," Mama commanded. "Don't *never* tell me where you git them chickens. What I don't know won't hurt me!"

"Oh, Mama." I sighed. "I'm glad you said that."

Then I hightailed it out into the night.

16

If you'd been lingering around outside Old Man Leverette's house in Bluff City on the night of October 30, 1914, you could have seen it all for yourself. Delayed by Mama somewhat, I wasn't there a moment too soon, but a slicker operation was never pulled off.

Though I'm not used to approaching that particular house from the front, I slipped like a shadow across the Leverette yard, swerved around a sugar maple tree that shades his porch, and nipped up to his parlor door. I rapped but once before the door opened, and Old Man Leverette let me in. I've rarely, if ever, seen him in a better mood.

Minutes later both me and him reappeared on the porch. My form was draped in various white bed sheets. My head was bound up in a pillow slip that fitted tight across my forehead and flapped behind.

My face was a work of art. Old Man Leverette had smeared my cheeks and chin with lampblack and a coating of goose grease to make my entire face shine like a raw wound. Under my eyes he'd painted

ghastly circles and bags with a red vegetable dye
he'd prepared especially. I was Barf City.

In my hand I carried a red railroad lantern with
the wick turned low. Under his arm Old Man Leverette carried a stepladder. He was chuckling and
snorting in advance, worse than a kid himself.

"If we don't show them boys a thing or two," he
wheezed, "you can call me a—"

"Never mind about that, Old—Mr. Leverette," I
replied, all business. "Just steady that ladder and
help me up that maple tree." Which he did.

I heard the ladder close below me and Old Man
Leverette's heavy footsteps as he tramped back up
on the porch and into the house.

The last leaf had fallen from the sugar maple, and
its branches were slick with the evening damp. I
needed to find just the right limb.

Flailing around in the tree like a big bird, I was
hampered by my sheets. A limb overhung the front
steps, but it was puny. I'd fallen out of one tree
lately and didn't wish to make a habit of it. I eased
into the gutter and rested from my climb. It was
dark that night and chilly up there on the porch
roof.

Turning up my lantern, I spied a stouter limb. It
too branched out over the front steps. Throwing
caution to the winds, I stood up in the gutter. Without looking down at certain doom or a broken leg at
least, I flexed my knees and took the leap.

The lantern swinging from my elbow threw weird
shadows across the yard. I hooked the stout limb

with an arm and a leg and hung there swaying. Then I pulled myself up to a sitting position. I might have been a large white owl gone to roost up among the bare branches.

I practiced my gymnastics then, arranging the folds in my sheets so they wouldn't trip me up. I meant to put on a ghastly show, but I didn't plan to hang myself into the bargain. As it happened, I had little time to practice. From down the unpaved street I heard the unstealthy footsteps of boys. Three boys.

From my high perch I saw these shadowy three scramble off the crown of the road and skulk along in the weedy ditch. Though I couldn't make them out, I figured Champ and Bub were the front ones and Alexander was bringing up the rear. My lantern burned low.

When they came even with the fence by the Leverette property, they bent double and skulked for the house. Through the pickets I watched these three toad forms moving up toward the porch.

They cut around then for the steps and were soon in a bunch right beneath my dangling feet. They were punching each other and snorting with laughter, which they muffled with their sleeves. I got a strong whiff of horse manure.

They eased onto the porch, crab-fashion. "Who brought the matches?" I heard Alexander ask. He can't ever plan anything since he never thinks a minute ahead.

I couldn't see them then because they were work-

ing up by the front door. Bub doubtless planted the paper sack of manure on the porch floor. Champ doubtless brought the match I heard struck. Alexander doubtless rang Old Man Leverette's doorbell.

"Trick or treat!" Alexander cried out in a breaking voice.

"Oh, shut up," Bub said. Then they must have set the sack afire, for the porch glowed.

Now was the moment when Old Man Leverette was supposed to jerk open the door, see a small fire on his porch, and jump on it to stamp it out. The boys were poised for flight the second they saw that front door begin to move.

They never saw it. While up above I hooked my legs around the branch, Old Man Leverette wrenched his front door open with lightning speed. Never setting a foot outside, he swung his shotgun just over the three boys' heads and let fly with both barrels.

Rock salt raked the porch ceiling and pounded in a hailstorm on the porch floor. The explosion was heard downtown. It was like the Day of Judgment, only louder.

This was followed by a piercing shriek which could only be Alexander. When they could move, Bub dived one way over the side of the porch, and Champ dived the other. They both vaulted over a matching pair of lilac bushes and lit, running.

There was a scuffling sound as Alexander's boots seemed to run into each other. Then he turned and

plunged down the front steps, just as he was meant to do.

At the last possible moment, I popped Mama's false teeth into my mouth. Being too big for my head, they made a wonderful show. With all my might I swung forward on my branch.

Just as Alexander hit the porch steps in wild retreat, my deathly face, upside down, swung level with his. I held the lantern, turned up full blast. It lit my awful black and red features. Mama's terrible teeth grinned at him, and that is some sight. The night breeze caught my drapings. I was a floating head, and my sheets were the shroud from some troubled tomb.

It stopped Alexander cold. He couldn't see my knees hooked over the branch above him. He could see only a face with the features upside down in red shadow, hanging inches before him.

A pitiful gurgling sound formed in his throat. His elbows were tucked up at his sides for running, but he was paralyzed. His face seemed to dissolve. He spun around in panic and pounded back up on the porch. Which was another mistake.

Old Man Leverette had doused the small fire with a bucket of water he had ready. Now he'd picked up the paper sack which had burned down to the manure. In both hands the old gentleman hefted up the soggy sack.

Alexander ran straight into it, face first.

17

Halloween Day dawned bright and fair, Indian summer as such weather is called. All the thoughts of us freshmen were upon the Halloween Festival Haunted House. Especially mine. But it was still a school day.

In homeroom Miss Blankenship took attendance as usual. Her daily *Hamlet* quotation was already on the blackboard:

I MUST BE CRUEL, ONLY TO BE KIND
Act III

We all sat restless in our rows, with scrubbed and shiny faces. Alexander Armsworth's face looked especially scrubbed.

But he wasn't sure whether he was speaking to me or not. I could read his mind like a book as he sat in the desk ahead of me. His ears glowed pinkish. Like Mama, he had some inkling of the mystery in the old abandoned Leverette farmhouse. But where I'd gone night before last when I'd walked through that fatal door, he couldn't be sure.

He also wasn't positive that it was me who was the ghastly floating red and black head which had caused him so much fear and discomfort last night. Hamlet himself had no more trouble making up his mind than Alexander.

But his ears were glowing redder. Just as the bell rang, ending homeroom, bells seemed to ring in Alexander's brain. He turned on me, hissing.

"Listen, Blossom, if I find out it was you last night you-know-where who made me get hit in the face with you-know-what, I will make you one sorry girl."

I looked back at him with wide and innocent eyes. But it didn't work. The bell had rung, and so I gathered up my schoolbooks and twitched up the aisle in Letty Shambaugh's way.

Alexander had not cooled off by history class. Long before the day was over, he had me tried and convicted in his mind.

"Listen," he hissed again, right under Mr. Lacy's nose, "you might as well come clean, Blossom. It was you up that tree because who else would pull such a disgusting stunt, you little—"

"Chill out, Alexander," I whispered sternly. "You had better keep your accusations to yourself until after tonight at least. That is, if you want any fortunes told in your so-called Haunted House."

This didn't calm him down, but it shut him up. "We have the reputation of the freshman class to consider," I added, sniffing.

All in all, it wasn't one of Alexander's better days. For one thing, he'd lost his freshman beanie someplace and didn't know where to find it.

I had it. Last night, when he'd received a faceful from Old Man Leverette, his beanie had shot off the back of his head, rolled down the porch steps, and come to rest under my dangling head. In the confusion that followed, Alexander had sped away, blind into the night.

I'd gathered up his beanie along with a plump fryer, cut up and ready for the pan, which Old Man Leverette gave me to remember the occasion by. Mama had made quick work of the chicken, but I still had Alexander's beanie. In such a mood as his, I didn't figure he deserved to have it back.

Mostly to hush us up, Mr. Lacy sent me down to the office with the attendance slip. As usual, I detoured past the girls' rest room to drop in on Daisy-Rae. Seemed like ages since I'd seen her last.

Much to my surprise, I found her out in the open, staring through the barred window by the sinks. You can't see anything through that window since it's frosted for modesty's sake. But Daisy-Rae's long face was turned to the sunlight filtering in.

"Hey, Blossom." She turned slowly to me.

"Hey, Daisy-Rae. Looks like you're getting braver." I gestured at the stalls. All of their doors were standing open.

"The sun felt so warm on my face," she said, mournful as a coot, "and I wasn't gittin' enough exercise in that place." She flapped a bony hand at

her favorite stall. "Anyhow, I bin thinkin' about givin' up this whole education idea. Roderick is gittin' to where he can find his way to Horace Mann school by hisself."

I sighed. It seemed like everybody was in a glum mood today. I wondered how we'd get up enough freshman class spirit to run a crackerjack Haunted House tonight.

Right then something began to dawn on me. I don't know if I Vibrated or not, but somehow the sight of doleful Daisy-Rae slumped there by the sinks sent me a signal. I racked my brain, but I couldn't quite think it through. Then the light began to dawn.

"Say, Daisy-Rae, you coming to the Haunted House tonight?"

"Well, you'ens is havin' it right out by our place. I expect Roderick will want to go. You know how he is. But we ain't got ten cents between us. Kin you git us in?"

"Oh, shoot, Daisy-Rae, you won't have to pay. I have an idea we might need you'ens—you and Roderick to help us run the place."

She drew back. "Well, I'm not rilly a freshman," she said, "and I cain't picture Roderick ever bein' a freshman, so I don't think it'd be our place to take part."

"Daisy-Rae," I declared, "you are one shrinking violet. Just make sure you and Roderick are available tonight, as I think you two might come in real handy."

I left her drooped by the sinks, but she was looking as interested as she gets.

*

Mama watched me like a hawk as I flitted around our place getting ready for the Haunted House. She'd been casting spells to while away the time. But she pushed aside all her little sacks of garlic and wolfbane and suchlike and took up a pack of cards.

"Looks to me like if they'd wanted a *real* fortune-teller, they'd have had me," she remarked.

"Well, Mama, you are not a freshman."

She sent a jet of tobacco juice onto the floor.

"Can I wear this?" I asked her, holding up her old purple washable velveteen shawl with the gold fringe. I'd already talked her out of a pair of hoop earrings for the evening and a black sateen skirt which she'd sewed silver moons and stars all over.

As if by chance, I slipped my hand into one of the many pockets of this skirt and drew out her set of false teeth.

"Why, looky here, Mama. You have stuck your teeth in the pocket of this skirt. You're getting awful forgetful and liable to leave them around most any-place."

Her eyes flashed and narrowed. "Gimme them things." She slammed her teeth down on the table. "I bin lookin' for them high and low," she grumbled.

I flitted away, seeming to busy myself. But I soon flitted back. Mama had just turned up the queen of spades, one of her favorite cards.

"Girl, what you know about tellin' fortunes I could put in my ear and still have room for my elbow."

"Well, Mama, I'm willing to learn if you have any pointers for me."

"It takes talent," she said, studying the cards, "which you ain't got."

"I'd hoped to make a good showing," I said, "as it might send some business your way."

Mama brightened somewhat. Her hand hesitated over the jack of hearts.

"There'll be grown-ups at the Haunted House," I observed, "with money to spend. As a matter of fact, one of the chaperons for the occasion is Mr. Lacy, the history teacher."

Mama grunted.

"Mr. Ambrose Lacy," I said.

"Who?"

"You heard me, Mama. I told you all about how Mr. Lacy was sparking both Miss Spaulding and Miss Fuller at the same time. You said Ambrose Lacy was trouble with a capital T and always had been. You said you knew him."

The jack of hearts seemed stuck to Mama's hand. She raised the card to her forehead and closed her eyes, seeming to receive messages.

"Ambrose Lacy," she said in a distant voice. "Ah, yes, here comes Wisdom from the Great Beyond. Lay it on me!"

There's nobody like Mama for pretending to receive a message she's known all along.

"I see in my mind's eye a young squirt down in Sikeston, Missouri, where we all come from. There is bad blood there, and bad blood will out! I see this young punk, name of Ambrose Lacy, bein' shot at by a local farmer for foolin' with his wife. And then along about 1905 or 1906 I see Ambrose Lacy gittin' married to the daughter of a prominent feed and grain dealer. Oh, yeah, I see everything."

"Married!" I muttered.

"That's right," Mama said. "This philandering dude married the former Blanche Potts in one of them two years."

"Well, I never," I declared.

"It gits worse," Mama said, her eyes tight shut. "I see a little stranger in their midst. A small son born to this mismatched pair."

"A small son," I breathed in outrage.

"You heard me," Mama said.

"What's the kid's name, Mama? Think!"

She flattened the jack of hearts against her forehead. "Leonard," she said.

"Leonard?"

"Leonard. And before this youngen was weaned, his hardhearted papa—I'm talkin' about Ambrose Lacy—deserted wife and child and skipped town. He hasn't bin heard of in them parts since."

The jack of hearts fluttered from Mama's hand. Her eyes opened and gazed into mine. "That any use to you?" she said in a voice normal to her.

"I wouldn't be a bit surprised, Mama." I tucked her shawl around me, ready to be gone.

She scooped up her cards. "You better take this deck with you, and the crystal ball, too. With yore puny Powers, you'll need all the help you kin git."

"Many thanks, Mama."

When I reached for the deck of cards, her hand closed over mine. I thought she meant to read my palm, but she only gave my hand a little squeeze. There is no charting Mama's moods.

Wedging the crystal ball under my arm, I vanished out into the night, my hoop earrings swinging free.

18

CLOUDS RACED BEFORE THE MOON, and the old abandoned Leverette farmhouse stood tall against the night sky. I was about tuckered out from walking every step of the way from town burdened by the crystal ball. There was a touch of winter in the wind that gusted right through Mama's shawl.

The old house glowed, though not with electric light. An eerie candle burned in every window, planted there by freshman hands. Grinning jack-o'-lanterns flanked the front door.

Lingering in the tall weeds, I thought of Jeremy-to-be. I strained to hear a distant *beep* or possibly a *pyong*. But I only heard the wind pump humming its familiar song. I stood there a moment between worlds and thought of how much time there is, and how little.

A large Packard touring car advanced up the lane, raising a cloud of dust and chaff. It drew up with a flourish before the broken steps of the farmhouse. Letty Shambaugh with all her club tumbled

out of the auto and ganged into the house under the sign that read:

REPENT WHAT'S PAST; AVOID WHAT IS TO COME

I had no doubt the boys were already inside the house, stretching Champ out on the drainboard and arranging the deadman's guts in the dungeon.

I hurried on, but not into the house just yet. Detouring around it, I made for the chicken coop. Except for details, my plan for drawing Daisy-Rae and Roderick into this evening's events was all but worked out. Without consulting the crystal ball, I foresaw a busy and productive evening for us all.

＊

By nine o'clock the old abandoned Leverette farmhouse was full of customers. Letty's committee manned the door to relieve one and all of the dime admission.

Garbed as ghosts, various freshmen led the unsuspecting to where Harriet Hochhuth in a trick harness was hanging from a fake noose in the china closet. The guided tour included everything from the attic, where Tess and Bess Beasley cavorted as twin bats, to the monster's kitchen and the deadman's dungeon and model torture chamber. The place was a regular beehive, and we were minting money. Even sophomores, juniors, and seniors had drifted over from their fund raisers to take a trip through ours.

I sat at a table in an upstairs room, Jeremy's room. Before me were the crystal ball, the pack of cards, and a guttering candle. Screening the broken plaster walls were several sheets draped to suggest the mystery of a Gypsy's tent.

Above the entrance was a hand-lettered sign clearly thought up by Alexander:

FOR A NICKEL EXTRA, MADAME
BLOSSOM TELLS ALL

Beneath this corn-fed sign I was at my post, wrapped in Mama's shawl, with a trick or two up my sleeve. Business was slow, but it was bound to pick up.

My first so-called customer was Letty Shambaugh, who popped in early to snoop. Big Maisie Markham was with her, since Letty doesn't like to face me alone.

The sight of both of them gave me a start. Maisie was costumed as Cleopatra, queen of Ancient Egypt. She wore enormous bloomers tied tight with silken cords around her thick ankles. A bejeweled jacket strained around her form and showed her middle. A chain of gold coins festooned her forehead. Embedded in the folds of her fat arm was a fake snake. She looked like three Cleopatras, all struggling for the throne.

Letty was tricked out as the new moving picture star Theda Bara of Hollywood. Her face was powdered dead white with arching eyebrows and a black rosebud where her mouth had been. She was all in

clinging black taffeta with a Spanish mantilla of silk cobwebs and artificial spiders.

I seemed to think of another girl of my acquaintance—a certain ballerina wielding her wand.

"Well, Blossom," says Letty, planting her little hand on her hip, "we are doing a land office business elsewhere in this Haunted House, while here you sit all by your lonesome. But never let it be said that the freshman class didn't give you your chance."

"That's right," said Maisie.

I shuffled my deck. "Which one of you . . . ladies wants to be first?" I inquired.

"First what?" Letty elbowed Maisie out of the way.

"First to have a reading," I remarked, laying out the cards.

Letty shrank somewhat. "Your job is to fool the public, Blossom, not us."

My gaze shifted sharply to the crystal ball like I'd just seen something real interesting in it. "I can offer you a choice of the cards or the crystal ball, or I can deal directly with your palm. Put up or shut up."

Curiosity overcame Letty. "Oh, well, Maisie, I suppose we ought to let her try. You better sit down and have a reading."

"Why me?" said Maisie.

"Because I say so," Letty replied.

Maisie flopped into the chair, which threatened to collapse under her. I made an interesting pattern with my cards.

"Cross my palm with silver," I told her.

"What?"

"Gimme a nickel, Maisie," I explained.

Maisie whimpered. She had nothing but the coins on her costume. But Letty was quick to fish a nickel out of her Theda Bara outfit. Letty probably figured I was going to scare Maisie out of her wits and ruin her digestion. She wanted to see how I'd do it. I decided to use Maisie for bait.

Slipping the nickel into one of my pockets, I reached for her hand. It was somewhat sticky and smelled strongly of licorice.

"Hmmmmm." I stared deeply into her palm, which was all hills and no valleys. Her Lifeline looked like a Parker House roll.

"That's real interesting, that is," I murmured. She tried to pull her hand away, but I had a good grip on it.

"See that little bitty line branching off there?" I asked, pointing at nothing. Maisie scanned her own palm. "That's your travel line. You will make no great journeys in your life, neither over land nor sea. You will look upon no foreign shores."

Above us Letty made an impatient sound, but Maisie was falling under my spell.

"And see that line right there?" I pointed at smooth pink flesh. "That's your romantic life. Would you look at the size of that thing!"

"Where?" said Maisie. The coins on her forehead jangled. Letty edged nearer.

"Oh, yeah, romance with a capital *R* is heading your way. It will sweep you off your feet. Better yet, it will last. I see four children in here, maybe six."

Maisie was staring holes into her own hand. "Six!" she breathed. Letty was peering baldly over Maisie's big bejeweled shoulder now.

"Who is my great love to be, Blossom?" She was quivering like jelly.

She had me there. I couldn't imagine. I thought of giving her Champ Ferguson or even Bub Timmons. But then I thought: *Oh, well, shoot, why get her hopes up?*

"My vision grows dim," I moaned, letting my eyes roll halfway back into my head. "Your palm is an open book to me, but the print is fine and growing faint." I let my head loll, but by now Maisie had a grip on my hand and was hanging on for dear life.

"Your great love is a mystery man who will reveal his identity to you and you alone. All I can make out is that he's a tall, thin fellow who—ah—likes big women."

"That's me," Maisie whispered, wringing my hand.

It was not my best work, but it did a job on Maisie. I blinked and sat up straight. "What did I say? Where am I? What time is it?"

Maisie slumped in a daze before me, staring off into space.

Letty fished up another nickel and slapped it on

the table. "Me next," she said, elbowing Maisie out of the customer's chair. I fanned the deck on the table.

"Take a card, Letty. Any card."

❖

While she was making her selection, I thought of what I knew of Letty's fate. Recalling the future, I saw Letty's granddaughter-to-be. I looked ahead seventy Halloweens and saw Heather, the spitting image of Letty. I saw Heather running her own little gang of girls at Bluffleigh Heights Magnet Middle School.

I foresaw Letty herself living to a ripe old age down in . . . Sun City, Arizona. Probably in the lap of luxury if I know Letty. I needed no crystal ball or deck of cards or palm for her.

But still, I pondered.

She turned up the four of diamonds, which is not an interesting card in itself.

"Hmmmmm, that's real interesting, that is."

"Quit stalling," Letty snapped, fiddling with her mantilla.

"Draw another card," I said, playing for time.

She twitched over the ace of spades.

"Whoops!" I jerked back and slapped my forehead. Letty flinched, too, and Maisie, looming over us, let out a little yelp.

"Can't be," I gasped. "Draw one more time. You owe it to yourself."

Her hand quivered as she turned up another ace

of spades. No wonder this is Mama's favorite deck.

Letty grabbed her throat, and Maisie grabbed her chins. I let my eyes roll all the way back. But I came to myself at once. Under all her white powder Letty's face had gone whiter. I swept up the three cards, reshuffled the deck, and slipped it into one of my pockets.

Fishing up a nickel, I flipped it on the table. "This here reading is at an end," I explained. "You can have your nickel back, Letty."

She took back her nickel quick enough. But her little black rosebud mouth trembled. "You better tell me, Blossom," she said in a tiny, tragic voice. "I better know what those cards are saying."

"Yes, she better know," said Maisie.

"Nobody thanks the bearer of bad news," I remarked. "Besides, I could be wrong. Possibly."

"Oh, I doubt it," Maisie blurted. "You were right on the button with me."

"Give me a hint anyhow," Letty said, twitching.

"I can't take the responsibility," I said. "I'll just have a squint at the crystal ball to double-check."

"Do that," Maisie urged.

I made a couple passes over the crystal ball. The flame from the candle reflected on the smooth glass. Back went my eyeballs till I was showing all white and seeing nothing.

"I see a peaceful scene and hear harps," I moaned mournfully.

"Oh, heaven help us," Maisie murmured. Letty was speechless.

"I see a group gathered around an open grave. Oh, how they're weeping and carrying on! But the floral tributes are lovely."

Maisie whimpered, but Letty wasn't breathing.

"Too soon, too soon," I lamented. "It's the grave of a young girl cut off in her prime or possibly sooner. A young *unmarried* girl, prominent in this community.

"My vision grows dim," I continued. "I can read this ball like a book; but it's clouding over, and we're spared from knowing the name of this deceased young . . . spinster."

My chin fell on my chest, but I jerked upright at once. "What did I say? Where am I? What time is it?"

But Letty was already at the door, and Maisie was struggling to keep her on her feet. "*She's a liar,*" Letty shrieked, throwing her arms around and grabbing air. "*It's a well-known fact. Ask anybody.*"

"Well, all I know is," Maisie said, "she was right on the button with me."

Cleopatra and Theda Bara went off down the stairs scared silly, which is about as good an advertisement for my business as I could get.

Before that Halloween night was over, I had customers waiting in line. I was passing out fortunes left and right and getting real good. I nearly worked the spots off Mama's cards, and my pockets bulged with nickels.

You can't go far wrong by giving the public what it wants and throwing in the occasional thrill.

19

It was near the witching hour of midnight before an important customer entered the Gypsy's tent and fell under my power.

Various teachers had dropped in through the evening to support our fund raiser and to keep an eye on us. Even Miss Blankenship had turned out. It was reported that she approved of the sign from *Hamlet* over our front door. But she hadn't come up to have her fortune told. Anybody as near retirement as Miss Blankenship isn't looking to the future.

But lo and behold, Mr. Lacy, the history teacher, as the official chaperon for this Haunted House, called on me. Clinging to his arm was none other than Miss Fuller of Girls' Gym.

"Better yet," I muttered, seemingly to myself, when I caught sight of her.

Miss Fuller was dolled up in a medley of flowing scarves. Her hair was swept up artistically above a colorful bandeau. Though her eyes are ever sad, they were bright tonight. She was riveted to Mr. Lacy's side.

He was in one of his natty outfits with matching haberdashery. "Well, Blossom," he boomed in his teacherish voice, "they tell me you have turned out to be the star attraction!"

He hovered there in the door with Miss Fuller hanging on him like a drowning woman.

"I hope you are a better student of the future than you are in my history class. Ha-ha."

"Oh, Ambrose," Miss Fuller simpered, "you are such a card."

I scooted my crystal ball into place.

"Good evening, folks," I said. "Step right in. Who's first?"

"Oh, ha-ha," booms Mr. Lacy. "I don't think Miss Fuller and I are in the market for any fortunes this evening. We have just stopped by to wish you well."

"Many thanks," I said, arranging my shawl, "but this is a place of business, and there are others waiting."

"Oh, Ambrose," says Miss Fuller, bending his sleeve, "go on and have a reading. These children need encouragement."

"Anything you say," he replied, giving her the old eye. Then he marched over to me, smirking.

"Take a chair," I told him. "You'll need it."

Smirking still, Mr. Lacy laid out his large white hand on the table. "I hear you are first-rate with palms," he boomed encouragingly.

"I'll just take a peek into the crystal ball if it's all

the same to you," I said. The candle was burning low now, and I'd counted on that.

Miss Fuller crept up behind where Mr. Lacy sat. Now she was looking fondly down at him. I rolled my eyeballs abruptly back, and both my customers started.

A breeze seemed to stir the sheets of the tent that enclosed us. The wavering candle threw long shadows. "Oh, my," Miss Fuller murmured.

I made a couple passes over the crystal ball, seeming to read it with the whites of my eyes.

"I don't think that can be good for her vision," Miss Fuller said.

"Hush, honey," Mr. Lacy replied.

I made a couple more passes over the crystal ball. "That's real interesting," I remarked, "but strange." My hands cupped my face, and I swayed from side to side.

"I wish she'd quit doing that with her eyes," Miss Fuller whispered.

My knee knocked the underside of the table, and the crystal ball jiggled, taking on a little life of its own.

Then I rolled my eyes back to a seeing position. A worried look crossed my face. "What we have here is an unusual situation," I explained to Mr. Lacy. "You don't seem to have any future at all to speak of."

"Oh, ha-ha," he boomed uncertainly. He began to rise. He wouldn't have minded leaving right then.

"Never mind, Blossom," Miss Fuller said kindly. "As I've often said in the locker room, you can't win them all."

"But poor student of history that I am," I continued, "I believe I'll try to delve around in your past, Mr. Lacy."

"Oh, a little personal history?" He smirked again, broader than before.

"You got it," I said. "After all, what is history but mankind's record where we look for guidance? We search the past for wisdom because the future is the Great Unknown!"

"I couldn't have put it better myself," Mr. Lacy said. The last of the candlelight gleamed in his yellow wavy hair.

"Here it comes," I said, peering deep into the blank ball. "Here comes Wisdom sharp and clear. Lay it on me!"

Fresh breezes seemed to whip the sheets around us. The screams of sophomores going through the deadman's dungeon far below our feet echoed upward.

"I see a small town, somewhat backward," I moaned distantly, "on the banks of the Mississippi River. I see steamboats drawn up to the wharf, taking on cotton and grain."

"How interesting," Miss Fuller remarked. Mr. Lacy said nothing.

"From the general condition of the place," I moaned on, "I'd put us back about 1905, or 1906 at the latest."

Mr. Lacy stirred.

"I see a festive occasion and half the town turned out for the event." My nose was practically flat against the ball by now. "A wedding!" I exclaimed. "They're throwing rice at a happy couple."

"How sweet," Miss Fuller said.

"The bride is not much to look at," I observed, "but the groom is one good-looking dude."

Mr. Lacy's white hand stole up to smooth his yellow hair.

I fell back in the chair. "My vision grows dim, dim," I nearly sobbed. "Dark clouds obscure this joyous scene.

"But hark!" Back my nose went to the ball. I was reading it like a book, and you could have heard a pin drop. "The groom is a husband now, and a bad one. I see the bride, now a wife, weeping in despair. She has been deceived and knows it!"

"For shame," Miss Fuller said.

"This poor deceived wife is tearing her hair and . . . rocking a cradle!"

"A *cradle*?" Miss Fuller plucked nervously at her drapings.

As if by chance, the fringe on my shawl swept over the candle, snuffing it out. We were in darkness now, within the swaying sheets.

"I can almost hear this abandoned wife and mother's voice," I said in rather a loud tone.

Silence fell.

I spoke again, louder. *"I say I can almost hear this abandoned wife and mother's voice."*

In a far corner of the darkened room something moved behind the sheets. It was only a shadow at first. Then there was the tiniest pinpoint of light, floating like a firefly.

"*Owwww*" came the weirdest voice you ever heard. Miss Fuller had Mr. Lacy in a hammerlock. Nobody breathed.

"*Owwww, Ambrose! Ambrose!*" The sheets stirred, and the pinpoint of lamplight grew to a glow. "*Wherefore art thou, Ambrose?*"

A lamp was held up by a bony hand. Its pale light filtering through the sheet fell on the frozen faces of Miss Fuller and Mr. Lacy. They stared in horror, and I had the willies myself.

There was only the hint of a wan and mournful face behind the sheet, for all the world like an abandoned wife and mother.

"*Owwww, Ambrose,*" the thing said, "*it's me, yore lovin' wife. Why have you run off and left me, Ambrose? Don't you know me, sweetheart? It's me . . . Blanche!*"

Mr. Lacy started from his chair. "Son of a—"

"Who?" Miss Fuller asked. "Who's Blanche?"

The thing went right on talking. "*And here beside me, Ambrose, is yore lovin' little child.*"

There was a short struggle behind the sheet. Another ghostly form, much smaller, was dragged up to our attention. "*Here is yore little boy. Wave to Papa . . . Leonard.*"

Mr. Lacy crashed back in his chair.

"Leonard?" Miss Fuller asked. "Who's Leonard?"

A bony hand reached up to turn the lamp down. It gleamed like a firefly floating and went out. The pair of ghostly figures, the big one and the little one, faded.

Then things went haywire.

We remained in dark silence for an instant. Then Mr. Lacy lunged my way. He fumbled for the crystal ball and grabbed it. Then he hauled off and heaved it toward the sheet. It exploded against the far wall with a deafening sound. Miss Fuller commenced screaming and wouldn't stop.

20

THE WITCHING HOUR HAD PASSED, and November was upon us. There was already gray dawn light in the east, and the old Leverette farmhouse was abandoned once more.

The last of our customers had departed, and the Shambaughs' Packard had long since called for Letty and her club. I had no doubt they were all snug in warm beds by now.

Still, I lingered in the upstairs room. I'd folded up all the sheets of my tent and pulled down my Madame Blossom Tells All sign. Now I was sweeping up the crystal ball that had shattered all over the room. Somehow, I wanted to leave the room neat for Jeremy-to-be.

Though I figured I was alone with my thoughts, I heard a footstep at the door, crunching on broken glass. I turned to see a shadow on the threshold. It moved and was Alexander.

He hesitated, still suspicious of this particular room.

"Blossom, you still here?"

"If I'm not, Alexander, you're looking at my ghost."

He peered from side to side. "Don't talk that way," he muttered. "I heard sweeping, so I figured you hadn't gone." He stepped cautiously into the room, carrying a couple of punch cups. "I was cleaning up the monster's kitchen and thought maybe you'd like a cup of grape juice. After all, you put in a pretty good night's work, I have to admit."

"Many thanks, Alexander." I propped the broom against the wall, and we settled at my table. It seemed empty without the crystal ball. Alexander placed a punch cup before me and withdrew his hand, fast.

"Don't worry," I said. "I've told enough fortunes for one night."

Alexander nodded. "That's what everybody says. You outdid yourself with Mr. Lacy. He took off like a bat out of you-know-where. Miss Fuller was right at his heels. She was screaming to beat the band and wouldn't stop."

"He was nothing but a philandering married man," I remarked wearily, "and he was sparking both Miss Fuller and Miss Spaulding. If he wants to save his worthless hide, he'll be on the milk train out of Bluff City this very morning."

Alexander considered this. "I hope they'll be in no hurry to find a new history teacher," he said, which is the way a boy thinks.

We sipped a little grape juice, and then he said, "Blossom, how did you get the goods on Mr. Lacy?

Did you use the crystal ball on him, or did you go off into one of your spells?"

I twitched my elbows slightly. "Well, now, Alexander, that's an interesting point. As you know, I have a number of Powers to draw on. And as I've often said, a Gift is a curse unless you put it to work. Now you take, for example, a deck of cards. I've done some of my best work this very evening with this very deck."

Reaching into a pocket, I withdrew the cards and fanned them on the table before us.

The room had gone from black to gray. In the cold light of dawn they were only ordinary playing cards, greasy from Mama's hand.

Alexander waited, almost politely, for whatever tall tale I cared to think up.

But Halloween was over, and it was just me and Alexander Armsworth there together. So I told him the truth.

I told him it was Mama who'd known about Mr. Lacy's shameful past. Naturally that brought in Daisy-Rae and Roderick, whom Alexander had already more or less met. I had to work them into this conversation, for Daisy-Rae played the role of Blanche, Mr. Lacy's poor, deceived wife. And Roderick played the role of his abandoned little son, Leonard.

It was lucky indeed that Mr. Lacy hadn't knocked one or both of them senseless when he let fly with that crystal ball. Even that polecat's aim was bad.

Of course, in the confusion that followed, Daisy-
Rae and Roderick had slipped off to their chicken
coop home and were doubtless fast asleep by now.

Alexander rubbed his chin for all the world like
Jeremy. "Blossom, do you mean to tell me that
Daisy-Rae sleeps in a chicken coop all night and
lives all day in the girls' rest room at Bluff City High
School? Is that what you're telling me?"

The trouble with the truth is that it's hard to believe.

*

But by and by I got Alexander convinced. It was
time we headed for home. The sun was all but up.
Though I hadn't liked to leave this room, somehow I
didn't mind with Alexander by my side.

We were climbing down the creaky stairs to the
cobwebby hall. "Now that Daisy-Rae has helped out
at our Haunted House fund raiser," I said, "I think I
can convince her to be a regular freshman. A little
nudge or two, and I'll have her attending classes."

Alexander nodded his approval of this plan.

"If Daisy-Rae's going to be a real freshman," I
observed, "she'll naturally need a beanie. But I'll
find one for her somewheres."

Alexander reached up to his bare head. "I've lost
my beanie," he said, "somewheres."

"Is that a fact," I remarked, and he gave me one
of his most suspicious looks.

His suspicions deepened when I led him to the

dining room. It was bare in there except for some burned-out jack-o'-lanterns and the old gasolier fixture hanging down. The china closet door stood open.

He saw that Roderick was not lurking inside, ready to scare him out of a year's growth again. Still, he was puzzled when I said, "I'd be obliged if you'd check around in that china closet for a loose floorboard."

He went down on all fours and peered inside. "All the floorboards are loose," he said in a hollow voice.

I reached into one of my many pockets and fished up the spelling medal. "Just hide this medal of mine under one of them boards."

When he'd wedged it tight under the floor, he sat back on his heels. "How come we're burying your medal, Blossom?"

"I've left it as a token of friendship," I told him, "for a kid of my acquaintance."

"A boy?" Alexander wondered.

I nodded.

"Is it anybody I know? It's not Champ, is it? Or Bub?"

"Mercy, no, Alexander." I shook my head till the hoops swung in my ears. "It's a boy yet to be. He won't be born for many years."

Alexander rubbed his chin in thought. "And yet you know him, Blossom."

I nodded.

"There are more things in heaven and earth,
Alexander,
Than are dreamt of in your philosophy."

"*Hamlet*?" he inquired.
"Act One," I answered.
Then me and Alexander Armsworth walked out into the bright November morning, almost hand in hand.

Richard Peck was born in Decatur, Illinois. He attended Exeter University in England and holds degrees from DePauw University and Southern Illinois University.

In 1990, he received the American Library Association's Margaret A. Edwards Award, which honors "an author whose book or books, over a period of time, have been accepted by young adults as an authentic voice that continues to illuminate their experiences and emotions, giving insight into their lives."

His other books include *The Ghost Belonged to Me*, *Ghosts I Have Been* (both about Blossom Culp), *Are You in the House Alone?*, *A Long Way from Chicago*, which was both a 1999 National Book Award Finalist and the 1999 Newbery Honor Book, and its sequel, *A Year Down Yonder*.

Richard Peck lives in New York City.